UNRELENTING

by JESSI HONARD and MARIE PARKS

DEDICATION

To friends close enough to call family,
and family close enough to call friends.

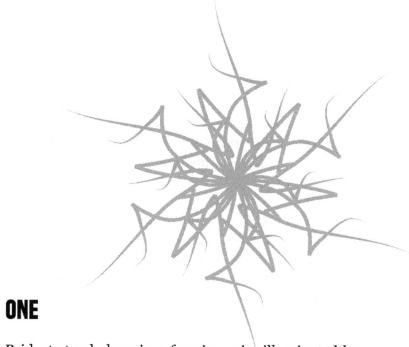

ONE

Bridget stood alone in a freezing rain, illuminated by a flickering streetlight. Droplets hovered in midair, and a fine mist left everything damp. The sun struggled to escape the clouds as it sank over a disjointed horizon of jagged skyscrapers.

Streaks of red, green, and yellow reflected off cracked pavement, alternating with the traffic signals above. As the light changed, cars sped to life and threw curtains of spray onto the sidewalk.

Bridget chanced a quick glance up, hoping for clear skies on the horizon. Icy raindrops splattered on her forehead, and she saw no break in the low-hanging clouds. Her red peacoat was soaked through, and she shivered as she tucked back damp blond hair. She wished she'd remembered to pack an umbrella.

This city is miserable, she thought, tightening her fingers around a paper coffee cup and cradling its warmth. Bridget had never understood her sister's decision to abandon North Carolina for a college in Ohio. It was such a dreary choice for Dahlia, especially in contrast to the sunnier schools of the South—scholarship or not.

And it had cost her so much more than tuition. Bridget pushed back a familiar wave of anxiety. Dahlia was still missing. Nine months had passed since she'd vanished without a trace, along with her boyfriend. When his car was found submerged in the Cuyahoga River, the detective had suggested Bridget and her mother move on. If the bodies had been swept into Lake Erie, they'd never be found.

Her mother had taken the news to heart, becoming sullen and despondent. She had begged Bridget to live as normal a life as possible. Get a better job. Finish her degree after six years of floating from one major to another. Maybe go on a date for once. She didn't want Bridget to miss her future, too.

Her mom didn't understand. No one did. Bridget had always made Dahlia her own responsibility, after all. And the contentious way their last call had ended gnawed on her insides. Returning to work or graduating wouldn't stop her flood of guilt. And as for dating—did her mother even know her?

No. She *had* to find her sister and make things right between them.

At first, she'd called the Cleveland police every day, demanding updates until Detective Ivanova told her to back off. Then, she'd set up a tip line website and shoveled every penny she could into missing person posters, digital ads, and her investigation fund. As the months trudged onward, her restlessness—and guilt—only grew.

And then last week, everything had changed. A new, unsolicited lead had surfaced, after months of dead ends. She'd booked the first flight out of Greensboro with the intent of meeting with the detective—whether she was welcomed or not. She was willing to be a thorn in Ivanova's side if it meant faster progress.

The squeal of brakes drew her attention. The city bus lumbered towards her, the glow of its headlights distorted by the rain. A wave of warm exhaust rolled over her as it stopped. The doors squeaked open, revealing a cramped mass of commuters inside.

Bridget stepped up and paid her fare, grateful to escape the rain. The bus lurched into motion, and she stumbled forward. She reached for one of the railings, clinging to her coffee. The bus was filled with suits and students, headphones in and smartphones out. They gazed down, avoiding eye contact with their fellow travelers. No one appeared to notice her near-fall.

Bridget's grip tightened around the metal rail as they hit a pothole. The ride from her hotel to the police station wouldn't be comfortable, but at least it would be brief. She contented herself with staring out the window as they rumbled along, watching neon signs and office buildings pass by. As the bus rocked to a stop, she shifted her weight to keep from toppling over, moving aside to allow several passengers to disembark.

She slid into a vacated seat and drew her purse onto her lap. The man beside her rested his head against the window. His eyes were closed, and his breath fogged the glass. The whole city felt like it wanted to crawl into bed and sleep.

But not Bridget. Maybe it was the latte, but she was on edge. This wasn't going to be like past conversations with Detective Ivanova. No more dismissals. No more brushing Bridget off. No more, *We're doing everything we can.* This time, she'd look the detective in the eye and demand she follow the fresh lead.

The bus hit a bump, jarring Bridget from her thoughts. Her seatmate slumped in her direction, and his head landed on her shoulder. Bridget stiffened and pulled away at the abrupt invasion of space, causing him to snort and sit up straight. He lifted a hand to wipe the drool from his mouth, and she turned away with a grimace.

The minutes dragged on, and Bridget stared straight ahead, hands clutched around her purse. Finally, the bus rolled to a halt, and a woman's pleasant, pre-recorded voice announced Bridget's stop.

Hurrying to her feet, she slipped past the other passengers and back into the rain. Cold, damp night air filled her lungs and Bridget pulled her soggy coat tighter around herself. Empty coffee cup clutched in her hand, she set off on the final two block walk.

The interior of the police station contrasted brightly with the gloom outside. Fluorescent lights gleamed off the shiny floor tiles and empty plastic chairs of the large waiting area. Bridget walked straight to the front desk, where an officer in uniform was scrolling on his phone.

Bridget cleared her throat, and he jumped. He set his phone down and blinked away his screen-induced stupor. Gaze finding Bridget's, he offered a belated smile. "Can I help you, ma'am?"

"Yes. I have an appointment with Detective Ivanova."

The officer pulled a clipboard from the top of a stack of manila file folders. "Name, date, and time. And I'll need to see some ID."

Fishing through her purse for her wallet, she passed her driver's license to the officer and exchanged it for the clipboard.

"Oh, you're here about the Keene case," the officer said as he read her name off her license. The words sent a jolt through Bridget. There was a terrible *officialness* to them.

"Yes." She passed the clipboard back to him.

"Uh huh." The officer punctuated the non-committal response by punching a command into his keyboard. The printer spat out a visitor's badge.

Rolling his chair over, the officer grabbed the paper

and offered it to Bridget, along with her license. "Take a seat. I'll let the detective know you're here."

Bridget gripped the badge so tightly the paper wrinkled. She turned and went to the hard plastic chair, dropping her empty cup in a wastebasket along the way. It fell in with a hollow *tap*. Once settled, she peeled the name badge off and stuck it to the front of her coat. What did they need name badges for, anyway? She was the only person visiting the station so late.

She pulled out her phone on autopilot and stared at the lock screen. It was a selfie of her and Dahlia. They were grinning at the camera, with Pilot Mountain in the background. Bridget swallowed and dropped the device back into her purse.

Hands fidgeting for something to do, Bridget set to folding the leftover paper from her name tag. She remembered Dahlia telling her, years ago, that it was impossible to fold a sheet of paper in half more than seven times. She took the paper and creased it down the middle.

Dahlia had always been like that: smarter and more driven than anyone gave her credit for. Everyone assumed she'd go to the local community college too, but Bridget knew better. Yes, Dahlia was free-spirited, but there was more to her than red solo cups and beach parties. No one else watched her pore over history books and doodle the National Geographic logo in the safety of their bedroom. Dahlia had long refused to crack open her drawing pad for anyone but Bridget, allowing only her sister to watch her progress from childhood scribbles to detailed street scenes.

Bridget folded the paper again, meticulous as she lined up the edges. If only Dahlia had stayed in North Carolina. Bridget had tried to show Dahlia how great Chapel Hill's archaeology program was. But when Dahlia set her heart on going out of state, Bridget had reluctantly encouraged her to follow her dreams. What she hadn't anticipated was the wedge it drove between them as Dahlia made new friends, explored a new city, and embraced her studies. Their daily texts turned into monthly phone calls. Bridget understood fewer of the references Dahlia posted online about her college life. They gossiped less and fought more, culminating in that horrible final argument. Bridget hadn't meant to hurt Dahlia. She'd only been worried about her. Now everything they'd had was gone. Maybe forever.

The paper strained against Bridget's fingers. It refused to crease an eighth time.

Her vision blurred, and she set the paper aside to wipe her eyes. She'd been thinking about her sister in the past tense. Maybe the dull acceptance of others was starting to rub off. *I can't give up on her.*

"Ms. Keene?" It was the officer at the front desk.

Bridget wiped wet fingers on her jeans and stood.

"Detective Ivanova is ready for you. Come on through the metal detector." Bridget's legs felt stiff as she approached and handed her purse to the officer. He gave the inside of her bag a cursory glance before returning it to her. "Through those doors, second room on the left."

Bridget nodded, though the officer was already turning back to his phone. *Typical. They've got a missing person case on their hands, and all he can do is play games.* She let herself through and into a high-ceilinged hallway, the sound of her boots bouncing off the sterile white walls. Most of the offices were closed for the evening. The room she was looking for, however, was lit up.

Bridget stopped outside and watched Detective Ivanova at her computer, focused on the screen. She was a thin, short woman with high cheekbones and dark hair pulled back into a tight bun. She was young for a detective, and she wore a permanent scowl. Her simple cardigan and slacks gave her an air of harmlessness, but Bridget knew better.

Bridget cleared her throat, and the detective looked up. "Sit down, Ms. Keene," she said in a severe voice before turning back to the computer.

Bridget took the empty seat opposite the desk. "Thanks for meeting me tonight." She set her purse on her lap.

"Could've waited until morning," Detective Ivanova pointed out, fingers still moving over the keyboard. "You're not my only case, you know."

Bridget bristled. "This is important. That video is the first new lead in months."

The detective finished typing and turned to face her. "Have you learned anything new about it that couldn't be shared with a simple email? What was so important you got on an airplane?"

Bridget's shoulders stiffened. She hadn't come halfway across the country to be dismissed outright. "You haven't *done* anything with the lead. I'm here to ask why not." She looked to a corkboard on the detective's wall. Ivanova had tacked on news clippings and photographs of other missing persons: an older Black woman, a middle-aged blond man. Along the edge of the board, Dahlia's section stared Bridget down. She recognized several articles about her sister's disappearance, pinned alongside her senior picture.

Bridget studied Dahlia's frozen smile. There was a resemblance between Dahlia and Bridget, but most of it was subtle—the curve of their lips, the shape of their cheekbones, the arch of their eyebrows. As half-sisters, their coloring was completely divergent. Contrasting Dahlia's dark hair was Bridget's blond. Brown eyes to blue. Petite frame to tall. Bridget felt like the foil to her sister in so many ways.

The detective spoke again. "We don't know that it's your sister in the video. All it showed was a dark-haired girl in an alleyway. Please don't get your hopes up."

"It *was* Dahlia." Bridget's fingers tightened around her purse strap. "I want to know when we're going to investigate."

The detective scoffed. "*We?* I'm going in the morning. You're not going anywhere. I told you not to come back to Cleveland until I sent for you, Ms. Keene. It's a waste of your time." There was an implied *and mine.*

Bridget straightened in her seat. "But I can help."

"Absolutely not." Ivanova leaned forward in her seat, hazel eyes narrowing. "Not only is it against regulations, but I'm here to protect you and your mother during this investigation. Let me do my job. Stay away."

"You can't keep me from this. The only reason we even *have* a new lead is because I set up that website."

The detective sighed in exasperation and dropped her arms to the desk's surface. "I appreciate your determination, and I know you're eager for news. If I find anything, I'll give your mother a call."

Bridget's face grew hot. "My *mother*? I'm the one who sent you the lead. I'm the one who's been keeping this investigation going." She pressed a finger down against the desk as her voice rose. "I'm not a child! We're supposed to be in this together. Aren't you on my side?"

Ivanova met her gaze. "Ms. Keene, please calm yourself. Of course I'm on your side."

"But you're not listening. Dahlia needs me."

"Ms. Keene, it's hard to lose a loved one. I know. And I assure you, I will follow this lead. Something may come of it, or it could be another dead end. Regardless, *you* are not the detective here. You're slowing down my investigation. All of them." She pointed to the board.

I'm the one pushing you on, Bridget thought, fists clenching. "I didn't *lose* her. And if you'd let me help—"

"No. End of discussion." Ivanova reached into her desk and pulled out a notepad, pushing it towards

Bridget. "Write down the dates you're in town. I'll be in touch tomorrow afternoon."

Angry tears burned Bridget's eyes as she wrote down the information and shoved the pad across the desk. It was clear from Detective Ivanova's expression that their brief meeting was at an end.

Bridget lurched to her feet. "It *was* Dahlia in that video. I know it."

Ivanova took the notepad. "I'll keep you up to date," she said, voice level. Her eyes turned back to her computer screen.

Bridget struggled to bite back a retort. She stalked out of the office, past closed office doors. It was all too obvious that Ivanova, like everyone else, had written Dahlia off.

Bridget was the only one who still cared. The only one who still hoped. She was finished with fighting red tape and dismissive detectives.

Cold, damp air slapped her cheeks as she stepped into the night. She cinched her jacket around herself. *I will find my sister,* she thought. *And I'll do it my way.*

TWO

Bridget hit play. Again.

A dark alleyway appeared on her phone's screen, its rough brick walls gleaming as a fine rain fell. A puddle reflected the single light that flickered above a worn metal door. It was the kind of scene that would kick off an old noir film.

In the fourth second of the clip, a woman stepped into the alleyway from the quiet street beyond. Her face remained in shadow, a hood covering her hair. She cast her gaze over her shoulder once before wrenching open the heavy door and stepping through. Dim, hazy light shone from the window, then faded. The video ended.

Dahlia. There was no doubt in Bridget's mind. Yes, the scene was dark and misty. No, the camera never clearly captured her face. But she would recognize that walk, that glance, that posture anywhere.

It was her. It *had* to be her.

Bridget adjusted the pillows behind her back and settled further into her hotel bed. Then she played the video again. And again.

As Bridget watched, she found herself repeating a familiar refrain. *It isn't your fault.* The words felt flatter each time. For the rest of her life, she'd never shake the angry, abrupt end to their last call. And all over a guy Bridget knew was bad news. Their fight had carved out a hollow place within her.

At first, the reigning theory was that Dahlia and her boyfriend, Dan, had run off together. But Dahlia wouldn't do anything so extreme without confiding in her sister, even after a blowout. Initially, Bridget thought Dahlia's silence must have been a form of punishment, but as the days and weeks stretched on, panic began to set in.

But she refused to give up hope. Even after Dan's car was found, Bridget knew her sister wasn't gone. She would've *known* if Dahlia was dead.

And now she had proof. The video's metadata told her the recording happened two months *after* Dahlia's disappearance. It hadn't arrived in her inbox until a couple of weeks ago, with the file attached. The first time she'd played those ten seconds, alone in her bedroom in North Carolina, it was a moment of vindication. Finally, she had confirmation her sister was still out there. Since then, she must have watched the clip a hundred times, relief giving way to frustration as Ivanova dismissed her.

She returned to her inbox, staring at her messages. She'd planned to send a follow-up to their meeting, but given the way Ivanova treated her, she doubted she'd get a response. The detective had made herself clear. Bridget should have known better than to trust the police.

But she had made herself clear, too. She wasn't giving up on this lead. She *needed* to find out what had happened to Dahlia. Maybe she could reach out once again to her sister's old roommate, Nicole. But they'd already emailed extensively, and nothing new had come of it. In fact, Nicole's last message said she was transferring to a school in Boston, to give her a chance to start fresh. Bridget didn't blame her. Nicole was the last person to communicate with Dahlia. She must feel traumatized by the entire experience.

With a steadying breath, Bridget returned to the email chain containing the video. It was a long back-and-forth by now, after two weeks of correspondence. The sender, a classmate of Dahlia's, had provided a spark of hope when everyone else had given up. Maybe he could help.

James, she wrote, I made it to Cleveland. Any chance we could talk in person tomorrow?

Bridget felt a small surge of satisfaction as she hit send and turned off the screen. She refused to keep waiting for news that never came. At least she had a plan. A loose, unformed plan, but it was better than nothing.

As she settled among the blankets, she hoped it would be enough.

The next morning, Bridget nursed her second coffee as she watched the crowds pass the café windows. The day was bright, but the sidewalks were still damp, and puddles lingered along the curb. It was warm enough that she'd shed her jacket, folding it over the back of her chair.

She pulled out her phone to check the time. The battery level indicator was yellow. After half a night of tossing and turning, she'd spent the early morning hours scrolling through her camera roll. Each photo of her and Dahlia was another twist of the knife, and it left her as drained as her phone.

James had been quick to respond to her email, but this morning was another story. Already, she'd been waiting ten minutes. She tucked her phone away to save the remaining battery and scanned the business casual crowd. She could have spent the morning seeing if the new tenant of Dahlia's former apartment would allow her to look around. Or maybe she could have tailed the detective or searched the campus. Instead, she was stuck watching for the Spiderman shirt James had told her he'd be wearing.

She was about to give up when a flash of red caught her eye. A young man with curly hair stepped into the shop. His bright t-shirt had a stylized *R* on the breast pocket. She watched him order at the counter. As he waited for his drink, he turned to scan the room. Hesitantly, she raised a hand. He smiled and returned the wave as he approached her with a steaming mug.

"Turns out Spiderman's dirty," he said, gesturing to his shirt. "You get Robin." He pushed heavy brown curls back from his eyes. "Bridget, right?"

She nodded, standing up and offering her hand. "James. Thanks for meeting me. I should've gotten your drink." He reminded Bridget of the kind of person who earned his high school letters from debate team and marching band.

James shook her hand and sat across from her. "It's okay. So, you came all the way to Cleveland because of my video?"

She returned to her seat, eyes on him. "It's the first real lead we've had in a while," she replied, wrapping her fingers around the ceramic mug.

He sat forward, eyes on her. "Did you *find* her?"

She shook her head. "No, I flew in yesterday. So far, all I've had time to do is go to the police station."

James' expression fell, and he looked so genuine, she felt a flutter of relief. She'd had a quiet, nagging worry that he was somehow involved, despite all of his help. But if he had anything to do with Dahlia's disappearance, he wouldn't want Bridget to find her.

"So... the police are looking into it?" James asked.

Bridget shrugged as she brought the coffee mug to her lips. "I don't know. They haven't told me much."

"That's not surprising. They like to ask questions, but they're not great at giving answers. That detective didn't tell me anything."

Bridget sat up a little straighter. So Ivanova *had* approached James. "What did you two talk about?"

He sipped his coffee. "She wanted to know why I was in that alleyway. If I knew your sister. Stuff like that."

"How well *do* you know her?" Bridget asked.

James lifted his shoulders. "We have a few friends in common, but we never talked much, except for a group project last year. I'm almost positive it was her in that clip, though."

"Yeah, it's her." She scooted forward and lowered her voice. "Which is why I need you to tell me where you shot the video."

He winced. "It's not in the best part of town. You're not planning to go there, are you?"

"I don't care if it's dangerous. Besides, *you* went there to film the video." Did he think she was helpless?

"Yeah, but that's because I needed that shot for my project."

"*That* shot. In *that* specific alleyway, in a bad part of town." Bridget sensed a lie.

He set his shoulders. "There was a good reason for it."

"Which was?" Bridget leaned closer.

He opened his mouth to respond, then faltered and buried his face in his coffee mug. To Bridget's surprise, a flush spread across his cheeks.

She folded her arms and glared at him. "Out with it. What aren't you telling me?"

James let out a quiet sigh, lowering his mug. "Alright, but don't laugh, okay?" He met her gaze until she nodded.

"The video *was* for a project for school, but it was also for, um... my own investigation."

"Your own investigation?" Bridget's heart leapt. "Did someone you know go missing, too?"

"No, no, nothing like that." James' cheeks reddened further. "I... look, I know it sounds ridiculous, but I'm in this group. Sort of a club, I guess. We're..." he trailed off.

"What?" she demanded.

He swallowed, fidgeting. "We're a paranormal investigation club," he said, voice small.

She stared at him. "So you're like... a ghost hunter or something?" He nodded, and her heart sank.

James didn't seem surprised by her reaction. "Or something. Cleveland is an old city, with a lot of history. You wouldn't believe some of the things we've found."

Great. He was delusional. No wonder Detective Ivanova was so cynical about the video. "Yeah. Okay, sure. But what does that alley have to do with anything? Are you telling me it's *haunted*?" It was impossible to keep skepticism out of her voice.

"No, not necessarily. There's more to the paranormal than ghosts. But there have been reports of strange activity there. Enough that I agreed to check it out, especially since I needed some stock footage for my videography class."

Bridget shook her head. "Did you tell the detective this?"

"Yeah. She wasn't impressed." He looked down at his mug, rotating in his hands.

"Was Dahlia in your club, too?" Somehow, Bridget doubted it.

He shook his head. "No. I don't know why she was there that night. I emailed you as soon as I realized it was her."

"And you didn't edit it or anything? Did you have a longer cut than those ten seconds? I wanna see the whole thing."

"I already sent the full file to the detective. There's nothing else, just half an hour of rain and a few raccoons digging through the dumpster." He shrugged. "You can't even see what's going on half the time because my lens fogged up. But I can send it to you if you want."

Bridget nodded. "Yes, please. And show me where the alleyway is." She pulled out her phone and set it on the table.

James eyed her. "You're not going to get yourself in trouble, are you?"

She shook her head. "I'll be fine. This is something I have to do."

James didn't press her further. Instead, he gave a resigned sigh and held out his hand. "Pull up your map."

Her throat tightened with nervous excitement. Finally, she was making progress. She brought up a map of the city and nudged her phone across the table to James. He peered at the screen, zoomed in, and tapped once before he gave it back to her. There was a fresh pin to mark the location of the alley. It was about two miles away.

"Thanks," Bridget said as she eyed the map. She downed the last of her coffee and put her phone away.

"Yeah, sure." James still looked troubled. "Um, do you want me to come with you?"

Bridget shook her head as she stood. She had what she needed. "No, I'm fine. Thanks, though. You've been a huge help."

"Yeah, okay." He nodded and shifted in his seat.

She slung her purse over her shoulder. "Hey, who knows," she said, "maybe I'll find my sister *and* some of your ghosts."

THREE

The city bus dropped Bridget off in front of a row of abandoned storefronts. Empty windows gaped at her, most covered with steel bars or haphazardly nailed boards. A lanky man in an oversized hoodie loitered at one corner, paper bag clasped between his hands. Bridget quickened her pace, feeling his doleful eyes on her.

She took out her phone and peered at the map. The place James had marked was less than a five-minute walk away. Urging herself onward, she kept an eye out for anyone following her.

Broken glass and bits of loose asphalt crunched underfoot as she made her way past red brick walls obscured by graffiti. She fought back the urge to hunch her shoulders and pull her coat around herself, despite the bright sunlight. James was right—this *wasn't* the best part of town.

Something important had to have brought Dahlia here. Something deeper than the gnawing guilt Bridget nursed. She mulled over the possibilities as she walked, trying to distract herself from her discomfort. Drugs? No, she would've known. A hidden place to hook up with her boyfriend? But even for someone who cared about that sort of thing—which Dahlia definitely did—that didn't make sense. Cleveland was full of hidden nooks and crannies, and many in far safer parts of the city.

The only thing Bridget could guess was that Dahlia was caught up in something dangerous. Dangerous enough that she'd avoided asking for help.

The entire street was abandoned, except for the man she had passed. She couldn't hear anything more than the distant roar of freeway traffic. Puddles darkened the gum-stained sidewalk, and she quickened her stride.

Unease settled low in her gut by the time she reached the pin on her map. Two multi-story brick buildings lined the alleyway, casting deep shadows. Bridget felt a pang of disappointment as she peered into it; it was as empty as the streets behind her. Some small, fanciful part of her had expected to turn the corner and see Dahlia waiting for her.

At least there was no sign of Ivanova. No surprise there; the detective had wanted to check it out first thing, and it was almost noon.

Bridget had seen this alley hundreds of times, captured on film during a dark, wet night. Now, in the light of day, déjà vu hit her in a wave. It was as if she had stepped through her phone screen and into the video that had become her obsession.

A utilitarian bulb hung over the alley's only door—the one Dahlia had gone through. The walls on either side were cracking, and the mortar had begun to crumble. There had once been two windows framing the back entrance. One was now filled in with bricks, the sill jutting out. Boards covered the other.

Sucking in a shaky breath, Bridget crept into the alleyway. Buildings stretched upward on either side like canyon walls. She pulled her coat tighter around herself.

As Bridget approached the door, she could see that it had once been red, a detail the video hadn't shown. A few chipped paint fragments clung to the metal. The hinges were brown with rust and a spider had spun a web across them since the last rain. It didn't look as if it had been opened in decades.

She reached for the handle, and the cold of the metal seeped into her fingers. She tugged.

It didn't budge.

She pulled harder, but to no avail. With a frown, she dropped her hand and took a step back to size up her options. Maybe she could try the front door. Before she turned away, her gaze wandered to the boarded-up window nearby. There were wide gaps between the warped wood planks. Just past them, she could make out grimy, broken glass.

Maybe she could pull the boards free and force the

window open. Bridget grabbed the end of the board nearest her and yanked. The wood bent with a soft groan of protest, but it held firm. Bridget gave it a second tug.

A sharp stab of pain made her jerk back. She bit her lip to keep from crying out and looked down at her hand. A splinter had wedged its way into the skin of her index finger. With a grimace, she pressed her thumbnail beside the thin sliver of wood and worked it out.

So much for removing the boards. She rocked onto her tiptoes and peered through a gap between two of the planks. Beyond was a litter-filled hallway with a concrete floor and shadowy walls. A broken light fixture hung from a wire overhead.

She was about to turn away when a faint thud made her pause. She tilted her head closer to the window, listening.

Nothing.

And then, faint voices. They were too far away for her to make out through the holes in the glass, but the building definitely wasn't empty.

Her heart thumped as she held her breath to listen. Distant footsteps accompanied the low murmur of conversation.

"... your fault."

"Rude of you to blame me."

"Why shouldn't I?"

A woman and a man. They were coming closer. Or at least getting louder. Bridget stood on her tiptoes, trying to get a clear view of the hallway. It still empty.

"What do you suggest?" the man asked.

"Nothing yet. Ugh, this place *smells*."

Bridget's breath caught. She *knew* that voice. It was Detective Ivanova. Through the small gap between the wooden boards, Bridget saw her step into the hall from somewhere deeper in the building. The detective was in profile to Bridget. She walked beside a man with red hair so bright, it stood out even in the shadowed hallway.

"Regardless, we should wrap this up," the man told the detective.

"Easier said than done," Ivanova muttered.

Bridget tensed, ready to bolt if they headed in her direction. But they turned the opposite way. She let out a quiet breath.

The detective took a few steps forward, then stopped in her tracks. Her companion paused with her, and they both stared at the wall for a long moment.

"Who put that there?" The detective's voice was sharp.

"None of us."

Ivanova reached out to run her hand along the wall's dusty surface. Then she started. "Do you see that? It's active."

Bridget inched forward, straining to spot what they were looking at. But the angle was wrong, and the dusty window made it impossible to see clearly. If it was some sort of clue, some indication of why Dahlia had disappeared, then she needed to get inside.

"Get back," the redhead said in alarm.

"I want to see what it does." She kept her hand pressed

firmly on the wall.

Movement along the floor caught Bridget's eye. It was impossible to tell through the grimy glass, but it looked like the edges of the cinder blocks were shifting and fuzzing. The haze materialized into smoke. It was dark and roiling, like a miniature thundercloud that bubbled as it spread outward.

Her heart gave an uncomfortable thud as the substance seeped from the seam where the concrete floor met cracked walls. It pooled around Ivanova and her companion's ankles, staying low. Focused on the wall, they didn't appear to notice the smoke as it began to advance down the hallway.

The man glared at the detective. "Let go. You don't know what it does."

Bridget watched, rooted to the spot. Was the building on fire? Maybe she should call out to them.

A sulfurous, heavy stench hit her, and she clapped a hand over her mouth to muffle a cough. She turned away from the window, trying not to gag, and froze.

Like a predator stalking its prey, the murky substance squeezed out from beneath the metal door beside her and slunk in her direction.

With a horrified gasp, Bridget turned and ran.

Inside the building, she heard a cry of alarm.

Before she could react, something snagged her ankle, tugging it backwards. Bridget pitched forward, arms windmilling and gut clenching. One hand caught the edge of a twisted rain gutter and she managed to stay upright.

She looked down; a tendril of smoke had lashed itself around her boot, clinging to her like a rope. As she watched, a second tendril shot forward with shocking speed to ensnare her other leg. It yanked her foot out from under her, and she collapsed to her knees.

Heart pounding in her ears, she grabbed the strange ropes.

Pain seared her bare palms as they came into contact with the smoke. She yelped and jerked back. An angry red mark stretched across both hands.

Bridget twisted and tried to scramble away. Her fingers clawed at the asphalt, but the more she struggled the more evident it became that she couldn't escape. The smoke crawled up her leg, and she scrambled for something she could use to fight it off. Her gaze landed on an empty beer bottle. She lurched forward and grabbed it, then spun and sliced through the bonds. They dissipated briefly, and she yanked one leg free. Before she could swing at the ropes holding her second leg, it surged forward.

Faster than she could react, the smoke clawed its way up her body. Its scalding heat pressed against her as it wound around her legs and reached towards her stomach. She opened her mouth to scream, but the rotten-egg smell made her gag.

Abruptly, the window exploded outward, and everything fell into chaos.

FOUR

The wooden boards burst free from the window, inches above Bridget's head. They slammed into the opposite wall of the alley and fell to the ground with a clatter. The force of the explosion ripped the smoke free from her ankles.

A rush of hot air drove Bridget against the brick wall. She clapped her arms over her head and bit back a scream. Shards of shattered glass rained against her coat.

The pandemonium gave way to abrupt stillness, pierced by a shrill, tinny ring in her ears. Beyond it, all Bridget could hear was the thudding of her heart. She drew in a raspy breath to steady herself.

Head throbbing, she peeked up from her crouched position. A faint haze lingered in the alleyway, but the strange smoke was gone. Hunks of brick and mortar were strewn about, and the dumpster was on its side. The boards that had been covering the window now lay on the floor of the alley. Rusty nails jutted out at awkward angles. If Bridget had been standing when the explosion hit, their jagged points would have slammed into her.

Don't think about that. She swallowed and forced down the grisly mental image. None of it was possible. None of it made sense. Smoke didn't move like that. It certainly didn't *capture* people. But it *had* moved towards her, and it *had* tried to capture her. Her palms stung, swollen and red where the smoke grabbed her.

One thing at a time. What first?

Ivanova and her companion. The powerful blast had come from inside the building.

Bridget sucked in a worried breath. What would she do if they were hurt? If she called the cops, they'd know she was there. They'd want to know why she was skulking about where Ivanova had forbidden her to go.

But she couldn't abandon two people who might be suffering, or worse. At the very least, she should call an ambulance and file an anonymous report.

Bridget pressed against the still-warm bricks. Her scraped knees ached as she pulled herself into a standing position. The scorching ropes had left her weak and shaky, though at least they hadn't burned through her clothes. She leaned against the wall and looked towards the window.

All that remained of it was a gaping hole and a few jagged pieces of glass. She peered in.

The interior of the building was thick with stirred-up dust, and Bridget put a hand over her mouth to keep from coughing. The cinder block walls hadn't suffered much from the explosion, but the light fixture had shattered and fallen. Bits of glittering glass and metal decorated the floor.

Two dim silhouettes were visible through the drifting haze. Bridget breathed a quiet sigh of relief as she saw that they were both on their feet, standing near the wall they had been inspecting before the blast. The man smothered a flame licking the hem of his pants and muttered curses she could barely make out over the ringing in her skull. He straightened and coughed, covering his mouth with his sleeve.

The detective stood still and watched him. Her back was to Bridget, making it difficult to tell what was happening. Then, abruptly, Ivanova doubled over. The detective *was* hurt. Tearing her gaze away from the hall, she looked for her purse. She should call for help.

The leather bag was a few feet away, flattened against the side of the overturned dumpster. She stooped down and snatched it up, pulling her phone from inside. Enough power remained to make a call.

As she straightened and unlocked the screen, she chanced another look inside the building. Ivanova spasmed, her shoulders shaking as she rested her palms on her knees. The man put a hand on her back, even as he began coughing again. Bridget's fingers paused above the screen as she watched. The detective wasn't in pain, she realized. She was *laughing.*

"Did you *see* that?" Ivanova straightened, gasping for breath. Her voice sounded distant through the ringing in Bridget's ears.

The redhead nodded. "Felt it, too." Bridget couldn't see his face, but she got the sense he didn't share her amusement.

Bridget backed away from the window before they could turn and see her. They were alive. Ivanova was *laughing.* Bridget had never known the even-keeled, disapproving detective to so much as crack a genuine smile. Maybe the explosion had jostled her brain.

Not her problem. They were safe, and she needed to leave before they spotted her. Once she was back at her hotel, then she could try to piece together what had happened, and how it was connected to her sister. Still shaking, she turned from the window and hurried down the alley, stepping over shattered glass and bits of broken brick and wood. At the main road, she took one last glance back. She half expected to see the dark smoke creeping after her, but the gloomy space was empty. She hurried out into the sunlight once again.

Cold water ran over Bridget's red hands as she held them under the faucet. They were still shaking. She had spent the entire ride back to her hotel forcing herself to remain calm, despite her brush with disaster. Now that she was back in the safety of her room, she could barely keep her eyes open.

She turned the faucet off and looked up to meet her own gaze in the mirror. Blond hair hung around her face in a tangled mess, and a few pieces of broken glass caught the light. Her cheeks were colorless, her few freckles fading under the glaring fluorescents. Grasping her brush, she dragged it through her hair. The glass *pinged* into the sink.

Once she worked the snarls out of her hair, she undressed. The smell of sulfur clung to her rumpled, ripped clothes. She shook them out with a grimace. A few bits of gravel fell to the tile.

Bridget changed into a fresh pair of jeans and an unsmudged shirt, her movements robotic. Finally clean, she settled onto the hotel bed.

She sat for a long time, staring at a blank spot on the wall while she tried to piece together what she'd witnessed. The smoke from the building had moved unlike anything she'd ever seen. It had acted almost *alive*, moving with unsettling purpose. Its touch had burned her skin raw, and it was somehow both strong as rope and ephemeral as mist. And the *smell*.

Bridget fought back a shudder. She glanced at her phone poking out of her purse and reached for it. Maybe she could find answers there. She plugged it into the charger and opened her email. There was a new message from earlier that morning. It was the full video file from James.

She opened the file and hit play. The image on the screen jostled, and she could hear the sound of breathing from behind the camera. Then the image stilled and the pattering rain swallowed the sound of his retreating footsteps. Pale fog curled around the edges of the dumpster, and Bridget scanned the scene. It looked normal.

Bridget kept her eyes fixed on the screen. It really was unremarkable. The buildings were poorly maintained, and the walls were darkened with years of soot. It was hard to imagine the place bustling with workers in years past.

Ten minutes in, Dahlia approached. This time, instead of watching the frame for her sister, Bridget eyed the door itself. Was that the black smoke near its base or mist from the rain? She couldn't be sure.

Bridget let the video play out. There were the raccoons James had mentioned. The image grew progressively milkier as the lens fogged up. Finally, James stepped back into the shot. He cursed, wiped the glass clean, then ended the recording.

She sat back. What on earth had Dahlia gotten herself mixed up in?

Bridget swiped away the video and pulled up her web browser. The search bar stared at her, waiting. After pausing to gather her thoughts she typed *sulfur smoke* and hit enter.

A few hundred thousand results popped up. She scanned the first page, reading headlines about harmful pesticides, deadly smog, and volcanic eruptions. None of it matched what she had seen in the alley. She started a new search. This time she tried *sulfur smoke Cleveland.* She had even less success, only managing to scrounge up a few articles about car fires and a science fair experiment gone wrong.

She prowled around the internet, looking up everything from chemical reactions to conspiracy theories. Even ghost stories. Nothing. The more she searched, the more her frustration mounted. The sun sank in the sky, and her inbox remained empty. No word from the detective. Enough waiting. She called the police station.

"Can I speak to Detective Ivanova?" she asked the officer who answered. As she waited for the call to connect, she drummed her fingers on the comforter. The phone rang twice and then clicked over to voicemail.

"Detective, it's Bridget. I'm following up on the lead you promised to investigate today. Please call me back as soon as possible."

She ended the call and lowered her phone, no closer to answers.

She had to go back. It was the only way to learn more about the smoke. Maybe *that* was the strange, paranormal activity James had referred to. Now his claim didn't seem so far-fetched.

James. Now there was an idea. Would he have more information?

But she wasn't sure she could fully trust him. She

didn't think he was involved in Dahlia's disappearance, but she'd resolved to search for her sister alone.

She faltered. She needed answers, and James might have them. She could hear from the detective at any moment, reporting back on her investigation. Bridget wanted more information before that happened, and James was the only person who might have some insight.

Besides, she didn't need to continue getting his help. Once she had what she needed, she could thank him and continue on her way.

She searched farther back until she reached the first email in the chain. There, under his name, was his cell number.

She tapped it.

The phone rang once. And then a second time. "Come on," she muttered, eyeing the number beneath his name. She needed more information, and he was the only one offering it.

A third ring.

"Hello?" He sounded distracted. She could hear the electronic chiming of a video game in the background.

She sat forward. "James? It's Bridget. We need to meet again. Now."

FIVE

"Wait. Tell me again, from the beginning." James watched Bridget with an intent expression, his fingers wrapped around an unopened can of cola. He was wearing the same superhero shirt from that morning.

"Do you really need to hear it again?" she griped in a quiet voice. "Don't you believe me?"

He shook his head. "No, I do. I definitely do. I just want to make sure you didn't forget anything."

She stared at him in disbelief. "How could I forget murderous smoke? Especially when it did *this?*" She held her hands up, palms outward, to show him the burn marks. They continued to throb, no matter how much cream she rubbed into them.

"I know, I know. Sorry." Despite his apologies, James was grinning at her, as if her near-death experience was the best news he'd ever heard. It wasn't hard to imagine him on one of those cheesy ghost hunter shows.

The sun was down, and the city buzzed with evening activity. They'd avoided the crowds by meeting at a pizza diner that hadn't seen an update since the nineties. The carpet tiles' black background and geometric neon shapes hid decades of stains. There were several arcade machines across from their booth, half of which sported *out of order* signs. Two plastic plates sat in front of Bridget and James, awaiting the arrival of their food.

"Does the smoke sound like something from one of your stories?" Bridget asked.

"Maybe. Tell me how it moved," he said.

She toyed with the tab of her drink can. "Slow. But almost like it knew where it was going. It felt intentional." Bridget shook her head. "I know it sounds completely nuts."

"No, it sounds completely awesome," James corrected her, earning an eye roll.

Before Bridget could respond, the server came over and placed a hot pepperoni pizza on the metal stand between them. The smell of melted cheese and crispy dough hit her hard, and her stomach gurgled.

"Awesome or not, what matters is Dahlia," Bridget said as she took a slice. Cheese pulled away in strings as she set it down on her plate and sprinkled on parmesan and pepper flakes. "It was like the smoke was protecting something. I need to know what was on the wall that the detective was so interested in, and I need to know what all of it has to do with Dahlia."

"You couldn't see anything?" James picked up his own slice. He brought it straight to his mouth and took a bite, expression thoughtful as he chewed.

"No. The angle was bad, and the smoke showed up while they were looking at it. But it seemed important." Her brow furrowed as a detail came back to her. "She said something strange. Something like, it was active. Activated."

He frowned. "That's weird. Sounds like tech. Or magic." She raised her eyebrows, but he was still talking. "What are you going to do?"

She spread her napkin across her lap. "Go back. I have to know what they were looking at."

He hesitated, then offered, "We could go together."

"We?" she echoed, followed by a sharp shake of her head. "No."

"Isn't that why you wanted to meet with me?"

"I wanted to meet with you to see if you knew anything about what I saw." Bridget sipped her drink.

"Well, the answer is a firm maybe. I'll have to get closer to know more." He grinned. "Besides, I wouldn't mind getting more footage."

"This isn't about hunting ghosts," Bridget said.

"I don't know about that. You've seen for yourself that there's something very weird in that alleyway."

Bridget couldn't deny that. Still, there had to be a rational explanation. "It might be dangerous. Flammable gases or something. There might be another explosion."

James frowned. "You know, that's a good point. I wonder if anyone reported the incident. Even if the building was abandoned, people would've heard it."

She shook her head. "Ivanova was there. I'm assuming *she* reported it."

James wiped greasy fingers on his napkin and tugged his phone from his back pocket, setting it down flat on the table between them. He pulled up the Cleveland Police Department's website.

"Looks like we'd have to put in a request to even see if there was an official statement. You sure you don't want to ask her?" He lifted his head to meet her gaze again.

"Definitely not. Then she'd know I was there."

He nodded and switched apps. "I'll check the local news."

Bridget took another bite of pizza as she watched James scroll through articles. Maybe she was blowing things out of proportion. Now that it had been a few hours, her fear and desperation felt distant.

"Nothing," James finally reported. "You're probably right about the detective. It's likely she didn't want the news to find out. I bet she wants to avoid bad publicity." He grinned. "That's good for us. I doubt there will be anyone there when we go check it out."

"*We* are not doing anything. And definitely not at night. It was scary enough at noon."

"Do you want to know what's on the wall or not?" James took a long drink of cola, then covered his mouth to hide a belch.

Bridget fought the urge to wrinkle her nose. "Of course I do. I'm also not going to creep around a crime scene in the dark. I'll go first thing tomorrow."

"It's not a crime scene if nothing was reported," James pointed out. "Besides, it sounds like the only real crime was to the building itself. No one got hurt."

"Not for lack of trying," Bridget muttered, rubbing her palms.

James eyed her over his slice of pizza. "Look, I'm sure Detective Ivanova will have said *something*, right? I mean, this was supposed to be a lead about your sister, and there was an explosion. And nothing?"

Bridget shook her head. "I haven't heard from her."

"Yeah. So, if you want *real* information, you're going to have to take matters into your own hands."

Bridget narrowed her eyes. Why was he so adamant about coming? "I get that you want to find a ghost or whatever, but this might be dangerous."

He looked down at his plate, expression turning contemplative. "I want to help. Dahlia was always nice to me. Besides, I know what it's like to lose someone you care about. It's awful, especially when the people in charge are making it worse." A forced smile crossed his face. "You came to Cleveland for answers, right?"

"I don't need help. You've already done enough," Bridget said automatically.

James reached for a second slice of pizza. "I can at least go with you to the alley. If there's another explosion or something, someone should be there to call for help.

Besides, Dahlia was sort of a friend."

He was right; going by the book wasn't enough. From North Carolina, nothing had happened fast enough for her. And now that she was here, she was still being told to wait in a corner.

She considered James. He *did* have some decent points. Besides, she was helping him, too. If nothing else, he'd scratch his ghost hunting itch. "Okay. You can come with me. How about tomorrow morning?"

He grinned. "Perfect. I don't have class until noon."

"Alright." Bridget took a bite of pizza. A vague plan was better than no plan. "Why don't we meet at the alley at nine?"

James nodded. "Sounds good." He slurped his soda can dry.

Back at the hotel, Bridget sat down on the edge of her bed. Her phone had a new voicemail. Detective Ivanova.

"Ms. Keene." Her curt tone was all business. "I looked into the lead you provided today. I'm sorry, but I found nothing noteworthy for the investigation. If you want to discuss it in further detail, stop by the station." *Click.*

Lies. Ivanova hadn't even hinted at the explosion.

She slipped under the covers and turned off the light. Half an hour later, she was still staring at the ceiling, worrying about what the truth actually contained. She couldn't stop hearing the detective's incongruous laughter in her mind. She drifted into an uneasy sleep as she wondered if Ivanova had already covered up evidence of the explosion.

The next morning, Bridget stepped off the bus and onto the sidewalk. She was back in her red coat and knee-high boots, hair pulled into a ponytail. She'd smudged concealer under her eyes, but it didn't do much to hide the dark circles.

James was waiting for her by the mouth of the alleyway in his Spiderman shirt. He looked far more awake than she felt, bouncing from one foot to the other.

"Hey!" His expression broke into a bright smile once he saw her.

"What's all that?" She eyed a black duffel bag that hung off his shoulder.

"I brought my gear." He patted the bag. "I've got my DSLR, a few extra lenses, a video camera, an EVP, a—"

"A what?" Bridget interrupted him.

"EVP. Electronic Voice Phenomena recorder. It lets me capture anyone's voice who might be trying to communicate."

She stared at him. "Right. Okay. Just... try not to make a scene." She gestured for him to follow her.

Bridget half expected to encounter yellow police tape blocking the alley, but there was none. She stuck close to the wall as she approached, James a few paces behind. He unzipped his bag and dug through its contents.

She peered down the narrow passageway. "Empty."

"Cool. Lead the way." He fumbled with his camera

lens.

A chill crept over Bridget as she stepped forward. The high, glassless windows gaped down at them like silent observers as they moved through the alleyway. Bridget stepped as softly as she could, but James' shoes crunched against the gravel. She bit back the urge to shush him.

It was fine. He was there to help. There was nothing wrong with that.

Bridget focused on the alley. Rubble still littered the back corner and decayed trash bags spilled out from the upended dumpster. Not only had the explosion gone unreported, but no one had bothered to clean it up.

"There," Bridget said, keeping her voice low. She pointed to the warped wood. "Those boards were nailed over that window. I was standing in front of it."

James let out a low whistle as he looked from the boards to the window. "You're lucky you didn't get hurt even worse." He lifted his camera and took a few shots of the building. "Okay, go stand by it."

"Stand by what?"

"Go stand by the window. Right where you stood yesterday."

"Why? What are you going to do with the pictures?" The last thing she needed was for Ivanova to find photos of her snooping around.

James sighed. "I want to recreate as much of the scene as possible. See if there's anything you missed."

"Oh, suddenly *you're* the detective?" Bridget asked.

"I'm not going to show them to anyone."

She frowned. "Fine, but this is a bad idea." Her heart fluttered as she approached the window, but a quick peek inside reassured her that it was empty. No sign of Ivanova or her companion. No sign of the dark smoke.

"I was standing here," she said, turning back to him.

"Looking in, right?" James asked as he fired off a few shots of his camera. "Could you face the other way?"

Bridget let out a slow sigh and turned towards the building. His camera clicked away as she rested her fingers on the worn brick edge of the windowsill. It was gritty and cool beneath her skin. The interior of the building was dark and silent. Broken glass winked at her, reflecting the outside light. Planks of wood and piles of broken furniture were strewn against the walls.

The camera shutter went quiet behind her, and James spoke up again. "So the wall you were talking about is inside? The one Ivanova was looking at?"

Bridget pointed. "They were standing right there."

Gravel crunched as he moved to stand beside her, adjusting his lens before snapping several more shots of the building's interior from outside. Then he let go of the camera, letting it hang from the strap around his neck as he reached for the door handle. He yanked on it, but it was still stuck.

"Even an explosion couldn't make it budge." Bridget shook her head.

James looked around until he spotted the pile of wooden boards. "Plan B." He bent over to pick one up and approached the shattered window. Brandishing the plank, he swiped away the remaining glass that protruded from the frame.

The noise was startlingly loud in the quiet alley. "Done this before?" she asked.

He shook his head. "Nope." Taking a step back, he let the board fall to the ground with a clatter. He inspected the window frame. "But I have watched movies before."

"Oh, great. Well, if you've watched *movies*."

James didn't respond, except to shoot her a grin. He pinned his camera against his chest and braced a hand against the sill. "Mind handing me my bag?" James asked as he climbed inside.

Bridget lifted it and passed it through the window. "Wait for me," she said with a furtive glance back and forth. With a deep breath, she hoisted herself up onto the edge of the window. The pressure sent a sharp twinge through her burned palms as she clambered inside. Her shoes hit the concrete floor with a slap.

Bridget stepped past James as he raised his camera. She peered about for the strange smoke from the previous day, but nothing moved in the dim light. Bits of concrete and empty beer cans crunched beneath her feet as she crept forward. The darkness pressed in, and the thin light from the window did little to reassure her.

She kept a close eye on the floor as she walked. Any shadow might be camouflaging the prowling smoke. Or Ivanova, coming to drag her away. She couldn't shake the nagging feeling she shouldn't be here. More than once, she pulled up short, convinced she'd seen movement.

Finally, unable to stand it any longer, she reached into her purse for her phone. She turned on the flashlight, flooding the hallway with bright light.

James made a disapproving sound. "That's ruining the photos."

"Yeah, well I'd rather not trip and ruin my face," Bridget said as she resumed her careful advance. "Keep it down, will you?"

Bridget stepped over a chunk of concrete and kicked up a thin layer of dust. She guided the light towards where Detective Ivanova and the redheaded man were standing when the black smoke had appeared.

"See anything?" James asked, still taking pictures of the hallway.

"Not really." A pang of disappointment hit her as she neared the wall. "Just some graffiti."

An intricate array of black strokes covered the worn cinder blocks. The artist had taken care to ensure the geometric pattern was precise, creating an expanding knot of swoops. It looked like the kind of design that would be difficult to create without a stencil. Something about it was familiar, but she couldn't quite place it.

James gestured for her to lower her phone then raised his camera to take a few shots. Each time his shutter clicked, the flash threw broken glass and wood piles into sharp relief. Dust motes hung in the air before being cast back into darkness. Bridget blinked to recover her vision.

He stepped forward to get a closer look. "It's cool. Kinda reminds me of fractal art." Letting the camera dangle from the strap around his neck once again, he brought out the thin, black recording device he'd called an EVP. He aimed it at the wall and pushed a button. A red light flashed as it started recording.

Bridget eyed the device. "What, exactly, do you think you're going to hear?" she asked. He shook his head and put a finger to his lips.

She fell silent and lifted her phone's light to the wall again. The graffiti stared back at them harmlessly. Was she overblowing what she'd seen? The burns on her palm told her that the smoke *had* existed, but it wasn't here now.

"Maybe we're in the wrong spot," Bridget said. She cast her gaze back to the window, then shook herself. She was here; she needed to search while she could. Moving deeper into the building, she left James to scrutinize the symbol.

The cracked cinder block walls didn't reveal much else. She passed by older, more faded graffiti and the tattered remains of a workplace safety poster. Chunks of the ceiling had fallen, leaving small piles of concrete for her to maneuver around.

"What else did the detective do when she was in here?" James asked.

"They looked around," Bridget said, stepping over a mildewed stack of magazines. "She complained about how it smelled."

"Anything else?"

"She touched the wall. Right before her friend said—

hang on." Something reflective had caught her eye. She stepped closer, scanning her light from side to side. Whatever it was glimmered again, amidst a pile of dusty, yellowed magazines and dead leaves. She bent down and pulled out a woman's sandal.

Coldness spread through her, radiating to her fingertips.

"James? I found something." Dirt and grime smudged the shoe, but she could still make out the silver of the straps. She turned it over and wiped away the grit to check the number on the bottom. Eight. Dahlia's size.

It could have belonged to anyone. In the video, Dahlia was dressed for cold rain, not a night out on the town. But she'd first gone missing in the summer. And the last anyone knew, she'd been on a date with Dan.

Maybe she was jumping to conclusions. It was just a shoe, after all. But if Dahlia *had* been here the day she disappeared, the missing shoe suggested she'd put up a fight. "What happened to you?" she whispered. She snapped a quick picture of it with her phone, then raised her voice again. "Hey, check this out."

"One sec," James called back.

Bridget pawed through leaves and rotting newspaper pages, searching for the sandal's match. Nothing. Still gripping the dirty silver strap, she straightened. Maybe the building held more clues. Her gaze fell on a closed door. She stepped towards it and turned the knob. The door swung inward on creaky hinges to reveal a dusty room; inside were several metal folding chairs and a busted lantern lying on its side under a coat of dust.

"Stop!"

The voice didn't belong to James.

Bridget's heart jolted. She spun around.

James was frozen, hand outstretched, touching the wall. His gaze was on the window they'd climbed through.

With James' attention away, he didn't seem to notice the graffiti under his fingers starting to glow.

"Drop your hand!"

The voice came from a man silhouetted in the window.

SIX

The man was backlit by faint sunlight, and although she couldn't make out his face, she could see his red hair. It had to be the same person she'd seen with Ivanova the day before.

James dropped his hand and shot Bridget an alarmed look. The graffiti's glow instantly fizzled.

Had she just imagined it?

And then there it was again—that horrible, sulfuric smell. A few wisps of inky smoke seeped from the wall.

"James!"

He spun to face her just as the wisps made a half-hearted attempt to snag his ankles, then dissipated.

They needed to take the sandal and run. Now.

The man's shadow moved away from the window towards the door.

Bridget glanced down the dim hallway. The ceiling was in even worse shape, and scattered mounds of cinder block hinted at an impending collapse.

"Come on!" she hissed, urging James towards her. "Hurry!" She had no idea where the hallway led, but there had to be another way out.

James turned and ran in her direction. He'd almost reached her when he cursed and skidded to a stop. "My bag—" His equipment sat beneath the window.

"Leave it!" Bridget cried.

He ignored her. Instead, he slipped the EVP into the inside pocket of his coat and dashed towards his belongings. Bridget's heart jumped in panic.

The door thudded against its frame.

James scrambled to his bag and tugged it onto his shoulder. Behind him, the redhead reappeared in the window. Before James could break into a run, the man's hand snagged the back of his jacket. "Let me go!" James twisted in alarm, trying to wrench free.

"Nobody move," the stranger commanded, and James froze. "That includes you, Ms. Keene." He locked eyes with her.

Bridget sucked in a surprised breath. He recognized her. Ivanova must have told him who she was. She watched as he hoisted himself through the window one-handed, keeping a firm grip on James.

"You two know each other?" James looked at Bridget in surprise, still trying to tug free.

"Not exactly." Bridget stared at the redheaded man.

She should have *known* that the detective would have the place watched. And with all the noise James was making, of course they'd drawn attention.

"Come outside," the man said, voice stern. "You're breaking and entering."

"No way!" James protested. "We were just looking!"

Bridget shook her head. She couldn't afford to get arrested when she was so close to answers. Her gaze darted to the floor. The sandal lay on its side at her feet.

"Let's go," the man said, and Bridget looked up again. With his free hand, he reached into the pocket of his jeans and pulled out an officer's badge. It glinted in the dim light, and she felt her resolve weaken. He put it away again.

The stranger kept a firm grip on James' shoulder, turning him to the door. "Give me the camera," he said as he reached over to slide the deadbolt free. He turned and extended an upturned hand towards James.

Reluctant, James pulled the camera from around his neck and set it in the man's palm. Then James faltered and went pale. He snagged the doorframe to catch himself from stumbling.

Bridget's eyes widened. He looked like he was going to fall over.

"Easy," the man murmured, voice low. The door squealed open. "Stay here, Ms. Keene." Then he guided James into the alleyway and out of sight.

Bridget pocketed her phone and wiped trembling palms on her jeans. If she was going to run, this was her chance. That's what Dahlia would do. But this stranger worked with Ivanova. If she cooperated, maybe he would give her fresh insight into the case.

The redhead returned with James' camera strap over his shoulder. "Now you."

"Is he okay?" She took a shaky step forward.

"A little lightheaded. Some people aren't made for creeping around. Come on." His eyes narrowed.

"What do you have there?"

She glanced down at the sandal and shoved it into her purse. "Nothing." The shoe was the only piece of evidence she had. She wasn't ready to hand it over. Not until she knew this man could be trusted.

He scoffed and gestured impatiently. "Come over here."

Bridget picked her way over busted pipes and hunks of concrete, fighting irritation. Who was this man to show up and tell her what to do? She'd never seen him before the previous day, and Ivanova had never mentioned having a partner. It made her wonder what else the detective was lying about.

As soon as she was close, the stranger stretched out his hand.

She frowned. "I'm fine."

"Give it to me." His eyes were on the sandal's heel sticking out of her bag. "I won't ask again."

"No." She put a protective hand over the bag. "It's mine."

His lips twisted with annoyance, and he stepped

forward, grabbing for it. He missed the shoe. Instead, his clammy fingers wrapped around her wrist. A hot spike of uneasiness rushed through her. The daylight shining in from the window abruptly seemed to brighten. She swallowed, throat suddenly dry.

Woozy, she tried to steady herself enough to pull away from him. Her cheeks burned with frustration as the redhead pulled her forward over a fallen light fixture.

Dahlia would have found her failed trespassing attempt hysterical. Bridget tried to shove aside the thoughts of her sister, but the heat of embarrassment ran through her all the same. In fact, the feeling only intensified with each step. The stranger's grip on her wrist tightened as sweat prickled along her forehead. Her stomach twisted with nausea. She drew in a breath, but it didn't help. The world tilted around her.

The man released her, and she sank to her knees. Distantly, she heard him ask if she was alright. She tried to respond, but it felt as if someone had wedged cotton down her throat. The edges of her vision darkened, and panic surged through her as she realized she was about to pass out.

A dull, persistent throb urged Bridget back to consciousness. Brightness assaulted her closed eyelids, leaving a deep pink glow. Bridget lifted a hand to shield her face from the onslaught of light. At first, she found it difficult to focus on anything. The well-lit room was a sharp contrast to the dark building she last remembered, and everything blurred at the edges. She blinked until her vision began to clear, revealing white walls, a wooden table, and metal folding chairs.

She was lying on a couch that looked as if it had come straight out of the seventies, with rough fabric and garish colors. Someone had placed a small, square pillow beneath her head. It was mustard yellow.

She remained still, trying to make sense of where she was and how she'd gotten there. She couldn't remember leaving the abandoned building with the detective's associate, only feeling dizzy.

With a quiet groan, Bridget pushed herself into a sitting position. Her head pounded in protest, and she reached up to rub her temples. Her fingers brushed against her fine hair, and she reached back to tighten her ponytail. She was still wearing her boots and, upon a disoriented glance, saw her coat folded on one of the metal chairs. There was no sign of James.

Wherever she was, the sparkly sandal wasn't here either. There was no way to know where that guy had taken it.

She coughed. Her throat was dust-dry. Water would be good, but there was no sink. A single wooden door led out of the room, and she pushed to her feet, pausing to steady herself. Bridget shook her head to clear it, and the world began to spin again. She squeezed her eyes shut and sank back down onto the couch.

Had she imagined that graffiti symbol glowing? That couldn't have really happened, right? She must have passed out.

But the smoke was real, of that she was certain. She couldn't have imagined it twice. And that *smell*. Though why it had fizzled so quickly this time, she wasn't sure.

"Oh, good. You're awake." Ivanova's voice broke through the throbbing in her head. Bridget hadn't even heard the door open. She risked peeking up, then ducked her head again, pressing the heels of her hands against the sides of her head.

"Aspirin?" The detective approached her. Bridget looked up again at the sound of pills rattling. The detective set a bottle on the table, along with a glass of water. Then she straightened her blazer, adjusting the collar of her white blouse underneath.

Bridget looked at the bottle with suspicion. "No thanks." She wasn't about to accept any favors from the detective.

Ivanova sat on the cushion beside her. "My associate brought you here. He said you passed out."

Bridget glanced around the room again. "Where is *here*?"

"You're at the station." Ivanova gave her a severe look. "What were you doing in that building, Ms. Keene?"

Bridget brought her hands down from her forehead. "I wanted to see it for myself," she said, hoping her gaze held more conviction than her pained voice.

Ivanova frowned at Bridget as if trying to figure out

what to do with her. "You got my voicemail, didn't you? I told you there was nothing there."

"Not nothing. I found a sandal. Your friend took it."

Ivanova scoffed. "A sandal is hardly consequential."

"But it's evidence! Why on earth would someone leave a fancy shoe in a place like that?"

The detective shook her head. "I don't know, Ms. Keene, but if I followed up on every odd item left by squatters, I'd never get anything done. It's not enough to go on."

Bridget bit back a retort. Arguing with Ivanova would get her nowhere. "Where's James?"

Disdain crept into her voice. "I've already spoken with him. He's been sent home with a warning. Breaking and entering is a crime, Ms. Keene. As is interfering with a police investigation."

"It was an abandoned building. I didn't hurt anything." She knew the defensive tone only made her sound guiltier, but she didn't care. If she had any hope of finding Dahlia she *had* to keep pushing. She forced herself to ignore her aching head and meet the detective's gaze.

Ivanova sighed, sitting back in her chair. "Abandoned or not, I want you to understand how dangerous it was to ignore what I said. Anything could have happened."

Bridget held Ivanova's eyes. "Like an explosion?"

Ivanova's expression hardened, and silence stretched between them. Bridget felt a thrill of victory at throwing her off her game.

"So you were there then, too. I told you not to investigate on your own."

Bridget shrugged in defiance. "And you told me there wasn't anything there."

Ivanova's jaw tightened, and she folded her arms over her chest. "Tell me exactly what you saw."

Blue eyes narrowing, Bridget replied, "You know what I saw. That... *smoke*. What was it?"

Ivanova chewed her lip, seeming to consider her response. "That's not for you to know. It's under investigation, as is the explosion."

Another deflection. Ivanova spent more time avoiding questions than finding answers. And Bridget hadn't even mentioned the glowing graffiti. "You lied to me. In that voicemail, you said there was nothing in that building."

"No. What I told you was that nothing in that building pertained to your sister's disappearance. This is unrelated, and it doesn't concern you."

Bridget scowled. "Well, I hope your new investigation goes faster than your attempts to find Dahlia."

The detective looked away. "On that topic, I'm afraid I have some difficult news. It's about the case. We're going to have to close it for now."

Bridget stared in disbelief. "What?" Surely, she had misheard.

"I was hoping to tell you under better circumstances, Bridget. There hasn't been a solid lead in months. I know this must be difficult." The detective sounded like she'd rehearsed the words.

No. It was one thing for Ivanova to push Bridget's attempts to help away, but to dismiss the case altogether? It had to be a joke.

The detective continued. "Unless something substantial emerges, we have no choice but to call an end to the search for Dahlia. I'm sorry."

A short time later, Bridget stepped out of the taxi the detective had called. She slammed the door closed behind her. Ivanova's words circled through her head on an endless loop. Nothing to be done. Missing for good. Go home and try to get on with your life.

The detective had turned her back on the entire case. Worse, Ivanova expected Bridget to give up, too.

Bless her heart. As if she would go home and let her sister fade into memory. *Especially* given what she'd found.

Frustration boiled inside of her, hot compared to the cold rain that fell. She looked up, and a droplet splattered on her forehead. Since her departure from the police station, the bright morning had given way to a dark afternoon. Charcoal gray clouds roiled overhead.

The rain sped up, leaving dark stains on the cement. A jagged arc of lightning splintered across the sky, illuminating the cityscape.

"Excuse me," a voice called out, startling her. The hotel's valet stood by the door. "Are you coming in?"

Bridget hurried towards him, out of the rain. "Yes, thanks," she said as she stepped into the busy lobby. A blast of over-circulated air sent a shiver across her damp skin. Eager to be alone, she ducked through a line of tired-looking professionals and families waiting to check in for the night.

She turned away from the packed elevator bay and pulled open the door to the stairs. The stairwell was like another world, all concrete and metal, with no windows to show the impending storm. The sound of her climbing footsteps rebounded off the walls, complementing a muffled rumble of thunder. Her thumping heart joined the racket.

When she reached the fifth floor, she paused on the landing to catch her breath, grasping the railing for support. How could Ivanova do this to her? She'd given up. She'd dismissed evidence. She'd actually tried to make Bridget feel *bad* for following her sister's trail. As if breaking into an old, empty building was a greater crime than abandoning Dahlia.

Evasions and distractions. That was all Ivanova had to offer.

Alone in the stairwell, gasping for air, angry tears finally spilled over. She yanked the door open, fumbling to pull her room key from her purse as she hurried down the hall. Her vision blurred as she swiped the key card for her room once, twice, three times before the light finally blinked green.

Inside, it was as cold as the lobby, but at least it was

empty. The housekeeper had changed the sheets and wiped down the counters, leaving behind the smell of disinfectant.

Her head still throbbed. She tossed her purse onto the bed and made her way to the bathroom. Outside, a boom of thunder rattled the window. She took two aspirin from her makeup bag and washed them down with tap water. Then she grabbed a washcloth and began to scrub away her makeup.

The search had to go on, regardless of what Ivanova said. But how could she find Dahlia when the so-called professionals were actively rebuking her? She *had* leads. Between the sandal, the smoke, and the glowing graffiti, she had more clues than she'd had in months. But for the detective to call them dead ends? Who did she think she was?

With an angry sob, Bridget bunched the scratchy face towel between her hands. She straightened, and another rush of lightheadedness made the room tilt and darken around the edges. Her head pounded in protest at the movement.

Rest first, she decided. She wiped her eyes and let out a shuddering sigh. As much as she wanted to resume her investigation, she'd be no use to Dahlia if she couldn't think straight.

She released the towel and made her way towards the bed, sinking down on the edge. Fat drops of rain spattered against the window, leaving smears that trailed downward in miniature rivers. At least she had *something.* Now she had proof she was on the right track. And if she went back to the building, maybe she could find more.

Her vibrating phone jolted her from her thoughts. She reached into her purse and peered down at the screen. It was James. "Hello?"

"Bridget?"

She was surprised by how glad she was to hear his voice. "Yeah, it's me," she said. "Hey."

"Are you sitting down, because you're not gonna believe—um." He cut off his rapid-fire speech and started again. "Sorry. Are you okay?"

"Honestly, my head is about to pound out of my skull." She leaned back against the pillows.

"Me too," James said in a hushed voice, as if worried about being overheard. "Listen, we need to meet again. Can I come to you?"

She shook her head to clear it. "What's this about?"

"The detective's full of shit. She doesn't care what happened to Dahlia."

"I know," Bridget said with a stab of annoyance. "She closed the investigation."

"Exactly. So she could get you out of her hair."

Bridget paused. "How do you know that?"

"I have proof she's lying."

Silence. From both of them. If true, this would confirm all her suspicions. The case wasn't cold—the detective was sabotaging it.

Bridget sucked in a tight breath. "Let's talk."

SEVEN

Bridget spent an anxious hour in her hotel room, all thoughts of rest pushed aside. She considered calling her mother with an update but dismissed the idea right away. It would make her worry, and she'd never believe stories about police conspiracies and creepy smoke. She'd tell her to come home, that the stress was getting to her.

No, if she was going to talk to anyone else about this, Bridget needed to get her hands on James' proof first.

Finally, a text popped up on her phone.

There in 20.

Bridget paced for the next quarter hour before descending to the lobby. The elevator doors dinged open and she stepped out, looking around expectantly. No sign of James. The crowd of afternoon customers had dissipated. Only the tired attendant remained. He looked up from his paperwork and gave her a nod.

Restless, Bridget examined the tourism brochures displayed in a rack beside the desk. Her eyes skimmed over advertisements for the Rock n' Roll Hall of Fame, Playhouse Square, and the Cleveland Metroparks Zoo. One of the pamphlets promoted a ghost tour of the city. She lifted the flyer, turning it over in her hand to read.

CLEVELAND GHOST TOURS: Explore haunted cemeteries, abandoned speakeasies, and even an old castle as we show you the most bone-chilling sites in the CLE.

Beneath the text was a series of photographs that looked altered. Was this the sort of organization James associated with? Could she trust evidence from someone who made a habit of seeing conspiracies where there were none?

On the other hand, did it matter? James was Bridget's only link to Dahlia at this point. Eccentric or not, he was useful. And he had information she needed.

"Hey, Bridget."

Her head lifted at James' familiar voice. She stuffed the flyer back in the rack and turned towards him. He lifted a hand in greeting as he crossed the lobby towards her. His curls had exploded into a frizzy, unkempt mess. Maybe it was the bad lighting in the lobby, but he looked pale, too.

"Hey. You alright?" She strode in his direction.

"Yeah, I'm good, if I ignore how sore I am. It's like I got hit with the flu," he said.

She nodded. "Yeah, my joints are aching."

"I told you something weird was going on. C'mon, let's go somewhere private." He started walking towards the elevator bay.

She didn't follow. "Why can't we just talk down here?"

James flushed, trotting back to her. "I want to get to a place where they can't listen in."

"Where *who* can't listen in?" Maybe he *was* just a conspiracy theorist.

"I'll tell you once we're in private." James beckoned for her to follow.

Bridget shook her head. She wasn't about to invite someone she barely knew into her hotel room. "Let's talk out here. The cafe's empty."

He turned around, then looked past her to the restaurant. It was vacant, except for a bored-looking barista behind the counter. He wavered, then strode in.

They chose the table farthest from the counter. Bridget slid into the booth, relieved to give her muscles a rest. Even standing left her tired. "Alright, tell me what's going on. You said you had proof that the detective is jerking me around."

"Yup." He pulled the EVP recorder out of his pocket and set it on the desk with a flourish. "This was still recording when I passed out."

Bridget sat up straighter. "You passed out, too?"

He nodded and tapped the recorder. "It's all in here. I

promise I haven't edited a thing. This is the original recording." His eyes were bright, expression intent. "It's too important to lose."

She nodded, eyes on the recorder. "Okay. Play it."

He pushed the button. The speakers crackled to life, and she heard her own voice say, "What, exactly, do you think you're going to hear?" The sound quality was poor, filled with static, and the volume was low to avoid prying ears, but she could make out the words.

"Sorry," James said, turning up the recorder's volume. "The sound isn't the best, but you'll get the idea."

She listened as the device played back their exploration of the abandoned building, picking up the garbled sound of their footfalls and Bridget's discovery of the sandal. Even though she knew it was coming, Bridget jumped all over again when the stranger's voice called, "Stop! Drop your hand."

Leaning towards the EVP, she closed her eyes to focus on the staticky sound of talking. She could only pick out every couple of words as Bridget called for James to hurry, followed by the thud of footsteps, then a brief scuffle.

"You shouldn't have gone back to get your bag," Bridget muttered. "Maybe we could have gotten away."

James looked up at her, incredulous. "It had all my equipment in it! Thousands of dollars' worth. I wasn't going to just leave it."

"Yeah, but—"

"Listen," James hissed, cutting her off. "This is the

important part."

"Give me the camera," the distorted voice of the redheaded man said. Then, a murmured, "Easy. Stay here, Ms. Keene." There was a shuffling sound, like a bag being dragged across the floor, followed by a thud.

"That was me passing out," James narrated in a hushed voice.

Silence followed. Bridget glanced up at him.

"Well?" she hissed, but he held up a finger.

The shriek of metal sounded over the speakers, followed by more dragging and a second thud. By this point, both of them would have been unconscious. More footsteps, and then the stranger's voice again, distant but intelligible.

"Eisheth? ... found two little mice." A pause. "The sister and a man, trespassing in the building." Another stretch of silence followed before he sighed in exasperation. "He touched the symbol. *Yes,* it came back. They'll be unconscious for an hour or two." A longer pause this time, then a curt, "Goodbye."

Bridget looked up at James. "Was he talking to the detective?" she asked. She fumbled for her wallet, pulling out the detective's business card. It read, *Elizabeth Ivanova.* Maybe he'd called someone else.

"There's more." James leaned forward and pressed a button. The vague sounds of scuffling sped up as he fast-forwarded the recording. When he hit play, the speakers crackled back to life in the middle of someone speaking.

"—not good, Gaul." It was Ivanova, Bridget was pretty

sure. "Aren't you... *us* not to act rashly?"

"There was nothing rash about it." It was the same voice that had been speaking before. Bridget glanced up at James. So the stranger had a name. Gaul. "They were dangerously close to hurting themselves."

Ivanova *hmphed*. "... pain." Bridget leaned closer to the recorder to hear, forehead wrinkling with frustration. It was hard enough to focus with the jackhammering in her skull.

"I agree. So send her home."

Bridget raised her eyes to James, brows lifting, but he was still watching the recorder.

"... think I've already tried that? She's obsessed... her sister... not as if I can halt an ongoing investigation." Ivanova's voice held a sharp edge.

"Can't you? Tell her it's closed... dragged on long enough."

A heavy sigh. "Fine. Put him... I'll take care of this."

Bridget stared at the recorder in shock. Fine? *Fine?* The detective hadn't even put up a fight.

Shuffling sounds followed, along with a quiet grunt. "We need to have a meeting," Gaul said a few seconds later.

"I'm busy," Ivanova responded. "I don't... listen to you drone on."

A pause. "Eisheth. I know you're worried, but... find him... cooperate."

"Because *you've* had... success," Ivanova snapped.

"Tonight at eight." There was no room for negotiation

in Gaul's tone. "I'm... someone to help."

James stopped the EVP and met Bridget's gaze. "After that, it's quiet for a while, and then Ivanova telling me to get out with a warning."

Bridget shook her head in disbelief. "So she just *told* me Dahlia's case was closed to get me off her back." She struggled to keep her voice low and level. *How could Ivanova sleep at night?* "There should be a record of something like that, right?"

He nodded. "I assume there's paperwork involved."

She clenched her fist. "The detective's lying. I want to show proof to her supervisor. Get the case moving again, and her ass fired."

"I think you're missing the more important point here," James said. "That guy somehow made *both* of us pass out. This is way bigger than a missing persons case."

"Nothing's more important than finding my sister," she retorted. Then she cooled, glancing up at the barista, who had yet to peel her eyes from her phone. "Granted, magically making people pass out *is* pretty weird."

"It's more than weird. It's *proof* something supernatural is happening," James said.

Bridget eyed him, considering. Should she tell him about the graffiti? And had he noticed the wisps of smoke? She hadn't said anything to the detective, but James was on her side. Right? Or would it just make him fall deeper into his conspiracy theories?

But then again, he hadn't broken her trust yet. Maybe it was worth the risk. "Did you notice anything weird about the graffiti?" she asked.

James shook his head. "It's cool artwork. Weird how?"

She hesitated. "When you touched that graffiti, I swear it started glowing."

"What? No way." James leaned in eagerly. "Bridget, that's even more proof!"

"I'm not sure I'd go that far," Bridget said. "It could have been a trick of the light. And as far as us passing out, what if he drugged us?"

"How? He didn't have a chance to."

With a huff of exasperation, she shook her head. "I don't know, okay?" There *was* a reasonable explanation, she was sure of it. But she didn't have enough information. "We need to listen in on their meeting."

"What?" James asked. The eagerness faded from his expression. "I was thinking we post this recording online or something. If the detective found you tailing her, she'd be pissed."

"This might be my only chance to find out what's going on. I'm not giving it up."

James hesitated as he pocketed the EVP. "How will you even find them? They didn't say where they're meeting."

Good point. Bridget hadn't considered that. "I'll go back to the police station. I can wait for the detective to leave and follow her."

"How? You don't have a car."

"True, but..." She looked through the windows at the parking lot. James' car had to be out there.

"Seriously?" he groaned.

"Look, maybe you can get a better recording with your EVP thing, and then you can put them *both* online."

James sighed and rubbed his cheek. "I have a bad feeling about this."

Bridget scowled. "What's the deal? Up until now you were excited."

"Yeah, but that's before we got hauled into the police station."

"Isn't that sort of the risk you run, breaking into abandoned buildings?" When he flushed, she pressed her point. "Don't you want to know what's *really* going on?"

"I do," he admitted. He drummed his fingers on the table and let out a short sigh. "Okay. I'll do this with you. Under one condition."

"What?"

"We do some research, first. It's what, four? Their meeting isn't until eight. We have time to figure out what we're up against."

"Whatever it takes, so long as we don't miss our chance."

James shook his head and held up his phone. "Like you said, if the detective is mixed up in something, maybe there's a record. There's time to look, at least."

Conspiracy theorist or no, she had to admit James was useful. Left to her own devices, Bridget wouldn't have thought to investigate further. She'd have spent the rest of the evening trying to corner the detective. But James was right; she didn't know what that would lead to. The more information they had, the better.

"Okay, let's do it," Bridget said.

EIGHT

"Officer Elizabeth Ivanova Promoted to Detective," Bridget read the headline aloud. "Serving as an officer for eight years, the newly appointed Detective Ivanova has been a model representative of the police force in Cleveland." She wrinkled her nose.

"This one is about some armed robbery she stopped." James tapped his phone. They were still in the cafe. A full cup of lukewarm hot chocolate sat beside Bridget. The whipped cream had melted, leaving tan fuzz on top.

"There's no dirt. Every mention of her talks about what a perfect cop she is." Her voice dripped with cynicism.

James chewed his bottom lip. "That's something in itself, though, isn't it?"

"How do you figure?" Bridget asked. She backed up to

the main browser and stared at the search bar.

"No officer's record is perfect. I mean, you know how cops are. And the news loves to report scandals and stuff. Why would they run all these stories about her great work? Aren't detectives supposed to lie low?"

Bridget hadn't considered that. "But that still doesn't tell us anything new, other than she *might* be covering up a bad reputation with reports about a good one. But we already know she's lying."

James shrugged. "It's a start." He lifted his cup for another sip of hot chocolate, then frowned when he realized it was empty.

Bridget responded with a noncommittal grunt. The detective's glowing reputation felt like salt in the wound.

"It's not fair," she said in a quiet voice.

James looked up from his phone. "What?"

"This. All of this." She set her phone on the table and rubbed at her eyes. "I'm not finding anything useful. And if I were the one missing, Dahlia wouldn't be holed up in a hotel lobby. She'd be out there *doing* something."

"We are doing something. I don't want to run into this without any information."

"You ran into the building this morning," Bridget pointed out.

"I'd been there before," he said. "So had you. And we still got caught. I don't want to take that risk again, not without knowing what we're getting into."

"Yeah, but we're not finding anything useful. I just..." She swallowed back a familiar lump in her throat. "I hate sitting around. I want to *do* something. I'm responsible for Dahlia, you know?"

James set his phone down. "I'm sorry." He didn't seem to know what else to say.

She studied him. "Do you have any siblings?"

He shook his head. "No, I'm an only child."

"There were times I wished I was. She used to drive me up the wall."

"Yeah? How so?"

Bridget looked down at her mug, smiling as a memory struck her. "I remember in senior year, I ran out of shampoo. So she grabbed me a spare bottle from under the sink. Only it wasn't shampoo."

His eyes widened. "What happened?"

She met his gaze. "She'd handed me the hair removal cream."

"Oh crap."

Bridget's cheeks felt hot with the memory. "I was furious. I lost half my hair and refused to speak to her for a month."

"Then what?" James leaned forward in his seat.

She rolled her eyes in exasperation. "She said it was a good look for me. And to prove it, she shaved *her* head so we'd both start the school year bald. By Thanksgiving break she'd inspired half her classmates to do the same. She was just a freshman, but she was more popular than ever, and way more insufferable."

James laughed. "Sounds like Dahlia. I think she could make anything popular."

Bridget nodded in agreement. "She has an uncanny ability to make people like her."

"Yeah. Are you like that too?"

Bridget snorted. "Definitely not. I've only ever had one or two friends, and we were never that close."

"Why's that?"

Good question. She'd asked herself the same thing many times. "I guess it takes people a while to warm up to me."

"I don't know. You seem pretty cool," James said.

Bridget shook her head. "I appreciate that, but I'm no Dahlia. High school was hell. Everyone had their little clique. Me? I just got through classes so I could take care of her." Her shoulders tensed at the memories. It was too easy to go back to that time, when she clung to the edges of the hallway, avoiding her classmates. "Bridget the Bitch. A few people called me that."

James rolled his eyes. "That's not even creative. They were probably intimidated by you."

"Maybe," Bridget said doubtfully. "They said I was stuck up. But I didn't mean to be. I was just quiet."

"I get it. I wasn't quiet, but... well, it's me. Where I grew up, most of the school spent their Friday nights at the football game. I spent my weekends exploring haunted buildings. People thought I was strange."

Bridget shifted uneasily, remembering the flyer she'd picked up. It hadn't been an hour since *she'd* wondered if he was a total weirdo.

"It's okay," James said with a self-deprecating smile.

"I get it. It's an odd hobby."

"No it's not," Bridget said quickly. When James raised his eyebrows, she sighed. "Okay, fine. It's a little odd, but who cares? So far, it's only helped the investigation."

"That's fair. So you spent high school taking care of Dahlia. What then?"

Bridget cleared her throat. "I decided to go to community college, so I could stay close. But then Dahlia graduated and went away to school and..." Her chest tightened. "It was hard. I really missed her."

"You must love her a lot." James' voice was gentle.

She nodded. "Until she moved to Cleveland, we talked all the time. Even when we fought, we'd always have each other's back. I figured we could come back from anything. Until she started dating Dan, anyway." Her vision began to mist and she cleared her throat. "What about you? Did you two spend much time together?"

"No way. Not outside of that class we were both in. She was way out of my league." He cleared his throat.

"You liked her," Bridget surmised. Of course he did.

He flushed. "I mean, as a friend. I kept asking when she'd join the Paranormal Investigative Club. I'm sure I came across as such a loser."

"It would've become the coolest club on campus," Bridget said.

"I'm still holding out hope," James grinned. "If we find something good, we're that much closer to figuring out where she is."

Bridget's smile faded, as James' words brought her

back to the cafe. She nodded and picked her phone up again. "So far the news reports aren't any help."

"Maybe we're going about this the wrong way," James said. "Here, why don't you try looking up the guy she was with. Gaul or whatever?" He picked his own phone back up. "I'll take the detective."

"Wish we had a last name for him. Or maybe Gaul *is* his last name." She typed it into the search bar. The top result was about a historic region of Europe. She scrolled down the page but didn't find anything more relevant. Backing up, she tried adding the word Cleveland to the search. Several profiles popped up. One was for a local bureaucrat, the other for a politician. Neither looked anything like the redheaded man who had stopped them in the building. "Find anything?"

He didn't respond, brow furrowed as he scrolled down his screen. His motions were swift and jerky, and his eyes zipped back and forth.

"James?" she prodded.

"Hang on." He kept scrolling a few seconds, then abruptly turned the phone to show her the screen. "Look at this."

Bridget squinted at the text. It was a news article with the title, Armed Robber Dies of Mysterious Illness in Jail, Raising Concerns of Outbreak.

"It's the same case from before. The one Ivanova stopped. Her name's in it," James said. "A day after she arrested him, he got sick and died. Sounds like dirt to me."

Bridget frowned. "It *is* weird. But it doesn't prove anything." She raised her eyes to him. "We need to be careful. She could be dangerous."

"Yeah," James agreed. He set his phone down on the table. "You're still planning to follow her, aren't you?"

"We're not finding anything this way. You're still doing this with me, right?" She pocketed her phone.

"Yeah. I don't like this, but you're right. Something strange is happening, and we need more proof." He glanced at his watch. "How late does the detective stay at the station? It's already after six, and their meeting is at eight."

"I don't know," Bridget said. "But we should go now. Before we lose our chance."

And before she lost her nerve.

NINE

Bridget leaned out the open window of James' parked car, grateful for the fresh air. His car smelled like mildew and French fries. She tilted the side mirror so it showed the glass doors of the police station entrance. They were lined by cement columns holding up a portico to keep off the rain.

"Do you think she left already?" James asked, craning his neck to peer through the rearview mirror. The thunderstorm had dissolved into a fine mist that fell over the parking lot. Beads of moisture fogged up the glass.

"No, I bet she's still in there." She sounded more certain than she felt. "Back when she was first assigned to Dahlia's case, she told my mom and me the best time to call her was in the evenings." She pulled a small bottle of hand lotion from her purse and spread it across her palms. They were still red from her encounter with the smoke, though they didn't sting as badly.

He leaned back in his seat as he unwrapped a granola bar. "Wanna make a backup plan in case we're wrong?" he asked over the sound of the crinkling wrapper.

"Yeah, if you have any bright ideas." The parking lot was almost empty. A streetlamp flickered on, as if realizing how dark it was. It cast a weak, yellow light.

He fell quiet, frowning. Evidently, new ideas were not forthcoming. They continued to sit in silence, waiting.

Bridget watched him as he chewed on the granola bar. His curls were a mop of frizz in the humidity. He shifted, fidgeting with his seatbelt. She could sense his anxiety, and a pang of sympathy ran through her. "Hey, um... last night at the pizza shop you mentioned you'd lost someone. I'm sorry."

James swallowed his bite and hitched a shoulder in a half shrug. "It was years ago." He kept his eyes on the misty parking lot.

"Still, I know that's hard." Bridget fell silent, not wanting to press further. She stuck her hand out of the window and let the cool raindrops hit her skin.

James cleared his throat. "It was my Saba. My grandfather. He, um... I mean, he got sick. He was old. It wasn't anything like what's happening with Dahlia."

Bridget nodded. "That still must have been difficult."

"I was close to him. He used to read me ghost stories when I was a kid. Every October we'd go to cheesy haunted houses." His laugh was soft.

Her lips curled into a smile. This, at least, explained his odd hobby.

James sighed and turned the granola bar over in his hands. "Even though he'd been sick, he'd insisted on going on a trip to Europe. When he died, he was in Italy. It was a nightmare. Mom had a hard time getting his—his body returned. I guess the paperwork was a big mess, and no one knew what they were doing. It delayed the funeral and..."

"I'm really sorry, James. That's awful."

He shrugged again. "It's sort of a big deal in Jewish families, you know? Burying someone quickly after they die."

She nodded. She'd only been to one Jewish funeral. Her friend's uncle had been buried the day after he'd died.

"My mom was a wreck. And it was all because no one could get their act together." He trailed off and picked at his thumbnail.

Poor guy. He was right. It was hard enough to lose someone, but the aftermath was sometimes even worse.

"Are we obvious?" James blurted. He glanced out the back window, despite the condensation that glazed it. "We're probably too obvious, huh? We should park somewhere else."

"We're okay," Bridget said, allowing him to change the topic. He was right; his loss wasn't the same. Losing a grandparent was sad but expected. A sister disappearing into thin air, her investigation halted by the police, was far from normal. Still, it was good to have companionship who cared. She turned her attention back to the mirror, wiping the glass with the sleeve of her coat.

"I'm gonna move to—" James started, then cut off as headlights swept across their car. He sank in his seat as a black Prius pulled into the parking lot. Bridget pulled her hand into the car and slouched lower. She caught a quick impression of the driver—a man with wavy hair. The car pulled into a parking spot in front of the police station, its headlights illuminating the building. It sported a French flag bumper sticker.

There was a soft rustling sound as James set down his half-eaten granola bar, and then nothing but cars sloshing past on the road. Bridget was about to dismiss the Toyota when the door to the station swung open. She held her breath, recognizing Ivanova at once. The detective clutched a cardigan around her thin shoulders, and her usually tight bun drooped. She walked into the rain without hesitation. The driver stepped out, opening an umbrella and adjusting a long, dark jacket. He left the engine idling as he crossed the distance to the front entrance.

"—don't want that," Bridget could make out Ivanova's snippy tone as she marched past the man. The mirror was beginning to fog up again, and the detective looked like a wraith moving through the night.

"Who's the guy?" James whispered, drawing a nervous glance from Bridget. His gaze was fixed on his own mirror.

Ivanova and the stranger made their way to the passenger's side of the car. Bridget squinted at the two figures, watching as the man reached for the handle. Ivanova swatted his hand away.

"I don't have patience for your chivalry tonight." Ivanova's voice was louder now. Bridget strained to listen but couldn't make out the man's murmured response. The detective yanked the door open and disappeared inside. That left the driver to walk back around to his side of the car, shaking off his umbrella before sliding into his seat. A moment later bright red and white lights came to life as he pulled out of the parking spot.

"Okay," Bridget said, sitting back up, "let's go."

James gave a nervous laugh as he turned the car on. "Yeah. Time to stalk a police officer. No big deal."

"Just don't make it *look* like we're stalking her." Bridget clicked her seatbelt into place and rolled up her window. Finally, they were making progress. She clasped her hands tightly to keep them from jittering.

Mist clung to the windshield between wiper swipes, and James' headlights reflected the gloom as they pulled out onto the main road. It was still an hour before sunset, but the thick clouds had forced the city into a premature twilight. The rain transformed all the cars into smudges, and the Prius' red taillights were their beacon as they joined the line of evening traffic.

The driver made his way east, past the campus Dahlia had called home and further from the heart of the city. Bridget bounced her leg, watching as the car pulled ahead of them. "Hurry." She inched forward in her seat as if it would make the car go faster.

A sudden roar came from their left. Bridget jumped as a bright blue Camaro sped around them. It slid back into their lane and cut them off as they approached an intersection.

James slammed on the brakes and Bridget jerked forward against her seatbelt. "Crap!" he cried. The car sped away and the traffic light turned red. James groaned and came to a halt. Bridget chewed her lip as she looked for the Prius, but it was nowhere in sight. It must have made it through the light.

"We lost them." Bridget turned to James. "What do we do?"

"I can catch up. Assuming it's a short light."

Bridget drummed her fingers on her legs as the seconds dragged on. James muttered with impatience. "C'mon, c'mon."

The wipers screeched across the windshield. Cross traffic continued to streak through the intersection. Then it slowed.

The instant the light turned green, James punched the accelerator. The car leaped forward. "See them?"

Bridget strained against her seatbelt, twisting to look. James kept his foot on the accelerator, going well over the speed limit. Now *they* were the ones cutting off other cars.

Finally, she spotted the sedan with its tell-tale sticker. It was turning onto a side street ahead of them.

"There! Go right!" she pointed.

James let out a relieved breath. "Good catch." He switched lanes but drove past the street. "I'll swing around the block so they don't see us."

"We might lose them again!"

"It's better than getting caught," James said.

She craned her neck, watching the Prius continue away from them until it was out of sight. *Please let it be the same car*, she begged silently. James turned right at his next opportunity, thrumming a nervous rhythm on the steering wheel over the gentle patter of rain. They continued in a circle, passing rows of two-story houses. Most of them had lights on inside and cars in the driveway. Bridget caught a glimpse of a family sitting on the couch, watching television.

Finally, James turned back onto the same side street where the Prius had disappeared. Bridget strained to see into each driveway as they rolled slowly past.

"There! A few houses up." Bridget pointed towards the car, silent and dark in the driveway of a single-family home.

She let out a sigh of relief as James pulled up against the curb. "Thanks, by the way," she said as she unbuckled.

He gave her an anxious grin. "It's an adventure, right?" He pulled the key from the ignition and pocketed it.

She returned the smile. "Yeah. Ready?"

"One sec." James rummaged through the bags that

populated his backseat.

"What are you doing?"

"Getting my equipment." He pulled out his camera. Bridget couldn't tell if it was the same one Gaul had confiscated in the alleyway or a new one.

She shook her head and glanced towards the house. Interior lights glowed in the front windows. "Not this time," she said, stuffing her purse under the passenger's seat and flicking her phone to silent mode. "What will the neighbors think if they see you lugging camera equipment around and peering in windows? Bring the recorder and use your phone if you need to take pictures."

James balked. "But the camera—"

"Is too obvious," Bridget insisted. "Come on, hurry. We might be missing something."

She stepped out into the drizzle, closed the door, and started towards the house.

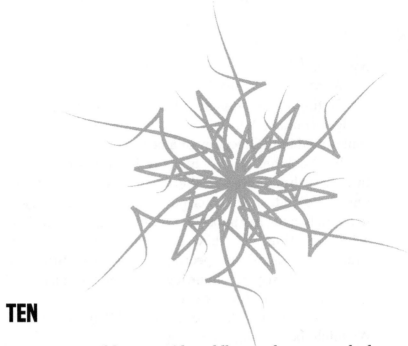

TEN

It was impossible to avoid puddles, and water soaked through Bridget's boots. She slowed her pace as she neared the house. Two cars sat in the driveway—the black Prius they'd followed, and a classic Mustang painted a deep red. Both vehicles' lights were off, their interiors empty.

The house was brick and wood, gables crowned by tired shingles. Its yard was well-maintained, but barren. There were no homey touches—no floral wreath on the door or potted plants on the stoop. The front windows had gauzy curtains drawn, allowing light to escape, but concealing the interior.

A loud splash made her turn. James arrived behind her wearing an apologetic smile. She held a finger to her lips and gestured to a thin line of trees that separated the house from its neighbor. He nodded in understanding, and the two of them crept forward, using the foliage for cover and keeping to the shadows. Fat drops of water dripped off the branches and onto her head. She stayed low, finally coming to a stop when she was even with the side of the house.

"Now what?" James whispered as he crouched beside her. He lifted his phone and snapped a picture.

Bridget strained to listen, but there wasn't anything to hear. "I don't know." In her mind, the plan had been simple. Follow Ivanova, eavesdrop on their conversation, and use the information to find Dahlia. She hadn't thought about exactly *how* to eavesdrop.

"We need to get inside," she realized.

"What?" James exclaimed, loud enough that Bridget shushed him. "No way," he said in a quieter voice. "This time we'll get arrested for real."

She chewed her lip as she considered their options.

"Not if we don't get caught. Or... well, there's nothing illegal about knocking. We could demand answers. After what we heard, we're entitled to know."

"After all this, you want to invite yourself in?" he asked, incredulous. "Why didn't you go to her office, if you were just going to ask nicely?"

"Do you have a better idea?"

"I don't—" James cut off at the loud whine of hinges, followed by the thump of a wooden door swinging shut.

Bridget's eyes widened. The sound had come from the back of the house. She beckoned for James to follow and started to move deeper into the property. There was no fence, and they slipped into the backyard without difficulty. It was as clean as the front, with a few waterlogged pots and a concrete stoop. Standing on it, sheltered by the eaves, was the man who had driven Ivanova to the house, still wearing his jacket. He cupped his hands around his mouth, lighting a cigarette. Weak light from inside spilled out onto the stoop, casting the man's shadow across the back yard.

Bridget shared a glance of nervous excitement with James before she looked back at the man. There was a creak as he leaned against the stoop's wooden railing. Smoke rose from between his lips as he exhaled. He was in profile to them, gazing into the thick stand of trees that lined the backyard.

Was he Ivanova's boyfriend? Bridget had a hard time imagining the detective in a romantic relationship, but it was possible—especially given his attempt at courtesy. Maybe this was their house; he seemed comfortable enough, slouched casually against the wooden railing, ashtray at his elbow. If that were the case, who did the other car belong to? Bridget had a feeling Gaul was inside since he'd been the one to mention a meeting on the recording.

James poked Bridget in the arm and she glanced over at him. The rain had flattened his curls, and water dripped down his cheeks. He gestured for her to hold back one of the tree branches so he could take a picture with his phone. She gave a sharp shake of her head.

Before James could respond, the door creaked open again. Bridget turned back to see Gaul step onto the stoop, immediately recognizable by his red hair. He stepped over to the rail and took the cigarette from Ivanova's driver, giving it a long drag. Then he offered it back. "We're getting started, Jean-Marc."

The curly-haired man gave him a betrayed look. "Do *not* call me that."

Gaul responded with a dark laugh. "You look particularly French when you smoke. Come on." He disappeared inside and the screen door slapped shut behind him.

The other man clenched his jaw tightly then ground out his cigarette in the ashtray. With a stiff back, he followed Gaul into the house.

Bridget and James exchanged an anxious look. Coming to a wordless agreement, they both hurried out from the cover of the trees. Bridget's heart pounded as she darted for the edge of the house, sticking close to the brick wall.

James stayed close behind her as she inched forward, and they both came to a halt next to the stoop. The lingering smell of cigarettes hung in the air, mixing with damp grass, potting soil, and rosemary. Bridget kept low, fingers gripping the edge of the stoop for balance. The inside door was still open, and the low sound of conversation drifted through the screen.

"—a seat, Eisheth." No sign of humor now. Gaul sounded as commanding and impatient as he had on the recording.

A pause, and then another voice. It was the man who had been smoking outside, Jean-Marc. "Are you trying to text Danel again?"

"As if it were your business," Ivanova growled. There was a scraping sound, then an extended silence before Ivanova demanded, "Well? *You* called this meeting, Gaul."

"So I did. I trust you're up to date regarding the incidents?" Gaul asked.

Bridget pressed herself closer to the stoop, glancing at James. He slid the EVP up onto the stoop, out of the rain. Its red recording light blinked.

"Which part?" Jean-Marc asked. "The murderous smoke, or the murderous explosion?"

"The explosion wasn't *murderous*. It saved us," Ivanova said.

"In any case," Gaul continued, "interpreting that symbol is beyond my ability, so I've called in Ret to lend his expertise."

"Will Ret help find Danel, too?" It was Ivanova again. There was a clink of glass and the faint sound of liquid pouring.

"*Ret's* expertise isn't in missing persons," Gaul said. There was no mistaking the pointedness of his tone.

Bridget heard a clicking sound, like the snap of fingers, and then Gaul's noisy sigh. "Put that out."

"It's not a bad idea, actually," Jean-Marc spoke up again. "The girl was spotted at that building, correct?

Perhaps what Ret discovers can lead to finding both her and Danel."

They kept mentioning a person named Danel. Could that be Dan? She strained closer.

"What makes you think they'll still be together?" Ivanova asked. The detective sounded bitter. Almost jealous.

"What matters is finding Danel before he gets himself in even worse trouble. Dahlia was never our concern," Gaul said.

"Speak for yourself," Ivanova muttered. Bridget leaned in, trying to make out her words. "She's been a pain in my ass since the beginning. It would've been easier if she'd drowned in that car."

Bridget gave a short exhale, lips parting in shock. *That bitch!* She clenched her fists as fury flooded her. Finally, she had proof of what she'd suspected since coming to Cleveland: Ivanova couldn't care less about Dahlia's case.

"Ret's first priority will be the symbol. And I expect your full cooperation." Gaul's voice was like iron. Bridget had been wrong to think of him as Ivanova's assistant.

There was some muttering she couldn't make out, then Gaul added, "And don't go running after Danel while Ret is visiting. We need to mop up one mess at a time."

They had to leave with the evidence, and fast. She tapped James on the shoulder and jabbed a thumb towards the street.

James nodded, slid the EVP back into his pocket, and

crept backwards. His curly hair was matted around his head, ends dripping with water. She started after him, wincing at the stiffness in her legs. It wasn't until she was back under the relative shelter of the trees that she let out a hissing breath.

"Did you *hear* them?" she demanded in a low voice.

"Yeah," James whispered back. "Think we can figure out what this Ret guy knows about the smoke?" He seemed oblivious to Bridget's fury.

"No, we need to go. We have everything on your recorder—"

"EVP," James interjected.

"Whatever. We need to take it to the police station. Show it to Ivanova's supervisor or something. Then they'll *have* to re-open the case." And with any luck, fire her in the process.

"But the symbol. You think he's talking about the graffiti we saw? What if—"

Bridget grabbed his arm and hauled him further down the tree line, away from the backyard.

"Keep it down," she whispered in a harsher tone. "You're going to get us caught. If you want to come back and spy on them, be my guest. But I came here to help my sister. I don't have time to chase ghosts." Immediately, a flush rose to James' cheeks, and Bridget felt a pang of regret.

He tugged his coat free from Bridget's grip. "This stuff is all connected. I thought you'd care about that."

"I do care, but I have to focus on Dahlia." She knew

she wasn't being fair to James, but Ivanova's words still rang inside her head. "If you want to stay, stay. I'm going."

She turned on her heel, keeping close to the trees as she stalked back towards the driveway. She hadn't gone far when James' footsteps caught up to her.

"I drove," he explained, not quite meeting her gaze. "I can't let you walk home."

"I'm fine. I'll just call a—"

Bridget cut herself off. The front door to the house swung open, shining bright yellow light across the yard. They hunkered behind the empty cars, eyes on the porch as Ivanova stepped out.

Dammit. With a frantic gesture, Bridget motioned for James to sneak back towards the trees. They retreated from the driveway into the muddy side yard, the ground squelching underfoot. If they could stay out of view, they could—

"You don't give up, do you?"

Bridget shrieked in surprise, spinning around. Gaul was behind her, blocking their escape.

"Oh no," James whispered.

Gaul's eyes narrowed to slits. He advanced on them, and Bridget staggered back a step.

"Asinine child," Gaul growled. He lurched forward and seized her by her jacket sleeve.

Bridget yanked her arm towards her chest, leaving him with an empty sleeve. She tucked her shoulder to run, but he seized her around the waist. Her frantic gaze met James'.

"Go!" she cried. She didn't know how far she could trust him, but if he could escape with the EVP, they could prove what they'd heard.

James took off running, tennis shoes slapping against the concrete of the driveway. He had one hand clapped against the EVP in his pocket.

"Eisheth!" Gaul snapped. The detective tore after James.

Gaul's upper lip curled back to show his teeth, and he tugged Bridget around. She stumbled, and he pinned one arm behind her. His hand moved to her wrist.

The instant his fingers touched her bare skin, a wave of nausea ran through her. Her stomach turned to lead. Her knees gave out, and she sagged, throat tightening as she was overtaken by a hacking cough.

"Gaul!" A sharp voice cut through her darkening, spiraling world. "You'll kill her!"

"*And?*" Gaul asked. A spike of fear shot through Bridget. She tried to lift her head, but another round of coughs left her clutching her abdomen with her free hand.

A thud resounded above her, and the fingers gripping her wrists let go. Bridget collapsed to the ground and sucked in a thin breath. Her forehead pressed against the cool, damp concrete, and a shiver snaked down her spine. She tried to push herself upright, but all she could do was cough and retch. Bridget heard voices arguing, but they felt far away.

Hands grasped at her. She tried to protest, but her body wouldn't respond. She was lifted up and tucked against something warm. The heavy musk of cigarettes brought on a fresh bout of coughing. In the distance, James cried out.

"Wait—" she whispered.

And then unconsciousness claimed her.

ELEVEN

Bridget opened her eyes. A cracked plaster ceiling came into focus. *Where am I?* She turned her head to get a sense of the dim space. As her eyes adjusted, she made out the shape of a nightstand a few feet away. She was lying on a four-poster bed. Wood paneling covered the bottom of the walls, and the top was painted white. It felt dismally old-fashioned.

She tried to sit up, but a sharp jolt shot up her arm, halting the movement. Bridget was handcuffed to one of the bedposts.

Her breath caught. She brought up her free hand and tried to pry off the cuff. It rattled against the wood, and the metal scraped against her wrist, but it was too tight for her to slip free. Giving up, she looked around for the key. That's when she noticed the curled-up lump at the foot of the bed. Her heart leapt into her throat.

"James?"

There was no mistaking that curly mess of hair poking out from a thin gray blanket.

Her breath caught as she watched his unmoving form. "James!"

"Ngh?" He stirred at the sound of her voice, then jerked upright. "Wha—Bridget? You're awake!"

She let out a shaky sigh. "You scared me."

"I'm alright," he assured her. He leaned against the bedpost closest to him. One arm was twisted behind his back, handcuffed to the post. "Are you okay?" He rubbed at his face with his free hand.

"I think so. How long was I out?" Faint light filtered through the curtains. She struggled to piece together disjointed memories of their failed attempt to spy on Ivanova. She recalled red hair and cold fingers. Narrowing vision. Rough concrete and pain all over. A whiff of cigarettes.

She took stock of herself. Her headache was gone, and there was no sign of nausea. In fact, she felt better than she had in months. Except for the fact she was trapped.

"That man, Gaul," she whispered, remembering his angular face and dark scowl. "He did something to me."

James dropped his hand to his lap and nodded. "Yeah. Again." He winced. "I think he makes people sick. Remember the news article I found?"

"About the robber who died?"

"Given what we know now, I'd bet money Gaul killed

him. Covering for the detective or something. I'm sorry, Bridget. We should've left when we could."

There was no going back now. "What happened after I passed out?"

He watched her closely. "There *is* something supernatural going on."

"I don't know about—" Bridget started, but James shook his head and she cut off.

"Look at your hands," he said. She turned her gaze down to her free hand and turned it over. Ever since she'd touched the acrid smoke both palms had been red and raw. Now the skin was unscathed.

"How?" she asked in wonder. She looked up at James. "How long have I been out?"

"Only overnight," James said. He leaned in and lowered his voice. "One of them *healed* you."

She struggled to sit up, scooting towards the headboard so she didn't hurt her wrist. "What?"

James glanced at the closed door to the bedroom and lowered his voice. "Gaul made you sick, and someone else healed you. They've got *magic*, Bridget."

"Magic," Bridget echoed. She wanted to laugh at him, but the sound wouldn't come. Instead, as she watched his intense expression, cold fear trickled over her skin. "You realize if that's true, we're in even bigger trouble than we thought, right? We're *prisoners*." She lifted her cuffed arm. With her other hand, she searched her pockets, but her phone was gone. "We have no way to call for help— and who would we call? The police? Ivanova *is* the police!"

James' shoulders slumped. "But that guy healed you. That must mean they don't want to hurt us. Right?"

"Or it means they're not finished with us," Bridget said, voice losing its fervor. She took a few deep breaths to calm herself. "Tell me about who you saw."

James shook his head as if to clear it. "He dressed like he'd come from an office or something. Nice clothes. Dark hair."

"Did he say anything? Did he come in here alone?" She needed to get a sense of who they were up against. There was the detective and Gaul, plus the smoker. Now there was a fourth man. How many people were covering up Dahlia's case?

"He didn't answer any of my questions. He just told me he was going to make you feel better and not to worry." James leaned in closer. "It was wild, Bridget. Before he came in, I thought you were dead. You were so pale."

Bridget tried not to let James' words bother her too much. She *wasn't* dead, and she needed to focus.

She looked to her restrained wrist. There was no way she could escape the room without a key. There had to be something she was missing. Some way out of this mess. "The EVP. Where is it?"

He winced. "The detective has it. She took it, along with our phones."

Dammit. Even their evidence was gone.

"There has to be *some* way out of here," Bridget said.

She tugged at the handcuffs, but it was no use. She examined the bedpost instead. The thick wood looked too sturdy to break without a tool. She tugged anyway, ignoring the scrape of metal cuffs against her wrist.

"I don't think that's going to—"

The click of a key sliding into the door interrupted James. Bridget tensed as the knob jiggled. She scanned the room for a weapon. The only object nearby was an old, dusty lamp on the bedside table. She reached over and wrapped her fingers around its wrought-iron stand. With a grunt, she tried to lift the lamp one-handed. It didn't move.

The bedroom door creaked as it swung open, and Detective Ivanova stepped in. Her hair was back in its tight bun. She'd changed out of her cardigan and into jeans and a blouse—an oddly casual look.

She fixed the two of them with a look of disdain.

Bridget let go of the lamp and clenched her fist in her lap. "You kidnapped us," she accused. Ivanova didn't respond. She strode over to James and unlocked his cuff from the bedpost. With a swift, practiced movement she snapped it around his free hand.

"Up." She yanked him into a standing position.

"Ow! Hey! Where are you taking me?" James asked as he staggered to his feet.

Ivanova forced him towards the door.

"Stop!" Bridget cried as she tried to tug free. "What are you doing?"

Ivanova spared Bridget an annoyed look, but

otherwise ignored her as she hauled him out of the room. Their footsteps retreated.

Bridget strained forward to listen, but she couldn't hear anything. The door hung open. Beyond it, all she could see was an empty hallway.

"Hello?" Bridget called. No answer.

She flexed her trapped hand. It was twisted back at an awkward angle that left her fingers tingling. The detective couldn't keep her strapped to the bed forever. She tried not to picture what Ivanova might be doing to James. Would he disappear, just as Dahlia had?

Bridget was close to yelling for help when she heard the rhythmic groan of old wood. The footsteps came closer, and Ivanova turned the corner once again.

Bridget spoke the instant she spotted her. "Where is he? What the hell is going on?" Ivanova made her way to the bed, and Bridget pulled back. "Stay away!"

"Don't make this harder than it needs to be, Ms. Keene," Ivanova said in a low voice. She pulled a small silver key from her pocket and Bridget tensed. This might be her only chance.

The lock clicked. As soon as the cuff loosened, she jerked her hand back. She swung her other fist at the detective. Her swing slammed into Ivanova's cheek with a satisfying *thwack*. Sharp pain exploded through her knuckles. The detective's eyes widened, and her grip loosened. It was enough. Bridget bolted out of the bed and darted for the hall.

She heard a low growl behind her. She'd made it out

of the room and into the dark, wood-paneled hallway when Ivanova collided with her and she fell hard, the wind forced from her lungs as she hit the floor. The detective's weight bore down against her back, and she wrenched Bridget's hands behind her, locking them back into place. The cuffs ratcheted down tight this time.

She tried to scream, but a hand clamped over her mouth. "Fight me and you'll regret it," Ivanova hissed in her ear.

Bridget whimpered, and the weight eased off her back. She panted against the floor until the detective hauled her upright by her arms. Her cheek stung and her hand throbbed. Ivanova towed Bridget through the hallway and down a flight of wooden stairs. It was all she could do to keep from falling.

They emerged into a small foyer, and she recognized the house's glass front door from the inside. To the right of the stairs was a study. Three men crowded around an old mahogany desk, inspecting something she couldn't see. Behind them, floor-to-ceiling bookshelves dominated the room, and a fire crackled in the hearth.

One of the men, a brown-skinned man in a suit, was a stranger. He stood beside the smoker from the porch. The third was Gaul.

Her attacker faced the other way, but she would be hard-pressed to forget that flame-red hair. Even now, she remembered his touch—cold and clammy. It sent an overwhelming sense of *wrong*ness through her.

"Come *on*," Ivanova growled, giving Bridget's arm a

sharp tug. She bit back a cry of pain, falling into step as the detective dragged her to the back of the house.

The downstairs wore the same musty decor, with wood paneling and faded oil paintings on the walls. They passed two more open doors before Ivanova pushed Bridget into a bright kitchen. A heavy wooden table dominated the room, with six chairs arranged around it. James was sitting in one. His eyes lit up when he saw her, and her shoulders sagged in relief. He looked unharmed.

"Sit." Ivanova walked Bridget around the table and forced her into the chair beside James. With two quick clicks of the handcuffs, Bridget found herself trapped once again. The detective stepped back and regarded the two of them.

"This is illegal," Bridget said. Her voice was raspy and she sucked in a wavering breath. She couldn't let herself sound scared. That would give Ivanova what she wanted. "Let us go."

"Not likely, Ms. Keene." Ivanova helped herself to a chair across from them. Her cheek was red where Bridget had punched her. "You're in more trouble than you know."

"You've been lying all along. About Dahlia, about the case, about everything."

"You're not going to hurt us, are you?" James asked. His voice cracked as he tried to wriggle free. "We didn't *do* anything!"

Fear settled in Bridget's chest, tight and cold. She forced herself to meet Ivanova's gaze. "We deserve answers."

The detective responded with a steely glare. Then she called out, "Gaul! We're ready for you."

TWELVE

"What?" Bridget froze at Ivanova's words. "Why does he need to be involved?"

Ivanova's expression was withering, but she didn't respond.

"Detective," Bridget said in the calmest voice she could muster. "I'm sure we can come to some sort of understanding, just the three of us." She glanced at James for support, but he had fallen silent, his skin pale. "Gaul tried to kill me. Please. I don't want him near me." Her voice edged louder.

"I assure you, the feeling is mutual."

Her heart jumped into her throat at the low voice. Gaul stepped into the kitchen and fixed his eyes on Bridget. Beside her, James tried to scoot his chair back. It scraped against the tile floor.

Bridget swallowed as she looked between Ivanova and Gaul. "You can't keep us prisoner." Her voice trembled, and she hated that it betrayed her fear.

Gaul leaned against the doorway, watching them.

The detective turned to Bridget. "No? Since arriving in Cleveland, you've been nothing but a pain in my ass. You've ignored my warnings, trespassed, eavesdropped, and interfered with a police investigation." She ticked off each item on her fingers.

"But—"

"Your excuses are useless here, Ms. Keene. Tell me why this encounter shouldn't be our last," Ivanova said.

"Are you going to kill us?" James' gaze darted between them.

Gaul folded his arms across his chest. "It's an option."

Bridget opened her mouth to respond and found it dry. She cleared her throat. "Look," she started, voice thin. There was nothing behind the word. Nothing but fear and uncertainty. She glanced towards the back door. If they could break free...

But no. Escape didn't matter. At least not yet. These people knew something. The conversations she and James had overheard proved that much. She had to learn more.

Figure something out, she ordered herself. It wasn't only their safety on the line. If something happened to her, then there would be no one left to look for Dahlia.

No one, Bridget realized, except more police. And that would be a bit of an inconvenience for Ivanova, wouldn't it?

She met the detective's gaze. "If you hurt us, or if we disappear, it won't stay a secret. People will find out and trace it back to you."

It was a believable argument. There was a record of her visiting the police station since arriving in Cleveland. If anything happened to her or James, it would reflect back on Ivanova—especially since the detective was in charge of Dahlia's case.

Bridget's mind raced to put together the pieces of what she knew. As much as she hated to admit it, James' theory of magic was far too plausible, given all she'd seen and experienced. That, coupled with the fact that Ivanova was eager to shove Dahlia's disappearance under the rug, meant something.

But what? Part of the conversation she had overheard the night before nagged at her.

She looked up at Ivanova. "This isn't about Dahlia at all, is it? It's about Dan. You're only searching for her because she might lead you to him."

Ivanova started, and Bridget hid a victorious smile. She was right.

"That is none of your business." Ivanova's voice was stiff.

"No, I think it is," Bridget said. "I heard you talking last night. I heard what you said about wishing Dahlia had drowned."

"You certainly eavesdropped quite a bit." Gaul's interjection drew Bridget's momentum to a skidding halt.

He didn't look impressed. If anything, he seemed even more annoyed than before.

"We know you have magic," James said, gaze flickering between them. "But you still have to deal with society's rules, don't you?"

Bridget forced herself to meet Gaul's gaze. "You don't want people to know about this group, right?"

Ivanova snorted in derision. "If it's not clear, your poking around *has* been quite an irritation."

"But we already know a lot," James said, picking up the thread. "So why are you trying so hard to keep us away?"

Bridget nodded. "We all want the same thing. We could help each other."

Ivanova responded with a sneer. "Help? You're a *liability*. Nothing more."

"This entire case has been a liability. There's a reason our kinds don't mix," Gaul said.

"You're wrong." Bridget hoped she sounded more certain than she felt. "I *know* my sister. I'm guessing you know Dan. Together, we stand a better shot at finding both of them." She tried to lean forward, but the cuffs halted her movement.

The detective appeared to be considering her words, though her forehead wrinkled in skepticism.

"Your secret is safe," Bridget added swiftly, "I won't tell anyone about you, or what you've done to me. Neither will James. Right?"

James shot her an alarmed look. She could almost feel

his panic at the idea of being unable to share his discoveries as soon as they escaped. Then he swallowed and nodded. "I won't tell anyone."

"You're going to have to deal with us either way," Bridget said. "I'm not going to stop looking for my sister. So either we'll be sticking our noses into the investigation, or you'll get rid of us and have a fresh one on your hands. Aren't you tired of wasting energy on us?"

"Decidedly," Ivanova said, then looked at Gaul. A silent decision passed between them, and Gaul nodded.

He turned his narrow gaze on Bridget. "Fine. But I want your silence guaranteed. Promises aren't enough."

Renewed fear shot through Bridget. "What does that mean?"

Gaul didn't provide an answer. Instead, he turned to Ivanova. "Eisheth, ask Nuriel to come in. Tell him to bring his supplies."

Bridget exchanged an alarmed look with James. "Supplies? What supplies?"

Ivanova inclined her head and stood from the table without answering. She disappeared into the hallway.

Bridget and James were left alone with Gaul.

The kitchen didn't seem so bright anymore. Bridget's breath shortened. The victory she'd earned while negotiating with Ivanova evaporated. She was still a prisoner, and the word *silence* conjured up horror movie torture scenes. She struggled in her chair, but the metal cuffs bit into her skin.

Tap tap tap. Bridget glanced beside her. James was

watching Gaul, his knee jittering up and down so the sole of his sneaker rapped against the floor. She stretched her leg over and pressed her foot on top of his.

He stilled and turned his attention to her. She saw her own fear reflected in his eyes. But there was also a whiff of excitement.

Figures, Bridget thought. Handcuffed to a chair and surrounded by supernatural police officers, some small part of James was enjoying himself.

She looked back to Gaul. He hadn't moved, staring down his nose at her.

Bridget sucked in a slow breath. "Why do you hate us so much?" she asked.

Gaul scowled. "We don't have time for the litany." Then he let his arms drop to his sides with an exasperated sigh. "Don't give me that look. It's not about *you* in particular."

"Who, then?" she asked.

He shook his head. "Forget it."

"You almost killed—" she started, then silenced herself as Ivanova stepped back into the kitchen. The dark-haired man she'd seen on the porch the previous night followed. He brought with him the scent of cigarettes and a small satchel. Gaul had called him Jean-Marc, but he had rejected that name.

Ivanova gave them a curt nod. "Ms. Keene, Mr. Schuster, this is Nuriel. He's our Artist." The way she said it implied a capital 'A,' a title rather than a hobby or profession.

Nuriel smiled warmly as he stepped up to the table.

"No need to be so hospitable," Gaul told Nuriel, eyeing his friendly expression.

Nuriel glanced at Gaul, sighed, then placed the satchel on the table.

Bridget eyed his bag, trying to shove back images of blades and needles that surely were inside. Nuriel began to remove the contents one by one. A vial of ink, several calligraphy brushes, and a folded sheet of paper. He handled each with care, placing them side-by-side on the table.

Finally, he flattened out the paper and uncapped a brush. Then he dipped it into the ink and began to draw.

James leaned closer. "What is all this for?"

"Shh," Ivanova glowered at him. "He needs to concentrate."

"It's fine," Nuriel said, but the detective's sour expression indicated otherwise.

An uneasy silence fell over the kitchen. Bridget looked from the artwork to Nuriel's face. He had the same furrowed brow Dahlia would get when she sketched.

Over the course of a few minutes, he worked an elaborate, star-like shape onto the page. It looked strikingly similar to the graffiti.

Nuriel lifted his gaze to meet hers, then James'. "This is a type of security contract. It's written in our language, and it carries the abilities of the person who seals it. In this case, Gaul."

"Wait, you're saying your language is magic?" James

asked.

Nuriel tilted his head. "If you want to think of it that way."

"You'd be very wise to follow its terms," Ivanova said, folding her arms across her chest.

James spoke up. "What happens if we don't?"

Gaul straightened. "Our contracts are binding. If you discuss our people and the truth of this investigation with any outsiders, you'll face my capabilities again."

Bridget swallowed as a memory of the previous night resurfaced: her forehead against the cold concrete as she struggled to remain conscious, aching and terrified. "You'll make us pass out."

"You'll fall ill," Nuriel clarified. "He can infect you with any disease in a heartbeat."

"And this time it will be far worse than the flu," Gaul said in a low voice.

Bridget's lips parted in shock. What kind of horrifying power was that?

Every ounce of self-preservation told her to say no. She'd already experienced Gaul's abilities twice, and twice it had left her unconscious.

But she was so close. She was finally on the verge of figuring out what happened to Dahlia. All her months of searching were finally paying off, and this contract was the only obstacle between her and real answers. Her sister had somehow gotten caught up in something supernatural, so striking a supernatural alliance could be her best chance of finding her.

If Bridget wanted to help Dahlia, she needed to see this through, and that meant playing by their rules. Having her sister back was all that mattered.

Bridget looked up to Ivanova. "If I sign this, you promise you'll share all the information you have on Dahlia? You'll let me be a part of the investigation?"

Ivanova gave a reluctant nod. "Yes. I'll share what I know."

"And is it reversible?" she asked.

Ivanova looked to Nuriel. "It's p—"

"No," Gaul cut in firmly, folding his arms again.

Bridget's jaw tightened, and she looked between them. It was still her best choice. "Alright. I'll sign it."

She glanced at James. He fidgeted in his seat. "I don't like this."

She didn't blame him. If Nuriel was telling the truth, they'd never be able to tell anyone about what they'd discovered. And he wasn't a part of Dahlia's family. The only reason he was there at all was because Bridget had needed someone to drive her to the station.

"Can he leave if he doesn't want to sign?" Bridget looked between Ivanova and Gaul.

Gaul paused. "I suppose. He knows so little at the moment, he'd hardly be a threat."

She looked to James. "You should go. I can take it from here."

James chewed on his lower lip, considering. Then, he shook his head. "No, I'll stay."

"James—"

"We're in this together. No matter what you say. Besides, if I go back now, I'll always wonder what I was missing out on." His smile was rueful.

Gaul gave an impassive shrug. "Let's get on with it, then." He stepped back and gestured to Nuriel, who moved to the chair beside James.

"Eisheth, if you would," he said, glancing up at Ivanova.

She strode over to James. From her pocket, she procured a silver key and leaned down to free James. He let out a quiet breath and rubbed at his wrists.

"Give me your hand," Nuriel said. When James hesitated, he went on. "I'm going to draw a copy of the symbol on your skin."

"Why?"

"We have our own way of sealing a contract," Nuriel responded. "Stay still."

James looked uncertain. "Will it hurt?"

"No," Nuriel said, dipping his brush into the ink.

James placed his palm on the table and Nuriel began to draw. His brushstrokes were slow and precise. They left dark streaks that he connected to form a perfect replica of the symbol on the paper.

When he finished, he looked up at Bridget.

She bit her lip, then nodded. *This is for Dahlia*, she reminded herself as Ivanova approached to unlock her cuffs.

"How does it work?" she asked Nuriel. There was a click, and the metal cuffs fell away. She brought her freed hands up to her chest and rubbed her wrists. Her fingers still ached from punching Ivanova.

"Our written language carries power," Nuriel said as he moved to the chair next to hers and set up his supplies again. "It grants us abilities, for one." He placed his hand, palm up, on the table. Hesitant, Bridget set hers atop his. His skin was warm, and the brush tickled as he drew out the pattern. Now that he was close, the scent of cigarettes was almost overpowering.

"Abilities," she echoed, watching him make his practiced lines.

"Maybe we can give you a demonstration soon. One that doesn't involve the flu." Nuriel straightened and set his brush aside. Wet ink glistened on her skin, all spirals and interlocking lines.

"Gaul?" Nuriel asked, turning to him. "Will you seal it?"

He approached, and Bridget started. "Wait, he has to touch us?" she blurted. "Isn't that how he makes people sick?"

Nuriel nodded. "Yes, but not this time. Physical contact will activate the security contract without harming you." He stood to make space for Gaul.

"Unless you break it," Ivanova reminded them.

Bridget stayed rigid in her seat as Gaul reached forward and placed two fingers on the freshly-inked design. Unlike Nuriel, his skin was cold, and goosebumps broke out on her arms. She braced herself, but no nausea came. Gaul reached out to touch the identical mark on

James' hand.

For a heartbeat, nothing happened. Then, gold light laced around the black edges of the paint strokes, just like the symbol in the abandoned building. The light danced towards the center until the whole symbol glowed. Bridget was struck by the beauty of it. Then the entire design faded, sinking into her skin as if her body was absorbing it.

Gaul pulled his fingers away, and Bridget exhaled a trembling breath. She pulled her hand up to examine it but found no trace of the ink. It was as if the drawing had never existed.

"It's done," Gaul said, nodding in satisfaction. He turned to Ivanova and Nuriel. "They're your responsibility now. Ret and I have more important matters to tend to." Without so much as another glance at Bridget, he turned and left the room.

Bridget looked to James. "You okay?"

He tore his gaze from the back of his hand. Above the anxious twist of his mouth, his eyes gleamed with anticipation. "I think so. You?"

She nodded. It felt as if she'd passed some hidden test. No more secrets. No more lies.

The true search for Dahlia could begin.

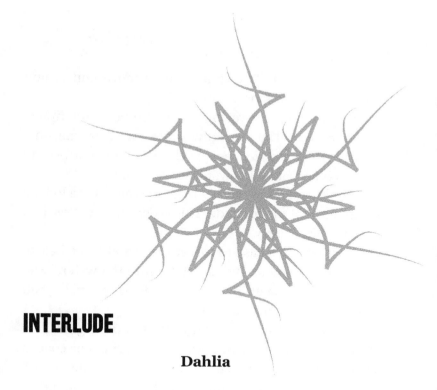

INTERLUDE

Dahlia

One year before...

The sun sparkled off Lake Erie, which stretched past the horizon. Dahlia shaded her eyes with a hand. "Should've brought my sunglasses."

"Told you. It's not *always* gloomy here," her roommate, Nicole, said. She propped herself up on her towel and squinted across the beach. She'd already stripped down to her bathing suit, the rare sunlight glinting off her dark skin.

"Mm-hmm," Dahlia's attention drifted from the horizon to two men walking past, shirtless. "It's definitely not."

Nicole snorted. "We've been here ten minutes, and you're already stalking your prey."

"Not stalking. Surveying." She grinned and tipped back her beer. The two guys were far from the only options. Several dozen people dotted the small private beach—some Dahlia knew, most she didn't.

"Thanks again for inviting me," she said as she lodged her can upright in the sand. "This is definitely better than the dorm pizza party."

"Yeah, well, it's easy to forget Cleveland has a beach. May as well enjoy it. Just don't get into the water." She wrinkled her nose at a small group tossing a volleyball back and forth, waist deep in the lake.

"You know it's not actually dangerous, right? Just freezing." Dahlia said. She was still wearing her coat in the evening, even though it was May. If she hadn't adjusted to the weather yet, she probably never would.

"If you end up with a flesh-eating parasite, don't come crying to me."

Dahlia rolled her eyes in response and settled back on her towel, pillowing her head with her hands. The sky overhead was clear blue. Not a cloud in sight, for once. Seagulls squawked in frenzied circles, waiting for an opportunity to pick through leftovers.

Unfortunately for the seagulls, there was no sign of the party letting up. The host—a student Dahlia had never met—hauled driftwood into a huge pile for a bonfire. It wouldn't be long before they lit it; the sun was low in the sky.

"Hey, Nicole! Dahlia!" a voice called. She glanced up. It was a mutual classmate, a lanky freshman with curly brown hair. He waved as he approached and plopped beside them in the sand.

"Hi James," Nicole said, giving Dahlia a pointed eye roll.

Dahlia hid a laugh and waved back to James. Then she threw an arm over her eyes, letting Nicole take the conversation. He was nice enough, but she wasn't in the mood for his weird conspiracy theories today.

While the two chatted, she allowed her thoughts to drift to the next few weeks. Everyone was gearing up to head home for the summer, but Dahlia would be spending it in the city. The idea of going back to North Carolina's heat and humidity made her want to crawl in a refrigerator.

Bridget hadn't understood her decision. Evidently, Dahlia had dashed all sorts of grand plans when she'd announced she was staying in Ohio. Bye bye, Outer Banks vacay. Oh well. Instead, she would enjoy the next three months exploring the city, free of the burden of classes, and without her overprotective sister breathing down her neck. Even better, most of her friends lived close by. She was certain this wouldn't be her only trip to the beach.

The combination of bright sun and cheap beer left her feeling fuzzy and light. She listened to the sound of the gulls and let the conversation fade into a lull. There was a soothing rise and fall to the voices, and a soft wind blew off the water, pushing strands of hair out of her face. She let herself drift, wondering if she'd remembered to stock her new apartment pantry with anything to eat.

A cool breeze picked up and Dahlia opened her eyes. The sun had dropped out of sight, leaving only a few lingering streaks of purple in an otherwise dark sky. Everyone had abandoned the water, and a chilly breeze swept over her bare arms. She must have dozed off.

Sitting up, she rubbed at her eyes and looked around. Nicole was gone, though her towel was still stretched out on the sand beside Dahlia's. The bonfire was tall, and a group gathered close, savoring its warmth. She caught a whiff of hot dogs cooking, and her stomach grumbled to remind her she hadn't eaten since lunch.

Dahlia reached into her tote bag for her cardigan. She tugged it on, then checked her phone. Five unread messages, all from Bridget. Dahlia bit back a groan. Once, the two of them had been inseparable. But ever since Dahlia had left North Carolina, something had shifted. It was almost as if Bridget *resented* Dahlia for breaking free from their boring old town and empty old house. Did she really have to know what Dahlia was up to every freaking night?

She tucked her phone away without responding and ran a hand through her dark hair, trying to work the sand out of it. No use. She'd be fighting that particular battle for days.

Her remaining beer was lukewarm and flat, so she stood and tossed it into a nearby trash bag. The breeze picked up, and Dahlia rubbed her shoulders. She sauntered closer to the flames, watching as an older student tossed more driftwood onto the blaze. A shower of sparks burst upward, and the people close by gave a giddy scream.

"Hungry?" a short brunette asked. She was standing at a portable grill, turning the hot dogs.

"Yeah." She accepted a paper plate and the hot dog that followed. As she ate, she wandered in a wide circle, searching for familiar faces. She spotted Nicole, who was engaged in a conversation with a redheaded girl from one of their classes. She had one arm casually looped over her shoulders, and they were leaning in so close their noses almost touched. Dahlia rolled her eyes and moved on, taking another bite of her hot dog. Sure, *she* was the one stalking prey.

A man with sandy blond hair by the bonfire caught her eye and smiled. She returned the expression, but continued walking, finishing the last of her dinner and dropping her empty plate into a trash bag.

Dahlia relaxed as the warmth of the fire washed over her, and she let her cardigan slip off her shoulders. Her gaze wandered to the flames. They wove around each other in a mesmerizing roar, throwing the rest of the beach into blackness.

She'd always been partial to campfires. Once, when she was seven, she'd begged to go to sleepaway camp. Her mom couldn't afford it, so Bridget had taken it upon herself to recreate the experience in their backyard. She'd pitched a tent and built a small fire pit, where they'd roasted marshmallows and told scary stories. That happy memory burned bright.

This bonfire was far more impressive than the small one she'd shared with her sister, and it marked the perfect end to her first year of college. She'd survived, and now she was ready to enjoy a few months free from nagging professors and piles of homework.

"Drink?"

Dahlia jumped, realizing that she'd been staring, transfixed, at the flames. She turned to see who had spoken. It was the blond man she'd noticed earlier. He was holding out a can of beer, still wet from the cooler.

She studied him. His blue eyes seemed friendly, and his hair was an agreeable mess that fell to his collar. Jacket open, the tight shirt beneath hinted at a gym-goer's body. He looked a little older—maybe mid-twenties? It was hard to tell. She'd always sucked at guessing ages.

"Sure, thanks." She reached out for the can and popped it open.

He nodded. "I'm Dan. And you are...?"

"Dahlia." She took a sip of the cold beer, watching him curiously over the rim.

"You a student, Dahlia?" Dan asked, sizing her up.

"Yeah." She glanced to the side of the bonfire. Nicole was still there. Her laughter carried over the sound of crackling flames. "I'm here with my roommate."

Dan nodded and moved to stand beside her. The fire bathed his face in a red and gold light. "Lots of students here tonight. Celebrating the end of the semester, I guess."

She scrutinized him, meeting his gaze straight on. "Why are you here, then? Aren't you too old for college?"

"I know Eric." He must have noticed her blank expression. "The guy whose parents own this place."

"Oh." She hadn't even thought to ask whose property this was. She'd just given Nicole an immediate *yes* when she'd extended the invitation. "So, what do you do?"

He rolled his eyes and took a swig of his own drink. "Come on, that's only the second-most boring question after, 'Nice weather, huh?'"

She couldn't help but smile. True. Who wanted to think about work on a night like this? "Okay, let me take another shot. Tell me your deepest, darkest secret."

He smirked. "Somehow I don't think you'd believe me. That, or you wouldn't want to continue this conversation."

"Why, are you a mass murderer or something?" Dahlia asked. She leaned in conspiratorially. "Or worse, an undercover cop?"

Dan snorted. "Yes, because only at a party full of underage drinkers would an undercover cop be *worse* than a serial killer."

"Well, if I got arrested for drinking, my sister would murder me. So either way, I'd be dead."

That got a laugh out of him. "This is an astoundingly morbid conversation. Is this how you always strike up new friendships?"

She raised her eyebrows. "Well, you didn't answer my first question." She took a long swig of beer.

Dan nodded, watching her. "I suppose I had it coming." As she lowered the can, he reached over, gesturing to her wrist. "Let me see your tattoo."

"You like it?" she asked, holding her arm out so he could see. The firelight illuminated the inside of her wrist, where an intricate circle of interlaced lines and curves was inked in black.

Dan leaned in as he inspected it, expression unreadable. "How long ago did you get it?" His skin was pleasantly warm, and she bit her lip.

"A couple of months back, after spring break. I went on this cool trip to Tunisia, and I wanted something to remember it by."

"Tunisia? What were you doing there?"

"It was a field experience thing for archaeology majors," Dahlia said with a shrug.

He ran his thumb over the tattoo then released her wrist. "Interesting. And what does that have to do with the design?"

She let her hand lower. "We found a bunch like it etched into a stone tablet on the dig, and I thought they looked cool."

Dan nodded, straightening. "It does. You have a good eye."

Dahlia shrugged. "I like art. If I didn't have such a full schedule, I'd double major. But at least I can still sketch things out in my field notebook."

He considered her, then asked, "Want to go to the Museum of Natural History sometime? I've been meaning to go."

She scrutinized him. "Are you asking me out?"

He gave her a small, crooked smile. "Maybe. Is that a bad thing?"

She pursed her lips and tapped her chin in mock thought. "That depends. Do you swear you're not a serial killer?"

"Back to morbid, I see," Dan laughed. He glanced across the fire. "Looks like your friend is trying to get your attention." Nicole was shooting Dahlia and Dan an interested look, and when Dahlia caught her eye, she nodded to him and mouthed the word *hottie*.

"Uh," Dahlia said, looking back at Dan. "Why don't you give me your number, and we'll go from there?"

He nodded. "Fair enough. I'll text it to you." He slid his phone from the back pocket of his jeans and looked up at her.

She watched him, considering whether she wanted to give her real number. She'd been to the museum plenty of times, but Nicole wasn't wrong. He *was* cute. "Sure." She recited the digits, and he entered them in.

"Alright, check your messages."

She pulled her phone from her bag and looked down at the screen. One new message. "Got it. Talk soon. Maybe." She flashed him a teasing wave and stepped backwards to join Nicole.

"Good meeting you," Dan told her with a warm smile.

She felt his eyes on her as she walked away.

Three months later...

Dahlia stood in front of the full-length mirror, a pile of clothes on the bed behind her. She scrutinized her current selection: a black dress that landed above her knees, its shape slim and form-fitting. Her dark, wavy hair fell over her shoulders and framed her face.

It was amazing how much better she felt after hanging up on Bridget. Seriously, could she *not* stick her nose in Dahlia's business all the time?

"So, are you finally going to do more than flirt with Dan tonight?" Nicole asked. She was stretched out on the bed, feet propped up on discarded dresses. Her dark, tight curls splayed out around her head like a crown.

Dahlia rolled her eyes and gave Nicole an exasperated look through the mirror. "As if it's any of your business. We're going to dinner."

"It's gonna be somewhere nice," Nicole predicted. "And I bet he finally takes you back to his place afterwards."

"I doubt it. He has roommates." Dahlia reached for her silver sandals.

"So?" Nicole asked. "Not like they all share a bed."

She gave a long-suffering sigh. "No, but he's weird about it. I'm having fun, alright? Let me sweat the details." Her phone pinged, and she checked her notifications. "He's here." Finally, something to get her mind off this obnoxious, long day. She twirled to face Nicole. "How do I look?"

Nicole rolled her eyes with a smile. "You *know* how you look. Go knock him dead."

Dahlia grinned. "Plan on it." She grabbed her bag off a hook on the wall and waved goodbye to Nicole. Humid late summer air greeted her as she stepped outside. Dan's silver Lexus idled next to the curb.

"Hey," she said as she opened the door and took a seat.

"Looking good," Dan said with a smile.

He didn't look so bad, himself. He'd dressed up, trading jeans for dress pants and a t-shirt for a button-down. His hair was its usual mess, blond strands looking windblown. In the three months they'd been dating, she doubted it had seen a comb. She didn't mind; it reminded her of where they'd met.

"So what mystery restaurant did you pick?" she asked as she buckled in.

"How do you feel about paella?"

"I have no idea what that is. Let me guess. Seafood."

He laughed in response. Dan's taste in food had become a joke with them. On almost every date, he had ordered fish.

"It's a Valencian rice dish. And yes, it usually has mussels and shrimp. There's a great little place downtown that I haven't been to in ages. I thought it might be a nice way to celebrate."

"Oh? What are we celebrating?" Her heart gave a little leap of excitement.

He grinned, pulling out into traffic. "You'll find out. Did you bring your sketchbook?"

"Yeah." She patted her bag, where the pad nestled between her wallet and her phone. "I still haven't figured out why you're so interested in it."

His smile remained in place. "You'll see soon enough."

Smooth electronica thrummed through the speakers as they made their way towards the city's center. They passed empty office and municipal buildings, noisy clubs, and crowds of dinner-goers in comfortable silence, save for the beat of the music. She watched other cars pass by, streaks of light in the night.

It was nice to be out of the house, away from Nicole's teasing questions. Now if she could only escape Bridget's judgment.

They'd argued over the phone that afternoon. Again. Since when was it her sister's business who she dated? Sure, Dan was older, but she was an adult. She could make her own decisions. What did Bridget know about their relationship? Hell, what did she know about relationships, period?

Couldn't Bridget see how stifling she was being? Even separated by hundreds of miles, she was still trying to control Dahlia's life. Every conversation turned into a lecture.

Whatever. She didn't need her sister's protection.

She turned to look at Dan. He was bobbing his head to the music, one wrist slung casually over the steering wheel as he navigated traffic. On an impulse, she reached over and rested her hand on his leg. Bridget wasn't going to ruin her evening.

Dan glanced at her and smiled. Her stomach fluttered in response. He was the best thing to happen to her since moving to Cleveland. He was smart, handsome, and could afford to dote on her. He'd taken her to every museum in town and gotten them third-row seats to several musicals at Playhouse Square. He'd even taken her sailing a few times. More than that, when she told him about her dreams to join archaeological digs around the world and have her discoveries placed in museums, he listened. His eyes stayed fixed on her, and he spoke words of encouragement.

He got her. Maybe he even loved her.

Finally, he turned into a lot and parked. The Terminal Tower was lit before them, dominating the skyline. It didn't matter how many people joked about Cleveland being the "mistake on the lake"—she'd loved its charm from the beginning. She especially loved it on clear, summer nights like this one, when everything thrummed with life.

The parking lot was almost full, and she knew from experience that the rooftop bars would be packed with people enjoying live music and craft beer.

"Hope you're hungry," Dan said as he stepped out of

the car and into the warm air.

Dahlia followed, adjusting her bag on her shoulder. She sucked in a deep breath. "Smells good." The scents of a dozen competing restaurants filled the air. Saffron, paprika, and sausage mingled with onion and steak.

Dan nodded in agreement and swiped his card at the pay station. Then he slipped his hand into hers and gave it a squeeze. She couldn't help but feel a thrill of excitement as their fingers locked and they set out towards the restaurant.

Diners filled its patio, laughing, talking, and sipping from wine glasses as they enjoyed the evening. Dahlia soaked it in, unable to help smiling. She let him lead her to the entrance, and they stepped into a small, crowded lobby.

The hostess greeted them with an apologetic smile. "Two? I can put down your name, but we have a wait. It's almost an hour."

Dan stepped up to her podium. "We have reservations. Dan Bridgeport, party of two." He gave Dahlia a smile as they waited for the hostess to check the list.

"Oh! Your table's ready. Come on back," she said, gathering menus and gesturing for them to follow.

Dahlia smiled as she slipped past the long-suffering patrons—most of whom were too busy scrolling through their phones to notice them. Flickering candles lit the place settings, and white china stood out against the black tablecloths. Soft guitar music thrummed under the chatter of patrons. The servers wore tuxedos, maneuvering trays of food and wine with practiced expertise.

"Here we are," the hostess said. She gestured to a table for two near the back of the restaurant. It was isolated from the others, affording them a bit of privacy.

She glanced at Dan, who only grinned back.

"Shall we?" he asked. The hostess set their menus down before walking away.

A waiter took her place, pulling out a chair for Dahlia and draping a cloth over her lap. Dan sat across from her.

"Anything from the drink menu tonight?" the waiter asked as he poured water from a carafe.

"The house chardonnay for me," Dan said. He slid his driver's license across the table.

"Oh, um," Dahlia eyed the wine list, but it would be another two years before she could legally indulge. "Water, please."

"Of course." The waiter nodded to them before walking off.

Dahlia glanced over the menu. "This all looks amazing. And way too fancy."

Dan smiled. "Not for you. How about that seafood paella?"

"Sounds perfect." Setting the menu aside, she fixed him with an appraising look. "So, you said something about a celebration?"

"I did." He sipped his water. "Have you finished the sketches?"

"The ones you asked for? Yeah, hang on." She twisted

in her chair, pulling her sketchpad out of her bag and sliding it across the table.

He lifted the pad and flipped through it.

"They're not perfect," she shifted in her chair. "I mean, I had to base them on my field notes, which are a mess. The only one I had time to sketch in detail was the one on my wrist."

"They're good," Dan said, looking up at her with a smile.

The waiter returned with his wine. "Still need a few minutes?"

"Seafood paella for two," Dan responded. The waiter gave a nod and collected their menus before leaving again.

Dan slid his glass across the table with a conspiratorial wink.

She glanced behind her to make sure the waiter was gone and took a sip. "So does that mean you'll tell me why you had me wracking my brain to remember what the hell they looked like?"

"I've got a collector friend who's interested in them," he said.

Dahlia lifted her eyebrows in surprise. "You told someone about these? But there's nothing to collect. The actual artifacts are still in Tunisia, and they're definitely not for sale."

"No, he's interested in the sketches themselves. He likes modern art inspired by antiquities."

Dahlia blurted a laugh. "Art?" she echoed, pushing the

wine back towards him. "These aren't art. They're doodles."

He smiled. "They're very good doodles, and when I told my friend about your tattoo he wanted to see more. He's opening a new exhibition soon."

She stared at him. "And?"

"*And* he wants to consider featuring your sketches." He lifted his glass in the universal gesture for *cheers*. "Surprise."

Dahlia scoffed. "That's ridiculous. I'm not an artist. I'm not even an art student."

"He takes a lot of pride in discovering new talent. I showed him the picture you posted online of your tattoo. He wanted to see more." He smiled, leaning forward. "So... will you meet with him?"

"Dan, I don't even know if it's legal to share these publicly," Dahlia protested. "A tattoo's one thing, but an art exhibit is another. I'd have to ask Dr. Patel."

"Tannin has experience with this sort of thing. He wouldn't display any sensitive information without going through the proper channels first. But that takes time and money. He wants to talk to you before he starts the process."

She wrinkled her nose. "How do you even know this Tannin person? Is he an old flame of yours?"

Dan's laugh was loud enough to draw a scandalized look from a nearby table. "You know me too well. But no, he's not my type."

"Yeah? What is your type, then?"

"You." He met her gaze and her stomach exploded into butterflies. She knew it was cheesy, but damn he could be romantic sometimes.

"I meant when you date men." She took a hasty sip of water to cool the heat in her face.

Dan shrugged. "Depends on the man. The same sort of things I look for in a woman. Someone interesting. Someone who can handle themselves." He tilted his head. "You're changing the subject. With this exhibit, you'd be paid, of course. Not to mention, you'd get some monumental bragging rights."

The waiter returned with their food then, giving Dahlia a reason to continue delaying. He set a large dish between the two of them, the sauce bubbling cheerfully. The bowl overflowed with rice and shrimp and mussels. The smell made her mouth water.

"I'll take a second glass of wine, too," Dan said. The waiter nodded and ducked away.

Dahlia spooned a helping onto her plate and took a bite. Her eyes widened at the burst of shrimp, saffron, and garlic. "Mm. This is ridiculously good." She shoveled in a second mouthful.

"Isn't it?" He grinned at her enthusiasm and passed her sketchbook back. She set her fork down with some reluctance and slid the book back into her bag, where it wouldn't fall victim to their meal. Considering their conversation, the tattered notebook felt much more valuable. It was absurd to think some stranger was interested in her sketches. But in the three months since meeting Dan, he'd surprised her with his connections. She still didn't know exactly what he did beyond "trading," but it kept him rubbing shoulders with the wealthy. He must have pulled some strings to get her this opportunity.

"So, when does this Tannin guy want to meet?" Dahlia asked after they'd each taken a few bites.

"Is that a yes?" A smile appeared on Dan's face, and Dahlia felt a thud of affection for him. "He wants to meet you tonight."

"Seriously? On a Friday night?" She glanced towards one of the dark windows at the far end of the restaurant.

He nodded. "He's only in town for a couple of days. May as well strike while the iron is hot." He sipped his wine, watching her over the rim.

She sucked in a slow breath, then a smile spread over her face. "Okay. Let's do it."

Throughout dinner, Dahlia continued to mull over Dan's words. She had to admit, his attention to her hobbies was endearing. Could she really consider herself an *artist*? He thought so. Maybe she should give herself more credit.

For as long as she could remember, Dahlia had loved to draw. When it came time to choose a college, she'd agonized between a local fine arts school and one renowned for its archaeology program. In the end, she'd opted for the route that got her out of North Carolina.

But maybe she could have both. Maybe she could be a scientist *and* an artist. Surely that was possible.

Dan continued to offer her sips of his wine, and by the time dinner ended she felt pleasantly warm and light. They returned to Dan's car and, as he pulled out of the parking spot, she sent off a quick message to Nicole—*Wait 'til I tell you what happened at dinner.* She leaned back against the headrest and closed her eyes. The soft vibrations were soothing.

"I want to know more about you, Dan," she murmured, eyes still closed.

"Yeah?"

"Yeah. Tell me, what's your family like? We've been dating for months, and you never talk about them."

He paused a long moment before answering. "I don't really have a family."

"No family?" She tried to imagine that but couldn't manage to conjure up the experience. Sure, her dad had skipped out when she was a kid, and her mom was busy all the time, but she'd always had Bridget.

Of course, now that they were fighting, maybe she didn't have family either.

"Well, I do have one person. A... a niece. We're estranged, but I make sure she's provided for."

"Provided for? You make it sound like her parents died."

"They did."

That sucked, but she found herself smiling. As much

as Dan might want to project the image of a cultured party boy, he really was good to the people he cared about. Like her.

Her head drooped as she nodded off to the peaceful rumblings of the car.

The Lexus hit a pothole and she sat upright, blinking her eyes open. They'd left the bright lights and bustle of the city behind, driving into an older area of town.

She glanced at Dan. He looked content, nodding his head in time with the music. "Are you sure this is right?" she asked as they passed a liquor store wedged between two pawn shops. She didn't see anyone on the street. "Why would your friend want to meet in a place like this?"

"He's eccentric," Dan told her. He turned down the music and cracked the windows to let in the night air. "Don't worry. I've known him for years."

She could sort of imagine an art collector choosing to stay in this part of town, particularly one interested in relics. There was a tired, industrial feel to the buildings they passed. Then again, for all she knew, they were being repurposed into chic lofts. Cleveland was like that, these days.

Finally, Dan parked against the curb, in front of yet another stretch of nondescript brick buildings. The closest one was a multi-story structure of soot-stained brick and broken windows. It looked like it had once been an old school or an office building, but it was long since abandoned. Dan's was the only car parked on the street. Even the liquor stores had thinned out.

"Here?" Dahlia peered up at the building.

"This is it. Hop out." Dan stepped out of the car.

Dahlia's eyes narrowed as she regarded the building. "This is a dump."

"Yeah, it kind of is," he admitted as he surveyed it. "Maybe it's nicer on the inside."

She chewed her bottom lip. Exploring dilapidated buildings was *not* what he'd promised. "Why don't we come back during the day? I'm not dressed for this."

Dan bent down to meet her gaze through the open car door. "I've got to work tomorrow, and then he's leaving town. Want me to ask him if you can come by on your own?"

She shook her head. "There's a zero percent chance I'm coming back alone. The place looks abandoned. I think your friend is messing with us, Dan."

He pulled out his phone and glanced at the screen. "This is the address Tannin gave me." He looked up at her. "What do you want to do?"

Dahlia hesitated. Leaving was the safest choice. But how often had she played it safe? Safe was boring. Safe was so *Bridget*. Besides, Dan had never given Dahlia any reason to doubt him. She twisted the seat belt in her hands, weighing her options. "Let's try."

Dan shot her that crooked smile she loved. "Great." He closed his side and walked around to pull the door open for her.

"You *do* know if this turns out to be some sort of joke, you're going to pay for it, right?" she said as she slid out of her seat.

"Noted. Here, I'll carry your bag for you." He hooked it over his shoulder as she stood. "Don't worry. If anything makes you uncomfortable, we'll go."

Despite their surroundings, he appeared completely at ease. He led her up several crumbling steps flanked by empty concrete planters and onto a landing. In front of them was a tall, faded door. It was wooden, set deep into the red bricks and topped by a curved, Romanesque archway. Dahlia could imagine the aged building having once been far grander, with its carved window trim and patterned brick inlay. Maybe it was being renovated.

Dan pushed the door open, sending paint flakes fluttering to the ground. Its hinges shrieked in protest, and Dahlia flinched back. She peered past Dan into a dark, dusty entryway. The door opened on what had once been an atrium. Years of abandonment had reduced it to peeling paint, rough concrete floors, and piles of discarded office supplies, all coated with a sheen of dust. Broken furniture lay in disjointed heaps, and grime-coated beer bottles littered the entrance. A stairway curved upward to a second floor. It looked rotten enough to collapse under a toddler's weight, and its carpet runner was shredded. On the main floor, a single dark hallway led deeper into the building.

Her stomach flopped. "Dan, there's *no* way I'm going in there. I thought this was going to be a converted apartment or something, but this is totally serial killer territory."

"You really have to stop listening to true crime podcasts," he sighed. "Look, I agree with you, but I'd hate for you to miss out if he's around the corner. It'll be fine."

"No." Dahlia shook her head. "No way. I'm not up on my tetanus shots."

The joke fell flat, and Dan sighed in disappointment. "Alright. Just wait in the car. I'll be right back." He stepped into the atrium.

"Dan, wait," she hissed.

"Hang on," he said, making his way over a pile of discarded wooden beams. He glanced back at her. "You sure you don't want to come?"

Dahlia shook her head. "Not a shot in hell."

He shrugged. "Suit yourself." He turned and disappeared down the hallway.

Fear stabbed through her as the darkness swallowed him. "Dan? Dan!"

She stood still, watching the space where he'd vanished. He'd *left* her! Despite his assurances, he'd slipped into the building and abandoned her alone in the dark.

Well, there was no way she was following him. She turned away from the building, already mentally writing a text to Nicole. *Oh, yeah. Dan thought he'd be a real Romeo and take me to a decrepit old building, probably full of asbestos.*

Dahlia stalked to the car and tugged on the door handle. Locked. "Dammit," she whispered, going around to the driver's side. Same luck. With an irritated grunt, she kicked the tire with her sparkly sandaled foot. "This is so not cool." She reached for her cell phone, then remembered—Dan had her bag.

"Shit." She moved back to the sidewalk and glared at the dilapidated building. How *dare* he leave her out here alone! It was dark, and half of the streetlights were burned out. There was nowhere to wait, not even a bench.

She leaned against the side of the car, crossing her arms and glaring at the building. Now what? She couldn't get ahold of Nicole—or anyone else for that matter— without her phone. Dan had said he'd be right back, but where was he?

A crash of breaking glass rang out. Dahlia spun towards the sound. Three young men turned the corner, laughing and shoving one another. As she watched, one bent to pick up a rock from the sidewalk. Then he hurled it at a building, and another window shattered.

Dahlia shifted her weight, now wishing she hadn't worn such a form-fitting dress. She did *not* want to attract the attention of Cleveland's miscreant population, thank you very much.

"Hey!"

Dahlia tensed. One of the men had spotted her. He nudged his friends and pointed. All three turned, and she felt their eyes rake over her.

Suddenly, the building didn't seem so bad. *Screw it.* Without making eye contact, Dahlia hurried back up the steps.

"Where are you going? We just want to talk!"

Dahlia slipped through the open door. It squealed loudly as she yanked it closed. Outside, the shuffling footsteps and laughter came closer.

"Come on out," one crooned.

Biting back a retort, Dahlia fumbled for the deadbolt and clicked it into place. As much as she wanted to tell them exactly where they could shove it, she knew from experience it would only encourage them.

"What are you doing out here alone? Do you need a ride?" a second voice called out.

The door rattled. Dahlia stepped back, nearly tripping over a discarded piece of plywood.

"It's locked."

"Don't be scared, we just wanna hang out," the first one said.

A third voice spoke up, lower and less slurred. "Come on, let's get out of here."

"Whatever, man."

Dahlia let out a relieved breath as their footsteps moved away. She rubbed her sweaty palms on her hips, then turned to cast her gaze into the building. At first, it seemed completely dark, but then a glimmer of light caught her eye. It came from the hallway where she'd last seen Dan.

Okay, she told herself. Get the keys. Get your purse. Get out.

She stepped forward and began to pick her way across the room, hands held in front of her. The ground felt gritty underfoot, and rotten boards and metal poles littered the floor, threatening to trip her. The place smelled of mildew and rust.

As she moved into the hallway, the light brightened. Peering down its length, she could see it shining from beneath a closed door. Beyond, she heard the low murmur of voices. She paused to listen. At least two people, maybe three. She couldn't make out their words, but one was definitely Dan. He'd left her out there to talk with his friends. Irritation urged her down the long, graffiti-covered hall.

She shoved the door open and stepped into a small room. Dan sat with two strangers in a ring of metal folding chairs. The room was illuminated by a single camping lamp that flickered atop a scratched wooden desk. She ignored Dan's companions and stalked towards him.

"The car's locked," she snapped, fingers clenching.

"Oh, sorry," he said. His easy smile faded. She spotted her bag, draped over his knee. "Since you're here, have a seat. Tannin's looking through your drawings now." He gestured to the man with her sketch pad.

He looked to be about Dan's age, with chestnut hair and copper skin. Despite the ragged surroundings, he was dressed for a business meeting. He wore a tailored navy suit accented with a gray tie and matching pocket square. Even his shoes were straight out of a catalog, leather shining in spite of the grit that covered the floor. He paused in flipping through the pages to study her with a curious gaze.

He didn't *look* like a serial killer. In fact, with an outfit that posh, Dahlia could easily picture him coordinating art exhibitions.

"You must be Dahlia," Tannin said with a warm smile. He stood, handed the pad to the other man, and extended a hand to her. "It's wonderful to meet you. I'm Tannin, and this is my associate, Kai." He gestured to the third man, who wore a weathered trench coat on top of a black shirt and fitted jeans. He had a hawkish nose, which stood out all the more thanks to his slender frame. "As I'm sure Danel has told you, we are art collectors and restorers." He tilted his head towards the sketchbook. "We've heard quite a bit about your work."

She paused, uncertain. He had an accent she couldn't quite place—almost English—and in light of his politeness, her outburst felt silly. She shot Dan a conflicted look, and he responded with a nod of encouragement.

"I'm surprised you're interested," she finally said. She regarded his hand for a moment, then reached out and accepted the handshake. "I'm not a trained artist."

"I would never know," he said, keeping hold of her hand and turning it so he could see the inside of her wrist. "Is this the tattoo?"

"Yeah, that's it." She extricated her hand.

"And your sketches," Tannin said, returning to his seat. "They're drawn from memory of actual artifacts?"

"Yes. And crappy field notes." Why were they meeting here? She scanned the room for anything to indicate that

Tannin was erecting a studio or cleaning up the place. But there were no tools or construction materials, and the only light came from the lantern. The space was dusty, battered, and smelled like someone had used the corner for a toilet.

She shifted uneasily. Something wasn't right, she could feel it in her gut. "I want to go," she told Dan in a low voice. Glancing back up at Tannin, she reached for her bag. "I'd be happy to talk about this some other time. Some other place."

"Just a minute," Dan said. He pressed his fingers against the strap of her bag to hold it in place. "Tannin went out of his way to meet with us tonight."

Her eyes narrowed in frustration. Why was he so determined to keep her there?

Tannin's gaze never left her. It was almost as if he was critiquing *her* rather than her art. "The one on your wrist," he said with a nod towards her arm. "That wasn't done from memory, correct? It's true to what you saw?"

Dahlia stepped back. "Look, I'm not interested in your exhibition, alright? We're leaving. Give me my bag, Dan."

Dan watched her for a moment, then looked to Tannin and said, "She told me it was. It's the most accurate of the lot. Of course, you can refine the others if we're in agreement over the price."

Price? Dahlia frowned. "What is wrong with you?" she hissed. "Let's. Go. There's no agreement. I'm not negotiating anything."

The third man, Kai, laughed. Until now, he'd remained

silent, focused on Dahlia's sketchpad. Now he looked up at her, his eyes glittering with amusement. "Child, we're not in negotiations with *you*."

She gaped at him. "Excuse me?"

Tannin turned to him, ignoring Dahlia. "Can you replicate it?"

Kai's attention shifted to Dahlia's wrist and the small symbol there. "It shouldn't be a problem. Assuming it works."

Dahlia's eyes tracked between the group, lingering on Dan, who was too busy watching Tannin to return the gaze. Her hands curled into fists at her sides. "Forget it, I'm leaving." She turned to hurry away. Car or no car, phone or no phone, she had to get out of there.

"She already did it for you. It's there, in the sketchpad. You don't need her," Dan said.

She didn't turn back, shaking with anger as she hurried in the direction of the atrium. She would walk home if she had to.

"Actually," Tannin said, "we do."

She'd almost made it to the atrium when a deep rumble filled the air. She stopped short. It sounded like an oncoming freight train deep within the walls of the building. Bits of concrete and flakes of rust jumped and rattled.

The ground bucked beneath Dahlia's feet. She stumbled as the cinder block wall beside her fractured into a spiderweb of cracks. A chunk of the ceiling fell in her path, and she jumped back in alarm.

Earthquake? In Ohio? Heart jackhammering, she recoiled and whirled around to look the way she'd come.

There in the hallway, a dozen feet away, was Tannin. He brushed a bit of dust from his suit and smiled at her, unperturbed by the ominous thunder that filled the building.

Another chunk of the ceiling sagged and broke free. It hit the ground with a crash, and Dahlia staggered forward. With a grunt, she broke into a run. If she could shove past Tannin, surely she could find another way out—a back door or a fire exit.

The floor continued to buck and tremble, and the light fixtures above swung wildly back and forth. Another crack raced along the ceiling, as if pursuing her.

"What are you doing?" Dan's voice was almost drowned out by the roar. He appeared in the hallway only a few feet away. They locked eyes, and Dan took a step towards her. Then he suddenly skidded to the side, as if pushed by an invisible force. He hit the wall hard and fell to his knees.

Dahlia pulled up to a halt. "Dan!"

Kai stepped into the hallway, hands extended in Dan's direction. *What...?*

The rumbling ebbed, and the floor stilled, allowing Dahlia to catch her balance.

"This wasn't part of the deal," Dan growled. He pulled himself back to his feet, using an overturned file cabinet for support.

"I'm not buying a product until I'm certain it works,"

Tannin said, voice calm. "Kai, would you please contain the situation?" He turned and stepped back into the room.

Kai smiled at Dan, then rushed forward. He threw a punch at Dan's gut, and Dan blocked it with a swift arm. Dan whirled with a kick that made Kai double over. But the dark-haired man made a swift recovery, swinging an uppercut aimed at Dan's jaw. It connected with a crunch.

Dan lurched backwards, looking woozy. Kai flicked his hand. Dahlia staggered as a sudden blast of wind came from nowhere, blowing Kai's trench coat forward. The full force of the gale hit Dan, and he flew into the wall again. His head slammed against the cinder blocks with a sickening *crack*. He fell to the floor and his chin dropped to his chest. He groaned, struggling to stand.

"Dan!" Dahlia cried again. She took a step towards him, then stopped. What could she do? He weighed too much for her to carry him; it's not like she could pull him to safety while fending off Tannin and Kai.

She pressed herself against the wall. Kai was still focused on Dan. If she hurried, she could escape and call for help. She broke into a run, scrambling around them as the wind slammed Dan into the wall again. Her stomach clenched at the sound, but she forced herself to run faster, down the hall.

Suddenly, her ankle twisted beneath her. She cried out as she fell, knee scraping the ground. One of her sandals had lodged between two broken hunks of concrete. She pulled her foot free, leaving the shoe behind.

Straightening, she pressed ahead. The hallway was dark, but she spotted faint light around the corner.

Kai turned back to Dahlia and stalked in her direction. Behind him, Tannin stepped back into the hallway. To her horror, he was followed by a writhing, black mass of smoke. It bubbled and seethed, like a hungry dog ready to attack.

Dread welled up within her, cold, tight, and deep in her stomach.

The stench of sulfur hit her hard. *Go!* she ordered herself. She turned and began to run again, grabbing for the wall to steady herself in the dark hallway. She clapped her other hand over her nose and mouth. Her eyes stung, and her ankle throbbed.

Abruptly, a scorching sensation erupted across her foot. Her leg was yanked out from under her, and she fell to her knees with a hoarse scream. Agonizing spikes of pain shot through her leg. She twisted to see a tendril of the dark smoke wrapped around her bare skin in a vice-like grip. Beyond, Kai advanced towards her.

"What do you want?" she cried out. Kai didn't respond. Behind him, she saw Tannin watching, her sketchbook in his hand. He almost looked bored.

She reached down to yank at the bindings, but the same burning sensation scalded her palms. Dahlia pulled back with a yelp of pain and rolled onto her chest, reaching for anything that could help her escape. Her aching fingers grasped metal, and she tugged a loose piece of rebar free from the rubble.

With a loud, wordless cry, she swung it at the ropes tethered around her ankles. The rebar cut through the smoke, separating it from the column. It dissipated, releasing her. Dahlia drew her stinging legs towards herself and fought back tears.

Kai was almost to her. She used the wall to help herself stand, then gripped the bar of metal like a baseball bat. With a strangled cry, Dahlia swung the metal rod towards him. He threw up an arm to block the blow.

"Finish it, Kai," Tannin's voice was calm. "This is taking too long."

Kai nodded. His hand darted forward and seized Dahlia by the shoulder before she could pull away. With his other hand, he beckoned towards himself.

At his gesture, the air rushed from her lungs. Her muscles seized, and she choked. Panic coursed through her. She couldn't breathe. The rebar fell from her hand and rolled away. Kai kept his grip on her as she sank back onto the floor.

Dahlia clawed at her neck, desperate tears streaming down her face. She tried to call out, but the words couldn't make it past her throat. Her vision swam, muscles seizing.

She sagged lower on the broken floor. How had everything gone so wrong? The swanky restaurant felt like decades ago. She'd had such high hopes for the night. Dan had looked so handsome in his button-down. Even Bridget would've approved.

Bridget. Would she ever see her sister again? Would

Dahlia's last words to her be angry? Desperation wove through her, and she tried to push herself up, but she'd lost control over her body.

"It will be over soon." Kai's voice was distant. "Rest."

Hot tears rolled down her cheeks. Dahlia's vision blackened around the edges as her fingers fell away from her neck.

The sounds, the pain, the light—everything faded.

THIRTEEN

Slam!

Ivanova dropped an enormous stack of papers in front of Bridget and James.

"You've been keeping all of this from me?" Bridget demanded.

"You didn't need to know," Ivanova said.

On top of the pile was a security camera still of Dahlia with Dan, and Bridget sat forward to inspect the image. They were at a museum. Dahlia looked happy. She was smiling up at him, holding onto his arm. Dan looked down at her with a smile of his own, his sandy hair tousled. Neither seemed interested in the painting they were standing in front of. "Did you ever figure out why Dan's car was in the river?"

"Danel," Ivanova corrected. "And no, we didn't."

"When you found that car, you said it meant they were likely dead." There was a quiet accusation to her tone.

"In a normal investigation, that would be true. In this case, I believe the car was meant as a distraction."

Bridget exhaled slowly. Lies upon lies. At least she wasn't the only one who believed Dahlia was alive.

James considered the photograph. "Does he have magic, too?"

At Ivanova's matter-of-fact nod, Bridget's lips parted in shock. Had Dahlia known she'd been dating someone supernatural?

"Abilities," Ivanova corrected. "'Magic' sounds childish. In any case, Danel appeared to be infatuated with Dahlia, for reasons beyond my comprehension. Danel has run off before. But he typically lets me know first."

Nuriel stepped into the room as she spoke, chiming in, "And he doesn't often leave a months-long police investigation in his wake."

Ivanova's mouth twisted into a sour expression. "Because I'm on the force to cover for his recklessness. It was only a matter of time before he got in over his head."

"This isn't the sort of trouble he usually gets himself in. But then again, Danel isn't usually so taken." Nuriel glanced at Ivanova, who glowered at him, then swiftly added, "By humans, that is."

Goosebumps prickled along Bridget's arms. They didn't even consider themselves human? They looked like anyone else—and clearly Ivanova was still capable of a normal emotion like jealousy. So, what were they?

"When are you going to tell us what you are?" James asked, following a similar train of thought. His gaze pingponged between the two of them.

Ivanova shot James an annoyed look and stood. Her chair squealed against the tile floor, and she walked to the kitchen counter to measure out coffee grounds.

Undeterred, James turned his gaze to Nuriel. "Well? We signed your contract."

Nuriel glanced at Ivanova, but she was focused on the coffeemaker, her lips pressed into a thin, irritated line. He turned back to Bridget and James. "We've been called by many names over the years, but the name we have chosen for ourselves is Grigori."

The word didn't mean anything to Bridget, though James repeated it under his breath. She could practically see him wracking his mental encyclopedia of supernatural creatures.

"What does it mean?" Bridget asked.

Nuriel considered her before speaking. "Literally, it means 'watchers,'" he said.

Her forehead wrinkled as she waited for more, but he said nothing else.

"What are you watching?" James asked.

"Reruns, mostly," Ivanova muttered from beside the coffeemaker.

Nuriel hid a smile. "Your people."

Bridget shook her head. "That's creepy. Why?"

"It's not important," Ivanova cut in. "Nor is it relevant

to the case."

"But we did promise to share," Nuriel said. Ivanova huffed in irritation as he continued speaking. "Humans and Grigori have coexisted for a long time, but not always peacefully."

"Coexisted, as in, you all knew about one another?" Bridget asked.

Nuriel nodded. "Long before we called ourselves Watchers, we were more involved in human affairs. It didn't go well. There was a war, and our people were nearly wiped out. Ever since then, we've lived in hiding. We adopted our new name as a reminder to stay away from humanity."

Bridget let that sink in. An entire people, forced to live in secret. It must have been a terrible war. She wondered why she'd never heard about it. "How long ago was the war?"

"Millenia," Ivanova said curtly. "And we don't have time to go over it. Ask Ret later if you want."

"Who?" James asked.

"A colleague," said Nuriel. "You met him upstairs when he healed Bridget. He's also a scholar of Grigori history."

"Are your abilities all different?" James asked. He leaned forward in his seat, eyes bright.

Nuriel responded. "Not all. There are commonalities. Take Gaul, for example. There are others like him, who can spread sickness with a touch."

"What about you?" James asked. "What do you do?"

His smile faded and he shifted in his chair. "Oh, uh..."

"Go on, show them. You did offer earlier." Ivanova tugged open a cabinet, pulled down a coffee mug, and filled it from the tap. "Give them their answers." She set the mug in front of him, along with a packet of tea.

Nuriel sighed and turned his gaze to the cup of water in front of him. He tore the tea packet open and placed the sachet in the cup. Bridget and James exchanged a confused glance.

Nuriel wrapped his hands around the mug. A few seconds of silence passed, then the water inside began to simmer, steam curling up from the surface.

Bridget watched in surprise as the scent of lavender reached her. "You can boil tea?"

His cheeks darkened as Ivanova barked a sharp laugh. The bubbling stopped. "Water," he explained. "One of my abilities is manipulating water."

"Woah," James breathed. "But how does it work?"

"I can change water's temperature, which means I can change its state. And I can also move it around."

"Why are you embarrassed? That's cool!" James said.

"Well, it's very limited," Nuriel replied. "Right now, I could turn this into a waterspout. But if you put a lid on it, I wouldn't be able to do anything at all. Even the weakest container is like an impenetrable wall to me. Hopefully, I'll eventually get stronger."

James scooted eagerly to the edge of his seat. "Okay, so who gets what abilities? How many do you have?"

Ivanova made a dismissive gesture. "We agreed to

help you with the case, not turn this into a physics class."
She paused, then cleared her throat. "Ms. Keene, are you
alright?"

Bridget blinked. She was still staring at the mug,
which Nuriel had lifted to his lips. "Sorry. I—yes." It felt
as if she'd fallen through a rabbit hole. "It's all too weird."

"I think we should answer James' questions," Nuriel
said. "They deserve to know what they're up against."

Ivanova pursed her lips but didn't protest further.
James looked to Nuriel, bright-eyed.

"We each have two abilities." He gestured to the mug
of water. "But one's always more powerful—more natural
to use—than the other. For example, I can also suppress
emotions."

Bridget stared at him. "What does that mean?"

He lifted a shoulder, then gave Ivanova a good-
natured grin. "I'd probably find it useful if I were better
at it. Maybe I'd make Eisheth less perpetually irritated."
She huffed in response.

"What can you do?" James asked Ivanova, turning his
eager gaze to the detective.

She rolled her eyes. "I'm not here to perform party
tricks. Nuriel's demonstration should be sufficient to
continue our conversation."

"I don't understand how you've kept this under wraps
so long," James marveled.

"We're careful and don't often invite in people like
you," Ivanova shot back.

Heat rushed to Bridget's cheeks. She ignored the jab,

instead asking, "Why Cleveland, of all places?"

Nuriel set down the steaming mug. "Why not Cleveland? We're spread all over the world. This city happens to have personal importance for Gaul."

"Yes, but I don't recommend asking him about that," Ivanova said. "It's a tender subject. Something about an old boyfriend here he's too stubborn to make up with."

She frowned. It was hard to imagine Gaul caring about anyone that much. "What about the rest of you?"

"We're still in training," Nuriel said. "He's our mentor."

"Training. Okay, so... what does it all mean?" Bridget asked, forcing herself back to the matter at hand. "For my sister?"

"What it means is this investigation is about more than Dahlia," Ivanova said.

Nuriel added, "We don't know exactly what's going on yet, but both your sister and Danel are tied up in it."

"It was my video, wasn't it?" James cut in. He sat on the edge of his chair. "That's what changed things."

Ivanova gave a long-suffering sigh. "Yes. Your video of Dahlia led us to that building. I don't know why she was there when you filmed it, Mr. Schuster, but given the symbol we found, it stands to reason that her disappearance has something to do with the place."

"What does the symbol do? Is it another contract?" Bridget asked.

"All symbols are contracts. They bind objects—or people—to a set of rules using our abilities. As far as what that specific contract does, we don't know," Nuriel said, looking troubled. "As an Artist, I'm trained to read and replicate them, but I've never seen this pattern before. We're hoping Ret can help."

"You don't think Danel put it there?" Bridget tapped the photo of him.

"No, definitely not," Ivanova scoffed. The detective's gaze lingered on the photograph, then she turned away.

She really cares about him, Bridget realized.

Nuriel nodded in agreement. "He couldn't. Our writing is highly complex. Artists are few and far between, and it took me years of training. Whoever did this has Ret worried. I've known him for a long time. He's a difficult person to scare."

Bridget sucked in a slow breath. "How much danger is Dahlia in?" she asked in a hushed voice.

"I'm not sure," Nuriel admitted. "But I'd prepare for the worst."

Hours later, Bridget still sat at the kitchen table, poring over the papers. Ivanova had left for work, hitching a ride with Nuriel. Ret and Gaul remained locked in the office. No one seemed concerned about her running away now that the contract was sealed.

In her hasty attempt to learn as much as possible, she'd destroyed Ivanova's original organization of the documents. Instead, she'd created her own system: a stack for photographs. A stack for transcripts. A stack for Ivanova's handwritten notes. Even after hours of work, she'd barely scratched the surface. There was so much she hadn't fully explored yet—information Ivanova had kept to herself for months.

Familiar frustration bubbled up as she tried not to think about how much time she'd lost. It would take forever for her to connect the pieces. And all because Ivanova hadn't wanted a public search for Danel.

Bridget turned to a page covered in Ivanova's tidy handwriting. It was a list of dates, beginning the months before Dahlia disappeared. May 7 - Dahlia and Danel meet. She frowned and turned her gaze back to the picture of her sister and Danel. Their last call had been so awful. And all because of this jerk.

She'd worried Danel was using Dahlia, but she'd never imagined this. Had their whole relationship been a scam? Had he cared for Dahlia at all?

The paper crinkled beneath Bridget's tight grip. She cleared her throat, trying to focus on the timeline. Ivanova had listed each of their known outings, from the time they met to that final night. Danel had taken her on dozens of expensive dates.

It left a bitter taste in Bridget's mouth. So much had changed, and so quickly. Only a few months stretched between Dahlia's early days in Cleveland—when she would video chat Bridget as she tried on outfits—and those final days when they barely talked. Ivanova's list was proof of how distant she and her sister had become.

The detective knew so much more about Dahlia than she did.

August 13 - Last contact with Danel. Last contact. Whose last contact? Ivanova's? Dahlia's? Nicole had reported her sister missing two days later, when she hadn't returned to their apartment.

"Making progress?"

Bridget jumped. Nuriel stood in the doorway, pulling off his jacket. Sticking out of the front pocket was his pack of cigarettes. She let out a slow breath. "You startled me."

He stepped into the kitchen. "Sorry. I'm surprised you aren't in the living room with James. It's more comfortable in there."

"I got immersed," Bridget said, gesturing to the paper-laden kitchen table. James had taken a small selection of the paperwork for himself—the official files Bridget had already seen—to familiarize himself with the details of Dahlia's case.

Nuriel nodded to Bridget's sorted piles. "You've been busy."

"I'm catching up on everything that's been hidden from me." Bridget sat back in her chair.

"I know this must be frustrating for you." Nuriel pulled out the chair next to hers and sank into it. He smoothed his navy sweater before folding his hands on the table. "I hope you understand why Eisheth withheld information."

"Yeah, to protect your secrets."

Nuriel lifted a photograph and gave it a cursory glance.

"You're not the first person who's found out about us, and it usually hasn't gone well. Even now, even with the precautions of the security contract, we're taking a risk. I'm surprised you were able to convince Gaul."

Bridget glanced down at her hand, remembering Gaul's fingers on her. "It's not a risk if it ends up helping all of us," she said. "What's Gaul's deal, anyway?"

Nuriel shrugged. "He's suspicious of humans. He doesn't mean anything personally."

"Then he could stand to be nicer," she responded firmly.

Nuriel laughed quietly. "I've been trying to convince him of that since I met him. I don't think he could ever have a job like mine, interacting with the public."

"What do you do?"

"I'm a docent at the fine arts museum. I enjoy the work, and it helps me stay on the lookout for any of our symbols."

She tried to imagine Gaul dragging crowds of tourists from painting to painting. The idea almost made her laugh. "You're right, he'd be terrible at that."

Nuriel flipped through the manila folder on the table while Bridget watched. She knew nothing about this man. And yet, where Gaul and Ivanova had been cautious, Nuriel remained kind. He'd answered her questions and responded to James' speculations with patience. Even now, his concern seemed genuine as he looked through the papers. He was likely good at his work, she decided. There was a casually professorial air to him.

She cleared her throat. "Thank you, by the way. You've been way more helpful than the detective."

Nuriel gave her a faint smile in response. "Eisheth is a little rough around the edges, but she means well. Trust me when I say she's as invested in this search as you are, if for different reasons."

Bridget glanced at the photograph of Danel and Dahlia. "She and Danel are close, aren't they?"

He responded with a noncommittal shrug. "Their relationship is complicated, but they've helped one another through quite a lot. Suffice it to say she's eager to know where he's disappeared to."

Bridget considered him before prompting, "She said something about keeping him out of trouble earlier."

Nuriel nodded and set down a photograph. "We try to stay hidden, and having Eisheth work at the police station is helpful. Unfortunately, Danel hasn't always been as careful as the rest of us."

"Why not? And why date someone like Dahlia?" Ivanova, at least, was closer to Danel in age.

"I don't know why he was with your sister. He likes his independence, and he often does things I struggle to understand." Nuriel shrugged. "His latest stunt is certainly keeping Eisheth busy."

"Maybe, but how do I know she won't just focus on him? What if we find him but not Dahlia?" Bridget asked.

Nuriel tapped the photograph. "She cares for Danel, yes. But she also cares for her work. This search is for your sister, too."

"Well, she'd better not forget it." Bridget wrinkled her nose in skepticism, but she plowed ahead anyway. "Now that I'm in, what can I do to make the search go faster?"

"You know your sister better than we do. Keep digging through these files and let us know what you think we might have missed."

It wasn't as exciting as scoping out abandoned buildings, but it was something. "I can do that. But I'm not going to just sit around reading reports forever. We need to make a plan."

"We'll have a clearer direction once Ret meets with us," Nuriel said. "He wants to update us on the symbol in that building. We'll hold a meeting after I pick Eisheth up from the station this afternoon."

"Can I have my phone back?" Bridget asked. "I want to let my mom know I'm safe. Otherwise, she might freak and call the cops or something."

"Yes, of course. You're not prisoners. I'll fetch it for you." Nuriel stood and stepped out of the kitchen.

Glad for the small victory, Bridget turned back to her work. She dug out a couple of pages detailing text messages between Dan and Dahlia, dated a month before her disappearance. Her eyes scanned the words, determined to find some sort of clue. A mention of the mysterious person who had created the symbol, maybe.

But it was just teasing banter between the two of them, edging towards scandalous in places. As she skimmed, her thoughts returned to Nuriel. His honesty was a breath of fresh air after months of back and forth with Ivanova.

But she had to wonder if there was a catch.

"Here." Nuriel stepped back into the room, handing her the phone.

"Thank you."

He nodded and went to the refrigerator, pulling out a carry-out box of leftovers. As he transferred it to the microwave, she looked down at her phone.

Someone had turned it off. She pressed the power button, waiting for the screen to come to life. Her mom was probably worried sick. She'd been sending her a quick message each night to let her know she was safe. Until the previous evening.

Several text messages appeared on the screen. She typed a quick response. Hey mom. Sorry I scared you, I fell asleep early. Well, it was true. She sent a quick follow-up message to steer the conversation elsewhere. How's Scout? Did you find a new dog walker?

There was another text message waiting for her. It was from Nicole, Dahlia's roommate. Hey, I heard you were in Cleveland. Perfect timing, I move to Boston next week. Wanna get coffee?

Bridget read the text several times. She hadn't heard from Nicole in weeks. In fact, she figured she'd already moved. As the last person who'd seen Dahlia, she'd already been extensively questioned by Ivanova and others. Even so, she'd been willing to help Bridget with her early attempts at finding Dahlia. She cared, Bridget sensed, but now she was moving on with her life.

Still, if Nicole was messaging her, that meant she still

had some interest. She wondered how she'd found out Bridget was in Cleveland.

Hey, not sure I can get away, she typed back, but maybe we could do a video chat. She had no idea what she'd tell her, but it didn't seem fair to ignore her completely. Bridget knew how it felt to be kept out of the loop.

She checked her voicemail next. There was only one new message, from a number with a Cleveland area code. That was weird; hardly anyone knew she was here.

As she brought the phone up to listen, Nuriel returned to the table and put a plate of steaming lo mein in front of him.

"Ms. Keene, this is Sam from the front desk of Leonardo Suites. I'm calling to leave a message from a gentleman who came asking for you tonight."

Bridget frowned. The only person in the city who knew where she was staying was James. She turned up the volume.

"No one answered your room phone, so I thought I'd try here," the concierge continued. "He wanted you to know your dinner reservations have changed to eight o'clock tomorrow at, uh..." There was a pause, and the distant sound of shuffling papers.

Dinner reservations? She hadn't arranged to meet anyone. The back of her neck prickled with unease.

"Here we go," the voice said. He rattled off an address.

Bridget's stomach dropped. She knew those numbers.

That was the abandoned building.

"Oh," the voice continued. "One more thing. He said your sister is looking forward to it. Have a good night."

FOURTEEN

Bridget's entire body felt numb. She lowered her phone and stared at the screen.

"Is everything alright?" Nuriel asked, setting his fork down. His eyebrows drew together in concern.

She didn't respond, trying not to tremble as she flipped through her contacts and selected the Cleveland Police Department.

A tinny voice answered on the second ring. "CPD Third District non-emergency number. How may I direct your call?"

"I need to speak to Detective Ivanova. It's Bridget Keene." Her voice shook.

"One moment."

Nuriel frowned. "What is it?"

Bridget drummed her fingers on the tabletop as she

waited for the call to connect. A moment later, Ivanova's familiar voice was on the line. "Ms. Keene?"

"I've got another lead. A voicemail."

Bridget expected Ivanova to jump at the information, but the detective responded with a heavy sigh. "Send me what you have, but bear in mind it might not be enough to reopen the case."

Bridget's brow creased. "But wait until you hear—"

"Calm down. Just tell me what the voicemail said."

At being rebuffed, Bridget's fingers curled into a tight fist in her lap. "It was someone from my hotel. A man came by to tell me about dinner reservations tonight with my *sister*. Eight o'clock. At *you-know-where*."

Silence, other than the tick of the kitchen clock. Then, "I'll contact you if it yields anything. Stay there and wait for me to return."

Bridget swallowed back a retort. "When will you be back?"

"In a few hours. I'll be in touch."

The line went dead. Bridget lowered her phone with stiff fingers. *Not* what she wanted to hear. And Nuriel wanted her to trust the detective? Not likely.

Nuriel's voice cut through her anxious thoughts. "That sounded serious. May I listen to the message?'

She gave a wooden nod and passed the phone to him. He lifted it to his ear and she heard the whisper of the hotel employee's voice. She stood, pacing the length of the kitchen. "Is it Dan?" she asked once the message stopped playing.

Nuriel looked up at her. "No, I don't recognize the voice. What did Eisheth tell you?"

"To stay here and wait for her." Bridget was unable to mask her irritation.

"That's probably for the best. I'm going to pick her up this evening. Ret wants to meet with all of us. We can bring this information, and all make a plan together."

She shook her head. "No, I have to do something now. I don't need her help for this." Not that there was much to do but wait. She glanced at the old wooden clock that hung on the wall. The supposed dinner reservations were hours away.

"I know it's hard, but trust her. You're on the same team." He paused, then added. "And don't return to the hotel either."

"My things are there," she said.

"Once this is resolved, you can retrieve everything. Right now, it's not safe."

Bridget swallowed. She couldn't afford to keep paying for that room indefinitely. How long would she be here?

"Who's to say it *will* be resolved? The detective hardly seemed interested."

His gaze was compassionate. "It's possible someone could hear her end of the conversation. She wants to protect you, and part of that means keeping this off the books."

Bridget supposed that made sense, but Ivanova's abrupt dismissal still stung. "What am I supposed to do in the meantime?" She looked at the piles of papers still strewn on the table. It felt like they had doubled in height. "Why don't you get some rest? There isn't much you *can* do right now."

"Rest?" Bridget stared at him. "How do you expect me to *rest* when someone is out there, looking for me?" Not to mention how much there still was to read and research. It was all too much. She could feel the sharp edge of panic welling up inside her. Everything was happening so fast. Magic, contracts, and revelations. New clues and new threats. It felt like her head would never stop spinning. Maybe she could go to the building on her own. But she had no idea who—or what—would be waiting for her. The thought made her shudder.

"Hey," Nuriel said. He watched her with a concerned gaze. "It's going to be okay. We'll do everything we can to help you."

His reassurance did nothing to loosen the knot in her gut. "I should at least update James." She stood, legs stiff as she made her way out of the kitchen and into the hallway.

On her left was the living room. James sat on a burgundy couch, half a dozen notebook pages spread out on the coffee table in front of him. "What are you doing?" She had to force her voice to remain steady.

He glanced up at her. "Taking notes. Here, look." He didn't seem to notice how anxious she was.

She walked closer and lifted one of the papers. *Ivanova*, one read across the top in James' blocky writing. Beneath it, he'd written a haphazard list.

Powers: Unknown. Secret Identity: Detective Elizabeth Ivanova. Real Name: Eisheth. Source: Kabbalah.

Bridget looked up at him. "Kabbalah?"

James nodded. "Jewish mythology. Eisheth ate the souls of the damned."

Bridget grimaced. "Lovely." She turned her gaze to the other papers.

Each sheet contained a similar list. There was one for Nuriel, Gaul, and even Ret. His phone sat on the table, displaying an article about various mythologies. Bridget cocked an eyebrow at him.

"Just because I'm not supposed to tell anyone about this, doesn't mean I can't have my *own* record. You wouldn't believe some of the stuff I'm finding," he said.

Bridget set the page down and sank onto the couch beside him. She pulled over the pages and flipped through without really seeing them. After a few seconds of distracted reading, she turned her gaze back up to him. "James, I need you to listen to something."

She opened her voicemail and passed the phone to him. As he listened, his expression grew more concerned. "Who...?" he asked, looking at her.

"I don't know. But once the detective's back, I'm going to find out." She tore a page from the notebook and held out a hand for her phone.

James returned the device. "Maybe it's smart to wait for Ivanova. It sounds pretty dangerous, honestly. Whoever it is could have powers like the others."

"It's worth it if I learn more," she said, trying to sound

firm. She cleared her throat and nodded to his notes. "What have you found out?"

"Remember how Nuriel said the Grigori inspired old stories and stuff? Well, I've found plenty of those." He rifled through the papers and turned them to face her, pointing at each as he spoke. "The names Eisheth and Nuriel both come from the Kabbalah. Get this, Nuriel's an angel of hailstorms."

Her eyes widened and she looked up to him.

He was already on to the next page. "But Ret and Gaul... that's a bit harder."

"Gaul is a region of France, right?" Bridget asked, remembering her own search back at the hotel's cafe.

James nodded. "The Gauls lived in Northern France until the Romans destroyed them. Which is all interesting, but none of it matches up to what we've seen," he continued. "And the word *Grigori* doesn't *just* mean Watchers. It refers to a bunch of ancient fallen angels or something."

That sounded far-fetched, even given what she'd seen today. Bridget had a hard time imagining Ivanova or Gaul were angels, fallen or otherwise. *Focus, Bridget.* This was a problem to solve, just like any other. "Well, we know they have powers. Have you found anything about that? Are they born with them? Is there some sort of initiation?"

He shook his head. "I don't know."

"Let's keep looking." She opened a web browser on her phone.

An hour later, nerves still wound tight with anticipation, she checked her text messages again. There was a new one from Nicole. *Yeah, sure, I'm free this afternoon.*

That would make a nice change of pace. "Gonna make a call," she told James and unplugged her phone from its charger. Half an hour before, she'd retrieved the cable from where she'd left it in his car. Bridget stepped out of the room, through the empty kitchen, and onto the back porch. The screen door squeaked closed behind her.

She leaned against the railing, nudging Nuriel's ashtray out of the way. Outside, it was like another planet. Birds chirped cheerfully, puffy clouds floated by, and the sounds of kids playing carried on the breeze. It was hard to imagine the world going on without the knowledge Bridget now had. That, lurking among society, were mysterious magic users who could boil their blood or abduct their families.

Time to pretend she didn't know any of that. With a slow exhale she tried to set her jitters about the voicemail aside. Maybe Nicole would actually have some new information for her.

She clicked her name in the contact list, and the video call initiated. After a second, Nicole picked up. Her hair was pulled back in a ponytail, and there was a stack of moving boxes behind her. "Hey, Bridget."

"Hey. How's the move going?" It was hard to sound cheerful with the voicemail message replaying endlessly in the back of her mind.

Nicole flipped the camera around to show a strewn-out mess of kitchenware. "Pray for me."

Bridget forced a chuckle. "Yeah, moving sucks. How'd you hear I was in town?"

"Oh, James mentioned it a day or two ago." She turned the camera back to her face.

That's right, if James and Dahlia had been classmates, it stood to reason he knew Nicole, too. "Cool. Yeah, he's been a big help."

"He's a nice guy. A little weird, but nice." There was a beat, then Nicole asked, "So have you figured out anything new? What'd the detective say? How did James get pulled into everything?"

Bridget paused before responding. She'd promised Nuriel and the others that she wouldn't give away their secrets, but Bridget didn't have to go into specifics. If anyone deserved an update, it was Nicole. "James submitted something on that website I made, so I reached out to him."

"Really?" Nicole's expression was skeptical. "What does he know? It's not like Dahlia spent a lot of time with him."

"Uh, he'd filmed something. For one of his classes."

She wrinkled her nose. "Like an art class?"

"Yeah, videography. It was this moody art video of some really run-down old warehouse or something.

Anyway, it just happened to capture Dahlia on it."

"What?" She straightened, staring through the screen intently. "Are you sure? And *just happened to*? Bridget, that sounds so suspicious."

"I know, I know. But I've seen enough evidence that I believe him. We found more of her stuff in that building."

"Holy shit," Nicole breathed. "What did the cops say?"

Bridget scowled. "They closed the case."

"What?! Those assholes. What excuse did they give?"

"They said it wasn't concrete enough. That there was no way to prove it was Dahlia in the video. It was dark and raining, and you could only see her from the back. So I guess it wasn't good enough." A familiar surge of frustration rushed through her, even though she now knew exactly why the case had been dismissed.

Bridget expected Nicole to respond with a scathing comment about the detective, or the police department. Instead, the other woman considered her, lips pressed together like she was holding back her words.

"What is it?" Bridget demanded.

"Nothing. Just... what if they're right?" Bridget's eyebrows lifted and Nicole hurried on. "I mean, of *course* I'd love it if James had just so happened to shoot some video footage of Dahlia after she's been missing forever. But it sounds way too convenient. You know James is a total conspiracy theorist, right?"

"I know about his club, if that's what you're asking," Bridget said, bristling.

"Well, yeah. And when Dahlia first went missing, he

talked about it nonstop. He didn't even know her that well, but I guess the idea of having his own personal *Unsolved Mysteries* case was exciting."

"You make it sound like he's mooching off her disappearance. It's not like that. He's really stuck his neck out for me."

"I didn't know you knew him that well."

"I'm still getting to know him. But I trust him." *Maybe more than anyone else.*

Nicole didn't look convinced. "I just don't want anyone taking advantage of something so horrible."

"He's *not*. He sent me that video, he went with me to check out where it was filmed—"

"Probably looking for ghosts or something, right?"

"Yeah, but you know what? We found some *weird* stuff there, okay? A shoe that might have been Dahlia's, some freaky graffiti, this smokey substance that moved like a *snake*, right up until it..."

She stopped mid-sentence, sudden nausea making the porch tilt. Bile filled her throat. She tried to swallow it back, but more came up, and she hurriedly set the phone aside before throwing up over the railing. Sweat sprung from her forehead, and a wave of ice shimmered throughout her body.

Shit. The contract.

FIFTEEN

"Bridget? Bridget?" Nicole's voice sounded distant, like she was speaking through an old landline.

She gripped the railing, staring over the edge as she tried to catch her breath. The edges of her vision prickled, black spots sparking. She clamped her lips together. Maybe if she stopped talking now, the contract wouldn't take full effect.

Forcing herself to stay calm, she breathed in, then out. Slowly, the queasiness began to subside. She straightened and wiped the back of her hand across her mouth. Goosebumps prickled up and down her arms as she considered what might have happened if she'd said more.

Rather than dwell on the thought, she picked up her phone, bringing Nicole's worried expression into view.

In the tiny picture of herself in the corner, she could see how pale she looked.

"Bridget, are you okay?" Nicole's forehead wrinkled.

She fought back a hysterical laugh. Was she okay? She hadn't been okay in a long, long time.

But that's not what she said. "Yeah. Sorry, I should go. I don't feel so good."

"Okay, well, let me know if you find anything else out, okay? And let me know if I can help."

"It's alright, those boxes aren't going to pack themselves." She swallowed back the acrid taste in her mouth. The last thing she needed was to drag someone else into this mess. But then she paused. "Actually, you helped her pick out her outfit that night, right?"

"Yeah."

"If I send you a picture of the sandal I found in that warehouse, can you let me know if it's hers?" She paused but didn't feel nauseated again. Apparently, the sandal was safe to talk about.

Nicole nodded. "Send it over."

Bridget opened her images and texted the picture. It was a little bit grainy in the dark, but the sequins glinted, giving it a clear shape.

Nicole studied the picture for just a second before nodding, her eyes wide. "That's definitely hers. I was even with her when she splurged on them. She called them her bougie sandals."

Proof that this was Dahlia's shoe. And despite the surge of vindication, Bridget bit back the swell of jealousy. She and Dahlia used to do their shopping together.

"Okay. Thanks so much, Nicole. I really appreciate it."

Nicole nodded. "Yeah, of course. Let me know if you need anything else, okay?"

"I will." Bridget ended the call.

She leaned against the rail, sucking in cool air, not ready to go back inside. While she waited for her stomach to settle, she looked back at the image she'd sent Nicole. The once-sparkly sandal looked battered and limp in the dim light of the abandoned building.

Nicole had confirmed her suspicions. It *was* Dahlia's. And when she went back to the building that night, she intended to find out exactly what had happened to her.

Bridget passed the rest of the afternoon sitting beside James on the couch, searching for information. His excitement when she told him about the sandal only reconfirmed how gratifying it was to be taken seriously. He didn't question her; he believed her. Conspiracy theorist or no, he'd stuck by her.

They didn't make much progress researching the Grigori. Especially when, every half hour or so, Gaul would stop by to check on them.

Eventually, frustrated by her lack of success and not wanting to waste time, she turned back to Dahlia's casework.

Among them, she found a small piece of paper tucked among Ivanova's notes. Sharp, slanted cursive read, *Eisheth, something came up. If my recent tail comes knocking, tell her I've got a new job. I need her to back off, as much as my damned contract will allow. Be careful, I don't want you mixed up in her games. -Danel.* It was dated the same day as Dahlia's disappearance. She'd have to ask the detective what it meant later. Setting the note aside, she continued to dig through the pile.

Twenty minutes later, the front door clicked as it swung open. The sound brought Bridget to her feet, heart thudding. *Finally.* James stood as well, shuffling his notes into a loose pile.

Bridget hurried into the hall. "Detective!"

Ivanova was already halfway up the stairs. "Give me a second to breathe, Ms. Keene."

Bridget bit back a retort, turning instead to Nuriel. He'd cracked open the study door. "We're back," he said through the opening.

"Good." Gaul responded. "Gather everyone."

Nuriel pulled the door closed and caught sight of Bridget. "How are you doing?" he asked.

"Not great," Bridget said. She glanced back towards James, who was stepping into the hall.

Nuriel's gaze was sympathetic. "Come on. We'll meet in the kitchen."

Bridget returned to the living room to collect her papers and phone, then followed Nuriel and James. Stepping into the kitchen, the three of them took seats at the table—Bridget and James where they had sat to sign the contract and Nuriel beside her. Bridget hooked her ankles around the chair legs to keep her feet from drumming on the floor.

"How was the rest of your afternoon?" Nuriel asked.

The question was so normal, Bridget almost laughed. "Enlightening," she said, though she had more questions than ever. "We want to know more."

Nuriel's dark eyebrows rose. "Oh? Well, our conversation may have to wait until after the meeting."

But James jumped right in. "How do you get your powers? How many different abilities are there? Why is Eisheth named after some mythical soul eater?"

Nuriel blinked in surprise. "Um." He glanced towards the doorway.

"Well?" James asked.

Before Nuriel could respond, Gaul stepped in, his brows pinched together. The second man Bridget had seen in the study followed. His suit was rumpled, and his long, dark ponytail looked at risk of coming undone. The skin under his eyes was a darker shade than his coppery complexion, and he hid a yawn as he approached the table. He must be the Grigori who had healed her.

"Ret," Nuriel said hurriedly, appearing to jump at the chance to avoid their questions. "I don't think you've had a chance to formally meet our guests. Bridget and James will be helping us with the search for Danel."

"And for Dahlia," Bridget interjected with a glance at the kitchen clock. Just over one hour until she was supposed to meet the mysterious caller. She shifted in her seat.

"I'm sure Eisheth appreciates the support," Ret said, turning his attention to Bridget. "Are you feeling better?"

Bridget nodded. "Thank you. For, um, healing me."

"Of course." His smile was warm despite his tired gaze. Bridget wondered when he'd last slept.

Gaul folded his arms and leaned against the wall. "Let's begin. Eisheth can catch up."

"Wait," Ivanova's distant voice called, followed by the thump of shoes as she hurried down the stairs. She swept into the kitchen wearing a fresh outfit and her hair pulled back into a ponytail. She took an open seat across from Nuriel. Bridget tried to catch her gaze, but the detective ignored her.

Ret waited for her to get settled before he took a seat himself. "First of all, it's good to see you again, Eisheth."

Tap, tap, tap. Bridget's toe nudged the floor.

"What have you learned?" Ivanova asked. She wasn't wasting time with pleasantries. That was a relief.

Ret pulled a folded piece of paper from his pocket. He smoothed it out on the table. It was a photograph of the graffiti inside the abandoned building. "This contract is unlike anything I've seen in a long, long time. It uses an old dialect."

"You've seen something like this before?" Nuriel asked. "My training never covered anything similar to this."

"And what does it have to do with Danel?" Ivanova cut

in.

Ret looked between them. "Unfortunately, I don't know. But I *do* know who sealed it. Tannin."

An uneasy silence fell over the room. Nuriel's throat bobbed in a nervous swallow and Ivanova sat up a little straighter. Bridget exchanged a confused look with James.

"Hang on," James said, "aren't tannins something found in wine?"

"How do you know who did it?" Bridget asked.

"You can see his signature woven in the design here." Ret drew his finger across the outer edge of the spiraling shape.

"What does it do?" Ivanova asked.

"I'm not sure yet. But I can tell you it's important to him. Otherwise, his Artist wouldn't have embedded his ability in the symbol. The smoke is a security device. When it's enabled, it attacks anyone trying to get through," Ret said.

"Which, evidently, is how it interpreted your touch," Gaul said to James.

Ret nodded. "From what Gaul told me, you didn't touch the contract for long. You're lucky. The smoke didn't fully emerge that time."

"Who is this Tannin person?" Bridget asked.

Ret responded. "He is a particularly dangerous Grigori."

She bit her lip. Perhaps *he'd* been the person to leave the voicemail. "Dangerous how?"

"He's a collector," Ret said. Bridget shook her head, forehead wrinkling. That didn't sound particularly threatening.

"A collector of what?" James asked.

"Artifacts. Our people have a long history, and much of it has been lost to time. There are a few of us, myself included, who have taken interest in recovering what is missing. I prefer scholarly study and preservation. Tannin subscribes to the school of thought that objects of power can be looted with no regard for the consequences."

"Like a grave robber or something?" Bridget asked.

"What kind of power?" James' gaze was locked on Ret.

Gaul shook his head. "That's an impossible question to answer."

"Each contract is different," Ret said. "There are infinite possible combinations. Without seeing and interpreting them, we can't understand the scope of his collection."

"Remember the war I mentioned earlier?" Nuriel asked, looking between Bridget and James. "Afterwards, many of those old contracts were lost."

Ret nodded. "And with them, a significant piece of our own cultural heritage."

"Tannin doesn't care about our heritage," Gaul said with a scoff. "He cares about his own gain."

Nuriel slipped the pack of cigarettes out from his pocket and fidgeted with the top. "He's notorious for pressing Artists into service."

Ret spoke again. "For him, collecting new artifacts and symbols is about more than possession. He's using them to try and change the social order. Restore the Grigori people, I imagine he'd say."

Gaul rolled his eyes. "He already has abilities humans could only dream of. I've never understood why he'd feel the need for more."

"Some people are never satisfied," Ret said.

"Yes, and they're going to destroy all the hard work we've done staying underground over the years," Gaul grumbled.

Ivanova sat up straighter in her chair. "Let's rein it in. Ms. Keene, wasn't your sister studying archaeology?"

"She does," Bridget said with a nod. "But she's just an undergrad. She wouldn't have access to anything important."

"Tannin is ruthless," Ret said, holding her gaze. "If she *did* come into ownership of something he wanted, he would go to great lengths to acquire it, regardless of what harm he caused."

The room grew quiet again. Bridget met James' eyes, then looked away, tamping down a swell of panic. Maybe Tannin had sought Dahlia out because she had information he wanted. Or was she merely collateral damage in his dealings with Dan?

She grabbed her phone. They needed a plan, *now*. She'd just opened her mouth to speak when she felt a sharp pain in her ankle. Ivanova was glaring at her from across the table. The detective had *kicked* her! Ivanova gave the tiniest shake of her head. Bridget swallowed her words.

"This is dangerous ground," Ret said. "Before we do anything else, we need to know what this symbol does and why it's there. Until I have more information, I suggest you pause your search." He raised his head, fixing Ivanova with a frown. "And do not, under any circumstances, return to that building."

Bridget held Ivanova's gaze across the table. The detective's expression was hard, and she tilted her chin in a curt nod. Neither would be giving up, no matter what Ret had to say about it.

SIXTEEN

The meeting adjourned and Bridget shot out of her chair. She had less than an hour to get to the abandoned building.

"Ms. Keene," Ivanova said. "Come upstairs. I have some paperwork that will interest you."

Bridget nodded. "I'll be right there." She gathered her notes, then grabbed James by the wrist, tugging him into the living room.

"Stay here, okay?" she told him, voice hushed.

James nodded. "We've gotta hurry. It's almost time."

Bridget paused. "Are you sure you want to be a part of this? You could stay here. Research some more."

He gave her a small smile. "And not find out who your mystery caller is? Or if Ivanova will eat his soul? No, I'm in. I signed the contract and everything. I want to help."

She felt a surge of appreciation. Despite everything, he still wanted to help. Maybe she'd been too hard on him. Sure, he was eccentric, but he was also earnest. She was closer to finding Dahlia than ever, and he'd been a part of that. It felt good to have someone actually believe her.

"Alright. I'll be right back." She released his hand and made her way up the stairs.

Bridget found Ivanova waiting for her in the first bedroom. It was a mirror of the one Bridget had woken up in, with the same kind of tired furniture and old artwork. It looked lived-in, with rumpled clothing tossed on the bed and a few books on the nightstand. A miniature flag, with three horizontal bands in white, blue, and red, stood atop the wardrobe. The detective sat at an old-fashioned desk in the corner, laptop in front of her.

"Close the door," the detective said.

Bridget complied, noticing an enamel tube decorated with Hebrew letters fixed to the doorjamb. Then she crossed over to the dresser to deposit her pile of papers. "We're not waiting."

"No, of course not," Ivanova said, and Bridget relaxed a little. "Let the scholars drudge through their books. We have a solid lead, and we're going to follow it. Give me your phone, Ms. Keene. I want to hear that message again."

Bridget tugged it from her back pocket and pulled up the recording, passing it to Ivanova. While the detective listened, Bridget looked down at her notes. Despite the hours she'd spent organizing and summarizing them, there was too much to take in. Her brain felt stuffed full of new information, and the brief meeting with Ret had added even more elements. Mysterious contacts aside, each of the Grigori seemed wary of Tannin. That fact alone made her uneasy. Who could be so dangerous that even *Gaul* was uncomfortable?

"Detective Ivanova," Bridget said, looking up at her as she lowered the phone. "Is it him? Tannin?"

She shook her head. "I don't know, Ms. Keene," she admitted. "I've never met him. I only know that Danel has tangled with him before, and it didn't end well."

"Is that what his note was about? The one about someone on his tail?"

"You found that, did you?" Ivanova sighed. "It's possible. He has a tendency to make enemies." Then she sighed. "Call me Eisheth, will you? It's such a mouthful, otherwise."

"Then stop calling me Ms. Keene, and let's get on with it." The detective gave a curt nod and Bridget pressed on. "What did Dan—excuse me, *Danel*—do to piss so many people off? Dahlia said he was in the trading business. I thought she meant stocks."

The detective set her lips in an annoyed line. "Collectors like Ret and Tannin don't gather their acquisitions alone. They hire people to do all the hard work. People like Danel. And when he bends the rules of a contract, his clients get upset and *I* have to help him clean up the mess."

"If Dan is so prone to making messes, why does he still have this job?" Bridget asked. "It doesn't make sense. Why work with people like Tannin if it's just going to put himself in danger? What does he get out of it?"

The detective scowled and consulted her watch. "We don't have time to discuss Danel's many shortcomings. Nuriel and I will drive you as close to the building as we can, and you will meet this man. I'll be waiting nearby. Once we have him in custody, we can bring him to a safe place to question him."

Bridget stared at her. "You're using me as bait?"

"You wanted to be in on this investigation, Ms. Kee— Bridget. Didn't you?"

"Yes," Bridget said. "But—"

"But we have limited time and choices. I'm not wasting this opportunity to get closer to your sister and Danel. Sending you in is the best option, but Nuriel and I can go on our own if you're too frightened."

"Of course I'm frightened," Bridget said. "If Gaul can make people sick with a touch, what can *he* do?"

"You already tangled with his smoke. And I understand your hesitation. It's frankly well-founded. But Tannin—or whoever left that voicemail—will be expecting *you* to show up. They'll be far more suspicious if they see me there, too."

The memory of the burning smoke was still fresh in Bridget's mind. She didn't want to relive that experience, but Ivanova was right—her mystery caller would expect to see her. "It's your choice, of course." Ivanova's expression softened. "I *do* know what I'm doing. Nuriel and I will protect you."

Bridget bit back a scowl. They didn't have time to argue. "Okay. Let me go tell James."

Ivanova's forehead wrinkled. "James should remain here. I don't care to endanger both of you."

She shook her head. "No. He wants to come. He should get to decide for himself."

Ivanova paused, then sighed. "Fine. Let's just go."

"How are we going to get out of the house? Ret told us not to leave."

"Ret and Gaul may be my seniors, but they aren't my babysitters. We'll tell them we're going to your hotel to gather your things," Ivanova said.

Bridget nodded. "Alright. When?"

Ivanova glanced at her watch again. "As soon as you're ready."

Bridget sucked in a rallying breath and turned, letting nervous energy guide her down the stairs and to James.

Night had fallen. Bridget watched through tinted windows as cars and traffic lights whirred by, streaks of color in the night. Inside the car, the tension was palpable. Even James was silent, choosing to stare at the glowing screen of his phone rather than ask more questions. She heard the click of a lighter from the front seat, and Nuriel cracked his window open. The pungent smell of cigarette smoke filled the air.

Bridget put a hand over her mouth to hide a cough and rolled her own window down. Fresh air blasted her face. It wasn't raining, but the breeze was heavy with humidity, and she shivered in her seat.

"Sorry," Nuriel said, looking back. "I can put it out."

"As if that would help," Ivanova said in a terse voice. "The entire vehicle reeks."

"It's fine," Bridget said. She felt queasy regardless.

They fell quiet again, and Bridget watched the time tick closer to eight. Her fingers tapped out a nervous rhythm on her leg, and she tried to distract herself by watching the buildings pass by. They had left the quiet neighborhood behind, skirted the bright lights of the city, and driven south. The closer they got to their destination, the more run-down the buildings appeared. Many had metal grates covering the windows, or boards hammered over the doors.

Finally, Ivanova stopped the car on a narrow side street. She unbuckled, turning so she could see Bridget. James put his phone away and looked up.

The car's clock read 7:55 pm. Five minutes.

"We're close," the detective said, "so pay attention. I have a microphone for you to wear under your shirt. It will transmit the conversation to me. You'll be my eyes and my ears out there, so communicate when it's safe, and otherwise, do as I say."

Nuriel bent down to dig through a bag Ivanova had brought, then handed Bridget a small leather case.

"Here."

Bridget accepted it from him. "You'll be close, right?"

"Very," Ivanova said. "Once you're far enough ahead, Nuriel and I will follow. But, just in case, make sure your phone is sending me your location data." Her expression was serious. "You understand there's some risk, Bridget."

She pulled her phone out and updated its GPS settings. "You'll get me out," she said, trying to reassure herself as much as confirm the plan.

Ivanova nodded. "I'll do everything I can to keep you safe. But we're going to need to be careful."

Bridget swallowed. *Great.*

"It's worth the risk," she said. She hoped she sounded convincing. Turning her attention to the case, she zipped it open. Inside was a tiny wireless earpiece and microphone.

James leaned over to inspect it with interest. "Where's mine?"

Ivanova's expression hardened. "You don't need one from the car."

"You mean he's not coming with me?" Bridget asked, looking up in alarm.

"Absolutely not," Ivanova said. "I agreed to James coming along, not to sending him out there with you. I'm not allowing both of you to run headlong into danger."

"But I can—" James started.

"It's okay," Bridget said as she checked the clock. Another minute had slipped past. "We don't have time to argue. I'll be fine."

She slipped the earpiece in and pulled her hair over it. Then she sucked in a deep breath and stepped out of the car and into the night.

The street looked as foreboding as she'd imagined. Each puddle was a dark, bottomless well. A nearby streetlamp flickered sporadically, buzzing with electricity. In the distance, freeway traffic hummed. The sound only made her feel more isolated.

"Go on," came Ivanova's voice in her ear, and she jumped in surprise. "You need to hurry."

Fixing her eyes ahead, Bridget set out down the quiet street. Aside from Nuriel's car, she was completely alone. She hurried from streetlight to streetlight, the dark spaces between them stretching on far too long. It wasn't hard to imagine someone lurking behind every bag of trash or telephone pole. She kept her stride long, not wanting to appear uncertain. When she reached the corner, she glanced up at the street sign, then down at the map on her phone. She turned right. Her rescue car dipped out of sight as she made her way forward.

You're okay, she told herself, wiping sweaty palms on her coat. Her entire body trembled and, despite Ivanova's promises, safety felt a long way away.

She watched the numbers on the old buildings as she passed, counting upward. The street itself was empty, with no sign of her caller—or anyone else. Finally, she came to a halt, matching the number to the address in the voicemail.

It was the first time she'd seen the building from the

JESSI HONARD and MARIE PARKS

front, and it wasn't any more impressive than from the alleyway. The facade was in the slow process of decay, its brick crumbling, half of the windows broken.

"I made it," Bridget whispered, hoping Ivanova would pick it up on her end. "Everything looks abandoned."

"Stay there," Ivanova's voice responded. "Nuriel and I are close behind, but I don't have eyes on you yet."

"Do you think he's late?" Bridget asked, her breathing short and shallow. She checked the time again. It was a few minutes past eight. She fought the urge to look behind her for the detective.

There was no response to her question, so she turned her attention to the faded door. It was tall and wooden, its paint peeling and handle rusting. On closer inspection, she could see that it hung open about an inch. A sliver of dim light shone out onto the stone landing.

"Hang on," Bridget whispered. "There's a light on in there."

"Stay quiet!" Ivanova ordered her. "We're coming."

Bridget inched up the stairs and onto the portico, taking care to make no sound. Stopping in a crouch, she craned her neck to see inside. Dark shadows resolved into the shape of broken boards and wrecked furniture. Creeping closer, the source of the light came into view. A single camping lantern sat on the floor, casting dark shadows among the rubble.

"Don't go in," Ivanova spoke up again. "I'm almost in place."

She didn't have to tell Bridget twice. Her heartbeat

throbbed in her ears. She straightened, intending to back away, but her trembling fingers brushed against the door.

It creaked open another inch.

The rusty hinges let out a shrill shriek of protest, and Bridget sucked in a horrified breath. The sound seemed to reverberate through the still night, raising the hairs on her arms.

"What was that?" Ivanova demanded.

Before Bridget could answer, a dark figure blotted out the light.

"Interesting." It was a man's voice. "You look so little like your sister."

SEVENTEEN

Bridget took a hurried step backwards. Terror lodged in her throat as she stood poised on the edge of the steps. Was this Tannin?

"I'm glad you came," the man said. Shadows hid his face. "Come in."

She shook her head, eyes wide.

"Bridget?" It was Ivanova's voice in her earpiece. "What's going on?"

The man pursed his lips and made a *tsk* sound. Then he lifted a hand and gestured, as if to wave her over. The wind kicked up and pushed against Bridget's back. Her hair blew in front of her face, and she staggered forward.

His hand shot out and grabbed her wrist, pulling her across the threshold and into the building, where the air stilled.

She was in a large atrium that once might have been a reception area. The dim lantern cast flickering, warped shadows across discarded paint cans, twisted metal, and a sagging desk. Near the back of the room, a dark hallway led into the unknown.

"Let go!" She yanked her hand back. To her surprise, he released his grip. She turned on her heel and darted towards the exit.

The door slammed shut with a bang, seemingly of its own accord. She jumped back with a yell of surprise and whirled around.

The stranger stepped towards her, and the lantern's light fell over his face. He had dark eyes and a black trench coat wrapped around his thin frame.

"Get away from me!" Bridget cried. She retreated until her back hit the door. She turned to yank it open, but it didn't budge.

"I assumed you would want to see your sister," the man said in a quiet voice.

Bridget froze at his words, turning to face him. He hadn't moved and watched her with a curious expression. "Where is she?" she demanded.

"I can take you to her." He stepped closer, and Bridget shook her head.

"Tell me where she is." She tried to keep her voice steady. If this man had answers, she had to find out more. "Is she okay?"

A loud thud shook the front door. Bridget jumped and

backed away. Another bang. The knob rattled.

The man's eyes narrowed. "So you did bring friends." White smoke crept into the room, curling around the edges of the door.

He was distracted. Bridget turned and bolted towards the back hallway, trying to put as much space between them as possible. Just then, the room exploded with red light, and a blast of heat washed over her. She fell to her knees and covered her head.

Flames hissed and crackled. Bridget looked up. The front door had exploded inward. Burning wood crumpled to the floor in white-hot pieces.

Through the wreckage stepped Ivanova, silhouetted against the fire. She surveyed the room as she brushed ash from her shirt. Her eyes locked with Bridget's. Then, she lifted a palm and rounded on the dark-haired man. A fireball appeared in her hand, tongues of vivid flames licking at the skin.

So *that's* what her power was. The heat was already stifling, and sweat broke out along Bridget's forehead as she crouched in the hallway's entrance. Ivanova only had to cuff him, and then they could find out what he knew. Bridget had done her part. Now she just had to follow the breadcrumbs to her sister.

Ivanova stalked towards him, arm cocked to throw the fire like a baseball. Behind her, flames climbed along the doorframe, lapping at the ceiling. The plaster cracked, and the paint bubbled.

"Who are you?" Ivanova demanded. "Tannin?"

The thin man watched the detective warily, staying away from the flames. "You must be Eisheth. You can extinguish that. There's no need to squabble."

"Where's Dahlia? Have you been hiding her all this time?" Fire licked at Ivanova's fingers greedily.

"I've been collaborating with her. It's not as nefarious as you think," he said.

She shook her head. "Bring her to us."

"I'm sorry, but I can't do that. Your human friend here wants to see her sister. I was just showing her the way. You're invited, of course. I'm sure Tannin would love to speak with you."

Not Tannin, then. Bridget tore her gaze from the conversation and dropped to her knees. With frantic hands, she searched the ground for a weapon. Her fingers landed on a chunk of concrete, but it was too heavy to lift one-handed. *There*—she dove for a piece of rusted pipe and hefted it over her shoulder. It was better than nothing.

"Screw you," Ivanova said over the crackling of burning wood.

He responded with a disappointed sigh. "How crude. Danel did mention you could be quite difficult."

Ivanova's flames burst higher. "Where the hell is he?"

Ignoring her, the man searched the room, his gaze landing on Bridget. "Come along." He raised a hand and made a pushing motion at her. Suddenly, a roar of wind rose up and shoved her into the hallway. Bridget yelped, scrambling for footing.

"Leave her alone!" Ivanova stalked towards the man in the trench coat.

He swept his arms towards the detective. This time, the wind came from behind Bridget, blasting into the foyer. Trash flew across the floor, and the lantern soared into the air, straight for Ivanova. She swatted it to the side, a snarl on her face. It shattered against the wall, its steady light winking out. The flames cast a wild red glow as they leapt higher. Smoke billowed along the ceiling.

Bridget opened her mouth to call Ivanova, but immediately began to cough. Doubling over, she covered her mouth with her sleeve. She backed away, down the dark hallway.

She'd made it only a few feet when a loud hiss startled her, and she lifted her head towards the atrium. The fire's churning smoke was overtaken by steam, and the flames around the entryway sputtered out. Water dripped from the frame.

Nuriel stepped through the remains of the door, waving his hand to clear the air of steam. Relief shot through Bridget as she hunkered down in the dark hallway, gripping the pipe with white knuckles.

The three Grigori were crimson-edged silhouettes against the weak flames that remained. The room became still as they eyed one another.

"Kai? Is that you?" Nuriel asked.

"Nuriel?" He sounded surprised. "I didn't expect to find you skulking after a stray human."

Bridget stayed low, peering into the atrium from the

hallway.

"You *know* him?" Ivanova demanded. She growled, a fresh flame licking at her palm. It cast enough light that Bridget could make out her livid expression.

"He's the Artist who trained me," Nuriel said. Bridget could hear the frown in his voice as he addressed Kai. "What are you doing here? Did *you* create that symbol?"

"Things have changed since you and I last met." Kai sized Nuriel up in the dim light. "Tannin needs talents like ours. Come back with me to meet him."

"You're *working* for him? Why? You know his reputation."

"Because it's the fulfillment of our purpose. You and I hold the key to taking back what's ours." One hand curled to a fist. "We can restore our people, Nuriel. Working alongside someone with Tannin's influence, we can finally come out of hiding."

"Ignore him," Ivanova said. Her ball of fire swirled in her hand. It illuminated her tight jaw and defensive stance.

"I don't understand." Nuriel said. "What kind of contracts are you creating? What is Tannin doing with them?"

"And where are Dahlia and Dan?" the detective asked.

Kai gave a low laugh. "Accompany me and I'll take you to them. They've joined our noble purpose."

"No one's going anywhere with you," Ivanova snapped, and the fire in her palm formed a crackling, hissing pillar.

Against the red glow, Kai lifted his hand. "Well, you're certainly not." Suddenly, Ivanova made a strangled sound that echoed in Bridget's earpiece. The detective's free hand came up to clutch at her throat. "I don't have much time, Nuriel. Decide quickly."

Bridget pressed against the wall in the darkness, starting to back down the hall. She had no idea what Kai was talking about, but right now she needed to get out of harm's way.

She kept a tight grip on her makeshift weapon, listening to the sounds coming from the atrium. There was a shuffling of feet and the soft thud of fists hitting flesh. Metal clanked and concrete thudded. Nuriel let out a wordless yell, and wind whistled through the space.

Bridget sped up into a run, one hand held out in front of her as she hurried down the dark hallway. Abruptly, her toe caught on something hard. She pitched forward, just barely catching herself against the wall. She took a moment to steady herself, then pressed onward.

A dim light guided Bridget to the end of the hall. She turned the corner, where she came to an abrupt halt. The light came from beyond a familiar, blown-out window. This was the hall where she and James had found the graffiti. She could just barely make out the dark, twisted lines of the symbol on the opposite wall.

All she had to do was let herself out the back door and into the alleyway.

Something grabbed her shoulder.

She gasped and tried to pull away, but sharp fingers

dug into her skin. Whirling around, she swung the pipe. The metal connected with Kai's arm, but he only tightened his grip.

"Let me go!" Bridget yelled, swinging again.

This time she landed a blow on his cheek, and his head snapped to the side. Kai let out a low growl. He gestured with his free hand, and a gust of wind blew the pipe from her grip. It clanged against the wall behind her. "Stop fighting me," he growled. A thin line of blood trailed along his jaw.

"Tell me where she is!" Bridget cried as Kai bore down on her shoulder, shoving her to her knees. She struggled against him but couldn't get the leverage to push him away.

Hurried footsteps approached, and Bridget turned to see Nuriel running at full speed towards them. In the distance she could hear Ivanova retching.

"The portal. If you want to see her, go through it," Kai said. With that, he let go of her and turned to face Nuriel. The two men collided, narrowly missing Bridget and slamming into the wall. She scrambled away as Nuriel rammed his shoulder into Kai. He groaned and raised his hands to send a gust of wind against Nuriel.

"What are you *doing*?" Nuriel demanded of Kai as he lost his grip, skittering back a few feet.

"Either come with me or stay out of this," Kai warned.

Bridget climbed to her feet and backed away from the two men. In the dim light, she saw sweat beading on Nuriel's forehead.

"Bridget is only human. There's no reason to harm her," he said.

Kai responded by holding a hand out to the side. Air whooshed from the floor, sucking a piece of rebar from the ground. It whipped into his open palm, and the wind settled. "I don't want to hurt you, Nuriel."

"Then leave her be," Nuriel pleaded.

"Then work for Tannin."

"I can't do that."

A flash of confusion passed across Kai's face. He lowered his arm a few inches. Then he blinked and gave Nuriel a bare laugh. "Do you actually think you're strong enough to toy with my emotions?"

He jumped forward and swung the rebar. Nuriel lifted an arm to block the blow, but the metal crashed into his forearm, and he fell back with a cry of pain. Twisting with unnatural grace, Kai struck again and again. He was like a self-contained tornado, feet skimming the ground as he spun around Nuriel in a blur. Papers, rusted nails, and bits of drywall joined the tempest. Bridget backed away, watching in horror as Kai forced Nuriel to his knees, hands covering his head.

Her back hit the wall and she glanced over. The graffiti was only a few feet from her. Go through the portal, Kai had said. Is this what he meant? Was that the contract's purpose?

A blast of heat tore through the hallway. A flaming missile hit the wall with an explosion of light. Ivanova stepped into view. The detective's eyes were narrow, angry slits.

"Get the hell away from him." She tore towards Kai at full speed and launched into her own attack. The detective was fire and fury, flames exploding from her hands.

In the midst of the fight, no one was paying attention to Bridget. The graffiti was right there. If it *was* a portal, and she went through, she'd be playing into his hands. It could easily be a trap. But if it led her to Dahlia, wasn't it worth the risk?

Ivanova ducked as Kai blew one of her own fireballs back at her, and it struck her in the shoulder. Smoke curled up from the fabric of her shirt, and she slapped at the flames until they sputtered out. She took a step forward but tripped on a loose piece of rubble. Her dark hair fell in front of her face as she grabbed the wall for balance. She was starting to look drained, her shoulders slumped. Kai sent another blast of air in her direction, and it toppled her. Nuriel was still on his knees, eyes half-closed and blood dripping down his cheeks.

But Kai stood straight-backed, fluttering bits of paper and dust falling around him. He held the rebar in one hand, his face flushed from exertion. His coat bore singe marks, but otherwise, he didn't appear injured. He turned to find Bridget. Their eyes met, and her heart thudded in fear.

"Come," he said, holding out his free hand. "Let's go see Dahlia."

A sudden scraping sound. Ivanova bent, unsnapping

the hidden holster at her ankle. Kai whirled around as she pulled her pistol free and raised it.

Bam! Bridget clapped her hands over her ears as the shot rang out. Kai staggered back, clutching his arm and dropping the rebar. Bright red blood stained his fingers. With a growl, he flung his hand towards Ivanova. The gun flew from her grip, hitting the wall beside the window and dropping to the ground.

Kai stalked towards Ivanova. He made a scooping gesture with his uninjured arm. A howling gale lifted her from the floor. She hovered, buffeted by the rolling air, her legs kicking frantically. Discarded wrappers and mildewed paper swirled around her.

"You don't want to hurt me," he warned her. "There are precious few of us, don't you think?" He tossed her to the side with a flick of her hand. She crashed into a rusty filing cabinet, denting it.

Movement drew Bridget's attention to Nuriel. He'd managed to crawl to his hands and knees, and was reaching for Kai's dropped rebar. Locking eyes with her, he mouthed, *Go!*

Bridget wavered. Running was the safer option, but she cast her eyes back on the graffiti. She had to know what Kai meant. Even if that meant unleashing that sulfuric smoke again.

As Nuriel got to his feet, Kai made a single sweep with his hand. The blast threw Nuriel backwards into the wall. He hit it with a sharp crack and fell to the ground. The rebar tumbled from his grip.

Bam! Another gunshot rang out, this one behind her. Bridget dropped to the ground and twisted to look back.

James stood just inside the window, the detective's pistol held in shaking hands.

Kai stumbled. Blood blossomed above his right shoulder blade.

"James—" Bridget gasped. He looked at her, then let the weapon fall from his fingers. His eyes were so wide she could see the whites around the edges.

Kai fell to his knees, emitting a low groan.

James frantically beckoned to her. "We have to go."

She took a step towards him, then stopped. If she ran, she would lose her chance to find her sister. What might be her *only* chance. Dahlia was close. She *had* to be.

"No," she said in a moment of decision. She turned back towards the graffiti.

"What?" He sounded dazed.

Bridget chanced a look at Kai. He was still on his knees, doubled over. His bloody shirt clung to his chest. Ivanova had found her feet. Fire flared up again from her uninjured hand. Kai straightened with a wordless growl, standing to face her. Nuriel was still down, and this time his eyes were closed. For the moment, she was ignored.

Through the portal. That's where Dahlia was.

She pressed her trembling hand against the swooping lines of the symbol and braced herself, waiting for the black smoke.

It didn't come.

In fact, nothing happened.

A pang of disappointment hit her, and she almost pulled away. But then the same golden ripple as before shimmered across the paint. It built up into a steady light that encircled the black lines in gold. A buzzing sound filled her head, as if the air itself was vibrating.

The light shone brighter and brighter, and she squeezed her eyes shut. An electric smell filled the air, and her hair stood on end. A strange tugging sensation urged her closer to the symbol.

"Bridget, no!" Ivanova's voice sounded distant and fuzzy.

"I have to," Bridget whispered. The golden glow washed over her, and she lurched through the wall and into the light.

EIGHTEEN

Piercing white light covered Bridget like a thick blanket. She opened her mouth to cry out, but her lungs refused to fill. The buzzing sound was all around her, like an electric current that filled the air. Brief flashes of black lightning ripped across the void.

She wasn't alone in this strange place-between-places. She couldn't explain how she knew, but with every bolt of inverted lightning, she sensed a thousand invisible eyes watching her, leering at her. The back of her neck itched, and she shuddered. Several seconds passed without lightning—all stillness, humming energy, and light. Bridget managed to pull in a thick gulp of air. It seeped into her lungs like glue.

And then another jagged dark line streaked overhead, and the oppressive feeling of being watched grew stronger. The hairs rose on her arms, an uncomfortable tingling spreading across her skin.

The light morphed from bright white into a brilliant gold, filling her vision, blotting out the lightning. There was a powerful lurch, and she fell forward. She slammed into something hard, landing on her hands and knees.

A second later, James crashed down beside her. He groaned and rolled onto his back. The buzzing subsided, and the unseen watchers faded away.

Bridget coughed and sucked in rapid breaths. Blood pounded in her ears as she oriented herself. She felt stretched and thin, as if a rolling pin had flattened her. Her arms trembled, and she clutched them around herself. "Why did you follow me?"

"I couldn't let you go alone," he said, coughing.

She blinked back dark spots as her eyes adjusted. She was in a long, narrow room. The ground beneath her was polished concrete, markedly different from the abandoned building. There were two doors, one in front of her and one to the left. Both were set into plain metal walls made of identical stainless steel. There were only two pieces of furniture: a tall metal tool cabinet and a stainless steel table with no chairs. The table looked like it belonged in an operating room, its metal gleaming under the sterile lights. She turned her head to take in the full length of the room; on the wall behind her was the same intricate symbol from the warehouse.

James climbed to his feet. He looked around with wide eyes before extending a hand down to her. She took it and stood.

"Where are we? Where *were* we?" he asked.

She shook her head, dropping his hand. "Kai said the symbol is a portal."

"And we went through it." James stared at the swirling lines. He sounded thunderstruck. "Is Kai the man I shot?"

"Yeah, he works for Tannin." She considered him a long moment then said, "Um. Thanks, by the way. If you hadn't distracted him, he might have killed the detective and Nuriel. And I wouldn't have been able to sneak in here."

James sucked in a slow breath. "You're welcome?" His voice cracked a little. "So... where are we now?"

Bridget reached for her phone to check her map, but her back pocket was empty. It must have fallen out during the fight. Her earpiece was gone, too. Bridget chewed her lip as she organized her jumbled thoughts. "Do you have your phone?"

He pulled it from his pocket. It took him several shaky tries to unlock it. "No service."

Unease settled over Bridget. Without service, there was no way to know how far they had traveled. Or contact Ivanova, if she and Nuriel were even okay.

"We should get out of this room," Bridget said. "I want to get a look around. Kai said Dahlia is here." Unless he'd lied to her. Kai might want her for his own purposes. She had no doubt that he intended to follow them, and she could only hope that Nuriel and Ivanova were keeping him occupied.

James nodded. A worried line creased his forehead, and he looked back at the portal. "Do you think we can go back the way we came?"

"I don't know." She glanced at him. "Why'd you get out of the car?"

"I wanted to see what was going on. You were gone for a long time. So, I snuck in through the alley. That fight..." He looked pale, and as he stuffed his phone back in his pocket, she saw his hands were still trembling.

"I've never seen anything like it," Bridget said. The image of the detective flinging fireballs while Kai whirled around her wasn't one she'd soon forget. "Or *that*," she nodded her head back towards the symbol. She turned away. "Let's go. If Dahlia's here, we need to find her before Kai comes back."

James nodded and followed her across the room. He paused beside the cabinet. It was almost as tall as he was and made of polished metal.

"What do you think this is for?" he asked.

"I don't know. Come on, before someone finds us."

"Wait." James slid the drawer open. Bridget peered over his shoulder, catching a glimpse of sharp, shining metal.

"Are those needles?" she asked.

James nodded, closing the drawer and opening the next. It held small bottles of antiseptic, ink, and cloth.

"What is it for?" he asked.

A quiet hum interrupted them. She spun towards the

swooping symbol and froze.

Golden light prickled at the edges of the shape. A ripple flowed across the design.

Her breath caught. "James, he's coming."

James slammed the drawer closed. In a rush, the two of them darted for the door on their left. He grasped the handle, and it swung open.

A wave of frigid air washed over Bridget's face. "A freezer?" she asked in confusion.

The hum intensified into a discordant buzz, and the symbol's glow filled the room. But there was no time to deliberate. She hurried in ahead of James, and he tugged the door closed behind them.

Bridget pulled her jacket tight around herself and strained to listen. Her breath fogged around her.

"Bridget?" James whispered.

"Shh!" she hissed. She couldn't hear anything on the other side. Was Kai in the room beyond?

"Bridget!" James' voice was more urgent this time.

"What?" She turned. Then she stopped and stared, stunned.

The freezer was filled with body bags.

Bare lights lined the ceiling. They gave off a quiet buzz and bathed everything in a harsh blue color. The walls were stark metal, and the floor was corrugated steel. Piled in the center of the long, narrow room were a dozen thick, black plastic bags. Each was five or six feet long, with a single zipper running down their length.

Bridget took a trembling step deeper into the space.

She couldn't hear anything beyond the hum of the freezer—nothing to indicate whether Kai would burst in at any moment. Her trembling exhale puffed around her face as she stopped in front of the first bag. She fumbled for the zipper and pulled it down.

Long, dark hair poked out from the plastic, and she felt her heart miss a beat. *Dahlia... oh god.*

But no. She tugged the zipper down further and saw that the woman inside wasn't her. Numb, Bridget zipped the bag closed, backing away and swallowing down nausea.

"What *is* this place?" James whispered from the door. He had one hand on the door handle, as if ready to bolt at a moment's notice.

"I d-don't—" Bridget stammered, but she trailed off with a shake of her head. Her nose was running, and she sniffed. Was that what Kai meant when he said that Dahlia was here? If she looked through each bag, would she find her sister, frozen solid? She swallowed back a sob, but she couldn't keep her eyes dry.

"We have to get out of here," James said. "This is messed up, Bridget. We need to get help."

"There's nowhere to go," she whispered. She wiped her eyes. "Kai could be out there."

"It could be the detective. Maybe they came through looking for us."

"Is it worth risking it?"

He chewed his bottom lip, then shook his head. "Let's wait."

She turned back to the pile. "Okay, then I have to know." She squeezed her eyes shut as tears fell down her cheeks.

"Yeah, but we need to be c—" He cut off, swinging his head towards the door. Bridget held her breath. She could hear footsteps outside.

They stood unmoving. Bridget's eyes darted around the freezer, but there was no other way out. The cold settled over her as they waited. She tucked her hands under her armpits.

A muted *slam* made Bridget jump. She ducked in reflex and James hurried towards her. They crouched together behind the pile of corpses.

They trembled, rooted to the spot. Several long moments passed, but the other room was silent. Beside her, Bridget could hear James' teeth chattering.

Finally, Bridget found her voice. "I think that sound was the other door closing. Whoever it was, they must've gone through." She straightened. "Come on. I think it's safe."

"There's nothing safe about this." James rubbed his hands together.

Bridget couldn't help but feel a pang of guilt. James hadn't wanted to come through the portal at all. He was only following her.

But no, he *had* chosen to investigate the phone call with her. He'd signed the same contract, and he'd insisted on riding with her to the building. He'd approached the window and fired the gun. He wanted to be here.

"Help me look," Bridget said as she straightened. "The faster we get through this, the faster we can leave." She returned to the body bags, reaching for another zipper.

"Oh man," James said, watching as she opened the bag. They found themselves face to face with a blond man's unseeing gaze. A gold necklace rested across his collarbones, a tiny cross glinting in the light.

Bridget wiped her cheeks dry, then closed the bag. James followed her as she made her way to the next body. Their sniffling and the quiet *shush* of the zippers were the only sound as they worked in silence. Bridget's entire body shook with cold, and her fingers had gone completely numb.

No one interrupted them. No sounds came from the room beyond the freezer. By the time they finished the last bag, Bridget's nausea had abated. She had seen twelve corpses in all, but none of them were Dahlia's. She rubbed her trembling hands together and turned to James.

He was paler than she'd ever seen him, and his lips were turning blue. "We have to go back. We gotta tell them what we've found. This is way too awful."

Bridget shook her head and stepped over to the door. A wave of warmer air washed over her as she cracked it open. The room was empty, and the symbol on the wall was black and inert. Fresh blood stood out, crimson against the polished floor. She nudged James and nodded to it.

He grimaced. "Kai?"

"Maybe. Nuriel was beat up pretty bad, too."

He eyed the symbol anxiously. "You think that will take us back?"

"I hope so. Look, you can go if you want." She couldn't. Not yet. Wrapping her arms around herself, she looked to James. "But Dahlia is here. I'm not leaving without her."

James chewed his lip and looked back at the symbol. He scrubbed his hands over his face. "I don't want to go through that thing alone. Let's at least see what's behind door number two."

Bridget nodded. Together, they moved past the tall table, following the droplets of bright red blood.

The room's second door was the same smooth metal, and Bridget paused to listen before reaching for the handle. Everything was silent, so she eased it open an inch.

It was dark on the other side. She urged the door open further. She could sense a large, open room in front of her. She stepped in and lights flickered on, making her jump in surprise.

"They must be on motion sensors," James whispered.

Rows upon rows of metal cabinets stretched in front of her. Each had a closed glass door with an LCD panel glowing in the corner. As she neared one, she saw it was giving readouts of temperature and air humidity. Inside was a heavy, leather-bound volume.

"Ret said Tannin's a collector," James said, peering into the cabinets. "I think we found his collection."

Bridget looked up and down the row. She saw more books, jewelry, pottery, weapons, papers, and stone tablets. Each cabinet had a number. She tugged at one of the glass doors, but it was locked.

"Hello?" A woman called out, from deeper in the space.

Bridget's head snapped up.

"Hello?" The woman shouted again, more urgent this time.

Bridget knew that voice.

She broke into a run, abandoning all attempts to stay quiet. The rubber soles of her boots squeaked as she rounded a row of cabinets, and the back of the room came into view.

To the left, the rows of cabinets ended, making way for a row of shiny metal cages that extended from the ceiling to the floor. They were all empty, except one.

Inside was Dahlia.

NINETEEN

Bridget froze. Her sister stared back at her with wide eyes. She looked as if she hadn't seen the sun in ages. Her skin was pale, and her dark hair was an oily, tangled nest. She wore a plain long-sleeved shirt and wrinkled pants that hung off her frame. There was a rumpled blanket on a dented metal bench behind her.

Bridget felt as if the floor had dropped out from under her. Dahlia *was* here.

Dahlia spoke first. "Bridget?" She moved to grasp the bars of her cage. Dark shadows under her eyes contrasted with jutting cheekbones.

After months of searching, of crying herself to sleep, of shoving down fears of the worst and refusing to give up, she'd done it. She'd found her. Bridget's knees almost buckled from relief, and she reached out to brace herself against one of the cabinets.

Footsteps approached behind Bridget. She glanced back to see James rounding the corner. He stopped when he saw Dahlia.

"Oh my god," he said, taking in the scene.

"Is that—James? From school?" Dahlia's eyebrow arched in an incredulous expression that was so familiar it made Bridget's heart ache.

She tried to find the words to respond. "Dahlia," Bridget whispered. It was all she could manage. Tears pricked at her eyes. She burst into motion, closing the distance between them. Her vision blurred and she sobbed as she reached into the cage for her sister.

Dahlia's hands came to her shoulders, and they embraced through the metal bars. Bridget's whole body shook, and she clung to Dahlia's thin frame, afraid her sister would vanish if she let go.

"You have to get me out of here." Dahlia's hoarse voice cut through Bridget's crying. Her fingers dug into the skin of Bridget's arms.

Bridget sucked in a gulping breath. "I will," she promised. The cage door was held shut with a heavy padlock. She looked around for something heavy enough to break through it. Nothing. Out of the corner of her eye she saw James, eyeing a trail of blood. It led to a closed door opposite where they'd entered.

Dahlia extricated herself from Bridget's grip. "Kai brought you here, didn't he?" she said in a low, angry voice. "That *asshole*." She knelt and began putting on a pair of sneakers tucked under her bench.

Bridget reached up and wiped away tears with shaky hands. "Not exactly. But he pointed the way. Dahlia, what's going on? Why are they keeping you prisoner?"

Dahlia shook her head. "I'll explain later. Right now, you've got to free me." She looked past Bridget's shoulder at James and hissed, "James, get over here. There's a camera."

Bridget whirled and spotted a security camera attached to the wall nearby. It pointed away from the cages, focused on the row of cabinets where James stood.

He followed their gaze, then hurried towards them.

Bridget drew a shaky breath. There was no way to know if anyone had seen them. "We have to get her out before Kai comes back."

"Is there a key?" James tore his gaze from the camera and gave the bars a sharp tug. The metal rattled without opening.

"Of course there's a key," Dahlia said in a sharp voice, standing back up. "There's a keyhole, isn't there?"

James' cheeks reddened at Dahlia's tone.

"Who has it?" Bridget cut in. She couldn't imagine the stress her sister was under. "Kai?"

"Or the guards," Dahlia's eyes fixed on the closed door. "I don't think Kai locked that door behind him—he looked pretty rough."

Bridget nodded. "James shot him," she said. Out of the corner of her eye, she saw him flinch.

"Good." Dahlia gripped the bars and looked between

them. "Injured or not, he's dangerous."

"Yeah, I know," Bridget said. They'd witnessed that firsthand. "How do I get the keys from him?"

"I don't know, but I'm not going anywhere without them."

"Okay. Don't worry. James and I will figure something out." Bridget reached for her sister's hands once again and gave them a squeeze. Then she froze.

On the inside of Dahlia's wrist was a small tattoo, full of familiar swooping lines. It was inked in black, its pattern symmetrical and complex. She remembered when Dahlia had gotten it, after her trip abroad.

"Is this—?" she breathed, touching it. It was a Grigori symbol. What did *this* one do?

Dahlia pulled her hands back and rubbed at her wrist. "It's the whole reason I'm in this mess. You should hurry. They might've already spotted you."

Bridget dropped the issue of the tattoo for now. They *had* seen needles and ink in the other room. Maybe some contracts required permanent markings. Still, she had so many questions.

"Why were you in Cleveland? And what about Dan-" she started, but Dahlia cut her off.

"I said I'll tell you later." Her sister's voice was harsh. "Go. Before they throw *you* in a cage."

Bridget winced. Dahlia was right. They were wasting time. "Let's go," she said to James.

Dahlia gripped the cage bars again. "Be careful. He's probably not alone up there."

Bridget paused. "Tannin?" she guessed.

Dahlia's expression tightened with anger. "Maybe. And his guards will definitely be there. This place is like a bank vault to him."

She nodded, aching to give Dahlia another desperate hug. "I'll be back."

She turned away from the cage and approached the door. Crimson blood streaked the handle.

"You okay?" James asked, coming up behind her.

Bridget cast one last glance back at her sister. "Yes," she said and pulled the handle.

As Dahlia had predicted, it was unlocked. Bridget peeked through, half expecting to find an army of guards waiting on the other side. But all that lay behind it was a black marble stairwell leading up. Polished chrome wall lights reflected splatters of blood. The trail led to another closed door at the top of the stairs.

Bridget and James made their way into the small space and pulled the door closed behind them. Muffled voices sounded from above. Bridget couldn't make out any words.

They crouched in silence, straining to listen for a few long moments before James whispered, "We found her."

His tone was reverent, and the truth of his words shot through her body like a thunderclap. Tears pricked her eyes. It was surreal to find her sister after all these months of searching. But she had done it. And not alone, either.

She turned to him. He was watching with a nervous

smile. On the plane to Cleveland, she couldn't imagine accepting help from anyone. But James had been there for her every step of the way.

She reached out and took his hand. "I couldn't have done it without you. Thank you."

He hitched a shoulder as if to say it was no big deal, holding her gaze a long moment. A flush crept up his neck, and he cleared his throat. "Maybe once this is all over, we could celebrate? Maybe, um, dinner?"

Oh. Her own cheeks felt hot, and she pulled her hand away. "Sure. Maybe all three of us could grab a pizza."

His anxious smile crumbled. He gave a valiant thumbs up. "Yeah. Sounds great."

Regret settled deep in her gut, familiar and bitter. "It's not you, okay?"

"Oh. Yeah, okay."

He sounded despondent, so she pushed aside the familiar flip of her stomach to say, "I promise it's not you. I'm asexual. Dating hasn't ever gone well for me."

Understanding flashed across his expression. "Okay, yeah. That's... thanks for telling me." She was relieved his smile didn't carry any trace of pity.

Eager to change the subject, Bridget looked towards the upstairs door. "Maybe if we get closer, we'll be able to hear what they're saying."

James, bless him, didn't press her. Without a word, he crept further up the steps. Bridget followed more slowly, avoiding the still-wet drops of blood.

"That's not English," James murmured when she was

beside him again.

"What language is it?"

He tilted his head towards the door. "I don't know. Something European?"

"That's Kai's voice," she said. It sounded like he was arguing. The words were indecipherable, but she recognized anger in his cadence. Whatever language this was, he appeared as comfortable speaking it as he did English.

"Bridget, I'm hearing at least three voices. That's not good odds."

James was right. No matter how injured Kai was, there was no way they could stand up to his abilities—and the others were an unknown. Who knew what they could do?

"Maybe there's another way." She turned and retreated down the stairs. James followed close behind.

At the doorway, he paused, touching her shoulder. She looked at him questioningly.

"I support you," he said. "And I'm really glad we've gotten to know one another. I hope we can stay friends after all this."

Bridget blinked in surprise, then reached over and gave James a quick, but firm hug. "Thank you. Me too," she whispered. There was more to say, but that could wait. Right now, they needed to hurry.

"What happened?" Dahlia asked as soon as Bridget stepped back into the collection room. She was still on her feet, gripping the bars. "Where's the key?"

"There are too many people up there," Bridget said.

She pushed the door shut behind her, cutting off the sound of voices. "I have another idea. James, remember the needles in the other room?"

He frowned, but then realization dawned on his face. "Yeah. Be right back." He turned on his heel, hurrying in the direction of the room with the portal. Bridget cast a worried look up at the camera. Kai had to know she was here. His injuries may have delayed him, but it was only a matter of time before he came to collect her. They had to work fast.

Bridget kept half of her focus on the stairwell as she approached the cage. The padlock looked too sturdy to break off, but picking it couldn't be that hard.

"I know what you're thinking, but it's not going to work." Dahlia's voice drew Bridget's attention. She looked up at her sister. Dahlia was watching with a frustrated scowl.

"Maybe we'll get lucky," she said. Her relief at finding her sister was leeching away, cold panic taking its place. Any second now, the men upstairs could burst in.

Dahlia responded with a quiet scoff. "Yeah, *luck.* Something I haven't had in months."

"I know. I'm so sorry, Dahlia. I never stopped looking for you. Even when I found out about all of this magical-" She cut off in sudden worry. This was exactly the kind of conversation that had activated Gaul's contract when she was talking with Nicole.

"Bridget?" Dahlia prompted, watching her closely.

She sucked in a slow breath, waiting. Nothing

happened. She must have stopped in time. Licking her lips, she changed tactics. "The police are involved in the cover-up."

At the mention of the police, Dahlia's gaze hardened. "Of course they are. The Grigori are everywhere. They're in everything. And now that they know you're mixed up in this, you're not safe either."

Bridget hugged her arms. "I'm starting to get that feeling."

Behind her, James' hurried footsteps returned. Wiping her sweaty palms on her jeans, she looked back as he rounded the corner. In his hand he clutched a thin, narrow metal box.

"Got 'em," he huffed, halting beside her. He slid the box open to reveal a row of silver needles inside.

"Have you ever picked a lock before?" Bridget asked.

He looked up at her, eyes wide. "No, you?"

She shook her head, then turned her gaze to Dahlia.

"It's not going to work," Dahlia repeated. "The needles are too flimsy. We need the key."

"We can't *get* the key," Bridget said in frustration. "Our only chance is breaking you out and escaping through that portal."

James nodded in agreement. "We'll be safe on the other side. We know people who can help."

Dahlia looked between them, skepticism plain in her eyes. Then she sighed. "Okay, fine. I hope you're right." She bent so she was eye level with James. "Look, I'm not exactly an expert, but I think you need to put a needle in there. Bend it first in, like, a zig-zag." She waited while he selected a longer one, then pressed it against the floor until it crumpled. He slid it into the padlock. "Now you need something small and flat."

James' brow furrowed as he looked around. Everything that could possibly be used as a tool was locked in a cabinet.

"The box," Bridget blurted. "Maybe that'll work, if you can break part of it off."

James nodded hurriedly, snagging the metal container and twisting the top edge. It bent backwards but didn't break. With a grunt of frustration, he dropped it to the floor and stomped on it, hard. A crack sounded as the metal snapped, and he hurriedly bent to rifle through the pieces. Grabbing a long, flat sliver of metal, he slipped it into the lock with the needle. He jostled both. Nothing happened. He tried again, then cursed as the needle slipped free.

"Hurry," Bridget urged. It was all she could do to avoid yanking the makeshift tools out of James' hands and trying it herself.

"Just a sec," James whispered, and he bit his bottom lip in concentration. The needle snapped in two.

Dahlia cursed. "I told you this wouldn't work."

"It's fine," James said, reaching for a fresh needle and bending it like the first. "I've got it." He eased the new length of metal into the lock.

A quiet, mechanical whirring started behind them. Bridget turned her gaze back and caught her breath. The camera was rotating on its base. Her heart thumped in fear.

"They know we're here," she hissed.

"Give them to me," Dahlia said.

"Hey—" Bridget began.

"Hang on." James gritted his teeth.

"Quiet!" Bridget shushed them. She could have sworn she heard a door opening at the top of the stairs. "They're coming." The padlock was still stubbornly locked.

"Here, let me—" Dahlia reached through the bars. Before she could grab the tools from him, there was a *click.* James let out a whoop of victory as the padlock came unlatched. He tugged it free and yanked open the cage.

Dahlia straightened. "You did it." She sounded shocked.

"Come on!" Bridget snagged Dahlia's hand and pulled her out of the cage. Her toe caught the edge of the needle box, and it skid across the floor. Together, they started down the rows of cabinets in an all-out run, James right behind.

They were almost to freedom. They just had to get out of—

Slam! The door burst open.

TWENTY

Hand still linked with Dahlia's, Bridget skidded into the room where they'd first arrived. Behind her, a man's voice cried out, followed by the sound of boots pounding against the ground.

Dahlia tumbled in behind Bridget, gait unsteady. She released Bridget's fingers and put a hand to her chest, gasping from the exertion.

James came to an abrupt halt, staring at the wall. Bridget followed his gaze. The metal was smooth and unmarked. The portal was gone.

"But how...?" Bridget's voice pitched up in panic. The footsteps were getting louder. "Close the door!"

James lurched forward and yanked it shut. He kept a tight grip on the handle. A second later, it rattled and inched back open.

"Help me!" He dug his heels in, pulling with both hands to keep the door shut.

Dahlia hurried to his side and added her weight. Together, they kept the door from opening further, but barely.

Bridget dove for the cabinet. Metal screeched on metal as she flung open the drawers one by one. Her fingers searched for a weapon. Ink, gauze, antiseptic. Nothing useful. In the last drawer, a glint caught her eye. A pair of silver scissors. She grabbed them and spun towards the door.

It *whumped* against the frame as James and Dahlia strained to hold it closed. Then it stilled. Bridget saw them exchange an uneasy look.

Abruptly, the door jerked open with enough force to pull the handle out of their grips.

On the other side were two men. The first had his hand wrapped around the door's handle. With light hair and a muscular build, he had to be at least twice her weight.

Behind him stood a thin, brown-haired man with a rat-like smile. With a cock of his head, he said something in a foreign language to the first man.

Bridget tightened her grip on the scissors, heart thudding in her ears.

"Get back!" Dahlia snarled.

The larger man surveyed their pitiful group.

"I think not," he said with a heavy accent. Then he darted forward and grabbed Dahlia by the arm. She cried out, trying to twist away.

Fury flooded through Bridget. They were *not* taking Dahlia back. She leapt into motion, running towards the large man with her scissors raised like a dagger.

Before she reached her, Dahlia twisted in the man's grip. She swung wildly at her attacker. To Bridget's shock, Dahlia's arm connected with a solid *thwack*. The man stumbled back with a cry of alarm, clutching at his jaw. It was hard to say who looked more surprised.

A sharp yell from behind Bridget made her whirl around. James had been knocked to the floor, clutching his stomach. The thin, bearded assailant stood over him. His back was to her.

"No!" Bridget yelled. She launched herself at him, latching on from behind. He grunted, thrashing to throw her off. James scuttled back on his hands and knees, eyes wide.

Bridget hooked her arm around the bearded guard's neck. He yelled and twisted to fling her away. Barely hanging on, Bridget swung the scissors around his side and drove them into his gut. He bellowed, and Bridget cried out in response, screaming in rage as she pushed against the scissors as hard as she could.

The guard doubled over, scissors protruding from his abdomen. Bridget released her grip and tumbled to the ground.

"Bridget!" She looked up at Dahlia's voice. The first man had pinned Dahlia's hands behind her back. She kicked but couldn't land a solid blow.

James regained his footing and took several steps

back. His eyes were wide, the whites showing all the way around. He locked gazes with Bridget, then turned and bolted through the open door.

"Wait!" Bridget clambered to her feet, going cold at the sight of him fleeing. She couldn't go after him while Dahlia was struggling to break free.

"Let go of her!" Bridget yelled. Lowering her shoulder, she rammed into him with all of her strength. She may as well have run into a rock. Bridget fell back, dazed by the pain that shot through her arm.

The guard fixed her with an annoyed glare. He swiped at her with one hand, and the force sent Bridget down hard. She landed on her back, the air exploding from her lungs.

Bridget stared up at the ceiling and gasped for breath. *Get up*, she ordered herself as she wheezed.

A shadow blotted out the light overhead. Something wet and warm spattered onto her cheek. The man she'd stabbed loomed over her, bloody scissors held by his side.

In the distance, glass shattered.

Bridget tried to roll away, but warm hands grasped at her arm. The guard yanked her upright. She scrambled to get her feet under herself, then froze as twin metal points pressed against the side of her neck.

"Fight and die." The bearded guard's breath stank of fish. He pushed her forward, keeping the scissors at her neck. With every step, the cold blades grazed her skin. She held back a whimper of terror, trying to stay as still as possible. Across the room she caught sight of Dahlia, grappling with the larger guard. Her sister fell to the floor with a cry of pain and the guard started to drag her towards the door.

A wordless yell pierced the room as James rushed back in. He held a sword, its shining tip raised towards the ceiling. Its honed edge tapered into a wicked point. Bridget caught a flash of a Grigori symbol etched into the hilt, just above where James gripped it.

James swung the weapon clumsily at Dahlia's captor. The sword bit through skin and muscle, and the guard cried out in surprise. His cry turned into a bellow as he recoiled and clutched at the wound, giving Dahlia an opening to pull free. She scrambled to her feet and ran towards Bridget. The guard's skin bubbled and blackened where the sword made contact.

The thin man holding Bridget stepped back, bringing her with him and shouting in another language. She grabbed his forearm and shoved it away from her. The scissors came away from her neck and she ducked beneath him.

Bridget turned. Without thinking, she rammed a knee upward and into the guard's groin. He doubled over with a grunt. The scissors clattered to the floor.

Dahlia skidded to a stop beside Bridget. "Asshole," she hissed. She gave the guard a kick of her own, this one in the stomach. He cried out and fell to his knees, clutching at his abdomen as fresh blood seeped from the wound.

Out of the corner of her eye, something flickered.

Turning, Bridget saw black, swirling lines appear out of nowhere on the flat metal wall.

"It's back!" she gasped. "The portal!" She bent to scoop up the scissors.

The larger guard snarled at James. Blood ran down his injured arm in crimson streaks. James raised the sword, preparing to deliver another blow, when his hair blew back. The weapon flew out of his hands and skidded away. It hit the wall with a clatter. His eyes widened and he spun around. "What—?"

Kai rounded the corner and stepped into the room. He had changed out of his heavy trench coat and stripped down to the waist. Scratches and bruises covered his skin. He'd bandaged his arm and shoulder; blood soaked through both gunshot wounds. Bridget took a step back, mouth dry.

Kai surveyed the room, and his gaze fell on the thin guard, who was curled up and clutching his bloodied stomach. "Dolos?" Kai sounded surprised.

Before either guard could respond, Dahlia let out a yell of fury and rushed towards Kai. He responded with a sweep of his hand. A blast of wind rose out of nowhere, forcing Bridget back. Dahlia slammed into the wall with a sharp crack.

"No!" Bridget gasped as her sister fell to the ground in a heap. Dahlia groaned, eyes unfocused.

Only an ashen James stood between Bridget and Kai. "The sword!" she hissed to James, then peeled towards her sister.

She knelt at Dahlia's side and gripped her shoulders. Dahlia cracked open her eyes. "I'm okay," she said woozily.

Bridget turned to look behind her. James and Kai were facing one another, James' eyes wide with terror. He took a jerky step towards the sword, but Kai gave a wave, and it skidded further away. James came to a halt.

Kai looked to the larger guard. "Ketill!" he barked, then gave him an order in their language.

The guard nodded. Golden light was creeping from his shoulder, working its way around the broken skin and muscle to sew it back together. He stepped towards his fallen comrade, Dolos, lifting him into his arms. With a dark look at Bridget, Ketill carried the wounded man back into the main room and out of sight.

Kai turned his attention back to Bridget. "You harmed my protégé."

Bridget stood from her sister's side and approached Kai with quaking steps, until she was nearly between him and James.

"You locked my sister in a cage!" Her fingers squeezed tight around the scissors. Her heart thumped out of control, and her skin was damp with sweat.

Before Kai could respond, James darted towards the sword. Kai growled and lifted a hand. A moment later, a roar of air burst through the space. It forced Bridget back, and James lifted off the ground, caught up in a miniature hurricane.

"I don't appreciate being shot," he said in a low voice.

He flicked his hand, and James flew into the wall with a thud.

James groaned and rolled onto his side. Arms quivering, he pushed himself to his knees. Slowly, he dragged one foot under himself, then another. Using the wall for support, he stood to face Kai. "You can't do this," he said. Despite his obvious fear, his voice was steady. "It's wrong."

The wind let up enough for Bridget to hear her own ragged breath. "Stay back, James. I've got this."

She turned around, planting herself between Kai and James, scissors clutched in her fist.

Kai's lips curled into a cold smile. "Do you?" He flicked his fingers.

A dart of wind stole the scissors from Bridget's grip, flinging them behind her. She whirled around to see them embed themselves in James' chest.

TWENTY-ONE

James looked down at himself, shock etched into his features. Blood spread outward, staining his Spiderman shirt. Then he collapsed.

"James!" Bridget burst into motion as he hit the ground. She knelt by his side, grasping his arm. He didn't respond, staring upward with wide eyes. His entire body convulsed.

"Oh God," Bridget whispered. The scissors stuck out of his chest, and she faltered. Should she pull them out, or would that make it worse? She pressed her hands around the wound to stem the flow of blood. James responded with a violent series of coughs, and she pulled back, hands coated in blood. The sharp smell of iron filled the room.

Behind her, Kai scoffed. "It's pointless to help him.

Come with me, before anyone else is hurt."

"No," Bridget whispered. James wheezed, and Bridget turned back to him. His lips were moving without making a sound. Blood soaked his shirt, and the stain was only growing. He turned his bleary gaze to her and sucked in a labored breath.

"Bridget," he whispered.

She gripped his hands with her bloodied fingers. They were like ice.

"It's okay," she said. Her voice caught with emotion. "I'm here. I'm going to get help."

Kai's slow footfalls approached Bridget. "Tell him goodbye." He wrapped a hand around her arm and hauled her to her feet.

Bridget shook her head. "No," she begged. She tried to tug free, but he only dug his fingers in more. "No!" She slammed her elbow back into Kai's chest, right where James had shot him.

Kai let out an angry hiss of pain and released her.

Bridget dropped back down beside James. She could save him. She had to save him. Her hands grasped at James' unresponsive body, trying to lift him. His head lolled to the side.

Kai didn't reach for her again. Instead, he shot his hand out, and a sudden wall of wind hit her. Bridget scrabbled for purchase, but her fingers slipped away from James. She skidded to a stop against the wall, streaks of blood marking her path.

"It's over," Kai said, stepping towards her.

The wind had rolled James onto his side, facing her. His eyes stared, blank and unseeing.

"No," Bridget wept.

Another blast of air came out of nowhere, and her head snapped backwards into the wall. Pain shot through her body, and then everything went dark.

"Bridget!"

Awareness returned to her in a rush. She gasped awake, sitting upright. Pain shot through her head, and her vision exploded with stars. She pressed her hands to either side of her skull, squeezing her eyes shut and curling her body around her knees. The back of her head throbbed. Her fingers pressed on the spot; it felt bruised.

She focused on her breath as the throbbing subsided. Finally, she cracked her eyes open again.

Recessed lights illuminated the space around her, and she squinted as she looked up. Surrounding her on three sides were the thick bars of a cage. Beyond them were the climate-controlled cases that housed Tannin's collection. The fourth side of her cage was a polished, uninterrupted metal wall. Her wrist throbbed.

"Come here." She looked towards the voice. It was Dahlia, back in her own cage. They shared a row of bars. Her sister was sitting on the bench, leaning forward. Her hair was still a tangled, dirty mess, and there was blood splattered across her shirt. A new bruise was above her left temple.

A shock went through Bridget. *James.*

"Oh god." She scrambled to her feet. The abrupt movement sent a jackhammer across her head. Gritting her teeth, she lurched to the door of her cage and tugged. It rattled but didn't open.

The scissors had flown right out of her grip. He'd bled so much, felt so cold. She looked down at her hands. They were stained a dull red. Her stomach gave a queasy lurch, and she clenched the bars to keep from vomiting.

"I have to help him," Bridget said. She reached through the bars to tug at the padlock. "I have to help him."

"Bridget, stop." Dahlia's voice cut through her haze. "Don't you think I've tried that?"

"But James—" Bridget could barely get out his name before her eyes watered and her voice cracked beyond the point of speaking.

Tears flowed down her cheeks as she sank to her knees, gripping the bars. She'd only spent a few days with James, but all he'd ever wanted to do was help.

A hand came to rest on her shoulder and Bridget looked up, sniffing. Dahlia had squatted down beside her and reached through the bars. "I'm sorry."

Bridget shook her head, blinking through her tears. She tried to respond but found that she couldn't draw a full breath. Her entire body shook.

"Why did Kai let *us* live?" she finally choked out.

Dahlia sighed and rested her forehead against the

bars. Her dark eyes watched Bridget. "Because of me. Kai needs me, and that makes you valuable, too. He went through the portal to bring you here."

Bridget raised the back of her hands to her face, wiping her eyes. "I don't understand."

Dahlia paused to glance beyond the cage bars, and Bridget followed her gaze.

The camera stared at them, red light blinking. Bridget turned away quickly, the movement sending a spasm through her aching muscles. She kept her back to the device.

Dahlia lowered her voice to a whisper. "Kai is Tannin's employee. My work hasn't been good enough for them."

Bridget scooted closer to Dahlia. "What work? What do they *want* with you? Why did Dan pick you for whatever it is Tannin is doing?"

"Because I have shit luck," Dahlia said, brows drawn in frustration. "Dan used me for my drawings."

"Drawings?" Bridget shook her head, trying to banish the stuffy, throbbing sensation within her skull.

"Yeah, like this." She tapped the tattoo on her wrist. "Remember that archaeology trip for school? It's what the team uncovered." She gestured towards one of the cabinets.

Bridget glanced at the rows of artifacts. In the cabinet nearest them sat a green sketchbook, its cover decorated with band stickers. She hadn't noticed it before, but now she recognized it as her sister's.

"So this *is* about their symbols," Bridget said.

Dahlia nodded. "I drew the ones we found on the dig. I used my field notes, at first. But then Dan wanted better versions. He told me it was for some friend's art show."

"An art show," Bridget said, unable to help the skeptical edge to her voice.

"I know, I never should have believed him. But I did. And I walked right into his trap."

A sharp blaze of fury shot through Bridget. Dan had destroyed Dahlia's life over a handful of half-accurate drawings.

"Their written language has power," she echoed Nuriel's words. "Why didn't he just steal them?"

Dahlia shrugged. "Kai's trained to draw the symbols, but I'm the one who actually saw them. I guess when Dan sold the images to Tannin, they decided to keep me around, too."

"Where is Dan now?" Bridget asked, hands curling into fists.

Dahlia's eyes narrowed. "Off doing Tannin's dirty work, I assume." She dropped her glare to the ground, then asked in a tight voice, "Are you going to say it?"

"Say what?" It scared her how bitter Dahlia sounded. It made Bridget's heart ache, thinking about what her sister had been through. All hints of that playful little girl, doodling pictures in their room, were gone.

And I wasn't there to protect her. Not when she needed me the most. Bridget hugged herself.

"That you were right about him. He's a creep."

"He's not a creep, he's a monster," Bridget growled.

But her outrage sputtered at the sight of Dahlia, looking abashed. "I'm just glad you're alive. I'm sorry about how our last conversation went. I haven't been able to stop thinking about our fight."

"Me neither," Dahlia said. Her dark eyes searched Bridget, and there was pain in them. "Let's forget it, okay?"

Bridget nodded, a fresh lump forming in her throat. "Thank you," she said. Then she drew in a sharp breath and changed the subject. "I saw you on a video James took." Her voice shook as she mentioned him, but she powered through. "You were in Cleveland *after* you'd disappeared. Alone. Why?"

"I wasn't alone," Dahlia said. "I'm never alone unless I'm in this damned cage. Because my drawings aren't accurate enough, Tannin sent me to see if I could get any photographs of the artifacts from the school." She shifted back from the bars. "Those weren't good enough either. That's why Kai went after you. To *motivate* me."

Bridget shook her head, staring at her sister. "And now that I'm here, this is your punishment?" She clenched her stained fists. "As if keeping you in a cage for months wasn't horrible enough."

"It's not getting you here that's the punishment," Dahlia said, voice quiet. "It's what they're going to do to you now that you're here."

A chill descended over Bridget. Her mind immediately went to James, and she shuddered. Kai hadn't wasted a second thought on him, but he'd taken care to knock

Bridget out and throw her in a cage. Dahlia was right; he wanted her alive. "We have to get out of here."

Dahlia let out a low, humorless laugh. "No kidding. Got any bright ideas?"

Bridget shook her head. "What if the portal is gone again?"

"No," Dahlia said. "It was there all along. I should've known better." At Bridget's puzzled look, she explained, "The smaller guard, Dolos? He can make people see things. Or not see things, I guess. He must have hidden it from view."

Bridget bit her lip. "If only we had those needles, we could break out again." A quick scan of the floor revealed the box James had used. It was far beyond their reach.

Dahlia sighed and reached up to rub her temple. She paused, looked down at her fingers, then up to Bridget. "You hurt your head, didn't you?"

Bridget nodded.

Dahlia gripped the bars, scooting closer. "I have an idea."

"You do? To get us out?" Her breath caught.

"To get *you* out," Dahlia said. "You'd have to come back for me."

Bridget stared at her sister. "What? After everything it took to find you? There's no way I'm leaving without you."

Dahlia scooted closer, casting a nervous look towards the camera. "James said you had friends in Cleveland, right?

"Yes, but—"

"Do you trust them? Would they help?" Dahlia asked.

Bridget paused. Her reluctance to accept help had already gotten one person killed. How far could she get fighting Kai alone? Or Tannin? Besides, Ivanova and the others weren't human like James. This was *their* world Dahlia had been sucked into. It was *their* kind holding her hostage and killing her friends. She didn't fully trust them, but Ivanova might assist her if she thought it would lead to Danel. Bridget couldn't be sure about the others, but Nuriel hadn't hesitated to join the battle in the abandoned building. And he, at least, seemed to trust Ivanova.

So long as they have a good reason, they'll fight. She had to admit their firepower would be an asset. Assuming they'd survived their terrible fight with Kai.

"They'll help," Bridget said, with as much conviction as she could muster.

Dahlia exhaled. "Then all you have to do is get through and convince them to come back for me."

"Get through the portal? What about the smoke?"

Dahlia shook her head. "Tannin's security system doesn't work on this side. He has no need to attack his own staff. But you'll have to deal with it coming back."

Bridget chewed her lip. "I really don't like the idea of leaving you here alone."

"You can't help me when you're stuck in a cage. Stay here and we're both screwed. If you go, you can bring back help and save us both." Her forehead was wrinkled, eyes intense.

"But—"

"Don't argue. This will work." Dahlia said. Bridget struggled to come up with a protest, but Dahlia was right. She was no help to anyone locked in a cage.

"Why can't you come with me?" she asked, voice quiet.

"I don't have a plan for that."

Bridget met her sister's gaze. "What will they do to you if I escape?"

Dahlia reached through the bars and wrapped her hands around Bridget's. "I've made it this long. I can wait a few more hours."

Bridget wavered, but she couldn't think of a better plan.

"Okay," she whispered. "Tell me your idea."

TWENTY-TWO

"Help! Help!" Dahlia yelled.

Bridget didn't know if the security camera picked up audio, but it didn't matter. Dahlia was screaming, the sound echoing through the vast room. With luck, her cries were loud enough for the guards to hear through the thick metal door.

Bridget didn't look up at her sister. Instead, she lay sprawled face-down on the floor of her cage. She'd spent the past fifteen minutes making a show of looking disoriented. Walking in vague circles. Looking around in confusion. Sitting on her bench and staring at nothing, ignoring Dahlia's pointed questions. And then she'd fallen to the ground, a few feet away from their shared wall of bars.

It was a simple, dangerous plan, but it was the only

one they had.

"Dolos! Ketill! Someone get down here!" Dahlia called, and Bridget imagined her waving frantically to get the attention of the camera. The minutes wore on, and Bridget's neck began to ache from the awkward angle. The metal floor was cool beneath her cheek. She remained still. Someone had to come.

Dahlia's voice was growing hoarse. How long would she have to scream before someone took notice? There was no way to know if anyone was even watching the camera.

The door at the bottom of the stairs finally banged open. She heard footsteps approaching, then an accented voice snarled at Dahlia from a few feet away, "Shut up."

Dahlia didn't. "My sister! Look, she's unconscious!"

"She is sleeping." His tone was dismissive.

Bridget kept her breathing light and eyes closed. She could feel his gaze on her. It didn't sound like Kai, but the other two men—the large one who could heal himself, Ketill, and the thin one who could create illusions, Dolos— both had heavy accents.

"She is *not* sleeping," Dahlia's voice cracked. "She hit her head during the fight. It messed her up. She wasn't making any sense when she woke up and then she just fell over."

A heavy sigh. "I will get Kai." He didn't sound pleased by the prospect.

The mention of Kai summoned images of James collapsing before her eyes, his blood pooling around the gleam of silver scissors. Her throat felt thick.

"Is she even breathing?" Dahlia demanded. "Please. Dolos, just check on her first."

The man gave an irritated grunt. Dolos. It was the smaller guard, the one she'd stabbed with the scissors. He'd apparently recovered from his injuries. "Why do you care so much? She is just a human."

"She's my *sister*. And Kai wants her alive. You know how much trouble he went through to get her here." A pause, and then her voice grew lower. "How would it look if she died while you were supposed to be watching her?"

"You're threatening me?" Dolos' voice was sharp. Bridget fought the urge to crack open an eye.

"No, I'm trying to *help* you. She needs a doctor. Please, I—"

A loud slam cut her off. It tapered into the clatter of bars.

Bridget could hear Dahlia fall back against her bench. Squealing, it slid along the floor. It took everything Bridget had to stay still.

"Enough! I don't need your help, child," he growled.

It's not going to work. Bridget's heart sank.

Silence. It continued for several long moments before Bridget heard a long sigh followed by the jangle of keys. There was a faint click—the unmistakable sound of a lock unlatching. It was working!

Bridget tensed as the door to her cage squealed open. Footsteps moved into the space, then came to a stop. She held her breath and waited.

Fabric rustled, and Bridget sensed Dolos squatting beside her. She couldn't screw this up—she would only have one chance. A hand touched her hair, pulling it away from her face.

Almost. He pressed two fingers to the side of her neck, checking for a pulse.

Now!

Her eyes popped open.

The thin, bearded guard hovered over her, inches from her face. His eyes widened as he realized she was awake.

Bridget lurched into a sitting position. Her head collided with his chin, and he cried out and fell backwards.

Bridget's head erupted with fresh pain and her vision blackened. Knocked off balance, Dolos fumbled for the side of the cage to steady himself.

Dahlia was ready. Her hand darted through the metal bars and grabbed the guard's wrist. With a swift movement, she jerked two of his fingers backwards. There was a sharp snap as they bent back to his wrist, followed by a scream.

"Go!" Dahlia cried, getting a firmer grip on the guard as he reeled in agony.

Bridget clambered to her feet, ignoring the throbbing in her skull. Throwing her weight into the door, she staggered out and slammed it shut with a crash. She clicked the lock shut.

It was then she realized her mistake. The keys were tucked away in Dolos' pocket. If they could get the keys from him, Dahlia would be free, too. She cursed herself for not thinking of it before. A quick glance back and Bridget saw Dahlia struggling to keep him held against the bars.

"Dahlia—" Bridget started.

"Hurry!" Dahlia called, interrupting her. "Go now!"

"Get the keys!"

"There's no time!" Dahlia grabbed Dolos' collar and pulled. He gasped, his breath cut off by his own shirt.

Bridget floundered with indecision. But getting Dahlia out wasn't part of the plan. Not yet, at least. This was Bridget's only chance to return to Cleveland and get backup.

"I love you." Tears made her vision hazy.

Dahlia's gaze flickered to her sister. "*Go.*"

Bridget ran. Her shoes squeaked against the metal floor as she rounded a row of cabinets. She sidestepped a pile of glass from a shattered case. James' sword had been placed inside.

Bridget ducked into the next room and came to an abrupt stop. It still bore the marks of the earlier battle. A streak of blood led to a dark, sticky pool. The cabinet lay on its side, drawers spilling out. Needles and ink lay scattered across the floor

Safety was so close. She crossed the room, avoiding the spilled blood, and pressed a hand to the swirling lines.

A buzzing sound filled her ears and golden light began to work its way around the symbol. She glanced back to make sure she wasn't being followed.

The freezer door caught her eye.

She faltered. He'd be in there, wouldn't he? In that moment, she knew she had to look. With a shaking breath, her fingers lifted away from the wall. The buzzing faded, and the light fizzled.

She yanked the freezer door open. Cold air washed over her, and goosebumps raced up her arms.

James' body lay sprawled on top of the pile of corpses. She put a hand to her mouth. Tears welled up in her eyes.

He hadn't even been given the decency of a covering. His eyes stared, open and blank. Someone had removed the scissors, leaving a dark hole in his chest. Blood completely obscured the Spiderman logo on his shirt. An empty body bag sat nearby on the floor, half unzipped.

With a whimper, she gauged her next move. Dolos wouldn't stay distracted forever, but she wasn't sure she could bring herself to leave without James.

Bridget let the door click closed behind her as she approached her friend. Hot tears rolled down her cheeks. She pressed a hand to her lips to stifle a sob.

His skin was an unnatural, pale gray. All the color was gone from his cheeks. When she reached out to touch his arm, it was cold and stiff. She looked away, a lump in her throat. James didn't deserve this.

A distant crash made her jump. Even through multiple walls, she recognized the clang of a cage door slamming shut.

Heart thudding in her chest, she slid her arms beneath James and hefted him. He was heavy. There was no way she'd get through in time. She set him back down.

Another slam, this time far closer. Someone had to be in the next room. Her breath came in short, terrified gasps. She'd made a mistake. Her need to see James had cost her the precious time Dahlia had bought. She looked around the small freezer. There was nowhere to hide.

Well, almost nowhere.

With a thrill of horror, Bridget grabbed the empty body bag. Casting a quick glance towards the still-closed door, she set the bag on the floor in front of her. Bridget sat down in it and slipped her feet down to the bottom. Trying not to think about what she was doing, she leaned forward to zip it up. With trembling hands, she lay down flat, tucking her hair in before she closed the bag.

Shivering in the dark, she shimmied closer to the pile of bodies, until she felt the weight of another bag slump onto her. She bit back the urge to apologize for disturbing whoever was inside. Something hard pressed into her chest—an elbow? A knee?

Outside the freezer, she heard faint footsteps. There was a squeal of metal as someone righted the fallen cabinet.

Entombed within the freezer of corpses, she held her breath.

TWENTY-THREE

The thud of boots paused outside the freezer. Hidden inside her body bag, Bridget sucked in a deep breath, willing the door to stay closed. The weight of a corpse pressed down on her, and she locked her limbs to keep from shivering.

Please don't come in, she begged. Please, please, please.

Bridget heard a handle turn, followed by the click of the latch. She squeezed her eyes shut and didn't move.

The corpse on top of her slid under the weight of the other bodies, and Bridget's breath caught.

Someone stepped into the room, then paused. She heard a low, frustrated mutter in that same indecipherable language. She recognized the voice; it was Dolos. Her heart thudded in her ears so loud she was shocked the guard couldn't hear.

The body slipped another millimeter across her stomach. Bridget summoned all of her willpower to remain still.

More silence.

And then the sound of footsteps retreated. The door thumped closed.

Bridget stayed still, listening. Another door closed and she allowed herself to breathe. As soon as her chest rose, the corpse slipped off of her. It landed on the floor with a dull thud.

She reached up with frigid fingers to unzip her bag. With a gasp of relief, she sat up, turning wide eyes on the door.

Bridget guessed the guard would return. He was probably going to retrieve Kai, or the larger guard. She couldn't be here when they returned. Moving with care, she extricated herself from the bag.

There was no way to tell how much time she had. Bridget straightened out the body bag and unzipped it all the way before she turned to James.

His glassy eyes stared unblinkingly up at the ceiling, arms stiff at his sides. A tear rolled down her cheek. He had been there for her every step of the way. He'd believed her when no one else had. He'd looked like a true superhero, wielding that sword.

"I'm so sorry," she whispered, touching his curls. Her breath puffed out in a white cloud.

Sliding shaky arms underneath James' rigid form, she

gathered her strength and inched him off the pile of bodies. He was heavy, and he slid from her grip, dropping a few inches towards the floor. She lunged forward to recover him, lowering him gently to the ground.

Even though she'd only known him for a few days, it was hard to believe James was gone. He'd never go ghost hunting again or crack another bad joke. He'd never slurp another soda or shoot another video.

Her tears were hot against her skin as she inched him into the bag. His body was stiff and heavy, and it took her precious minutes to maneuver him.

Hurry, she urged herself. Bridget couldn't afford to think about what she was doing. This was a task. Move the object into the bag. Get out before Dolos returned. She steeled herself and continued her work.

Finally, she had him situated. James' empty gaze stared past her. She fought back a sob as she pulled the zipper up, closing him off from the world.

All Bridget wanted to do was curl up and cry, but now wasn't the time. She needed reinforcements. Dahlia was counting on her. James deserved to go home.

She wiped the tears from her cheeks and approached the freezer door. A wave of warm air ran over her skin as she cracked it open. She peered out into a silent room.

Empty. For now.

She returned to James. She bent down and pulled the bag as hard as she could. It lurched forward. With a grunt of effort, she tugged again, and inch by inch she dragged him across the floor of the freezer.

She reached the door and pushed it open, straining to listen. In the distance, she heard a slam. A jolt of alarm rushed through her, and she redoubled her grip on James. Muscles straining, she continued to make slow, agonizing progress past the table and towards the portal.

Her entire body shook as she stepped over spilled ink and scattered needles. Nausea clawed its way up her throat when she reached the dark stain of drying blood, but she kept moving. She was almost there.

A sudden yell sent a shock through her. Dahlia. Bridget couldn't make out the words, but she recognized the furious tone of her sister in the heat of an argument.

It took her a considerable amount of willpower not to drop James and run to her sister's aid. But that wasn't the plan. *She's buying me time*, Bridget reminded herself. She seized the body bag and pulled with all her strength, straining at the effort as she dropped one side and reached out to slap her palm against the symbol.

Buzzing filled the room and drowned out the sound of Dahlia's argument. Brilliant light blocked the sight of the tilted cabinet, the needles, the blood.

And then Bridget fell forward, consumed by the suffocating whiteness. She tried to catch her breath, but the thick air choked her, and she coughed.

Black lightning streaked across the nothingness, and the deeply unsettling feeling of being spied upon returned. She hugged James closer, shrinking under him as her surroundings went white again. She clung to his body, sealed in its thick plastic bag. Each breath was a struggle, and the air sat in her lungs like water.

Another jagged fork of electricity cracked across the sky. She could have sworn that, just beyond it, were countless glistening eyes. They disappeared with the lightning. A sudden hook in her abdomen pulled her forward.

She fell to her knees on gritty concrete, losing her grip on James. He rolled to a stop a foot away.

Fresh air spilled into her lungs too fast, and she coughed, then turned her head and threw up. She drew a shaking hand up to wipe at her mouth.

She raised her head to survey her surroundings. Daylight filtered in through the broken window before her, illuminating a battle-scarred hallway. The cinder block walls around her were scorched, and the scent of metal and burned wood was sharp. She had made it. Dahlia's plan had worked.

Keep moving. Dahlia couldn't keep Dolos distracted forever. She needed to get far away.

Bridget pulled herself to her feet and looked around. The building was still. Behind her, the symbol faded from gold to black. She ran her fingers through her tangled hair and considered her options.

Under any other circumstances, she'd make a run for it. But she had James with her, and he was too heavy to carry. Besides, what would she do if someone stopped her? There was no way she could explain herself.

She needed to contact the detective—but her phone had been lost somewhere in the building. She scanned the piles of wrecked building materials, then picked her way down the hallway. Every few feet she paused to turn over a broken board or a chunk of concrete, searching for the familiar device that would connect her with the outside world. Enough dim light filtered in from outside that she could make out her surroundings.

Luck was on her side. She'd only been searching for a few moments when something reflective caught her eye, wedged between a crumpled filing cabinet and a tilted wooden chair. With a gasp of relief, she picked her phone up. There were dents all along the blue metal casing, and the screen was a spider web of cracks.

She held her breath as she tapped the screen, and almost sobbed when it came to life. In the upper corner, the battery indicator flashed red. She fumbled for her contact list and selected Ivanova's name. Trembling, she placed the call.

The screen went black.

"No," Bridget whispered, eyes wide. She tried to turn the phone back on, but it was unresponsive. "Come on!" She shook the device, then tried again. Nothing. She let out a frustrated growl.

A sudden scraping sound made her freeze.

She looked up, muscles tensing. Dolos? She strained to listen, breath held.

Another rustle came from the front of the building. As she listened, she heard a footstep. Another followed.

Bridget whipped her head back and forth, searching for somewhere to hide. She ducked into the nearest room, crouching inside. She recognized the tilted desk and scattered chairs from when she and James had first explored the building.

The hallway darkened, the dusty light blocked by a tall figure. It was in shadow as he took a step further into the building, approaching her. Bridget looked for something that could serve as a weapon. Her fingers closed over the neck of a broken beer bottle, the glass caked in dry mud. Was this how Dahlia felt, scared and huddling in the dust, when Danel lured her here?

Her gaze snapped back to the hall at the sound of more movement.

Grit crunched under the figure's foot, and she shrank back farther. And then a faint line of daylight illuminated his features.

She sagged in relief. It was Nuriel.

INTERLUDE

Danel

Nine months before...

Danel shifted in his seat and worked his jaw. It made a cracking sound. Wonderful.

He sat in a high-backed wooden chair in a sparse but well-appointed office. Tannin's. He'd only been here once before.

Before him stood a wide mahogany desk and large, organized bookshelves. Danel tilted his head to read the spines. Nothing of interest. A second empty chair sat beside him and a third behind the desk.

He'd woken up not long ago, hands tethered in front

of him with rough rope. Even better, each ankle was lashed to one of the chair legs. It was a weak attempt to prevent him from escaping. Danel regarded the knots that bound his wrists. Already he'd loosened them so they chafed less. It would be easy enough to break free, though he doubted he would get far. The door to the office was likely guarded.

He wasn't concerned with escape yet, though. The job wasn't done; he didn't even know what had happened.

Dozens of aches and pains shot through his body. Judging by the throbbing in his head and the gap in his memories, Kai had knocked him out. Last he remembered, the man had stood between him and Dahlia.

That had *not* been part of the deal. Tannin had told him to bring Dahlia's sketches to him. There had been no mention of becoming a punching bag in the delivery process.

He probed the inside of his mouth with his tongue. The jagged edge of a molar sliced it and he grimaced at the sudden taste of iron. Broken tooth. So that's what that aching was. He was fast collecting a list of grievances.

Muffled footsteps approached and Danel twisted towards the sound. The motion sent a spasm through his side, and he added broken ribs to his tally.

A lock clicked and the door opened. Tannin stepped in, unflappable as ever. He looked unaffected by the scuffle for Dahlia. His wavy hair was neatly combed, and he'd changed out of his dusty clothes and into a fresh suit.

Armani, from the looks of it.

Kai followed, favoring Danel with a look that bordered on disgust. He still had concrete dust in his dark hair, which made it look like he was going gray. His head was held high, and his nose wrinkled when he looked down at Danel.

Why did Artists always have to be so damned pompous?

"Oh good, you decided to stop by." Danel couldn't help the scorn that slipped into his tone.

Neither of them appeared hurt. Of course, they'd probably visited a healer for their injuries. A luxury they clearly didn't see the need to extend to Danel. How considerate of them.

Tannin gave Danel a thin smile, but Kai's expression remained impassive.

"Danel. I apologize for the precautions." Tannin walked around the desk and took a seat in the more comfortable, cushioned chair behind it. Kai straightened his coat and sank into the chair beside Danel.

"You think a bit of rope is going to hold me?" Danel asked.

"No, I don't imagine it will. Let's talk before you feel compelled to prove yourself, shall we?" Tannin folded his hands on the desk's surface.

Danel let out a sigh of exasperation. This was already taking too long. "Where are the sketches?"

"They're in our custody," Tannin said. He inclined his head. "Thanks to your diligent efforts."

"And Dahlia?" Danel asked. His last memory was of her struggling to maintain her footing in the wake of Tannin's small earthquake.

"Also in our custody," Tannin said in a smooth voice.

Danel scowled. "You didn't tell me you planned to terrorize the girl. What are you going to do with her?"

Tannin shook his head. "A discussion for another day."

Danel huffed in irritation. He'd put a lot of time and energy into gaining Dahlia's trust. For months, he'd planned dates, put up with Eisheth's scathing questions, and pretended to care about the sketches. Even then, he'd barely been able to convince Dahlia to meet with Tannin.

"Well, if you wanted her in addition to the sketches, you should've mentioned it. And I wouldn't mind an explanation for this." He nodded down to the ropes. "Why are you treating me like a criminal?"

"Because you got in the way," Kai said. Danel shot him a glare.

Tannin leaned forward, scrutinizing Danel. "I'm happy to compensate you for your grievances, of course. But before I do, I'm curious. What motivates you?"

"Not being tied up like an animal," Danel said.

Kai sneered. "Answer the question. You have to care about something beyond this little business of yours."

"It's not a 'little' business," Danel said, bristling. "It's my livelihood. Besides, what else is there?"

"History. Loyalty. Family." Tannin spread his hands, palms up, as if offering a buffet.

Danel rolled his eyes. "None of us have any family left."

None that know of our existence, at least.

"Don't you? Family goes deeper than blood. Especially since the war, considering so many of us were lost."

"Yeah, speaking of blood, I'm going to need a healer, too. You broke my tooth."

Kai gave an irritated scoff. "That's what you're concerned with right now? Dentistry?"

Danel turned to Kai. "It was a good tooth. I'd like to keep it."

"Stop thinking myopically, Danel," Kai said, voice dripping with contempt. "Tannin is trying to offer you an opportunity. A rare one for someone as young as you."

Danel opened his mouth to retort, eyes narrowing in disdain.

"You care for Eisheth," Tannin said. Danel looked at him with surprise, but Tannin just smiled.

"Is that supposed to be a threat?" Danel asked, all flippancy gone from his tone. He'd already faced enough of those.

"Not at all. Merely an observation. Family and loyalty extend beyond those we've left behind. You can *choose* your family. We all do, in the end. And I take care of mine." Tannin smiled thinly.

Danel's eyes narrowed. "Is there a point to this?"

"I want you to choose loyalty to me. Join *my* family." Tannin's voice was firm. "Changes are coming for our people, Danel. I want you to be a part of them."

Danel responded with a sharp laugh. "Let's think about this. You want my loyalty when you've covered me in bruises, knocked me out, locked me in a room, and tied me to a chair. And that's just in the past few hours—to say nothing of our past business arrangements."

"I understand your reservations," Tannin said. "But you've done good work, and our cause needs trustworthy, talented people. This would be a fresh beginning. And a profitable one, at that."

Danel rolled his eyes. "Yeah, your fresh beginning is off to a great start. I'm not working for you again."

"Not for, *with*." Tannin placed his hands flat on the desk, standing. "These new symbols have the potential to change our place in the world. To allow us to reclaim what we've lost."

"We haven't lost anything," Danel said. "Unless you're referencing my tooth."

Kai scoffed. "You know so little. Those symbols the human girl found could represent abilities that have been lost for *millennia*. They could rewrite the rules of—"

"Enough, Kai," Tannin said.

Kai fell silent, but his eyes remained bright with indignation.

"See," Danel said, shifting forward to rest his elbows on his knees. His ribs gave a sharp pang of protest. "This is how I stay in business. People like him." He nodded towards Kai. "People like you. Those symbols are only as important as the value you place on them. To me, they're a bunch of worthless sketches."

Tannin tutted. "That's unfortunate. Those worthless sketches will have a great impact on our people, yourself included. And you're as beholden to our contracts as anyone."

Danel snorted but didn't respond. As if he needed some prick in Armani to remind him of that.

"There is potential here for something very significant—far beyond a business transaction. Not only that, but *you* have potential, Danel."

Danel gave him a bland look. "I should hope so, or you wouldn't have hired me." He shifted in his chair and the rope pressed against his skin.

"I told you it was no use," Kai told Tannin. "He's got a smart-ass answer for everything. He doesn't care about anyone but himself."

"Kai, why don't you go see to the girl?" Tannin said sharply. Kai stiffened, but Tannin held his gaze. Setting his jaw, Kai rose to his feet. He sneered at Danel as he went.

As soon as Kai was gone, Tannin considered Danel. "What would you charge for me to become your only client?"

Danel shook his head. "More than you can afford."

"I doubt that. I want us to work well together. Like we did before."

"Before?" They'd worked together before, sure, but it had never been particularly smooth sailing.

"No, not what you're thinking. *Long* before," Tannin said. "If I have to pay handsomely to restore our positive working relationship, I am willing." He leaned forward and lowered his voice. "And I can override your current contract."

Danel kept his expression blank. How had word of that gotten to Tannin? "I don't know what you're talking about."

Tannin's eyebrows lifted. "No? So you haven't been trapped working for Eris? She knows you're here, even now. I can resolve that for you."

Danel stiffened at her name. Eris was another collector, but her application of the work was far less subtle than any other in the profession. Accepting a contract with her had been one of his worst decisions. Sure, it had allowed him to live well while also providing for his one remaining family member. Unfortunately, helping Eris in her single-minded hunt for symbols also meant becoming her accomplice in crimes far more serious than theft. And now he was glued to her through a contract that let her breathe down his neck.

As much as Kai derided him for his business, there was much more than mere profit at stake. He gave Tannin a level stare. "I don't negotiate while tied to chairs."

"Of course not," Tannin said. He reached into the drawer of his desk, pulled out a folding knife, and walked around to where Danel sat. Stooping, he opened the blade and cut the ropes at his ankles.

Danel cleared his throat and held out his hands.

Tannin sliced through the material. Danel wasn't fooled by his youthful appearance. He was a businessman, through and through. He wouldn't hesitate to use Danel, but the feeling was mutual. At least Tannin was influential and wealthy; Danel could turn that to his advantage.

"Triple what you paid for the sketches," Danel said. If he was going to allow Tannin to press him into work, he may as well be highly compensated. "And I want the contract with Eris broken."

Tannin met his gaze. "You know as well as I do that only she can deactivate it entirely. But Eris is an old friend of mine, and she'll back off whatever threats she's made while you work for me. I *do* have conditions, though."

Danel sighed noisily as he brought his hands to his wrists and rubbed them. Of *course* he had conditions. "Go ahead." Tannin straightened and sat in Kai's chair.

"First, I know Eisheth is a close friend of yours, but keep your distance during this engagement," Tannin said, crossing one leg over the other. "In fact, you're not to contact any of the Cleveland group."

"Why?"

"When it comes to these symbols, discretion is key. Even among those in your inner circle."

Danel hesitated. Dahlia's disappearance would most likely land in Eisheth's lap, which meant she'd be forced to cover for him. Again. She'd be *thrilled*. It might work to his advantage to give her some space.

"Fine," he said. If he *did* decide to contact Eisheth, there was no reason Tannin needed to know about it.

That was his own business.

Satisfied, Tannin continued. "Second, as part of you prioritizing your work with me, I'd like you to set up a home base here in Athens. I will provide you with accommodations."

Athens? How'd he get this far so quickly? He must've been knocked out longer than he thought. "Fine. I'll let you know if they're not to my satisfaction."

"Finally—and I recognize this may be difficult—cooperate with Kai," he said. "I value you both, and I believe you can accomplish much together."

He scowled. "I hope you've told him the same."

"I have." Tannin reached into his breast pocket and pulled out a piece of paper, where a pre-drawn swirling symbol had been inked. Presumptuous bastard. He'd already had Kai draw up a contract.

Danel scowled. "I want to add my own terms. Assuming you mean what you say about working *with* me."

Tannin lowered the paper to his lap. "Go on."

"I want protection from Eris," Danel held up one finger. "And not just for me. For another person, too. I'll give you their name and location, but I don't want any questions asked." When Tannin nodded, Danel exhaled slowly. So far, so good.

He lifted a second finger and continued. "When I'm not on a job, my time is my own. If you don't need me, I can do whatever I want."

"Very well, although I am serious about being your

sole client. Anything else?" Tannin asked.

"Yeah," Danel said. "I don't know what you need Dahlia for. It's not like Kai would ever train a human Artist. But she didn't ask for this, so treat her with some damned decency."

Tannin gave a mild smile. "You have a soft spot for her?"

"I have a soft spot for anyone who gets jerked around by assholes like Kai."

"I'm not a barbarian. And while she's far from my only plan, she's making an important contribution to our people. We are creating a better future for ourselves here."

Danel shook his head. He was used to well-funded Grigori who thought they were going to change the world. It never happened. "We'll see."

"Regardless, she'll be taken care of." Tannin said.

"One last thing. No contracts. I'll work with you, and I'll agree to your terms, but I won't be bound by another symbol. They're too much damned trouble."

Tannin raised an eyebrow. "Unconventional."

Danel's jaw clenched. "Take it or leave it."

Tannin held Danel's gaze. Then finally he crumpled up the piece of paper and offered his right hand. "Do we have a deal?"

Danel considered Tannin. He was just as dangerous as Eris, in his own way. But he, at least, was willing to negotiate. Danel could work with that. Especially if it protected what remained of his *true* family.

He reached out and clasped Tannin's hand. "We do."

Two months later...

Danel spun the leather-clad steering wheel and turned onto a busy Athenian street. A car horn blared at him. He stamped down on the accelerator, and the engine of his Jaguar roared in response.

Two months. It had been two months, to the day, since he'd made his deal with Tannin. In many respects, it was a straightforward job. All he had to do was hunt down artifacts for Tannin—specifically, the original stone tablets Dahlia had encountered on her school trip. Simple enough on the surface. Unfortunately, despite scouring Europe and North Africa, all he had to show for it was a sunburn.

This job is a complete waste of energy, Danel thought as he glided to a precision stop in his reserved parking spot. Unfortunately, he had few options. Tannin was an effective shield from Eris. From the moment they'd shook hands, her threats had halted.

Danel killed the engine and stepped out into the sunshine. The smell of souvlaki wafted from the restaurant across the street, and birds chirped from the branches of a nearby fig tree. Before him was a former bank building with walls of polished marble blocks. He clicked the lock on the Jaguar's key fob, then strode towards the bank.

A heavy bronze door marked the bank's entrance. Danel pulled it open to reveal a high-ceilinged atrium adorned with crystal chandeliers. The original marble floors were inlaid with intricate mosaics, and stone reliefs lined the walls.

Danel passed Dolos, standing at attention. The guard gave him a grudging nod that Danel didn't bother returning. Why pretend he was anything but a lackey? He crossed the open space where teller windows once had been, passing the plush chairs and tables that adorned the room. Beyond Dolos it was empty, and Danel's footsteps echoed off the walls.

The muffled sound of quiet conversation greeted him as he approached a closed office door. It was the same room where he had struck his deal with Tannin. Danel paused in the hallway, listening. It sounded like Kai, speaking in a hushed but intense tone.

Danel opened the door. "Good morning, gentlemen." The conversation died, and Tannin stood from the desk, immaculate in a dark Brioni suit. Kai remained sitting in one of the available chairs, wearing his signature black trench coat. He possessively clutched a loose stack of papers to his chest.

Tannin came around the table to greet Danel with a handshake. "I trust your recent travels went well?"

"The beaches in Djerba nearly made up for the tedium of the work." Danel looked between Tannin and Kai. "What's this about?"

"We've made some progress, but we also have a problem. I've called you here to discuss both," Tannin said.

"What sort of problem?" Danel asked. "I'm not going back to Tunisia, if that's what this is about. The artifacts aren't there anymore."

"You won't need to," Tannin said. He looked to Kai. "If you would explain?"

Kai nodded. "I finished a new symbol earlier today." There was a note of pride in his voice as he held up the stack of papers.

Danel shrugged. "That's not news. You finish symbols every day. Between you and Dahlia, you've probably finished a thousand." He hadn't seen Dahlia since that night in the abandoned building, but her name came up frequently when he spoke with Tannin and Kai. He knew she was hard at work, collaborating with Kai to replicate the Grigori writing she'd documented in her sketchbooks. So far, it had reportedly been a fruitless effort. It made Danel wonder why he bothered keeping her around. The sketches certainly weren't Tannin's only strategy for uncovering old contracts. Danel's recent travels were proof enough of that.

"The girl's contribution is unimportant," Kai said with a dismissive wave. "The previous drawings have been drafts. What *is* important is that this symbol *works*. It activates a functional contract." He gripped the stack tighter, eyes bright.

Ah, not so fruitless, after all.

"Good for you." Danel stuffed his hands into the pockets of his jeans. Kai scowled. What did he expect, a party?

"We don't know for certain that it works, Kai," Tannin said. "We need to test it first."

"It will work," Kai insisted.

"What makes you so sure?" Danel asked. "Nothing else has."

Kai bristled. He turned the top paper in his stack towards Danel. On it was a collection of swooping lines, drawn on graphing paper for precision. "This will. The dimensions are perfect. The subtle symmetry of the—"

Tannin cut him off. "It's based on a symbol we uncovered years ago, before we had the girl's sketchbook. The original allowed us to set the portal in place. It's close enough to the first that we're fairly certain it will activate."

"Okay," Danel said. "What's it do?"

"It's a derivation of that original design," Kai said. "It will allow us to set another point of entry or exit for an existing portal."

"Like a back door," Danel said.

"Precisely." Kai sounded surprised at his understanding. "The first portal was activated in Cleveland, to allow us access to the girl. With this derivation, we'll be able to synchronize the channels and—"

"Fascinating," Danel interrupted. "So, no champagne?"

Tannin interceded before Kai could respond. "Our celebration will be remote. I'd like to test this new symbol in Cleveland."

His brow creased. "But you already have a portal there."

"Having a back door, as you so elegantly put it, can only benefit us," Tannin said.

Kai nodded. "Once our business in the city is finished, we'll remove the portals and use them elsewhere. With both symbols, we can effectively set up operations anywhere on the planet."

Tannin nodded and stood. "Come with me, gentlemen."

Kai and Danel followed Tannin out of the office and back into the atrium where Dolos was. They walked past several closed office doors, moving deeper into the building, and came to a stop at a heavy metal door. A digital keypad glowed red beside it.

Tannin hid the numbers behind his body as he entered a code. The pad beeped and glowed green. He pulled the door open to reveal a set of marble stairs that led downward to the basement level, with a second closed door at the bottom. This was new territory for Danel.

Tannin led the descent. "This breakthrough couldn't have come at a better time. I was starting to have my doubts about this team, given the glacial rate of progress."

Danel's attention sharpened as he followed him down the stairs, Kai's shoes clacking behind him. "What is that supposed to mean?"

"It means I am not paying you to sit on the beach in Djerba," Tannin said, hand gliding along the rail.

"Hey, learning where something *isn't* is still progress." Danel couldn't risk his arrangement with Tannin disappearing on a whim. To his relief, Eris had stopped contacting him with her thinly veiled threats. He'd like to keep it that way.

"Not the progress I'd like to see," Tannin said coolly, not bothering to look back. "But Kai's success—assuming he *is* successful—has bought you more time. One working type of symbol is not enough, but it is a start. The portals represent a small sliver of what we could create for our people."

Danel rolled his eyes at Tannin's back but said nothing. He'd learned not to offer his opinion when Tannin or Kai began discussing Grigori destiny. "You still need the stone tablets from her dig," Danel said.

"As your efforts haven't yielded anything yet, we will resort to another method." Tannin turned to face him as they reached the bottom landing. Danel could feel Kai's smirk without even looking at him. "Dahlia believes that her university may house photographs of the artifacts. It's not as ideal as having the originals, but I'd still like to recover these images. You'll be going to retrieve them tomorrow."

"You're sending *him*?" Kai cut in. He was several steps behind them, watching with an offended expression. "Why? He might be recognized. And he can't put the new portal in place; he's no Artist."

"I need you here, continuing to work with Dahlia," Tannin said. "Until we're able to recruit more Artists to our cause, you're too valuable to go far afield right now. You can provide Danel with the necessary materials."

"You have so little faith in me, Kai." Danel smirked.

Kai huffed in irritation. "Is that why we're coming down here? To put my hard work in *his* hands?"

"Yes," Tannin said, matter-of-factly. "And to speak with Dahlia. The three of you have been working in isolation for long enough."

"Is Dahlia here?" Danel asked. His jolt of anxiety surprised him. He couldn't imagine she'd feel charitable towards him.

Tannin nodded. "We'll be including her in the conversation. And while we're down here, Kai is going to provide a stencil for you, Danel." He swung the door open.

"This is degrading," Kai muttered, shifting his papers.

A series of lights automatically flickered on, and Danel's first impression was a sleek, metallic underground museum. The room was vast, likely stretching for half a city block. Rows upon rows of glass cabinets boasted various immaculate ancient artifacts.

Ah. *This* was where Tannin kept his collection. Danel had wondered.

He stepped into the room to peer in a cabinet. Inside, there was a handsome dagger set, each one bearing an intricate symbol carved from its jade pommel. Kai followed, closing the door behind him.

"*Dan?*"

He spun towards the sound, recognizing the voice. He'd expected to find Dahlia at a desk, drawings scattered around her. And there *were* drawings. But there was also a cage. The steel bars ran from the floor to the ceiling, and the only furniture inside was a bench.

As for Dahlia, she looked awful. Her hair was a limp mess, and she wore a ragged sweater atop the very dress she'd been wearing the last time he'd seen her. Her eyes were filled with rage.

He let out a curse, hurrying to her. "Dahlia—" He whirled around to face Tannin, fingers clenching into fists at his sides. "You promised me she'd be cared for."

"So it's true. You're in on this, too." Dahlia clutched the bars.

"She has been cared for, as promised," Tannin said, voice calm. "She's been given a place to sleep, meals, and projects to keep her occupied."

"She's starving! She's in a cage!" Surely Tannin wasn't so out of touch with humanity that he thought *this* was legitimately caring for someone.

"It's not our fault if she refuses the food we give her," Kai snapped.

"We've given her every opportunity to work *with* us," Tannin said. "Unlike you, she has very little sense of self-preservation. We had to resort to persuasive—"

Danel interrupted him, pointing an accusatory finger at him. "You made a promise."

"I did, and I have followed through," Tannin said. He gestured at the cage. "If she refuses to cooperate, certain measures must be taken to ensure she does not harm our mission."

"That's bullshit. I—"

"Are you familiar with the phrase, 'don't bite the hand that feeds you'?" Tannin's voice was sharp. "Without me, your precious protections would be gone."

"Thinking only of yourself. Typical," Dahlia spat. She looked disgusted.

Now wasn't the time to offer her an explanation. He turned back to Tannin, eyes narrow. "You have no respect for our arrangement. You *know* this isn't what I meant when I said I wanted her unharmed. She doesn't deserve this."

"You can't speak to what she deserves if you haven't seen how she behaves," Kai said.

It took everything in Danel to keep calm. He couldn't afford to blow up at Tannin. He needed a new angle. With effort, he uncurled his fists. "Let's speak privately. Right now."

Tannin nodded. "Kai, get started on the stencil with Dahlia."

Grumbling under his breath, Kai turned to obey.

Tannin beckoned for Danel to follow as he made his way towards a door at the back of the collection room. He opened it and stepped through. Danel followed, looking around.

The room was smaller than the previous one. Here, a

tall metal table was bolted to the ground, and a single cabinet stood in the corner. The far wall was covered with a swirling Grigori pattern, its dark lines inactive. Kai's precious portal, most likely.

"What do you wish to say, Danel?" Tannin asked, stopping beside the cabinet and turning to face him.

Danel forced his breath to steady, though he could still feel angry heat in his cheeks. He fixed Tannin with a hard look. "I should call our deal off right now. I can manage on my own."

Tannin arched his eyebrows. "Tell me, what's so important about Morgan Bridgeport?"

Danel stiffened at the name. "How dare you bring my family into this?"

Tannin looked entirely unbothered. "I'm sure Eris would love to know that she's no longer under my protection."

Danel fought the urge to raise his fists. He'd learned long ago that violence would only make matters worse with people like Tannin. Still, he struggled to push down the tightness in his throat. He'd agreed to work with Tannin to get *away* from bullshit like this. He forced out a slow breath. "Leave her out of this."

Tannin spread his hands, palms up. "I would love nothing more than to do exactly that. I don't understand your fascination with her, but I do respect that she's important to you. I'm merely pointing out that you're in a precarious situation. You can only do so much to protect yourself, especially with Eris constantly asking after you. She's eager to get you back under her control."

Danel stiffened. "I haven't heard anything."

"Of course you haven't. Because I've been working hard to *uphold* our deal and keep her away from you. I'm shielding you, Danel. Don't think for a moment that she's happy about it, though." He sighed, shaking his head. "Honestly, I'd expect gratitude, considering how much I've done for you. We used to be so close, once. Before you changed."

Danel watched Tannin through narrowed eyes. Was he telling the truth? It was impossible to know. But if he was serious, Danel was backed into a corner. He couldn't risk putting his last family member in danger. Morgan was all he had left. "Fine. I'll continue to do your legwork. But Dahlia comes with me to Cleveland."

Tannin cocked his head. "Do you take me for a fool? You clearly still have an attachment to the girl. You'll cut her loose."

"No, I won't," Danel said. He hated the truth behind his words. Sure, he *wanted* to set her free. But that was impossible. She was in too deep, and he had his own hide to protect. "Dahlia hasn't done anything wrong. I *know* how important she is to your project, but you can't continue to treat her like this."

"Her treatment is entirely up to her," Tannin said.

"You want us all to work together? You're letting one of your most valuable resources waste away in a kennel. Dahlia needs a reason beyond her own survival to cooperate. Let me talk to her. Alone."

Tannin paused, seeming to consider his words.

Danel spoke again. "She won't escape. I can promise you that. Consider this your opportunity to *truly* uphold your end of the deal."

Tannin gave a slow nod. "I suppose you're right about one thing. It is time to begin investing in Dahlia, beyond her sketches." He fixed him with a firm look. "You leave with her tomorrow to recover the files and place the second portal. Any questions?"

Danel shook his head.

"Good. Go get Kai's stencil. And Danel? Don't make me regret placing my trust in you."

One day later...

Danel staggered forward and drew in a breath of fresh air, bracing himself against the wall. The golden glow of the portal lit up a familiar, debris-strewn hall. Dust motes floated in the air, and the floor was littered with broken planks of wood, empty glass bottles, and bits of twisted rebar.

Dahlia stumbled through behind him. He reached out to steady her, but she ripped away from his touch. The glow faded, and darkness enveloped them. He reached into his pocket and pulled out a small flashlight, clicking it on.

As she took in their surroundings, he watched her

expression turn stony. This is where she had been attacked. Betrayed.

Him too, he wanted to remind her. It's not like he was thrilled about the way things had happened.

He strode to a boarded-up window and peered into the alleyway beyond. It was raining, as usual. How could he forget Cleveland's temperamental weather so quickly? A fine mist hung in the air, reducing a nearby dumpster to a hulking shadow. Beyond that, Danel couldn't see anything. He pulled away and turned to the rusted door beside the window.

"This should be fun," he said as he turned back to Dahlia. She hadn't moved. He lightened his tone as he slid the deadbolt back. "Don't look so grim. This is better than that cage, isn't it? And I'm better company than Kai."

That only earned a tightening of Dahlia's lips. Her anger washed over him like a physical force. He didn't blame her. Maybe he could try a different approach.

"Dahlia, I know this isn't what you want, but—"

"Don't talk," she said. They were the first words she'd addressed him with all day. Her dark eyes met his. He could tell she was just waiting to lash out at him. Searching for the right move. The right moment.

He wanted to tell her that he was trying to *help* her. That he'd always been trying to help her, since the day they'd both been brought through the portal. Yes, he'd used her, but only for her drawings. He'd never intended to get her involved.

He had a fair idea how well that conversation would go. There was nothing he could do to change her mind, and they had a job to do.

He tugged open the metal door. Lifting the hood of his raincoat, he stepped into the night. Dahlia followed in tense silence. Their feet crunched on gravel and broken glass. When they reached the sidewalk, he cast a glance in her direction.

"Let's review," Danel said, earning a look of cold fury. He kept talking. "We go to the school and access the archival computers. Or, even better, the physical photographs."

"Digital is easier." Dahlia's response was curt.

He inclined his head. "See, this is why you're here. You're the reigning expert. Alright, we'll access the digital files then. Or rather, you will while I watch. Computers don't like me much."

Silence. There was a time when she would have laughed and responded with a teasing comeback. But now she only stuffed her hands deeper into her pockets, gaze on the broken sidewalk.

"You'll stay with me the entire time. Don't speak to anyone, and don't make me chase you through the streets," Danel continued, rubbing his hands together. "When we finish, we'll return here, and you go back through. Ketill will be waiting to receive you on the other side."

Her eyes narrowed. "You're not coming back, too?"

"Not immediately. There's another task Tannin needs

me to see to," Danel said. The stencil Kai had prepared was folded neatly and tucked away in his jacket pocket. A can of spray paint was there with it, making his jacket bulge. "We only have three hours to wrap this up before Tannin reactivates the symbol's security system, so let's hurry."

Dahlia lowered her head against the rain, and they fell quiet once more. She didn't speak again as they came to a main road. After a few blocks of walking, Danel took an old flip phone from one of the pockets of his raincoat. He snapped it open and turned it on. The screen glowed orange, and he entered the number for a local cab company.

It wasn't long before they were out of the rain, rumbling through the city in the back of a warm taxi. Dahlia sat beside Danel in the back seat. He glanced at her and saw she was trying to make direct eye contact with the driver's rearview mirror. Danel nudged her foot with his boot. She responded with a defiant glare, then lowered her eyes.

He ordered the driver to drop them off near the university. The brakes squealed as the car rolled to a stop next to the curb. Danel pulled out his wallet, thumbing through it for a few bills.

A latch clicked.

Danel looked up to see Dahlia throw the door open. She tumbled out of the car and took off in a sprint. The door hung open behind her, rain washing over the seat.

Dammit, Danel groaned internally.

Dahlia was a dark streak in the night, a smudge against the rain. Her hair whipped back behind her as she catapulted herself along the grass and up a hill.

Danel shoved a wad of bills at the cabbie. "Keep the change," he said. He stepped out into the rain, closing the door behind him. Then he walked to the other side of the car. "Sorry, she really doesn't like getting stuck in the rain," he said as he shut Dahlia's door. It wouldn't do for the driver to suspect Dahlia was a prisoner.

Fortunately, he simply raised his hand in acknowledgement and pulled away from the curb.

Danel glanced around, taking stock of his surroundings. They were on the edge of campus, but the dreary weather and late hour left it quiet. There were no students around. Good. No one to witness him.

Water streaked off Dahlia's raincoat as she barreled towards a distant blue light—a campus emergency station.

Danel took a deep breath, then tapped into his power.

The world slowed around him. In the early days of using his ability, he'd wondered if he could control time itself. But no, it was an illusion. When he moved with supernatural speed, he was no more than a blur to others.

In the distance, Dahlia's dash slowed to a crawl. She took another step, her leg suspended and her arm pumping backwards an inch at a time with the motion.

Danel tore forward, kicking sod out from under his feet. Raindrops glittered in midair, their trajectory halted. They exploded into thousands of sparkling diamonds as he ran through them.

It was almost unfair how easy it was to close in on Dahlia. He reached out to grab her arm.

It slipped from his grip, slick with rain, and she gained another few inches on him in an unexpected blast of speed. She raised her hand towards the blue-lit button as she neared it. He burst forward, and just before her hand came down, he threw his arms around her, tackling her to the ground.

They fell in a heap, Danel landing on top of Dahlia. Time whirred back to normal.

"What the hell do you think you're doing?" Danel growled, gripping her arms. "Do you want to get us both killed?"

"Let me go!" Dahlia cried. She gasped for breath, cheeks flushed from exertion. Her dark hair fanned out in soaked, bedraggled tangles around her head.

"Listen to me," he said, fingers tightening around her arms. "Listen! I don't care if you hate me, but you need to follow directions. If you escape, Tannin will find you, and he will do far worse than put you in a cage."

"The police—"

"The police can't help you. You should know that by now. Tannin might care about keeping you alive, but what about your family? Your mom? Your sister?" She flinched, and he plowed forward. "You know how fast I am. You can't outrun me, Dahlia."

He felt her sag, muscles relenting. "I just want to go home." Her words caught in a sob.

"I know." Danel loosened his grip. "I'm sorry. I truly am, Dahlia. I never wanted this for you." Damn Tannin and Kai for locking her in that cage. She'd never listen now.

"Then let me go." She was crying in earnest now.

"I can't. I'm sorry." He got to his feet, wiping the seat of his pants. His jeans were soaked through. He offered her a hand up.

Her expression hardened and she pushed herself upright on her own. He watched tremors run through her as she hugged herself.

He sighed. "Come on. It's this way, right?"

She wiped her tears and strode away from him without responding. He followed, allowing her a little space, trusting she was smart enough not to make another escape attempt.

Danel didn't blame her. He knew how she felt. He might not spend his nights in a cage, but he was trapped, too—by contracts and handshakes and prior agreements come back to haunt him. But that didn't change anything. For now, they both had to play by Tannin's rules.

Danel sped up, coming to walk alongside her. "I know it doesn't seem like it now, but you want this trip to be a success."

"Do I?" Her voice was like venom.

"Yes. The more you work with Tannin the more likely it is he'll treat you well. You deserve to live like a human being, not a trapped animal."

"That's rich, coming from the guy who got me in this

situation."

Danel bit back a retort as they continued across campus. Eventually they came to an old brick building with a soaring turret, like a small castle. They stepped onto the covered porch out of the rain, and Danel went straight to the door. He tugged the handle, but to no avail. Set into the wall was a keycard reader.

Danel pulled a card from his pocket. On the front was the university's logo and a small picture of Dahlia. He felt her eyes on him as he swiped the card.

"Dolos removed the identifiers," he said. The card still worked, but it wouldn't trace back to her.

Inside, Danel expected to find something modern and sterile, like Tannin's collection. Instead, he stepped into an echoey atrium with old linoleum floors. It was empty, save the bronze bust of some dusty, long-dead man, its nose rubbed gold. There was an old, musty smell to the place.

"Lead on," he said. She did so without hesitation, walking straight ahead. Together, they went through an open doorway opposite the entrance. The musty smell intensified as they stepped into a cold library. Books lined the walls and a dozen computers hummed quietly. It was, fortunately, also empty—no students or staff to spot them. Dahlia sat down in the closest chair.

Danel came to a stop behind her, watching as she shook the mouse to wake the computer from its slumber. The screen came to life, displaying a simple login prompt. *Library Archive Search,* it read. *Please sign in to use the system.*

Dahlia began typing in her student email address, but Danel put a hand on the back of her seat and tugged her away from the keyboard. "Wait. They'll see that you logged in. Let's use your professor's computer instead."

Dahlia glared at him and stood again. He followed her out of the computer lab and down one of the halls. They passed a series of dark classrooms and offices before they came to a stop at a wooden door labeled *Dr. Iris Patel.* She gave the knob a quick test, then shook her head.

"Allow me," Danel said, stepping over. He glanced up and down the atrium. Once he was convinced they were alone, he reached into his jacket pocket and pulled out a set of lockpicks. With practiced motion, slid them into place. The lock gave with a quiet click, and he smiled.

Inside was a cramped office. The bookshelves overflowed, and mounds of paper covered the desk. A single, ragged chair held a box filled with binders. How could anyone work in such a mess?

He flipped on the light and closed them inside. "Hurry."

Dahlia set the box on the floor and sat in the chair, shoulders hunched under her raincoat. When she shook the mouse, the monitor remained black. She frowned and leaned over. "The dock is empty. She must've taken her laptop home."

Danel remained in front of the closed door. "So that means no digital copies?"

"That's right, genius," Dahlia rolled the chair towards

the other side of the desk, carefully lifting papers, then replacing them, trying not to disturb whatever order there was to Dr. Patel's chaos. Given the state of things, Danel doubted the professor would even notice.

A framed photo sat on top of a stack of papers depicting who he could only assume was Dr. Patel. She knelt on the ground, her dark hair mostly covered by a wide-brimmed hat that kept the sun at bay. She was looking at the camera, holding up a small brush, grinning despite her dirt-smudged pants, and looking utterly in her element at the dig site. He set the photo aside and flipped through the documents underneath it. They were old tests, covered in bad handwriting and markings in red pen.

He placed everything back and glanced up at Dahlia. She was sifting haphazardly through the mess, her eyebrows pinched together. Given how she'd been treated, her bitter anger was more than understandable. If Tannin wanted her sincere cooperation, he was going to have a long wait on his hands.

All for the glory of the Grigori, Danel thought with an internal scoff. Whatever that meant. Tannin said it was about restoring their society to what it had been before the war. But as far as he could tell, his obsessive collecting of symbols and artifacts served only himself.

"Here," Dahlia said, drawing Danel's attention. He moved closer to peer over her shoulder.

Dahlia slid a handful of sheets from a larger stack. They were photo prints on high-quality paper, and depicted what looked like etched tablets, their surfaces worn and battered.

She leaned in to inspect them. "This is maybe a quarter of them, but they're not going to be any good to Kai or Tannin." She turned her gaze up to him, forehead wrinkling. "No wonder I can't make the symbols work. The damage to the tablets is worse than I remembered." She shuffled through the pages and checked the pile for more prints. Danel joined her, redoubling his search efforts. They couldn't find anything else.

Finally, Dahlia stood with a frustrated growl. "This is bullshit. I can't fill in gaping holes with absolute perfection."

"Having photographs has to be better than relying on memory," Danel said, glancing towards the hall. Now that they had the papers, he was eager to move.

"Barely." Dahlia shook her head. "This isn't going to work."

He shrugged. "It's the best we have right now. Let's go."

She looked vexed but didn't argue. Instead, she slid the images into a large inner pocket of her raincoat.

"Lift the hood, so you aren't recognized," Danel said.

She obeyed, and the waxy fabric hid her rigid expression.

It was another silent cab ride back to the mostly empty

industrial district, and they disembarked a quarter mile from the derelict warehouse. Danel kept his head turned against the drizzle as they walked. Cold rain dripped off the edge of his coat and rolled off his boots. Puddles decorated the sidewalk, and each streetlight cast a misty halo of light on their path.

They were a block from the building before Dahlia glanced up at him. Dark strands of wet hair clung to her cheeks. "You *could* let me go," she said in a quiet, terse voice.

Her words sent a surge of frustration through him. "You know I can't." That earned an angry scoff from her. "I can't. If I go back on my word with Tannin, both of us will suffer."

"Look, I can't help him," Dahlia said. "What we found back there is just more evidence of how hopeless this is. How am I supposed to finish these sketches? Those pictures are no help."

"You have to try." They came to a halt at the mouth of the alleyway.

Her eyes narrowed. "I've already lost everything. I could just refuse."

Danel shook his head. "If you'd already lost everything you wouldn't be so desperate to escape. People only fight when they think there's something worth fighting for."

Dahlia looked away and hugged herself. She glanced down the dim alleyway wreathed in mist. "This sucks," she whispered.

Danel couldn't help a quiet laugh. "I know. I'm sorry

things turned out this way. But right now, your best shot is to play by Tannin's rules. Finish the sketches and deal with whatever comes next."

"How do you know he won't just kill me when he doesn't need me anymore?" Dahlia asked.

"He won't," he said. "That's not how he works. You'll have to trust me on that."

She scowled up at him. "My trust in you is long gone."

He sighed. "Well, it's not like you have much of a choice right now." She started to protest, but he cut her off. "Go. And turn the lock behind you. I'll be waiting until you're through the portal."

Her jaw set. She held his gaze, eyes narrow. "Don't for a second think things are okay between us," she said in a low voice. Then she turned away. He waited as she stalked down the alley. She glanced over her shoulder at him, then tugged the door open and disappeared inside.

Danel stayed where he was, watching the boarded-up window by the door. After a few seconds, a golden light penetrated the darkness, then faded. She had gone through.

Part one of the job was complete, with mixed results. Some of the tension released from his shoulders, and he patted his pocket, reassuring himself that the stencil and can of paint were still there.

Dahlia's plaintive words returned to him. *I just want to go home.*

Home. He wasn't far from the house that Gaul had made their headquarters. The police station was even closer. It wouldn't be difficult to secure a private conversation with Eisheth and ask for her help.

But speaking to her would directly violate his agreement with Tannin. After their fight the previous day, Danel wasn't ready to anger him again. Not with the threat of Eris hanging over his head.

And if something happened to Morgan because of his own actions...

Home wasn't an option. As long as Tannin held Eris at bay, Danel had a leash around his neck.

He tilted his head back. A few drops of cold rain splashed on his face. He wished he could wash himself of this entire ordeal.

It was a nice thought, but he had work to do.

TWENTY-FOUR

Although Bridget begged Nuriel to return through the portal with her, he insisted they needed backup before attempting to free Dahlia. Together, they laid James' body across the backseat of Nuriel's car and covered the bag with a blanket.

Silent tears rolled down Bridget's face as Nuriel drove. Her nose was so blocked up she couldn't even smell the lingering odor of the ash tray. Each time they hit a bump or pothole, Bridget looked back to make sure James hadn't fallen.

When she managed to pull her thoughts from James, they went straight to Dahlia. She was still trapped on the other side of the portal. Every moment lost was a moment she was in greater danger. She sat on her hands to keep from wringing them.

Ten minutes into the drive, Nuriel spoke up. "Bridget, are you injured?"

She turned her head from the window and wiped her eyes. "I have some scratches. That's all."

She dropped her gaze to her lap and picked at the dry blood on her hands. She wanted to tell Nuriel to drive faster. By now, Kai must know Bridget had escaped. But Nuriel was already going over the speed limit and the last thing they needed was a police officer pulling them over with a corpse in tow. She fidgeted.

"Ret will help," Nuriel said, turning onto their street. She saw James' car, still parked against the curb, and looked away.

"We need to go back through the portal as fast as we can," Bridget said.

Nuriel pulled into the driveway, his car bumping over the curb. "Before we do anything, we need you to tell us what you saw."

Bridget responded with a numb nod and let herself out of the car. The sun was shining, but she shivered as she stepped into its light. Hugging her arms, she waited as Nuriel went to the backseat and lifted James.

They walked up the sidewalk. Before they reached the door, it swung open. Ret was on the other side. He looked shocked to see her. "Come in quickly."

Nuriel stepped in first, followed by Bridget. Ret shepherded her into the study on her left. Despite the warm day, a fire crackled in the hearth. Gaul sat behind the desk, looking up from the piece of paper he was writing on. His red eyebrows rose at the sight of her.

"We thought you'd been killed," Gaul said.

Ret urged her to sit by the fire. "Tell me what happened." He knelt nearby, expression anxious. He had traded his suit for a charcoal button-down shirt and black slacks.

Bridget sat on the edge of the chair. "I need your help. Dahlia is in trouble."

"Dahlia—you found her?" He sounded surprised. Then a look of dawning realization crossed his face. "The graffiti. It *took* you somewhere, didn't it?" He reached for her blood-stained hand.

She pulled back, flinching.

"I'm going to heal any injuries you have," he said in a gentle tone. She hesitated, then allowed it.

"It's a portal." Bridget struggled to keep her voice from wavering. "It took me through... something impossible. White light and black lightning and... What was that place?"

Ret shook his head. "I'm not entirely certain. What was on the other side?"

Bridget drew in a shaky breath. "It took me to Tannin's collection."

Ret and Gaul locked eyes. Then Ret turned back to Bridget with new intensity.

"What did it look like?" Light seeped from Ret's palm as he spoke. An itching sensation worked its way up her skin. The cuts and scrapes on her arm began to close and fade away, consumed by threads of gold.

She raised her gaze to his dark eyes. "The biggest room I saw was full of cabinets with artifacts. Books and pottery and... and swords." She swallowed. "There were also cages. Dahlia was being kept in one."

"Well, that's unsettling," Gaul said.

She flexed her wrist and turned over her arms. The cuts had closed up completely, and the dark bruises had faded. Even her headache was gone, leaving her more clear-headed than she'd felt since first going through the portal.

Bridget looked between them. "He's doing worse than that."

Footsteps announced Nuriel's return. Behind him was Ivanova, expression drawn. She went straight to Bridget. "Why didn't you listen to me? You could have died."

"I'm fine," Bridget said. "Please, we need to go. Dahlia needs us."

"Was Danel with her?" she demanded.

Bridget scowled. Predictable. "No. Dahlia didn't know where he was. Just that he was working for Tannin."

Ivanova's eyes narrowed. "That idiot."

Bridget looked from her to Gaul. "Tannin isn't only putting people in cages. He's *killing* them."

Gaul frowned. "How do you know?"

Bridget continued, throat constricting. "There's a walk-in freezer. It's full of bodies."

"What?" Ivanova demanded as Nuriel let out a soft sound of dismay. Gaul's gaze flicked back to Ret, who had frozen, eyes widening.

"I... I suspect I know what this is about." Ret strode to the bookshelf and selected a leather-bound volume and placed it on the desk where Gaul sat. "Tannin has been searching for lost Grigori contracts for almost as long as I've known him. It's his area of specialty. No one has used a technique like that portal in millennia. But as powerful as it is, however, there are even stronger symbols."

"Do we really have time for this?" Bridget asked. She stood from her chair and paced over to the desk. They were wasting time. Dahlia needed her.

"This is important," Ret said as he flipped through the pages. "Some symbols create more Grigori." He stopped on a particular page and tapped it.

She shifted her weight, then sighed and bent to look. Swirling Grigori script covered each page. "What do they mean?"

"They're our true names. We have our chosen names—like 'Eisheth'—and then we have these." He gestured to the page. "When tattooed into our flesh and activated, they give us our powers and anchor us to this world. There are a few thousand of us."

That, Bridget realized with a start, must be what the needles and ink in Tannin's collection were for. Ret went on, pointing to the book. "That one is Tannin's. Here's mine." He turned the page. "Gaul's." He flipped forward towards the end of the book, passing more and more emblems. "This is Nuriel, Eisheth, and Danel."

"Are you implying he found more?" Ivanova asked.

Ret traced one of the symbols with a finger. "As far as

I know there *are* no creation contracts beyond those in this book. They were lost in the war."

Bridget shook her head. "There might actually be some new ones. Dahlia's sketches." All eyes turned to her. "She found a bunch of tablets covered in symbols on an archaeology dig in Tunisia last year. She drew sketches of them and Danel sold them to Tannin."

Silence descended on the study as the Grigori all exchanged uneasy glances.

"Those contracts could do anything," Nuriel said. "We've created countless symbols over time."

Ret shook his head. "Perhaps. But modern-day Tunisia isn't far from the African front of the Grigori-Human War. It's not unreasonable to imagine someone may have found a Grigori graveyard. And if Tannin is collecting bodies, it's safe to assume he believes some of those symbols may represent lost names." Ret's forehead creased in worry.

"But what does creating new Grigori have to do with..." Bridget trailed off as the pieces clicked into place. She could feel the color drain from her skin.

Gaul's lips twitched into a grim smile. "Yes, we were all freezer fodder once." He glanced at Ivanova. "Some of us have remained more frigid than others."

Ivanova looked too preoccupied to bite back.

"But..." Bridget began, but she couldn't find the words to continue. The Grigori weren't simply supernatural. They were revived corpses. She hugged her arms around herself.

"It's alright." A gentle hand fell on her shoulder. She sucked in a swift breath as she pulled away. Nuriel winced. "Sorry."

"If you're finished, I believe Ret was sharing *useful* information," Ivanova said.

"Bridget, do you want to sit back down?" Ret asked, his eyes on her. He didn't *look* like a dead person. The bodies in the freezer had been gray and unresponsive, their eyes unseeing. By comparison, Ret's skin was a healthy ochre.

"No, I—I'm okay."

Ret didn't press the issue. "If Bridget's right, then it stands to reason that Tannin intends to create more Grigori using Dahlia's drawings as a guide. He could be looking to bring back his allies who were killed in the war."

"You know I respect our customs," Nuriel said, "but could this actually be good? It's been centuries since we ran out of known names, and humanity's population has grown. Surely a few more Grigori won't pose an issue."

Bridget gaped. *Centuries?*

Ret and Gaul shared a dark look. "It will. When Gaul brought you to this world, Nuriel, it created a momentary rift in the fabric that separates our worlds. Doing so with dozens at once could be catastrophic. Especially if they aren't connected to a truly viable candidate."

Nuriel frowned, and Gaul said, "Imagine you're on a ship and it springs a leak. You can plug the leak and the ship remains intact. But if the hull takes on too many leaks at once, the entire structure gives way."

Ret nodded. "Additionally, if Tannin is trying to revive Grigori, that could draw attention to us. From what Bridget has said, it doesn't sound as if he's exercising caution."

"No, it sounds like he's building an army," Ivanova said.

Bridget's head spun. It was the sort of information James would have loved, but all it did was leave her with a lump in her stomach. *Don't dwell on it now,* Bridget chastised herself. "Look, I know this is all important, but we don't have time to waste."

"Right. Your sister." Ret cleared his throat. He looked from Bridget to Ivanova. "How long has Dahlia been in Tannin's custody?"

"Nine months," Ivanova said. "Assuming she went there directly after disappearing."

"So why store the bodies? Why hasn't he already created more of us?" Nuriel asked. "He has Kai, so he isn't lacking an Artist."

Bridget spoke up again. "The sketches aren't right. Tannin and Kai want her to make them perfect."

Ret nodded. "That makes sense."

"Then we need to recover those drawings and any copies before she's able to *make* them perfect," Gaul said.

"Agreed," Ret said. "Or both our worlds could be in terrible danger."

Bridget looked around the room at each of them. "I can take you to Dahlia. She's right through the portal, and

she might know where the drawings are being kept."
Assuming she's in any condition to tell us. Bridget
stomped down the thought.

"Okay," Ret said. "Let's make a plan."

TWENTY-FIVE

The plan, as it turned out, didn't include Bridget.

"But I'm the only one who knows what it's like on the other side," she protested. Four unyielding pairs of eyes stared back.

It was Ivanova who spoke, in her brisk, no-nonsense manner. "Ms. Keene, you are not going anywhere." So they were back to last names. "You need rest."

"I do not need rest."

"You'll be in the way," Gaul said. He stood and slid Ret's book back on the shelf. "We have enough to worry about without protecting some fragile human. I'm going to go start the car." He turned and left the house, letting the front door creak closed behind him.

Heat rose to Bridget's cheeks. After everything she'd gone through, she was being pushed aside. This is what she got in return for asking for help?

She rounded on the others. "You're more interested in Dahlia's sketches than saving her."

Ret shook his head. "I assure you, we will do everything we can to extract your sister."

"That's not good enough," Bridget snapped.

"Bridget, please believe me. I am truly sympathetic; I've suffered my own losses," Ret said, tone gentle. "I'll do everything I can to reunite you two. Nuriel, if you'd stay with her."

Nuriel's apologetic expression turned to surprise. "What? Why me?"

Ret gave him a compassionate look. "You've been watching that building since I healed you. When's the last time you sat down? Besides, someone needs to keep her here, out of harm's way."

Bridget bristled. "Oh, so I'm a prisoner now?"

"You're not a prisoner, Bridget, but both you and Nuriel need rest," Ret said. "And we need Eisheth to help us figure out how to handle the smoke."

"Can the three of you handle them on your own, if it comes down to a fight?" Nuriel asked. "Kai is bad enough, but if Tannin is there, we'll need all of our strength."

"I've known them both for a long time," Ret said. "With luck, they'll listen to reason."

"Reason?" Bridget echoed, voice shrill. "Kai murdered James!"

"Gaul and I have more strength than Kai." Ret reached for his jacket draped over the desk chair.

Nuriel didn't argue. "Be safe."

Bridget shook her head. "I can't stay here. Dahlia needs me."

"No, she needs *us.*" Ivanova looked to Nuriel. "Don't let her sneak away." The detective stepped out of the study and into the front yard after Gaul.

"You've already done more than enough," Ret told her gently. "You've been brave. You've given us a great deal of information. Let us take it from here." He smiled, no doubt in an effort to reassure her. Instead, it just made her feel like a child.

"I don't know if I can trust you," Bridget said plainly. "I came here to get your help, but Dahlia is still my responsibility."

"Bridget," Nuriel said. "As much as I hate to admit it, they're right. At this point, we'd be more hindrance than help."

Ret stepped towards the hall. "Perhaps take a hot shower. Get a change of clothes."

She looked down at herself. She'd forgotten what a mess she was, in the midst of her emotional return. But while Ret's powers had healed her cuts and scrapes, they hadn't done anything for the spatters on her clothes and hands. James' dried blood. Her throat tightened. She couldn't lose both of them.

She had to get back to Dahlia. Just because she needed their help didn't mean she could accept being benched. But this conversation was dragging on too long.

"Promise me you'll do everything you can," Bridget

said, meeting Ret's gaze.

"Bridget, I've spent my entire life trying to preserve everything that's decent about my people," Ret said. His brown eyes met hers. They were warm with compassion, but she also saw pain in them. "People like Tannin think they're helping, when all they do is cause more pain. I don't want anyone to be a part of that. Your sister deserves her freedom."

Bridget searched his expression. He seemed earnest, but that wasn't enough. Even as she nodded in agreement, she resolved to find her own way forward. "Fine. I'll stay."

"Thank you." Ret gave Nuriel and Bridget one last nod, then followed Gaul and Ivanova outside. The front door latched behind him.

Bridget waited until the sound of the car engine faded into the popping of the fire in the hearth. When she was sure they were gone, she turned to Nuriel. "Alright, our turn."

"What?" Nuriel looked at her in surprise.

"Isn't your car still out there?" Bridget asked. "We can follow them."

"Bridget, no." Nuriel said in a soft voice. "They know what they're doing. Besides, Eisheth and I share a car. The only one still here is Gaul's, and I don't have the key."

Bridget glared up at him. "You really believe they care about Dahlia as much as I do? I'm wasting time here. We should've all gone together."

"They're faster and stronger, Bridget. I don't like being

left behind any more than you, but there's truth to what they said. We need to recover."

He was no help. If she was going to get back to the collection with the others, she would need to leave the house on her own. She just needed to figure out how, and small talk with Nuriel wasn't going to help matters.

Bridget scrutinized him. "Fine. Where's the shower?"

"Upstairs," Nuriel said, looking relieved to see her drop the argument.

With a nod, Bridget stepped into the hall. A shower would buy her time to think. She took the stairs two at a time and looked around. The bathroom was across from the room where she'd initially woken up with James, handcuffed to the bedpost. Had that only been a day ago? So much had happened, it felt like weeks had passed. She ducked into the bathroom and pulled the door shut behind her.

She needed to figure out her next steps. Bridget reached for the old-fashioned faucet, and it squealed as she twisted it on. As she waited impatiently for the water to heat up, she turned to study herself in the mirror. Her eyes were bloodshot, shadowed by dark circles. Dust from the abandoned building had settled in her tangled blonde hair, and it looked dull and grey. Dried blood crusted under her fingernails and made her clothing stiff.

Her fingers curled around the edge of the porcelain sink. After all the fear and horror she'd faced, a small part of her wanted to listen to Nuriel and the others. She felt as if she could curl up on the cracked tile and sleep for days.

But that wasn't an option. As steam fogged the mirror, she peeled off her shirt and jeans, then stepped into the shower. Her skin prickled from the heat, and the water ran off her in brown rivulets, swirling down the drain. She raked her fingers through her hair, scrubbing so hard her scalp burned.

Bridget had promised Dahlia she would return to Cleveland for backup, and she'd done that. But Ivanova had proven for months she didn't really care about her sister, no matter what she said. She barely knew Ret, and Gaul hadn't exactly endeared himself to her. Even Nuriel was taking their side. It was Bridget's responsibility to make sure they stayed on task and freed Dahlia. She had to get back to the portal.

Maybe she could take a bus, she thought as she rinsed her hair. No. It would take too long. And if she used a rideshare, she ran the risk of dragging other innocents into danger.

Her fingers stilled. James' car. It was still parked along the curb in front of the house.

She began to form a loose plan as she turned the shower off. Water dripped to the floor as Bridget pulled on her filthy clothes. Working through her tangled hair, she hurried back down the stairs.

She found Nuriel in the living room, sitting on the couch. He held a piece of paper covered in James' scribble. As she watched, he flipped it over to read the back.

"What are you doing?" she asked.

"It's amazing what you can find online these days," he said as he set the paper back down on the stack of James' research and offered it all to her.

She snatched the pile from him and held it against her chest. "And? How much of it is accurate?"

"Not much, I'm afraid. Eisheth sent a message while you were upstairs." He slid his phone across the coffee table. The text on the screen said, *We've arrived at the building. Tell her we haven't forgotten her sister.*

Bridget let out a long breath. "Good." But not good enough. "Can I ask a favor?"

"Ask away." Nuriel took his phone back.

"I'd like to see James," she said. "Where did you put him?"

Nuriel cleared his throat and nodded. "There's a freezer downstairs."

She flinched. "You have a giant walk-in freezer here, too?"

"Nothing like that," he assured her. He stood from the couch and gestured for her to follow. With the papers still tucked against her chest, she stepped into the hallway behind him.

Nuriel crossed the hall to a door beside the kitchen entry. Bridget had assumed it was a linen closet, but it swung open to reveal a staircase that led down into darkness.

Nuriel flipped a light switch and a single bulb flickered on. It cast a weak, yellow light across unfinished wooden stairs. A spider skittered out of sight. She shivered.

Nuriel's boots made a hollow thump on the stairs as he descended. *It's a cellar, nothing more*, she scolded herself. She steadied herself and followed Nuriel, one hand on the wobbly wooden banister as she stepped downward.

The further down she went the cooler it became. The drafty air raised goosebumps on her arms, and she fought down the urge to turn and run. It all felt too much like walking back into that horrible freezer.

Bridget stepped down onto the concrete floor where Nuriel waited. The basement was a single, unfinished room that ran under a large portion of the house. The only furnishings were a few stacked boxes in one corner and a chest freezer against the wall in front of her. Strewn around it were haphazard piles of frozen peas, packaged chicken breasts, and pizzas, all left to thaw on the floor.

Bridget rubbed her arms. "He's in there?" she asked, eyeing the freezer.

"Yes," Nuriel said.

She stepped forward, picking her way past the bags of frozen food. Nuriel hung back near the base of the stairs.

She bent down to set the papers on the floor, then straightened to touch the cool metal with the tips of her fingers. Poor James. He deserved safety and protection, at least in death if he hadn't had it in life. Steeling herself, she lifted the lid.

The black bag took up the bulk of the space within. James was taller than the freezer's length, and Nuriel had laid him in on his side. She could make out the impression of bent knees pressing against the bag.

Her throat tightened. "Can I have a moment alone with him?" The question came out wavering.

"Take your time," Nuriel said quietly. She waited for the sound of his footsteps retreating up the stairs. When none came, she glanced over her shoulder. He'd wandered to the back of the basement, busying himself with the boxes there. It would have to be good enough.

Bridget leaned forward and grasped the bag's zipper. She dragged it down, tooth by tooth.

His face came into view, and she stalled. His stiff, blank expression made her want to slam the chest shut and run upstairs. Tears spilled over as she pulled the zipper past the bloody hole in his chest. She stopped when she reached his waist.

A glance back told her that Nuriel was still turned away. Throat tight, she reached a hand into the bag and touched James' frozen clothes. *Just find the keys.* She slipped a trembling hand into the fabric of his pocket. Empty. She checked his back pocket. Her fingers closed on his wallet, but nothing more.

Swallowing, Bridget slid a hand beneath his side, reaching between him and the bottom of the freezer until she found his other pocket.

There. Her fingers brushed metal. She slipped her finger through the ring and pulled it free. It clinked, and she gripped the keys in her fist to silence them.

Moving quickly now, she slipped the keyring into her

own pocket and closed the bag. The freezer lid shut with a thud.

She sucked in a tight gasp, a shudder running through her. She'd done it. Now all she had to do was escape when Nuriel wasn't watching.

"Thank you for putting him somewhere safe," she said to Nuriel as she stooped down to pick up the papers.

"Of course," Nuriel said. He turned away from the boxes and stepped back towards the stairs. "I'm very sorry."

She lowered the lid and turned to him. "What's going to happen to him?" she asked, wiping at her cheeks.

Nuriel nodded. "Eisheth will use her role with the police to get him home."

She gripped the papers. She could imagine the detective's matter-of-fact expression as she delivered the news to his mother. It made her chest tighten. He deserved better than lies and cover-ups. He deserved better than to have died.

Maybe he didn't have to stay dead. Her brow furrowed and she looked to Nuriel. "You," she said. "*You* were dead once."

Nuriel paused. "Yes." His tone was wary.

Bridget pressed on. "Those names Ret showed me. They really bring people back from the dead?" She'd been so focused on Dahlia, that she hadn't paused to consider what her sketches might mean for James.

Nuriel shook his head, expression pained. "I'm sorry, Bridget, but there are no new names. It's like Ret said:

there hasn't been a new Grigori in centuries."

"But if one of the ones Dahlia found works, could you help me bring him back?"

Nuriel shifted his weight. "The process doesn't work that way. Why don't we go upstairs? I'll tell you more once you've had a chance to rest a bit."

She took a few steps towards him, looking up at his face. "Tell me now. I need to know."

He searched her gaze, then sighed. "For one, candidates to become Grigori are hand-picked before their death. Not every body is a good match to be contractually bound to a Grigori."

"What makes a good candidate?" she asked.

Nuriel shrugged, and wrinkles creased his forehead. "I'm afraid I don't know all of the specifics. You should speak to Ret about it." He turned to make his way back up the stairs.

Bridget didn't move, clinging to James' papers. She glanced down. The top page was a list of each Grigori's name.

Nuriel was halfway up when she asked, "What's your real name?"

Nuriel turned back, brow furrowed. "Pardon me?"

"James and I looked up all your names," she told him. "The name Nuriel belongs to an angel, doesn't it? And that's your... what did Ret call it? Your 'chosen name.'"

"I'm hardly an angel. But yes, it's my chosen name as a Grigori. I was rather drawn to that particular bit of mythology, early on."

"So, what's your real name, then?" she asked again.

"You saw the symbol. It's only a written language."

She frowned. "When I first saw you on the back porch, Gaul called you something different."

"Jean-Marc," Nuriel said in a quiet voice. "I didn't know you overheard that." He let out a slow breath. "That was this body's name before it became a Grigori. I don't use it anymore."

"You mean it was your name before you died."

Nuriel inclined his head. "And another reason why reviving James is more complicated than you can imagine. I'm not who I was before. I look the same, and I have Jean-Marc's memories, but Nuriel is who I truly am."

Bridget gripped the rough banister. "When did you die?"

He remained quiet, looking uncomfortable. She said nothing, waiting him out. Finally, he sighed. "It happened during the French Revolution."

Bridget started. "The French Revolution? Wasn't that..." She trailed off, trying to remember what she'd learned in her history class.

"I was created in 1794," Nuriel said.

Bridget stared at Nuriel. If he was telling the truth, she was talking to a man who was centuries old. She looked down at the pages again. Nothing in James' research even came close to the truth.

"The others?" she asked faintly.

"Ret already told you a little. He was there, during the

Grigori-Human War."

Bridget winced, asking, "So when was *that*? Before your time?"

He shook his head. "Much. It was millennia ago. Ret was created just after the war broke out. One of our factions was rounding up humans, slaughtering them, and creating new Grigori to act as infantry. Ret was created as a healer. He doesn't talk about it much."

Bridget tried to imagine being alive that long, living with the memories of a brutal war that drove your entire kind into hiding. No wonder he was so passionate about preserving their culture.

"Ret made it sound like Tannin was around then, too."

Nuriel nodded. "He was. The two of them have a long history, one I don't entirely understand. But Tannin, like Ret, came away from the war determined to make sure our people survived. They just went about it in very different ways."

"What about Ivanova and Gaul?" she asked.

Nuriel shook his head. "Their stories are their own to tell," he said. "Suffice it to say, I'm one of the younger Grigori. Which is part of why I have so few answers for you."

"But you remember who you are," she said. "You're still Jean-Marc. If we used one of the new names, James would still *remember* being James."

"Bridget." The dim light in the stairwell cast dark shadows over Nuriel's face, hiding his expression. "I am *not* Jean-Marc, and even if I were, there are no names to spare. I'm sorry."

Bridget set her jaw. Nuriel was skirting the answer. It didn't matter if that ratty old book had no new symbols— not when Dahlia had a sketchbook full of them. He was lying to her. None of them could be trusted. She clenched her fist. "Listen—"

Before she could finish, a colossal crash of breaking glass sounded from the front of the house.

TWENTY-SIX

Bridget jumped at the noise. Nuriel turned and bolted up the remaining stairs, bursting into the hallway. She shoved James' research into her waistband and followed in a rush.

"Get back!" Nuriel waved her into the kitchen. She hurried onto the tile, then rocked onto her tiptoes to see past his shoulder.

Icy wind rushed through the hallway, and footsteps crunched towards them. The hairs on Bridget's arms stood on end.

Kai stalked in their direction. His trench coat billowed out, writhing in the wind that he himself created. Behind him, the glass of the front door had shattered inward.

Bridget's heart thumped in her ears. This man was responsible for killing James. He was responsible for imprisoning Dahlia. And now he was here. Did that mean the others had failed?

"Kai," Nuriel said stiffly.

"Last chance, Nuriel. Don't make a foolish choice."

He shook his head. "This isn't our way. Tannin—"

Kai cut him off with a single flick of his wrist. Nuriel flew into Bridget, who fell backwards. He slammed into the table and hit the floor with a grunt.

"Nuriel!" Bridget got up and staggered towards him.

He climbed to his feet. "Go," he urged without taking his eyes off Kai. But Bridget stood rooted to the spot, her heart thudding against her chest as the two Grigori men glared at one another.

"This *was* our way," Kai growled. "Before humans interfered, we were numerous, and we used our powers without fear. Haven't you ever wondered what that would be like?"

"You know I have," Nuriel said. "But that doesn't mean I sink to murder."

Kai scoffed. "The boy? He was a human. His life was already short and meaningless."

Bridget exhaled sharply, clenching her fists. How dare he?

"This is wrong, Kai," Nuriel said. "I don't care how badly you need more Artists. I'm not joining you."

"Then so be it. I've given you plenty of chances. All that's left for me is to take the girl and go." He swept his left hand forward, as if pitching an invisible baseball.

Shards of glass lifted from the remains of the front

entry and hurtled towards them. Bridget darted backwards out of the line of fire. Nuriel dove to the side, but the glass tore through his sleeve and carved a jagged line in his arm. Nuriel clasped a hand over the injury, and blood seeped through his fingers.

Bridget rocked her weight from foot to foot, hovering in indecision. She could make a break for James' car and drive to the abandoned building. But that would leave Nuriel at Kai's mercy. On the other hand, if she and Nuriel could keep Kai distracted here, that would hold him off long enough for the others to rescue Dahlia.

Bridget burst into motion. She rushed to one of the cabinets and yanked open a drawer. Tea towels and oven mitts. She cursed and moved to the next drawer. Spoons, forks, and a set of butter knives. Nothing useful.

She risked a glance over her shoulder.

Nuriel ran towards Kai, but a small hurricane of wind lifted him off the ground. Kai made a pushing gesture, shoving Nuriel into the wall with the wind. He hit hard, and the nearby wall clock fell to the floor with a crash. Kai kept his hand outstretched, pressing him against the plaster while Nuriel's feet kicked helplessly.

"Do you think we deserve the lives we've been given?" Kai's voice was barely audible over the roar of wind. "Have we been granted immortality only to spend it hiding in shadows?"

Bridget gripped the edge of the counter to keep from losing her footing in the gale. The dish rag hanging from the oven door whipped past her face. The trash can toppled over with a clang, scattering broken eggshells across the floor.

"You still intend to stand against me?" Kai asked. Nuriel didn't respond, fighting against the wind as Kai reached out with his free hand to summon more jagged shards of glass. They glinted as he beckoned them closer.

The fragments hovered before Nuriel, buffeted by the wind. Kai cocked his arm, poised to launch them forward. The glass would tear into Nuriel, just like those scissors had torn into James. She had to act quickly. If nothing else, she could distract Kai.

She shoved the drawer closed and turned to face Kai, back rigid, body tense.

"Leave him alone!"

Her voice drew Kai's attention. He glanced at her, and a glass shard pinged to the floor. "Be quiet," he growled. The rest of the glass crashed to the ground as he stretched his hand towards her and closed it into a fist. With a rush, her lungs deflated, the air sucked from them. Fiery pain erupted in her chest. She doubled over, knees smacking into the kitchen tile. She clawed at her throat. Black spots erupted in front of her.

"Come with me and I won't harm Nuriel." Kai stepped towards Bridget. He kept one hand outstretched towards him, keeping him pinned. She couldn't respond. Her muscles spasmed. In a panic, she thrashed.

Her eyes locked on Nuriel. His gaze met hers, lips moving. The gale pushed against him and stole the words from his mouth as he braced against the wall, trying to gain traction. Against his back, the plaster cracked, a jagged line running up to the ceiling.

Focus, she told herself. But she couldn't breathe. She was suffocating.

Bridget struggled to clear her mind. She needed to think. Her heart pounded in her ears, each beat pumping fire through her lungs. Beyond that, all she could hear was the torrent of wind. Kai had managed to immobilize them both in under a minute. If only they had some way to fight back...

Her blurring gaze found the kitchen sink. A single drop of water hung from the spout.

Water.

With her remaining energy, Bridget lurched upward and snagged the kitchen counter then turned the tap.

She collapsed back to the floor. James' papers jabbed into her ribs. Her limbs were slick with sweat, and everything was dark around the edges. A fine, cool mist fell over her. Her head lolled onto her chest, and she closed her eyes. Ret had told her to rest. Maybe that wasn't such a bad idea after all.

Her drifting was interrupted by a thud followed by a distant cry.

Then the invisible hand around her throat released. Fresh, unexpected air rushed into her lungs.

Bridget gasped, eyes opening wide. She sucked in a frantic breath, then immediately doubled over as her stomach twisted. Searing pain tore through her chest as she retched. Spitting, she gulped the precious air.

Water continued splashing over her and she looked up. The kitchen faucet had burst clear off, and water gushed from the plumbing into the basin at an incredible rate.

Kai's bellow of pain pulled her attention back to the room. He was doubled over, clutching his cheek. Beneath his fingers Bridget could make out an angry, red burn.

Nuriel was back on his feet, a spinning ball of water hovering inches above his palm. It frothed and bubbled, its edges coalescing into steam. With a swift throw, Nuriel sent it flying towards the other man.

Kai swept his arm to the side, and a gust of wind blasted the ball apart. It exploded into individual boiling droplets that fell in a scalding rain. He let out a cry of pain and fell back.

Move, Bridget ordered herself. Limbs leaden, she used the counter to pull herself up from the wet floor. Her entire body was trembling. She felt like someone had rubbed her lungs with sandpaper. Each breath was a struggle.

Kai fell back into the hall, groaning.

With eyes locked on Kai, Nuriel drew the water gushing from the sink towards himself. It obeyed without hesitation, shimmering like a silvery snake that stretched into his outstretched palm. With the finesse of a sculptor, he coiled the water into layers, one on top of the other.

A wall, Bridget realized. He was using the water to build a barrier between them and Kai.

Out of the corner of her eye, Bridget spotted her

phone, charging in the corner. Miraculously, the windstorm hadn't blown it away. Instead, it was wedged behind the coffeemaker, cord still attached.

"You've gotten stronger," Kai said to Nuriel. "You were so opposed to using your abilities when we first met." He raised his hands and sent a fresh barrage of glass hurtling towards Nuriel. Nuriel twisted out of the way, and the meager wall of water fell to the ground, sloshing over their shoes.

Nuriel swept the scalding water up towards his palm. He abandoned the wall and instead sent fresh balls of boiling water careening in Kai's direction. He continued to pull water from the ground and the faucet, adding to his arsenal.

Kai fell back a few more feet, his lips curled back in a furious snarl. The skin on his face was red and blistered. He swept a hand over his head in a circle and the water projectiles twisted on their axis, exploding against one another. In seconds, Kai had created a steaming, sputtering waterspout. It spun between himself and the kitchen, filling the hallway.

The whirlwind of water edged towards them along the hallway. It threw up an angry spray, soaking the oil paintings on the wall. The miniature hurricane sucked up a lamp and an old rotary telephone. A *brrrring* sounded out as it crashed into the doorframe. Bridget fell back, holding up an arm against the deluge.

Nuriel stretched one hand forward, fingers splayed as he pushed the water back. His other hand drew fresh ammunition from the faucet in a steady stream. Blood dripped from his injured arm.

He planted himself between Bridget and the water. Kai was a dim shadow beyond the twirling waterspout, growing clearer as he forced his way forward.

Nuriel brought both arms out towards Kai. He planted his feet against the tile, then he clenched his extended hands into tight fists.

The temperature plummeted. Bridget shivered, goosebumps racing across her arms. The water in the room cracked as it froze in a circle extending outward from Nuriel. The entire room—anywhere touched by the water—was suddenly coated in a fine layer of sparkling frost. Her teeth began to chatter, and with her exhale, she puffed out a cloud.

The waterspout gave off a sharp hiss. The edges crystallized into ice, throwing up an angry, jagged spray. The frantic spinning of the waterspout slowed, then ground to a slow halt.

The column of water was frozen solid, a blue-white barrier that separated her and Nuriel from Kai. There was a muffled shout of irritation on the other side of the wall. Several thuds slammed against it in succession.

Bridget watched with wide eyes, her body wracked with shivers.

"Don't be a fool, Nuriel!" Kai called out. "This is for the good of our people. Give me the girl!"

Nuriel didn't respond. He still had his hands balled into fists, and his full attention was on his frozen creation.

Another thud sounded, and Bridget jumped back. The icy pillar groaned while Nuriel panted with exertion. There was a loud crack, like a gunshot, and the wall began to buckle inward.

Bridget gasped for breath, her lungs still burning. *We can't beat him alone,* she realized. They needed help. The thuds continued, encouraged by the breaking ice.

"I'm going to get backup!"

Nuriel glanced at her, concern etched into his features. "Be careful—" he started, then cut himself off. With his lapse of focus, the icy barrier crumpled further.

Bridget made a dash for her phone, yanking it free from the cord. Then she turned and bolted for the back door, skirting around a toppled dining chair. The cold metal of the doorknob prickled her fingers as she yanked it open.

Spring air rushed in, and Bridget hurried onto the stoop. She spared one last glance back. The wall of frozen water was holding, but barely. Nuriel's back was to Bridget; she could see in the set of his shoulders that he was fighting an uphill battle.

She pushed back a pang of fear and ran.

TWENTY-SEVEN

Bridget's boots squelched as she rounded the front of the house and sprinted past the red Mustang in the driveway. The porch was a mess, its railing completely demolished, and the front door was blown in. Angry as Kai was, what if he had taken his fury out on Dahlia before coming for them? Her gut tightened at the thought.

She tugged James' keyring from her pocket and sprinted towards his vehicle several houses away. With a frantic swipe at her cracked phone screen, she called Ivanova. She kept running, phone held to her ear. *Come with me and I won't harm Nuriel,* Kai's words echoed in her head.

The call went to voicemail. "Detective," Bridget gasped, voice heavy as she ran, "we need you now. Kai is here!"

She ended the call and dialed again. First Dahlia was kidnapped. *Ring.* Then James was killed. *Ring.* Now Nuriel was risking his life for her. *Ring.*

Even if she got through, there was no way Ivanova and the others would get to the house in time. Nuriel and Kai would destroy one another first.

"Hello—"

"Hello, Detective? It's Kai, he—"

"You have reached the voicemail of Detective Elizabeth Ivanova. I'm not available at the moment. Please leave a message at the tone."

Bridget cursed and ended the call, then immediately dialed again. It rolled to voicemail again. And again.

Halfway through her fifth attempt, the ring cut off.

"Yes?" The sound of the detective's familiar, irritable voice was such a relief Bridget almost dropped the phone.

"Detective," she said. She came to a breathless stop in front of the car. "Kai's at the house. Nuriel's in trouble."

"Kai's *there*?" Ivanova cursed under her breath. "He must have come through before we arrived. No wonder the smoke didn't appear. Are you hurt?"

"No, I'm okay," Bridget said. Her hands shook as she tried to find the right key. "I snuck out the back. Nuriel is holding him off."

Ivanova cursed. "He's not strong enough to fight Kai alone."

"I don't know what to do," Bridget said. She found the key, slid it into the car door, and twisted. The lock popped.

"Get out of there. You don't stand a chance against him."

"What about Nuriel?" Bridget asked as she sat in the driver's seat. "He needs help."

There was a long pause. Then Ivanova sucked in a breath. "I doubt I can get there in time. I'm halfway across town."

"But he'll be killed," Bridget said, eyes on the house.

Ivanova responded with a frustrated snarl. "Why is Kai there? What does he want?"

"He's here because of me. Dahlia told me he wants to take me back to Tannin. I... I don't think he wants to hurt me." *Not yet, anyway.* She paused then ventured, "What if I turn myself in?"

"*What?* Are you out of your mind?"

"He'll have what he wants," Bridget said, stomach flip-flopping. "He'll leave Nuriel alone and bring me to the portal. Then you can step in."

"Or he could kill you," Ivanova pointed out.

"He'll kill *Nuriel* if he has his way," Bridget retorted.

It was a terrifying risk. Kai could change his mind and destroy her. Dahlia could end up in even more danger. Nuriel could still die.

But it could work. It was better than guaranteeing Nuriel's death. Kai wanted her, and the others were paying for it. She had to try.

"I'm doing it," she said. "If I'm right, he'll lead me straight to you. You can take it from there."

"This is a terrible plan," Ivanova said.

"It's the only one we have. If you'd let us come along in the first place, we wouldn't be in this situation."

Ivanova made a sound of frustration. "You would have been in the way."

Bridget shoved back a flare of irritation. *Focus.* "Any news on Dahlia?"

"Gaul and Ret went through. I don't know anything yet."

"Be ready for us." Bridget ended the call.

In the silence that followed, a tremble went through her. She gripped the steering wheel. She couldn't just go in helpless.

Her eyes dropped to the center console. A half-eaten granola bar still rested in one of the cup holders, right where James had left it. A crumpled McDonald's bag crunched under her heel. Something stabbed at her side. James' research, folded in half and poking out of her waistband. She tugged it free. The edges were damp, but her shirt had saved it from getting soaked through.

She popped open the glove compartment and shoved the papers inside. Then she turned and searched the back seat. A camera bag. Old cassette tapes and CDs. A shoe box full of flash drives.

Her eyes fell on a small black tube of pepper spray. She grabbed it and tucked it into her pocket. Better than nothing.

Gathering her strength, Bridget stepped out of the car and hurried back towards the house. When she reached the driveway, she crouched behind the cover of the

Mustang. There was no more obvious damage to the house than before. Bridget wasn't sure if that was good or bad news. Maybe Nuriel had gained the upper hand, despite her and Ivanova's worries.

A strangled yell sounded from inside. The hairs on her arms stood on end. It was impossible to tell whose voice it was.

Bridget darted towards the backyard. Halfway there, she passed a small waterfall cascading down the side of the house. Water seeped from a window frame, dribbled along the brick siding, and pooled at the ground. She took the back porch steps two at a time and burst into the kitchen.

The ice was gone. Instead, a fine layer of mist hung in the air. Condensation fogged the windows, and water dripped from the table. The sink was still gushing.

Another shout sounded from deeper in the house. Bridget sprinted through a puddle into the hallway. The carpet runner squelched underfoot. Bridget came to an abrupt stop at the entrance to the living room. Inside, the couch was upside down and shoved against one wall. The wooden coffee table had been obliterated. She stepped over a shattered lamp and onto the waterlogged rug.

Nuriel stood in the center of the room, his back to her and hands outstretched. His arms trembled, as if holding them up took every ounce of energy he had. He was still bleeding, and his shirt was in tatters. His full attention was on the corner of the room, where a massive ball of water churned. Within it was a shadowy, thrashing figure. Kai had been completely consumed.

Nuriel was winning. A thrill of hope rushed through Bridget. Maybe she wouldn't have to lure Kai to the abandoned building after all.

But as she watched, the watery prison shimmered and expanded outward. Kai pulled himself up off the ground, and she could make out the distorted shadow of his arms pushing upward. The ball of water thinned, a growing bubble of air forcing it back.

Before Nuriel could get his hands up, the air pocket Kai had created broke through. The bubble burst outward, spraying the entire room. Water washed over Bridget, soaking her all over again.

Nuriel stepped back, then his foot slipped out from under him.

Kai knelt, clutching his right arm to his stomach as he caught his breath. Blisters covered his neck and arms. He lifted his gaze and locked eyes with Bridget. A thrill of fear went through her. He lifted his hand, lips curling into a victorious smile.

"Wait!" Bridget cried.

Nuriel whipped his head around at the sound. There was a long slice down his right cheek, and blood trickled down his jawline. "What are you doing here?" he demanded.

Her voice sounded clearer than she had expected. She raised her own hands, palms forward. "It's okay. I surrender."

Nuriel stared at her in shock. His dark curls were

plastered against his forehead and his breath came in exhausted gasps. "What are you doing?"

"Ending this," Bridget said. She kept her gaze on Kai, her hands lifted.

"Wise choice." Kai pulled himself to his feet and stepped towards her.

With a desperate shout, Nuriel drew water from the floor and shoved it at Kai. All it took was a flick of Kai's wrist to send the water and Nuriel flying. Nuriel hit the wall with a thud and sagged to the ground.

"Nuriel!" Bridget started towards him, but a gust of wind sent her stumbling into the hallway.

Kai advanced on her. "Nuriel isn't your concern. Come with me."

She straightened, fingers curling into tight fists. Bitter tears pricked the corners of her eyes. She wanted nothing more than to grab the pepper spray and douse him with it. It was only a small taste of what he deserved. But she couldn't attack Kai. Not yet. *Play along,* she told herself. If she could get back to the abandoned building, everything would be okay.

"I'm coming," Bridget said, lowering her hands. Kai strode up to her and grabbed her arm.

Bridget bit back a protest as his fingers dug into her skin. He pulled her forward, and she almost tripped over her own feet. His jacket, heavy with water, swung against her as he forced her forward another step.

A shadow fell over the foyer, dragging her attention away from Kai.

A lean figure stood in the open gap where the front door used to be. Hazy gray light glinted off sandy blond hair. Bridget had only seen him in photographs, but she recognized him immediately.

"Danel?" Kai asked. "You're not supposed to be here." His eyes narrowed in irritation.

Bridget heard footsteps behind her. She looked back to see Nuriel stagger into the doorframe. His gaze landed on Danel. "You're back."

Danel ignored him, instead addressing Kai. "I hope you're not taking her back to the building." He leaned against the wall, the picture of ease in a brown t-shirt and distressed jeans.

Kai paused. "What do you know?"

Danel's gaze flickered to Bridget. She shook her head, silently begging him to stay quiet.

"It's a trap," he told Kai. "Eisheth and the others are waiting for you there."

TWENTY-EIGHT

Bridget's breath caught. *No.* She had to get away. With a sharp tug, she tried to pull free from Kai, but his grip only became more vicelike.

"Is that so?" Kai asked. He shot Nuriel a glare. "I *thought* it was too quiet here."

Danel stepped further into the house, taking in the wreckage. "Have you been decorating again, Nuriel?"

"What are you doing?" Nuriel asked. He sounded pained.

"What else did you see?" Kai interrupted.

Danel's expression soured. "It looked like Eisheth was standing guard. Gaul went through. He had Ret with him."

Kai sneered, then looked at Bridget. "Thought you were being clever, did you?" He turned to Danel. "Take me to the backup portal."

Bridget's breath caught. There was another one?

Danel's eyes narrowed. "I thought you didn't trust anything I drew."

"*I* drew it. You traced it. Take me there, and bring him," Kai said, eyeing Nuriel. "Let's hurry. This has already taken too long."

Danel arched his eyebrows. "We don't need Nuriel."

"He is a threat to this entire operation," Kai said.

Danel's lips twisted into a scowl. "He doesn't seem like a threat to me."

It was true. Nuriel clung to the corridor wall, swaying where he stood. He looked more likely to fall over than attack.

Kai fixed Danel with a look of irritation. "Are you willing to risk harm coming to Tannin? You would lose his charity."

Danel muttered under his breath as he straightened. "Fine."

"No," Bridget growled. Her plan was falling apart at the seams. Not only would she fail to bring Kai to Eisheth, but Nuriel was in more danger than ever. She fumbled with her free hand, trying to yank the pepper spray free. "Leave him alone! It's me you want, not—"

A sharp slap cut her off. Her head snapped to the side, and pain blossomed across her cheek. Lights flashed in front of watering eyes.

"Tannin made no stipulation as to what condition you're in," Kai said. He pulled her into motion, and she staggered forward.

She caught a glimpse of Danel, staring down Nuriel. "Are you going to come quietly, or do I have to haul you out too?"

"Please, don't hurt him." She reached for the banister as they passed the stairs, but Kai yanked her away.

"That's up to Nuriel," Danel said. "So, what'll it be?"

Nuriel responded with a growl. He swung his arm forward with enough force that he almost toppled to the ground. A battering ram of water, as big around as a tree trunk, hurtled around the corner.

Danel jumped to the side. The column of water flew past him and continued on a collision course with Bridget and Kai. Bridget tried to pull free, but Kai held his ground. He lifted his free arm and the projectile hit a wall of wind. The water disintegrated around them, throwing spray back towards Danel and Nuriel.

Danel shook out his hair and gave Nuriel an annoyed look. "Wrong choice."

And then he simply disappeared.

Bridget's breath caught, but before she could say a word, Nuriel doubled over with a pained grunt. Danel appeared beside him, hand curled into a fist.

Then he was gone again. This time, Bridget made out a blur against the soggy portraits. Nuriel slammed into the wall. Blood sprayed from his mouth and splattered the wallpaper.

"Stop!" Bridget yelled. Kai lifted his hand and smacked her cheek again. Heat rushed up the side of her face, and she tasted iron.

Kai didn't even need his powers. In his grip, Bridget was helpless. *Think*, she told herself, but it was hard to focus with her head ringing. Kai dragged her onto the porch, and she lost sight of Nuriel.

Pepper spray. She needed the pepper spray.

Kai forced Bridget down the stairs. She let him pull her along, digging her free hand into her pocket. There was a new car parked in the driveway, a black BMW with the engine idling. Kai tugged her towards it.

Movement caught her eye. Across the street an old man stepped onto his porch, watering can in his hand. He stopped and stared, slack-jawed, at the scene.

Maybe he could call for help. She raised her hand in a telephone gesture.

The old man dropped the can, shaking his head, and hurried inside. He slammed the door so hard the window blinds swayed.

Bridget's throat clenched. So much for that idea. She needed to use the only weapon she had.

Kai reached the car and pulled the back door open. "Get in."

Instead of responding, Bridget yanked the pepper spray from her pocket and aimed it at Kai. Her finger punched down on the button, sending a stream of liquid at his face.

"Ahh!" Kai dropped his grip on her and clapped his hands over his eyes.

The heavy smell of pepper invaded Bridget's nose. She

staggered away in a sneezing fit.

When she looked up, Kai was inches from her. Tears streamed down his cheeks and his teeth were bared. "Get in!"

Bridget bolted down the driveway.

Her boots thudded on the concrete. James' car was so close. If she could just—

A blur, and then Danel appeared in front of her. She tried to dart around him, but before she could blink, he crashed into her. She hit the ground hard, the wind whooshing from her already sore lungs. Danel was on top of her, swatting the pepper spray from her hand.

She kicked and squirmed beneath him. "Let me go!" Danel hauled her upright, breath heavy in her ear. The world blurred around her in a nauseating whirl.

Everything came back into focus with a lurch. She was next to the BMW. Before she could get her bearings, Danel pushed her inside. She hit the leather seat hard. Frantic, she searched the back seat. A weapon. She needed a weapon. But the car was clean and empty.

She couldn't escape. The door was still open, but Danel stood in front of it, blocking the way. He'd turned his back to her to face Kai, but there was no way she could get by him. She scooted deeper into the car and tried the other door. Nothing happened. *Child locks*, she thought, panic building.

She eyed the driver's seat. The car was already running, the engine sending soft vibrations through the soles of her feet. If she was quick enough, she could crawl into the front and drive away.

"Nuriel's unconscious," Danel said to Kai. Bridget bent to peer around him.

"Put him in the trunk," Kai snapped as he wiped at his eyes.

Danel wrung out the bottom of his shirt. "Don't give me orders. *You* put him in the trunk. He isn't exactly light."

Bridget inched towards the center of the bench seat, eyes fixed on Kai and Danel. They hadn't noticed her movement, too preoccupied with their argument. She slid over another inch, trembling with nervous energy.

Kai lifted a hand towards the house and made a beckoning gesture. Bits of dirt and rock skittered in his direction, caught in a sudden breeze. The gauzy curtains blew outward. A few seconds later, Nuriel's limp form floated through the entryway and onto the porch. Bridget covered her mouth in horror. Blood covered his face and his head lolled to the side.

Danel grabbed Kai's arm. "Don't do that in public!" He glanced down the empty street.

Kai growled as he pulled away. "You don't give me orders, either. They'll all know what we are before long."

"Planning on the humans making a little shrine for you?" Danel growled. All the while Nuriel drifted closer.

"*You* just used your ability in public."

"I'm too fast to be seen," Danel said. "You're making someone levitate. That's a bit obvious, don't you think?"

She had to move. Now, while they were distracted. She

lurched forward.

"Kai!" Danel shouted. Bridget heaved herself between the center console and tumbled feet-first into the driver's seat. She jerked the gear shift into reverse and slammed down on the gas.

The car's back door was still open, and it swiped Kai as she barreled backwards towards the street. She caught a glimpse of him reeling from the blow and saw Nuriel's unconscious form tumble to the concrete.

As soon as all four wheels hit the street, Bridget cut the wheel sharply, hit the brakes, and threw the car into drive. The door slammed closed, and the car leapt forward, tires squealing.

And then the BMW jerked to a halt. Bridget slammed into the steering wheel. Her foot was still on the accelerator, pressing down so hard it touched the floor, but the vehicle wasn't moving forward. It wobbled, the scream of tires falling silent as the entire car lifted off the ground. Bridget let out a terrified yell, peering out the driver's side window to watch the street fall away. The car lurched to the side, and she spun the wheel to try and steady it.

Kai stepped in front of the car, both arms outstretched and bloodshot eyes narrow. His jacket blew forward, and his hair was a disheveled mess. He strained to lift his hands higher. The car groaned and rose a few more inches.

A flash of movement. Danel appeared beside Kai. She couldn't hear him over the sound of the engine, but he looked angry. Kai lowered his arms and the car slammed back down, sending a shock through Bridget. The wheels kicked up the sharp scent of burning rubber. Acrid smoke billowed upwards as the car remained trapped, shaking from the ferocious wind that held it in place.

"Go!" Bridget begged, foot flat against the gas pedal. Frustrated tears made their way down her cheeks as she urged the car to break free.

The driver's door flew open, and hands reached inside to tug her out. The world around her blurred as she fell from the car. She caught a passing glimpse of Danel taking her spot in the driver's seat.

She tumbled to the concrete, head striking the road. The engine's roar softened to a whine, and the whizzing of tires fell silent.

Bridget rolled onto her back, staring upward at the grim gray sky. Her breath came in short, stuttering gasps and the world spun around her. *Get up. You have to get up.*

A shadow fell over her. Kai. His face was dark with fury. "Why won't you *behave?*"

He bent down and hauled her to her feet. She sagged, disoriented from her fall. "Please, no," she whispered.

Danel appeared beside Kai and grabbed her other arm. Together, they forced her chest against the side of the car. She gave a gasp of pain as they yanked her arms behind her. A hand shoved her head down. Her cheek pressed against the cool metal of the BMW as hot tears streamed down her cheeks.

"Get the rope," Kai said. This time Danel didn't argue. With dizzying speed, he lashed her wrists together. She pushed back, but Kai thumped her head against the car, and her vision wavered. "Stop fighting."

Danel tied her ankles as securely as her wrists. Together, the two men pushed her into the car and slammed the door closed behind her.

TWENTY-NINE

Bridget lay on her side in the leather back seat, head spinning. The car's gentle rumbling was at odds with the panic that tightened her chest. Ropes dug into the skin of her wrists and ankles. Each time she moved, they tightened.

Kai pulled open the passenger's door. "I wish you wouldn't make everything so difficult." She couldn't see his expression, but the way he rubbed at his eyes told her that he still hurt. Good.

The car jostled as the trunk popped open. A dull thud followed. The trunk banged closed and Danel slid behind the steering wheel.

"Let me go," Bridget said as he shut his door.

Kai turned around, bloodshot glare landing on her. His jaw twitched. "Be quiet." He wasn't going to offer any sympathy.

Danel put the car into gear, driving down the residential street. She could see a sliver of his face in the rearview mirror. His furrowed blonde brows were drawn together in frustration, and a bruise was beginning to darken his right cheek.

"I can't believe Dahlia ever cared about you," Bridget spat. Danel's eyes darted towards the mirror. He met her gaze for a brief moment, then looked back at the road.

"She *trusted* you," Bridget pressed. "You should have heard the way she talked about you." Danel's shoulders stiffened, but he didn't respond.

"Must I tell you again?" Kai turned in his seat to glare at her.

But now that she'd started, Bridget couldn't stop. All of the fear and anger and frustration of the past nine months—it all stemmed from Danel. This was all his fault.

"You lied to her. You led her on. You took *advantage* of her." Bridget's voice pitched higher as she gained steam. "And for what? What's worth destroying someone's *life*?"

Danel's face turned red. "I didn't—"

Kai cut in, "Ignore her."

"Don't tell me what to do," Danel snapped. The car jerked to an abrupt halt as he reached a stop sign. The movement rocked Bridget forward and drew an annoyed look from Kai.

Bridget sucked in a gulp of air as the car jumped into

motion again. Her head throbbed. She was shaking, on the verge of angry tears. She forced them back, knowing that if she lost it now, she might never put herself back together again.

"It doesn't have to be this way," she said to Danel. "You can still help Dahlia."

"Shut up."

Bridget's cheeks flushed in indignance. She started to retort but pulled up short as she saw Danel's scowl. She had touched a sore spot. She could use that. "What about Ivanova—Eisheth?" Bridget asked. "She's spent months looking for you, Danel. She cares about you. If not Dahlia, what about her?"

"I don't owe anyone anything." Danel's fingers gripped the steering wheel so tightly his arms trembled.

"I can think of a few people you owe," Kai said, tone snide.

Bridget went on. "You owe Eisheth an explanation. You owe Dahlia her *freedom*. Do you have any idea what I've been through, trying to find her? James gave his life trying to get her out of there. Jesus, aren't you even a little sorry?"

He didn't respond, except to stamp down on the accelerator.

Unable to wipe the tears away, Bridget blinked and tried to clear her vision. Danel wasn't budging. She was back to Plan A: Escape.

She struggled to sit up, pushing her elbow against the seat to give her leverage. Her bound fingers grasped the smooth leather to inch herself upward.

That amount of effort alone left her winded. She paused to close her eyes and lean against the side of the car. The cool glass of the window gave her something to focus on. She inhaled through her mounting fear. She could get out of this. She had to.

Cracking her eyes open, she assessed her options. Jumping out of the car was out. Danel wove through the highway traffic too fast for that.

She looked out the window to get her bearings. The blue-grey waters of Lake Erie extended outward on her left. That meant they were headed east. She looked behind her, through the back window. Cleveland's skyscrapers jutted up along the horizon. Railroad tracks ran parallel to the freeway. Behind those, dilapidated warehouses and factories stood guard, their facades crumbling.

A cell tower stood in the distance. Her phone. Maybe she could get a message out to Ivanova. Twisting her bound wrists, she dug the tips of her fingers into the back pocket of her pants. She found the plastic edge of the case and wormed it free, bit by bit.

She gripped it with one hand and swiped with her thumb. She couldn't tell if she'd managed to unlock it or not, and there was no way she could message Ivanova without seeing the screen. She hitched her shoulder to inch the phone towards her hip. It slid across the seat, and she turned. Her spine gave a quiet pop of protest, but she could see the edge of the glowing, cracked screen.

She tapped her messages, and Ivanova's name was near the top, just under James'. Biting her bottom lip, she brought up the keyboard and began to type.

H- She glanced up at the front of the car. Neither man was watching her. *E*- Would Ivanova have enough time to get to her? *L*-

The car jolted. Danel bumped over a pothole and the phone bounced from her grasp just as her finger tapped the *P*. It dropped to the floor with a dull thud. Bridget froze, her breath catching.

Kai looked back at the noise. His gaze dropped and he huffed in displeasure.

"I always forget about these infernal things," he said as he reached down and lifted the phone. Her heart sank as he slid it into his jacket pocket.

Danel took an exit ramp onto a bridge, and the lake dipped out of sight. As he came to a stop at the light, Bridget twisted her bound hands behind her. She grasped at the door's handle and tugged. Nothing happened. The child lock was still on.

They turned left and crossed over the freeway into another neighborhood. The houses they passed were large and stately. They bore signs of age, but had weathered elegantly. Ivy crept up crumbling brick walls, and tree-lined driveways wound out of sight behind wrought iron gates.

Danel drove past the neighborhood, which gave way to a wooded park. Trees soared overhead, blocking out what little sunlight managed to break through the clouds.

They had to be getting close to the lake, but Bridget couldn't make anything out beyond the foliage.

She looked around for someone, anyone, who might see her. But there were no joggers or dog walkers in sight. No police or school kids. No one would come to her rescue.

The road curved around a bend and then widened out into a parking lot. The trees thinned out to reveal a small park, empty except for a few worn out picnic tables and charcoal grills. Pine needles littered the ground, mixed with a layer of sand. A sliver of lake water gleamed beyond a row of pine trees.

Danel pulled into the remains of a parking spot, its white lines faded against the dark asphalt. He killed the engine

"It's in there." Danel nodded across the park. A few hundred feet away stood a squat cinderblock building. It looked like a public bathroom, or maybe a maintenance shed. A cracked concrete walking path connected it to the parking lot.

Kai stepped out of the car and surveyed their surroundings, sentinel-like.

Maybe she could still reach Danel. It wasn't too late. As soon as they were alone, Bridget leaned forward and hissed, "Danel, you don't have to do this. If you cared about Dahlia or Eisheth at all, even a little, you can fix this."

Danel glanced back at her. "I don't have a choice." His voice was a low growl. Bridget's heart thudded. It was the first time he'd acknowledged her earnestly.

"You do," she whispered back. She scooted towards him as best she could. "You can help us. Why are you working for *him*?"

He bristled. "I am *not* working for Kai."

"You could've fooled me," Bridget said.

The muscles in Danel's shoulders bunched. "You don't have any idea what you're talking about. I don't have much ch—"

Kai interrupted them. "Let's move them in," he said, peering down into the car. He slammed the passenger door shut. Bridget backed away from him as he wrenched her door open. His fingers closed on her forearm.

She aimed a kick at him as he tugged her from the car. She fell into a heap on the ground, unable to support herself with her ankles tied. Twisting onto her knees, she started to scream.

Sudden pressure clamped down on her throat. An invisible rope of air cut off her cry. Instead, she gagged, muscles spasming.

"You couldn't have shut her up in the car?" Danel asked, shooting Kai an annoyed look as he climbed out of the driver's seat.

"Letting her irritate you was entertaining enough," Kai muttered.

She sucked in a stuttering breath, but only a thin stream of oxygen worked its way into her lungs. Bridget closed her mouth and breathed in through her nose. Her heart hammered against her ribcage.

Kai raised his palm upward, cold eyes falling on Bridget. She let out a muffled cry of alarm as a sudden gust of air pressure lifted her from the asphalt. She rose a few feet upward, cushioned by the pillar of air, her feet several inches from the ground.

"Get Nuriel," Kai ordered. Danel went to the trunk with a grumble of protest and popped it open.

With a gesture from Kai, Nuriel's limp form floated out of the trunk towards Bridget. Ropes entangled his legs and wrists. His pale skin glistened with water and blood. Kai turned and began to stride across the parking lot. Bridget, struggling to breathe, floated behind him, and Nuriel after her. They made a sad parade as Kai walked towards the building, with Danel following.

They were in a major city, surrounded for miles by hundreds of thousands of people. And yet she was alone. Even the lake was empty, with only a few boats visible in the far distance.

She looked back to Nuriel. She couldn't tell if he was breathing. *Please wake up.*

Her eyes darted to Kai. He wasn't far. Maybe she could make him lose his concentration. She swung her bound feet, but he gave a dismissive wave of his hand and blew her farther away.

She drew her body in on itself, then kicked at the air. Twisting, she found Danel. His gaze was on the ground as he walked towards the building, hands stuffed in his pockets.

"Please," she gasped, the word no louder than a

whisper. "For D—" she cut off, coughing. "For D-Dahlia. For Eisheth."

He looked up at her. She couldn't read his expression. Was that frustration in the pinch of his eyebrows? But then he looked away.

Kai stopped at a heavy metal door that led into the building. "Get the door."

Danel huffed in irritation and stepped past Nuriel and Bridget. The door squealed in protest as he swung it outward, revealing the inside of a dim, empty building. The only windows were thin slits along the top of the walls, which illuminated glittering cobwebs and broken beer bottles. Bridget could make out a familiar intricate pattern on the far wall.

Kai stepped into the building, his feet crunching over shattered glass as he crossed the room. Bridget and Nuriel floated in after, and Danel followed.

Without a word, Kai placed one hand on the dark painted lines. The portal began to glow. The air pulsed around her.

"Danel, please!" She flung out her arms in a last, frantic attempt to break free. The motion spun her toward the open door.

Just as a black Prius careened around the corner.

It skidded to a stop, and the engine cut off.

Detective Ivanova stepped out, fire igniting in her palms.

THIRTY

Bridget's breath caught as the detective stalked closer, her expression livid and palms aflame. Behind her, Gaul and Ret stepped out of the car. Bridget had no idea how they had found her, but for the first time, she allowed herself a glimmer of hope.

That is, until she realized Dahlia wasn't with them. Hope turned to dread in an instant.

Bridget twisted to see gold light threading around the symbol. Kai, still facing the portal, hadn't spotted Ivanova and the others yet. The deep thrum of the portal pressed in on Bridget. In seconds it would carry her through to Tannin's collection. She needed to buy herself time. She drew her legs into her chest and kicked with all of her strength. Her boots hit Kai square in the temple. He cried out in surprise and wobbled, and his fingers lost contact with the wall.

In an instant, the wind buffeting her evaporated. The cement floor rushed up, and Bridget landed with enough force to knock the remaining air from her lungs. Nuriel struck the concrete beside her with a thud. She gave a wheezing cough and rolled onto her side, curling in on herself. She drew in a full breath, then coughed again.

Danel appeared at Bridget's side. Rough hands gripped her and hauled her upright. She sucked in another breath and got a mouthful of his cologne.

Red light burst in through the open doorway. An arc of fire lanced past Bridget's peripheral vision.

It hit Kai square in the shoulder, and he staggered back into the wall with a pained curse. Then he looked up and snarled.

Danel whirled around, dragging Bridget with him. "Eisheth?" His voice cracked in shock.

Ivanova stood in the doorframe. Flames danced from the palm of one hand. Gaul approached at a run, Ret just behind him.

Across the room, Kai beat the flames from his jacket. "Take the girl through," he commanded Danel. His full attention was on Ivanova, eyes bright with fury. "I'll deal with *her*."

"Let her go, Danel!" Ivanova shouted.

Danel looked between them. Bridget tried to jerk free of his grasp, but his fingers tightened. "Danel, please don't do this."

"Take her!" Kai insisted. In the same moment, he

threw out his hand and sent a hurricane of wind towards Ivanova. Bits of glass and empty beer cans zipped at her. A broken bottle sliced her arm, and she cried out in pain.

Danel's jaw tightened. "For the last time, Kai, you *don't* give me orders."

And then he was gone, a blur in the dim light. Free from his grasp, Bridget lurched. Her tied ankles failed her, and she fell to her knees with a burst of pain.

Kai doubled over, clutching his stomach. Danel stood over him, a satisfied curl to his lips.

Gaul stepped up beside Ivanova, narrow green eyes focused on Kai. Together, they blocked the doorway.

"What are you doing?" Kai demanded, glaring at Danel.

"Sorry," he said without sounding particularly apologetic. "A better offer came along."

Kai responded with a low growl. He swept an arm out, but Danel blurred and disappeared. The wind Kai summoned kicked up a cloud of dust and hit the wall. Bridget scrambled back from the pair as fast as she could manage. Her gaze swept the room in a panicked jolt. She was trapped.

Danel reappeared beside Ivanova. "Fancy seeing you here, Eisheth," he said, tucking his hands into his back pockets.

The detective shot him a murderous glare. "Shut up."

"Traitor!" Kai lifted a hand, then pushed it outward. Wind gusted forward with the gesture. Ivanova and Gaul staggered back, but Danel caught the brunt of it. He cried out as the blast threw him against the edge of the door. His head hit the metal and he dropped hard.

Bridget's breath came in rapid bursts, and she strained against her bindings. She had to get out of here.

Gaul snagged Ivanova's shoulder. "I'll draw Kai out. Ret, stay back."

With a snarl, she raised her hand. "I've got this."

The redhead didn't argue. Instead, he swung his gaze to where Danel knelt. The blond man sat with sprawled legs, clutching his head.

"Are you with us?" Gaul grated.

Danel grunted as he pulled himself upright. He managed a sarcastic salute, then jumped back into action. Appearing at Bridget's side, Danel tugged at her bindings, and her hands and feet fell free.

"Get Nuriel to Ret," he said. Then he was gone, leaving a breeze in his wake. He reappeared beside Kai, delivering a solid blow to his jaw that sent Kai careening away.

Bridget rolled onto all fours. Her hands and feet were pins and needles as she scurried to where Nuriel lay crumpled.

She glanced up at the battle raging around her. Ivanova circled Kai, blocking his path to the portal. Danel darted in to attack and then disappeared again. Gaul stood at the doorway, waiting impatiently with clenched fists. For the moment, they had the upper hand.

"Get back!" Ivanova yelled. Danel came to a stop behind her, panting. She swung her arm around, igniting the air in front of her.

Bridget grabbed Nuriel under the arms and dragged him towards the open air. He was dead weight, and each tug only gained them a few inches.

A spark landed on Bridget's sleeve, and she looked behind her. Kai had raised his hands in defense, fingers splayed. His wind pushed Ivanova's fiery attack outward in a spray of heat and crimson light. Bridget lunged out of the way, but a blast of flames hit her leg.

The fire burned a hole right through her jeans to the skin beneath. Bridget stared in horror. It didn't even hurt. It looked like it should.

Then the pain hit.

She screamed. It was as if someone had driven a thousand needles into her leg, then twisted. Everything around her faded—the broken bottles, the fiery heat, Nuriel's limp form. The world went dark, except for a tiny pinhole of light.

She slapped at her leg, but the fire was already out. Nothing could stop the searing agony. It felt like it was eating its way up her calf and down to her toes. More flames exploded against the ground nearby, and she rolled out of the way.

Hands grasped at her. She jerked in alarm, trying to ward off an attack, then caught a glimpse of red hair. Gaul gripped her beneath her armpits and dragged her out of the building. Cool air hit her, and she gasped, sucking it in. There was a vague sensation of being lifted up, then the world passed her by as a kaleidoscope of gray, brown, and green. She caught a flash of Gaul's eyes, of the blue sky, of Ret carrying Nuriel.

She looked down at her leg. The fire had burned clear through to the muscle. The skin around it was red and raw, bubbling with blisters. Bile rose in her throat, and she moaned.

Gaul jolted to a stop. She rolled her head to the side and saw they'd reached the parking lot. Ret knelt beside Ivanova's car, lowering Nuriel to the ground. A gentle glow illuminated them.

She was dimly aware of being set beside him. The asphalt was warm, and pine needles poked at her skin. She curled up, vision blurring as she fought back tears of agony.

"Stay here," Gaul said. Then he turned and ran back to the distant building that still raged with wind and fire. When he reached the doorway a few moments later, he darted inside.

Why would he say that? Where else would she go? Her entire world was on fire. The smell of her own burned flesh wafted up, and she rolled onto her side and threw up.

Then Ret was there, kneeling beside her. His fingers brushed the skin of her leg. Even the gentle touch sent a spasm of pain through her. But it was short-lived. Cool relief spread from his fingertips and into her leg. She let out a sob.

Finally, all that remained was the memory of the pain, accompanied by a bone-deep exhaustion. Her jeans were burned through, leaving a gaping hole in the fabric. But instead of blackened skin beneath, her leg was now pink and new.

"You're alright," Ret whispered. "Take a deep breath."

Bridget wiped her mouth, trying to calm her gasps. She looked around. They were shielded in the narrow alleyway created between the two parked cars. "N-Nuriel?"

"He'll be okay. He's asleep."

She sagged. He'd survived. And so had she. But that still left her sister. "Where's Dahlia?"

Worry creased his brow as he looked down at her. "Gaul and I saw her, but we couldn't break her free. Once this fight is over, we can finish the job."

"You *left* her?" Bridget stared at Ret in shock. "You made it through and then you left her there?"

"We didn't have a choice. We can talk about it later." He climbed to his feet, eyes on the building. They were far enough away that all Bridget could make out was the occasional burst of flame from the door.

"Why? Why couldn't you?"

"I'll explain after this situation is resolved," Ret said, voice steady.

"Forget it. I'm going in after her," Bridget said. "Now's the perfect time, with Kai distracted. I know where to go, and there's another portal here."

He was shaking his head before she finished speaking. "You can't. There will be a guard waiting for you."

"I'm not going to leave her. The entire point of this was

to get her out!"

Ret pressed his lips together into a thin line. Instead of arguing further, he gestured to Nuriel. "Help me put him in the car. He needs to rest."

Bridget gritted her teeth. With Ret's support or not, she *would* get to her sister.

She climbed to her feet, half expecting her leg to give out under her. It held as if the injury had never happened. She went around to Nuriel's shoulders and bent, sliding her hands beneath his arms. Together, they lifted him from the ground and maneuvered him into the Prius. He was out cold. His shirt hung from him, the tattered clothing and dried blood the only remaining evidence of his injuries. As she shifted him into the back seat, Bridget caught a glimpse of an intricate tattoo between his shoulder blades.

"Bridget," Ret said, pulling her attention away. He placed a hand on her shoulder. "Don't go after Dahlia. That's exactly what Kai wants you to do."

"I have to try," Bridget said, yanking free.

Ret shook his head. "Please, let us handle this. The keys are in the ignition. Take the car and get to safety."

"Are you serious?" Bridget laughed incredulously. "After everything that's happened? No. I can't run."

A loud crack of concrete made Bridget jump. Fire spewed from the blasted-out door of the building.

"We don't have time to argue. Get out of here." Ret took off at a run towards the building, lifting his hands as he went.

"Wait!" But he was gone, already halfway to the fight.

She clenched her fists. She wasn't running away. Not when she was so close. But if she didn't have a weapon, what could she hope to accomplish?

Abruptly, she remembered James framed in the abandoned building's window, the pistol clenched in his shaking hands. It had been Ivanova's gun. She was a cop, after all. Maybe she kept one in the car.

Bridget bent over to peer under the seats. There, under the driver's side, was a black case. The latches popped open easily, revealing several pieces of folded paper. Pushing them aside, she pulled out the pistol. She closed the case and returned it to the floorboards. Then she backed out of the car and shut the door, hoping that would shield Nuriel from the fight.

The gun weighed heavy in her hand.

Everyone else had some power to protect them. Wind. Fire. Speed.

Her fingers tightened around the weapon. Her determination was its own sort of power. And she was done feeling helpless.

THIRTY-ONE

Bridget hefted the gun, its metal cool in her hand. A strong breeze kicked up, and she hurriedly backed out of the car, looking towards the building. Ivanova and Danel had been forced from the building and onto the grass where Gaul and Ret waited. Kai followed, his coat flapping in the wind. She ducked behind the car and hunkered down.

The detective and Danel stopped beside Gaul. Even from where Bridget crouched, she could see their flushed cheeks and heavy breath. Ivanova teetered as a focused blast of wind barreled into her. Gaul waved the two of them back and stepped forward, Ret at his side.

Kai paused, and an unsettling silence filled the air. The wind stilled. He sized his two new opponents up. Said something that Bridget couldn't make out.

How is he still going? In the past twenty-four hours, she'd seen Kai fight multiple times and get shot twice. He'd taken a beating—his face was still marred with angry red blisters. But still, he advanced.

Gaul lifted a fist, and a sudden crack broke the silence. The ground between him and Kai ripped open. Bridget clapped a hand over her mouth in shock.

The force of the miniature earthquake sent Kai staggering backwards. Ret swept a hand forward and Kai flew into the outside wall of the building.

The detective raised her hand, tendrils of fire leaping to life at her command. At the same time, Danel zipped forward.

Kai threw both arms out and all four of them blasted backwards, skidding across the grass. His face twisted with effort as he used his power to lift a fallen tree branch and hurl it towards them.

Gaul rolled out of its path and raised his fist again. A deep rumble welled up from the ground. The dirt beneath Kai's feet shifted and cracked, knocking him off balance.

Ivanova was back on her feet. She strung a chain of fireballs into a long, glowing whip. With a quick movement, she cracked it towards him. It wrapped around Kai's ankle and tugged his feet out from under him. He fell to the ground with a choked scream.

Bridget searched for an opening, but she doubted she could get to the portal in the chaos.

Ivanova pulled the whip back and lashed out again. Kai rolled and it missed, slapping the ground with a brilliant spray of yellow and red sparks. He pushed himself to his feet as the detective dropped the whip and swiped her hand across her body. A six-foot wall of fire materialized and advanced towards Kai. He yelled, dispelling the wall into a burning spray. It arced high over Bridget's head, a miniature meteor. She ducked, and it exploded into a tree behind her.

She peeked over the car to see Danel blur to Gaul's side. The two men locked eyes, then knelt on the ground. As one, they pressed their fists to the ground. The grassy area bucked. From their knuckles, a five-foot wave of dirt, stone, and roots rolled towards Kai, like an ocean swell that crested in ragged rocks. It hit Kai and knocked him back a dozen feet.

Their fight had migrated farther from the tiny building, closer to the tree line. No one was paying attention to Bridget. The doorway to the building was unprotected. This was her chance to get to Dahlia. She sucked in a deep breath, then burst into motion.

Crouched low with the loaded pistol pointed at the ground, she darted away from the car. The ground steamed with soft globs of tar and pitch. Two pine trees were ablaze, their trunks blackening as eager flames lapped at the bark. Dark smoke rose from the top like a chimney.

A blast of heat and wind sent her stumbling into a weathered picnic table. She caught her balance and reoriented herself. Kai was back on his feet, teeth bared as he and Ret faced off. A ferocious wind spiraled between them, forming a whirling cone of dirt and stone.

Danel was nearby, hands on his knees and gasping for breath. Gaul stood beside him, speaking in his ear.

Ivanova was further back, away from the line of fire. Her dark gaze was directly on Bridget, and the gun in her hand.

Bridget flinched, hiding the weapon behind her back. She braced for Ivanova's snarl of disapproval.

But the detective gave a curt nod towards the building, mouthing, "Go." Then she turned back to the battle.

Bridget let out a long breath, then took off running again. No one else spared her a glance as she ducked into the building.

A rush of hot air slammed into her. She drew in a choked breath, and it burned her throat. Bridget blinked watering eyes and moved deeper in.

A shout came from the battle outside, followed by the thunderous crack of splintering wood. Bridget hurried across the room, forcing herself to ignore the voices behind her. Dahlia was her first priority. She lay her palm flat against the design, ignoring the flush of heat as she touched the concrete.

The portal activated immediately, gold light threading around it. A deep thrumming blocked out the sounds of battle. She clutched the gun in her right hand and lurched forward into the light.

This time, she knew better than to try and breathe. She kept her lips pressed tight as the air around her thickened. A bolt of black lightning tore across the whiteness, and she squeezed her eyes shut. She felt the pressure of a thousand eyes. *Don't think about it. Be ready.* Ret had mentioned guards. Her grip tightened on the gun. Her lungs burned.

The droning grew louder, and she opened her eyes. The light intensified, first at the edges of her vision, then splintering and growing, forming a cobweb of gold that coalesced together. With a grunt, she fell forward onto polished cement. She let go of the breath she'd been holding, and clean, cool air filled her lungs.

A hand closed on her arm.

It yanked her to her feet and spun her around. Ketill, the bulky guard who could heal himself, was in front of her. His uniform was rumpled, and blood streaked his forehead. His lips curled into a sneer.

Bridget swung the gun with all her strength. It hit him in the temple. He grunted and tightened his grip, unfazed. With a sharp motion, he yanked her around.

Her shoulder popped, and she gasped in pain.

She fumbled for the gun's safety. As soon as it disengaged, she pointed the weapon downward and pulled the trigger. A bang blasted through the room, and the gun kicked in her hand.

Ketill howled, releasing her. She scrambled away as he bent to grab his foot. Blood dripped from his fingers.

She'd *shot* him. But already, golden light was arcing around the injury. Ears still ringing, unable to draw a full breath, Bridget raised the gun and fired again. This time the bullet hit him in the chest, and he fell back against the wall.

Blood blossomed from the wound and he groaned, slipping down to the floor. Bridget spotted a key ring sticking out of his pocket, and she lurched for it. His bloody fingers wrapped around her wrist just as her fingers brushed the keys. His grasp was weak, but it still shot a spike of agony through her now-injured arm. He wheezed in a breath, and blood rolled from his mouth down his chin. Then, to her horror, glowing light began to spread across his torso.

She pointed the gun at his forehead. Healing ability or no, his magic wouldn't help him if she blew his brains out. "Let me go."

He watched her with narrowed eyes for a few long seconds, then finally released her. She finished pulling the keys from his pocket and darted back. Her shoulder throbbed with every heartbeat.

Dahlia. She had to get Dahlia. She darted past the tall table and into the collections room.

Several of the compartments were ransacked, their contents strewn across the floor. She hurried past, sidestepping a pile of shattered glass. Turning the corner, she staggered to a sudden stop.

Her way was blocked by a corpse. She gasped and jumped back.

It was the other guard—Dolos. Or at least, it had been. She recognized his thin frame and dark hair, but little else. Where his skin remained, it was blackened and dead. Whole areas of exposed muscle were eaten away, down to the bone and ligament. His mouth twisted into a permanent scream of agony, half of his jaw exposed. She put a hand to her mouth to keep from throwing up. The smell coming from the body was a sickly-sweet mixture of urine, sweat, and decay.

That explained why Bridget had only met one guard. Gaul must have taken care of Dolos. But why hadn't he and Ret saved Dahlia? They couldn't free her, but they'd had time to make this mess?

"Who's there?" Dahlia's voice dragged her from her thoughts, and she looked up towards the cages.

"Dahlia!" Bridget hurried past the body and rounded the corner. Her sister looked even worse than before, with dried blood marring one cheek and a black eye. But she was alive.

"You came back," Dahlia breathed, gaze locking onto her.

Bridget came to a halt in front of her cage and knelt. "I said I would," she whispered. She set down the pistol and grabbed the padlock, bringing up the keys. They all looked the same, and she tried one after the other, hands shaking and shoulder screaming from the effort.

"Well, those assholes you sent didn't do much. Come on, hurry," Dahlia urged. "Before he comes back."

"Kai's distracted," she said.

"Not Kai." Dahlia looked up at the security camera. "Tannin."

Bridget started. "He's here?" She tried another key. The padlock rattled in response, but it didn't open.

"He will be. The guards tried to contact Kai after those men attacked. They couldn't reach him, so they called Tannin."

Bridget released a slow breath. "How long do we have?"

"I don't know. Not long."

Bridget nodded and returned to her work. She'd almost gone through the entire keyring when the lock clicked open. Dahlia burst free immediately.

Bridget snagged the gun and Dahlia helped her to her feet. She reached forward with her good arm to pull Dahlia close. They held one another tight for a few seconds.

"We need to go," Dahlia said, pulling back.

Bridget nodded. "If Tannin's on his way, we have to warn the others." She grabbed her sister's hand. They took off at a run, skirting around Dolos' corpse. A second later, they reached the closed door to the portal room and came to a halt. Bridget's fingers were tight around Dahlia's.

"Ketill's in there," she warned in a low voice. "I hurt him, but he may have healed himself."

Dahlia paused, then pulled her hand from Bridget's. "Give me the gun."

Bridget handed the weapon over, grip first. She grasped her injured arm; it still throbbed.

"Stay back," Dahlia warned Bridget. Then she opened the door and slipped through.

Bam! Bam! Bam! The sound of multiple rounds going

off sent tremors down Bridget's spine.

She hurried into the room. Her sister stalked forward towards the guard, oblivious to Bridget. She pulled the trigger repeatedly until finally there was a *click*.

Ketill fell forward onto his face. A crimson pool spread from his body.

Dahlia offered the gun back to Bridget. "That felt good."

Bridget took the pistol with shaking hands, stunned into silence.

THIRTY-TWO

Bridget gripped Dahlia's hand as they passed through the portal. She only let go when they tumbled free, so she could catch herself against the dirt-strewn concrete. The shock sent a spasm of pain through her shoulder.

Heat slammed into her like a wall. When she inhaled, it scorched her lungs and left her gagging.

Outside the building the world was on fire.

The trees on one side of the parking lot were raging towers of flame. They spewed black smoke into the sky, blotting out the clouds. The roar was overpowering.

Silhouetted against the inferno, his back to Bridget and Dahlia, was Kai. He hovered a few feet off the ground, coat flapping in the wind. His hands extended outward, a miniature tornado keeping him aloft.

Dahlia tugged on Bridget's sleeve and mimed firing a

gun at him. Bridget shook her head and leaned over. "We're out of bullets," she shouted over the howl of wind and fire.

Dahlia's jaw clenched tight. A dark bruise splotched across her cheek. "Are there more?"

"Maybe."

The building's doorway afforded Bridget a narrow view of the park's lawn, and the broken parking lot beyond. She couldn't see Ivanova or the others, but both cars were still sitting beyond Kai. Maybe there were more rounds in the gun's case, tucked beneath the passenger's seat of the detective's car. Better yet, maybe she and Dahlia could simply drive away to safety. Ret had said the keys were in the ignition.

But the car was at least thirty feet away, and the flames were starting to move towards it, chewing through grass and picnic tables.

A start went through her.

Nuriel was inside the vehicle.

"Come on!" Bridget cried. The two sisters climbed to their feet, and Bridget tucked the gun into the band of her jeans. Crouched low, she rushed to the doorway and peered out. A glimpse of nearby gold light caught her eye. Just to their left, Ret knelt over Danel, whose blonde hair was caked with blood. It looked like he'd been thrown against the building wall.

Dahlia stiffened beside her. "Is that *Dan*?" she hissed in Bridget's ear. "What is he doing here?"

"Helping us, I think," Bridget said.

Dahlia's expression darkened. "Bull. He's working for Tannin."

"We'll deal with it later," Bridget said. Now wasn't the time to discuss Danel's loyalty. Half of the forest was a hellscape, and Nuriel was in danger. She turned her eyes towards the car he was in and stepped out from the building.

As soon as she did, wind whipped at her clothes and blew her hair back. The full scope of the fire came into view, and she gasped. It had consumed an entire side of the parking lot, turning trees into tinder and blocking the road out.

She ducked low, hoping Kai wouldn't notice as she ran for the car. Ivanova and Gaul came into view. They stood at the edge of the parking lot, heads tilted back to watch Kai. The detective's slumped posture betrayed her exhaustion. Gaul stood in front of her, fists clenched and eyes narrow. He didn't look as worn down as Ivanova, but his expression overflowed with anger and frustration.

Bridget tucked her injured arm against her chest and ran faster, Dahlia just behind. The sky overhead was black with ash, but at eye-level, the air was clear, thanks to the swirling gusts of wind. The air was a hurricane, and Kai was its eye. The same powers, unfortunately, were spreading the fire. Sirens wailed faintly over the rumble of flames.

She reached the cars and ducked between them, the gun digging into her skin as she knelt.

Dahlia skidded to a stop. "Did he see us?"

Bridget glanced over the hood. "No, I don't think so." Kai was still focused on Gaul and Ivanova. He lifted his hand, and a fiery tornado sent the detective hurtling backwards. She flew through the air, collided with a burning tree trunk, and fell to the ground. A shower of sparks went up. When it cleared, Bridget saw Ivanova crumpled at the tree's base, covered in bark and soot.

Ivanova and Dan were both down. Kai turned his attention to Gaul and a blast of wind flung the redhead across the parking lot.

There was no way she could get close enough to warn them Tannin was coming. But she could still get away with Dahlia, and maybe save Nuriel in the process.

Bridget reached for the driver's door handle, then snatched her hand back with a yelp. The metal had absorbed heat from the growing fire.

She tugged her sleeve over her palm and wrenched the door open.

Reaching in, Bridget twisted the key in the ignition. The engine gurgled impotently. She gave the key another turn, but this time the engine was silent.

She slammed her hand against the center console. How were they supposed to get out now?

Sweat plastered her hair to her forehead. Everything in the car was boiling hot—the leather seats, the floorboards, even the air. If they couldn't drive to safety, they needed to get Nuriel out of the vehicle.

She scrambled out of the driver's seat and yanked open the back door. "Help me!" she called to Dahlia.

Her sister didn't answer. Crouched a few feet away, she glared at Kai over the hood. Her jaw was tight, lips pulled back in a snarl of fury.

Bridget leaned into the car and grabbed Nuriel's leg, shaking it. "Wake up!" He didn't respond.

She sucked in a breath, then gripped his ankles and tugged. Her shoulder screamed in protest, but he barely budged. "Dahlia!"

Her sister tore her gaze from Kai and leaned into the suffocating space. Together, they slid Nuriel along the seat. The three of them fell onto the ground.

Recovering her breath, she rolled Nuriel on his back and knelt beside him. "Nuriel?" She shook his shoulder. Nothing. She turned back to Dahlia. "If we can't drive away, we may have to fight our way out. There's a black case in the car. Grab it."

Dahlia nodded and crawled back into the Prius.

A loud crash came from close by and she jumped. Leaving Nuriel's side, she crept towards the hood and peered over. Ivanova was still motionless at the base of the tree. Ret stood from Dan's still form, watching as Gaul reached back and tore a slab of concrete from the ground. He launched it at Kai. His opponent made a slicing motion with both hands, hurling it away.

"I've got it!" Dahlia's voice pulled Bridget's attention from the battle. She turned to see her sister crawling out of the car, the gun case in her hands.

Bridget pulled the weapon from her waistband. Another crash made her jump and turn. Smoke and sparks billowed up in a massive cloud. A tree had fallen, throwing up sand and pine needles in its wake.

Gaul flung another chunk of rock towards Kai. It catapulted forward, then slowed and came to a halt. For a moment, it hovered in midair. Then the rock changed directions and veered towards Ret. Bridget stifled a cry as it slammed into the cinder block building above his head. Dirt and gravel rained down on them, and he lifted his hands to cover himself and Danel.

Ret staggered to his feet and dragged Danel around the corner of the building. Then he took off across the remains of the parking lot, headed straight for Ivanova. Kai summoned a torrent of burning branches and launched them at Ret like fiery spears. The healer flung an arm behind him, and the projectiles veered off course, missing him.

If Bridget was going to be any help at all, she needed to reload the gun. She started to turn, but a flash of motion halted her.

Gaul was sprinting straight towards the still-hovering Kai. He skidded to a stop beneath him and raised his hands. In response, the parking lot quaked. Rock and dirt danced across the ground, and the car shuddered beneath Bridget's fingers. The noise became a thunderous roar as a pillar of earth broke free. It rose up beneath Gaul's feet, carrying him towards Kai.

Buffeted by the wind, Gaul crouched on the rising circle of asphalt. He lurched forward and snagged Kai's leg, yanking him closer.

Kai's shout carried over the parking lot. He pulled back, but Gaul held on. The redhead's feet slipped off the crumbling platform, but still he clung to Kai in midair. He scrambled to get a better grip on Kai's pants, feet flailing.

Kai dropped his arms. The wind stilled. Bridget's breath caught in her throat as the two men plummeted downward. Kai kicked downward with his free leg. The blow caught Gaul square in the chest. He let out a cry of alarm and released Kai.

The wind whooshed back to life. It buffeted Kai upward towards the ceiling of smoke. Gaul hit the ground, sending up a flurry of ash. The platform he had been standing on crashed to the ground just beside him with a boom, sending rock flying outward. Gaul covered the back of his neck with interlaced hands.

Kai ascended high above them all, his hair a wild halo around his head.

"Give me the case," Bridget rasped to Dahlia, coughing. She handed over the box, and Bridget set it on the ground. The car tire beside her gave off the acrid smell of burned rubber.

Near the building, Danel stirred. He climbed upright, using the wall for support. Ret struggled to drag Ivanova to safety, while Gaul shoved aside rocks and dirt to stagger back to his feet. He stood to face Kai, back hunched.

Then Kai turned his gaze towards Bridget and Dahlia. She felt his eyes lock onto them. A thrill of ice zipped down her spine.

Kai extended a hand towards them. The Prius trembled. An invisible force lifted it off the ground, and Kai's expression twisted with the effort. With a sideways jerk of his hand, Kai flung it across the parking lot. Exposed, Bridget grabbed the case and scrambled backwards with Dahlia.

The car flipped past Kai and straight towards Gaul. The redhead dove to the side. The Prius slammed into the tree where Ret knelt by Ivanova. The tree swayed and groaned, and then, with an ear-splitting crack, it fell. Fire and ash billowed into the air, and a wave of dirt flew up in its wake.

The car was a twisted mass of blackened metal and mangled wheels. Black smoke poured upward from the wreck as fire devoured it.

"Eisheth!" Danel blurred to the car.

She couldn't see any of them. Gaul. Ret. Ivanova. Gone.

Bridget's heart caught in her throat. It felt as if the ground had opened beneath her and dropped her into a pit. She was wrong, so wrong. She couldn't do anything, not against a person—a creature—as strong as Kai. If she didn't escape with Dahlia this instant, they'd be buried here, just like the others. Her eyes burned with tears, and she roughly rubbed them away.

"We need to get away from here," Bridget said, looking from Nuriel's unconscious form to Kai. He still hovered, but the cyclone of wind that held him aloft wavered. His shoulders sagged and he raked his sweaty hair back from his eyes.

She glanced behind her. The beach wasn't too far away. If nothing else, she could get Dahlia out.

She had to take the chance. They had to go. Now.

"Dahlia, come on." She reached for Dahlia's hand, but her sister didn't move. She was rooted to the spot, her eyes on the building. She pointed at it. "Look."

Oily black smoke spewed out from the doorway. Bridget stared. The building was the one place that *wasn't* on fire. The substance coalesced, tendrils snaking towards the parking lot as if they had a mind of their own. She took a stiff step backwards. She *knew* that smoke.

"It's him," Dahlia whispered. "It's Tannin."

THIRTY-THREE

Black smoke writhed from the building. Unlike the ashy
fumes that rose from the fire, this moved like a living
thing. It reminded Bridget of a thousand snakes, coiling
outward as they sought out prey.

A shadowy form emerged from the smoke. It gained
sharpness, tinged red from the blaze. Tannin.

He had an angular face framed by close-cropped
waves of brown hair. Tall and thin, he was dressed in a
gray suit with a blue pocket square. He stood at the center
of his smoke, taking in the fiery scene. His lips pressed
into a thin, angry line. His hard gaze fell on Kai, who had
turned to watch Tannin's entrance from his perch in the
air. Then he looked to Bridget and Dahlia.

"Run," Dahlia breathed.

"What?"

"Run!"

She grabbed Bridget's hand as the ground rumbled beneath them. The earth around Tannin buckled. It drew in on itself, rocks crunching and roots snapping as dirt and rock swelled upward. In seconds, a wall of earth towered as tall as the building itself. Tannin flicked his wrist and the entire mass burst into motion, careening towards Bridget and Dahlia.

They bolted.

Bridget made it a few steps before the wave of debris slammed into her and Dahlia. It knocked Bridget's feet from under her, and she crashed into the ground. She dropped Dahlia's hand, gun flying from her grip as she threw her arms over her head. Dirt and rock crashed down on her, bashing into her back and legs. She tumbled end over end, her entire world a roar of cascading dirt.

Then everything stilled.

She tried to draw in air but received a mouthful of grit instead. It clung to the inside of her mouth and made her gag. She opened her eyes but saw nothing. The sound of crackling fire was muffled. Jagged asphalt pressed her down.

She was buried alive. *Don't panic,* she told herself, fighting back the urge to scream. If she lost control, she might hurt herself more.

She listened but could only hear the muffled roar of flames. Shifting her weight, she pushed, testing the pile's give. Pain stabbed through her injured shoulder, but the loose dirt and rocks shifted. Crimson light filtered through the rocky prison. She shoved again. This time she broke free of the wreckage, spitting and sputtering. Sound returned, a roar of oxygen as the ravenous flames consumed it.

"Dahlia!" she cried.

"Here." Her sister's voice was hoarse. Dahlia crawled from a pile a few feet away, dirt caught in her hair and streaking down her skin.

"Where's Nuriel?" She couldn't see him. Not only that, but the gun and its case were gone, too. The parking lot was nearly unrecognizable, strewn with burning tree limbs, crushed slabs of asphalt, and shattered picnic tables.

Debris had been blasted outward in a massive circle, and at its epicenter was Tannin. Kai hovered beside him, ten feet in the air. Beyond, Danel was frozen near one of the fallen trees, watching with wide eyes as Tannin crossed the parking lot towards Bridget.

"We have to get out of here," she said.

Dahlia climbed to her feet. "I'll hold him off." She stood and turned to face Tannin, expression defiant. "You go."

"Dahlia, no! We can't fight him."

"I know," Dahlia said. "You go."

Bridget swallowed, mouth dry and heart fluttering. She stared at her sister. She'd always been so brave. Her chest swelled with equal parts love and terror. "I'm not leaving you," she said. Bridget ripped her gaze back to their assailants.

Tannin stepped around chunks of asphalt as he crossed the parking lot. Whorls of smoke advanced before him, and he kept his gaze locked on Dahlia. His living smoke continued to spread, and the smell of sulfur mixed with the scent of burning wood.

Kai's tornado ebbed. His feet touched the ground, and he matched pace with Tannin. Side by side, the two Grigori advanced.

"It's me they want," Dahlia said. "Go. Please."

Heart fluttering in fear, Bridget shook her head. "No."

The gun was gone. The case might have fresh ammunition, but it had disappeared too. Both had probably landed near the trees behind them. Bridget reached for her sister's hand. Dahlia's sweaty fingers gripped hers in return.

Tannin and Kai came to a stop in front of the sisters. The bubbling, dark mass of smoke pooled at Tannin's feet, waiting. Ash fell around them like dirty snow, and Bridget's throat burned.

Tannin's voice was calm. "Dahlia, you can stop all this by coming with us."

Dahlia's fingers tightened in Bridget's hand, then fell free. With a quick motion, she stooped down and grabbed a fallen pine branch, flames licking the end. Holding it between both hands, she shifted into a defensive stance. The sight would have been pitiful were it not for her straight back and the determined gleam in her eyes.

"I won't be your prisoner anymore," she said. Her words earned a scoff from Kai.

Tannin shrugged. "Alright, then. Force, it is." He lifted his hand, and the smoke coiled like a spring.

The second the sulfuric smoke connected with the flaming branch, an explosion blew Bridget and Dahlia back. Bridget raised a hand to shield herself from the shattered wood flying in every direction. She blinked woozily. It had been just like the explosion in the abandoned building.

As she got to her feet, a sudden blur crashed into Kai. Bridget jumped in surprise, and Tannin's head turned towards the commotion.

Kai slammed into the ground. Danel materialized on top of him with one knee pressed into his gut. He pulled back an arm and swung, his fist a blur. Kai's head snapped to the side and blood sprayed from his mouth. Even from where Bridget stood, she could hear the sound of bone crunching.

Tannin's smoke lashed outward. It moved fast, but Danel was faster. He dodged a tendril and drove his fist into Kai again.

Both Tannin and Kai were distracted. If she was going to find the missing gun case, now was her chance.

Bridget shook her head clear and staggered to her feet. Dahlia yelled, but Bridget didn't stop, sprinting towards the piles of debris. The gun and its case had to be around here somewhere. She skidded to her knees near the tree line and began to claw through dirt and rock.

Heart hammering, Bridget spotted the corner of the case peeking out from beneath a tree root. She lunged for it.

Dahlia's shrill yell cut through Bridget, distracting her from her efforts. She looked back to see Tannin's smoke encircling Dahlia's wrists and ankles. It crawled its way up her torso and wound around her like a boa constrictor. Her sister screamed again, a sound of pure agony. Tears streamed down her face as she thrashed against the bindings.

Bridget climbed to her feet and lurched towards Dahlia. Then she stopped. Her fingers were rigid around the case. What was she going to do, beat Tannin over the head with it?

She shook the case. A spare clip rattled inside. Now she just needed the gun.

Bridget turned back to her frantic search. She swallowed back bile as her sister screamed herself hoarse. *Focus. Find the gun.* Her shoulder ached with every inch gained. Hands probing the rubble, she found nothing but chunks of parking lot and blackened bark.

She paused to glance over her shoulder. Next to Dahlia's trussed form, Kai hurled Danel to the ground, his face a bloodied mask of fury. He swiped his hand to the side, a gust of wind blasting in its wake. The air flung Danel backwards into his BMW a dozen feet away. The door bent inward where he'd hit, and he fell to the ground in a heap.

Bridget scrambled farther from the fight, eyes wide. If she could just—*there!* It was dusty and half-buried, but it was the pistol. She lunged for it and ducked behind a sap-streaked tree trunk. There, leaning against the rough bark, she fumbled to disengage the spent clip.

Another strangled yell almost made her drop the gun. That didn't sound like Dahlia. She chanced a glance around the tree trunk.

A dark section of Tannin's smoke had wrapped itself around Danel's neck. Bridget watched in horror as it lifted him high into the air. Danel bellowed in pain, hands scrambling to push the burning tendrils away.

"I had high hopes for you, Danel," Tannin said over the din.

Danel couldn't respond. He kicked and writhed, red splotches appearing across his cheeks. Tannin gave him a grim smile and flicked a finger downward. The rope slammed Danel down with a sickening *thwack* that sent up an explosion of dust. When it cleared, Danel was still.

Bridget stared, mouth agape, frozen behind the tree. Dahlia screamed as she struggled to escape her smoky prison.

Bridget grasped the gun's grip with a sweaty hand and tugged, but the magazine held firm.

"Come on, come *on*," she hissed. Her scrabbling fingers found the release, and she pressed it. The clip fell to the ground. With a gasp of relief, she opened the case and shoved aside the folded pieces of paper. Her hand landed on the fresh clip. She grabbed it and slammed it into place.

Dahlia's screams cut off.

She snapped the case closed and dropped it to the

ground. With the loaded gun in hand, Bridget straightened.

She peered around the tree. Dahlia was held tight by ropes that wound around her arms and legs. They'd lifted her high into the air, and Bridget could see her head loll to the side. Tannin had a hand held in her direction, fingers spread outward. Kai was beside Tannin, bracing himself with his hands on his knees.

Bridget let out an involuntary whine. Her free hand gripped the bark of the tree she hid behind. "Dahlia," she whispered.

Tannin turned and began walking towards the building; the smoke was a leash that pulled Dahlia along.

No. *No.* She couldn't let Dahlia return to that horrible cage. Not after all she'd gone through. After all Bridget had done. After all everyone had sacrificed.

She took a deep breath, then stepped out from behind the tree.

"Let go of my sister!" she screamed. Kai's head snapped up. His dark eyes locked onto her. Blood ran down his face, and his nose was bent at a horrible angle— the remnants of his fight with Danel. He grimaced and spat out a tooth.

Bridget's chest sank like a stone as cold fear seeped through her.

Tannin paused. He glanced over his shoulder to meet Bridget's gaze, but it was Kai who responded. He let out a sharp laugh. "You think *that*'s your sister?" he waved a hand in Dahlia's direction. His shattered nose left his voice thick.

Bridget swung the gun towards Kai, hand trembling. "Stay back!"

"You're in a world you can't begin to understand," Kai said as he pulled himself to his full height.

Bridget thumbed off the safety and looked from Kai to Tannin. "Drop her." Tears rolled down her cheeks. Her knuckles were white around the grip.

Tannin watched her with the glittering, narrow eyes of a snake. He seemed more curious than worried.

Kai smiled. His teeth glistened red around the edges. One was missing altogether. Beyond was blackness.

"Your sister is dead."

THIRTY-FOUR

Despite the suffocating heat, a thrill of ice shot down Bridget's spine. *No.*

Kai took another step closer. A trickle of bloody spit rolled down his chin. "She's been dead for nine months." Another step. "Your sister is one of us now."

The icy feeling spread, and her heart thumped so hard her entire chest felt tight. Bridget's eyes darted to the swirling mass of smoke that covered Dahlia. "No," she whispered aloud. Then, with more force, "That's not true!"

His smile grew. "I killed her myself."

It was a lie. It had to be. Who else had she been fighting alongside? Speaking to? Holding onto? She tried to steady the gun, but tremors ran down her arm like an aftershock.

"Look at the chaos you've created," he said in a low voice. "For nothing."

Bridget shook her head, throat tight.

"Kai!" Tannin called, impatient. "That's enough. Leave her."

Kai scowled and turned away.

Rage prickled within Bridget.

She raised the gun. Taking aim between Kai's shoulder blades, she pulled the trigger.

The gun kicked in her hand and sent a violent jolt through her.

Kai spun around. His eyes narrowed on her. She cocked the gun and redoubled her grip. He lifted his hand in a dismissive wave.

She fired again, but his blast of wind flung her backwards.

The parking lot blurred, and wind rushed in her ears. She slammed into something hard and crashed to the ground.

Black spots dotted Bridget's vision. Pain shot through her dislocated arm. Her ankle throbbed. She sucked in a breath and gasped as her ribs twinged sharply.

She was lying against the BMW. Danel was next to her, eyes closed, and one arm flung at an impossible angle beneath him. Through her swimming vision, she saw Kai rejoin Tannin, Dahlia in tow. They were almost to the building, silhouetted by the angry flames.

A sob clawed free from her throat. In moments, Dahlia would be lost to her. Forever. Ivanova, Gaul, and Ret were likely all dead. And James...

The only person left was Danel. She reached for him, shaking his shoulder. "Danel, wake up. Please, I can't do this alone." Her voice cracked. He didn't move.

Kai was right. It was all for nothing.

Bridget slumped back against the warm ground. Hot blood trickled down the back of her head, matting her hair to her neck. She closed her eyes, listening to the dull roar of the fire.

Wait.

That wasn't just fire. It was a new sound, a low rumble that grew into a loud rush. She opened her eyes and propped herself up on one elbow.

A wall of water shot above Bridget, arcing over the broken parking lot. It slammed into Tannin and knocked him off his feet. Dahlia tumbled to the ground, freed from the smoke.

Shaking, Bridget pulled herself to her knees. Nuriel stood straight-backed behind the car. He held both arms out, one to siphon water from the lake, and the other to attack Tannin. His hair was matted with blood, and his face was covered in dirt and soot. She'd never seen a more welcome sight.

She swallowed the lump in her throat and turned back to Tannin and Kai. They looked somehow smaller, now that Nuriel was on his feet. Now that she wasn't alone. But Nuriel had barely held Kai at bay before. She had to step up.

The gun lay on the ground a dozen feet away. She

pulled a leg under herself. Pain shot up her ankle, but she gritted her teeth and powered through. Adrenaline propelled her towards the weapon, and she cried to Nuriel, "Protect Dahlia!"

He twisted his arm forward and the water spun, forming a cyclone around Tannin, blocking him from both Dahlia and the building.

Kai snarled at Nuriel and whipped his arms forward. Leaves and branches caught in the blast of wind and rocketed into Nuriel. He staggered back but kept his waterspout intact.

"I can't hold against them both!" Nuriel cried between gritted teeth. Bridget could already see the surge of water faltering.

Bridget shouted over the commotion, "Just hold Tannin off. I've got Kai."

Kai fixed his dark eyes on Bridget and bared his teeth. She couldn't hear him, but she could see his mouth form the words, *"Do you?"* Then he gripped the air and pulled it like a lasso.

Her breath sucked from her lungs in one burst. But without the heaving of her chest, her hands no longer wavered. She brought up the gun.

The world narrowed, everything blotted out, until it was just the barrel of the weapon and Kai.

She squeezed the trigger.

Kai jerked and slapped his hand against his neck. Bright blood spurted between his fingers. His body seized, and he gurgled as he collapsed to the ground.

Air rushed back into Bridget's lungs. She swayed in shock as she stared at Kai.

Beyond him, the waterspout encircling Tannin darkened into a thick, viscous brown. It exploded outward, raining down sulfur-laden drops. Tannin stood in the middle, arms outstretched. Boiling mud coated Nuriel, and he cried out. The lake water fell over him in a deluge.

Tannin's smoke rematerialized, covering Dahlia and dragging her unconscious body upwards. A second tendril shot towards Nuriel and looped itself around his neck, cinching tight. Nuriel spasmed as he tried to pry free.

Heart hammering, Bridget took off at a limping run towards Tannin.

He locked eyes with her. His lips peeled back in an irritated snarl, and he gestured sharply. The tendril of smoke holding Nuriel tossed him aside. He hit the ground and rolled to a stop.

Tannin turned and ducked out of sight within the building. Dahlia floated behind him, just outside the door.

A warm glow illuminated the entry, and strands of gold wove through the dark smoke, encircling Dahlia.

Heart hammering, Bridget sprinted past Kai. He was twitching in a puddle of blood.

Her every jerky step made her gasp in pain. She pushed it aside and quickened her pace.

The light grew brighter. A pulsing filled the air as she

closed in on the building. With a desperate cry, Bridget threw herself on top of the cable of smoke that tethered Dahlia to Tannin.

It was like diving into a lake of acid. Fire burned through her skin. She hit the ground hard, and a shrill, animal-like scream clawed out from her throat.

Then the sharp pain receded, leaving behind a dull ache.

She blinked her vision clear. She was lying face-down in the dirt, staring at soot-coated blades of grass. Tannin's smoke had disappeared.

She sat up, coughing. Then she squinted through the haze and found Dahlia, sprawled across the ground, unmoving. Her sister's skin was red and raw. Blisters covered her wrists and ankles. Behind her, Kai had grown still. Nuriel was unmoving on his side, facing away from her.

She pulled herself to her knees and started to crawl to Dahlia, setting the gun aside. Then she paused. The hum of the portal set her teeth on edge. As long as it was active, Tannin might still be here. With a groan of pain, she dragged herself to the doorway. She steeled herself, then peered around the corner.

The last puff of smoke curled into the portal. The golden light faded, and the hum ceased. The building was empty. Tannin was gone.

But only for a moment.

Bridget reversed course, returning to Dahlia's side. She grasped her shoulder. "Dahlia, please, wake up."

Slowly, Dahlia's dark eyes blinked open. She moaned and curled in on herself.

Bridget bent close. "I'm going to get you out of here." But they couldn't leave yet. Tannin would be back as soon as he realized Dahlia wasn't with him.

She had to destroy the portal.

THIRTY-FIVE

Bridget turned from Dahlia and crawled back towards the building. Ten feet away, a tree dropped a charred limb and sent up a shower of sparks.

She hurried into the building on all fours. A wall of heat met her head-on. Sweat trickled down her temples, and she gagged at the taste of ash.

Bridget forced herself towards the inert symbol. She reached the wall and grabbed a hunk of broken cement from the floor. Hauling herself upright, she rubbed it against the markings. Flecks of paint fell to the floor, but the symbol remained in place.

She scraped again, then slammed the chunk of cement into the wall in frustration. It thumped to the ground.

If she was going to destroy the portal, she needed help.

She staggered to the door, stopping just before she

reached Dahlia, and looked out at the parking lot. A thick cloud of ash swirled before her, obscuring her view and leaving her throat cottony.

When the air cleared, she found herself looking out on destruction. The parking lot looked like a demolition zone. Blackened pines rained down soot.

She'd lost sight of Ivanova and Ret when the tree had fallen. Gaul was buried under the burned-out car, which was little more than a smoldering ruin. Nuriel hadn't moved.

Then, out of the corner of her eye, she spotted Danel rolling onto his side. He was still sprawled beside his car.

Bridget turned back to Dahlia. "I'll be right back." Her chest tightened at the thought of leaving her, even for a second.

Dahlia didn't respond, expression twisted with pain.

Bridget began to limp towards Danel. He'd put the portal in place—surely he knew how to destroy it.

On her way, she passed the unconscious Nuriel, who had a horrific burn across his neck.

And then she skirted around Kai. He was lying on his back, eyes staring blankly at the smoke-filled sky. One hand was limp beside his neck, the other flung outward. Dark blood pooled beneath him, soaking into the dirt.

Bile rose in her throat. She swallowed it back and took a steadying breath. Turning away, she continued to advance towards Danel. She called his name as she got closer. He didn't move.

She crouched at his side. "Wake up. Please."

Desperate, she shook his shoulders.

His head thumped against the car door, and he gasped, eyes flying open.

She helped him into a sitting position, and he cried out in pain. "Danel, I need your help."

Danel blinked a few times and followed her gaze. His eyes were so wide she could see the whites around the edges. "What?" His voice cracked.

"The symbol. Please, we need to destroy it." She stood, and her ankle spasmed in protest.

Danel slid his feet under himself and leaned against the car. His arm dangled limply at his side, and his clothes were splattered with blood. Gasping for breath, he took in the parking lot.

His gaze fell on Kai. "He's dead?" He sounded shocked.

"Yes."

"Good."

"But Danel, Tannin escaped through the portal. I need help destroying it."

At Tannin's name, his face paled. Pushing away from the car, he took a lurching step towards the building. He steadied himself, but nearly fell again.

Bridget hurried after him and slipped her good arm around his back. She let him lean against her, grunting at the addition of his weight. Together, they stumbled forward.

Halfway across the parking lot a glow began to illuminate the building.

"We've got to hurry!" Bridget tried to urge them on faster, but Danel came to an abrupt halt.

"Stop."

"No." Bridget shook her head and tugged on his arm. "We can't stop. We can't—"

"Let go. I'm faster." Bridget started to protest again, but Danel interrupted her. "Trust me."

Heart thrumming in panic, she relented. He pulled away, swaying where he stood as he gauged the distance to the building.

The glow grew more intense.

Bridget's breath stuck in her throat as Danel closed his eyes, appearing to gather his strength.

And then he was gone, leaving Bridget wobbling. She caught her balance, looking around frantically. *There!* Danel reappeared beside the building, a few feet from where Dahlia lay. He dropped to his knees and drove his fists into the ground with a bellow. The earth splintered like a parched desert beneath his hands. It crackled outward, and as the ground bucked beneath her, it threw her to her knees. The building shuddered, and cracks raced along the joints between blocks, then burst the concrete apart.

The walls and ceiling caved in, concealing Dahlia from view. Bridget covered her face with her arm as an enormous cloud of dust billowed out and over her. She coughed, doubling over. Tears streaming down her cheeks, she wiped the back of her hand across her mouth and sucked in a fresh breath.

The rumble subsided. Dust settled, and the glow was gone.

Bridget staggered to where she'd last seen Dahlia. She climbed over chunks of concrete and twisted rebar, throwing them aside.

The rock cut her hands, leaving a smear of blood down her gray, dust-coated palms. Clouds of dust obscured her vision and choked her throat. Danel crunched through the debris to join her, coughing hard.

A spray of dark hair. Dahlia was huddled in a ball, her arms covering her face. The dust in her hair made her look like she'd aged twenty years. Danel continued to pull away pieces of crumbling rock as Bridget knelt beside her.

"Dahlia?" Bridget asked, frantic.

Dahlia lowered her arms from her ash-streaked face, coughing as her bleary eyes met Bridget's.

A thunderous crack sounded from the far end of the parking lot. A fire-consumed tree trunk split down the middle. It swayed, then toppled to the ground with a boom. A shower of burning pine needles and ash flew up in its wake.

Bridget looked up at Danel. "We have to get her out of here."

"I'm not leaving without Eisheth." He limped towards the detective's mangled car.

Bridget held her sister close, peering out over the parking lot. Her gaze fell on Nuriel, still crumpled in a heap.

If they wanted to get out of here alive, they needed his help. "Stay here," she whispered to Dahlia, then staggered past Kai's body. Falling to her knees beside Nuriel, she shook him until he groaned. "Are you okay?"

His eyes lifted to half-mast, and he coughed. Her heart thudded in relief. Ash fell around them like snow, and another tree gave an enormous pop as it splintered.

"Come on, get up," she urged him. He braced himself with both hands on the ground, then struggled to stand. She grabbed his arm to steady him.

"What happened to Tannin?" Nuriel's voice was raspy.

"He's not coming back. We need to go before the forest burns down."

"Where are the others?"

Bridget pointed towards Danel, who was still digging for the detective.

"Go help him. I'll get Dahlia," she said over the roar of flames. He nodded, and Bridget made her way back to her sister as he joined Danel.

"Found her!" Danel pulled Ivanova out from the wreckage. She staggered into his chest, hair askew and blood coating the side of her face. She clung to him for a few seconds, then wrenched herself away.

Bridget watched them, a lump of emotion lodged in her throat. Dahlia let out a moan, pulling Bridget's attention back to her. She knelt down and brushed dark hair from Dahlia's face. No matter what else happened, she was free. A tear dripped from her cheek and landed on Dahlia's cheek, turning the ash a dark gray.

Bridget bent to touch her forehead to her sister's. "It's okay," she whispered. "You're going to be okay."

THIRTY-SIX

"Firefighters continue to battle a deadly blaze that erupted on Cleveland's East Side today. Several acres of Lakefront Park have been consumed, forcing surrounding neighborhoods to evacuate. Let's go to Aaron Johnson, live at the scene."

The television cut from the news anchor to an on-site reporter. Behind him, an orange glow lit the night sky. Bridget muted the sound.

She shifted against the padded hotel headboard to look at Ivanova. The detective leaned against the laminated desk. Her fingers tapped out an irritable, irregular rhythm as she watched the single serving coffee pot gurgle out a cup.

"Do you think anyone saw us?" Bridget asked.

Ivanova looked back at her, expression drawn. "It's

hard to hide these days." She picked up the Styrofoam coffee cup and took a sip, then wrinkled her nose and ripped open a packet of creamer.

Dahlia sat at the end of the bed, her legs drawn up and arms wrapped around her knees. Bridget hadn't told anyone about Kai's final words to her. It was too big, the implications too impossible.

And yet, every time the thought surfaced, she stole a glance at Dahlia. How could she know for certain? She still *looked* like Dahlia. Thin and haunted, but Dahlia all the same. Her dark hair clung to her shoulders, still wet from the shower. The horrible burns left by Tannin were gone, thanks to Ret.

Bridget and the others owed a lot to the healer. He'd made their worst injuries vanish, even though his abilities didn't extend to himself.

Since arriving at the hotel, Ret had remained in bed in the next room over, nursing a broken leg and deep burns. Gaul was at the house collecting their essentials. With Bridget's urging, he'd promised to check on James' body. In the meantime, Nuriel was contacting someone who Gaul promised could help while also watching over Danel.

"Tannin will find us eventually, won't he?" Bridget asked. They'd paid for the room in cash, and Ivanova had used false identification. Even so, Bridget couldn't help but picture Tannin and that horrible smoke advancing on them. "How long do you think we have?"

"Some time," Ivanova said. "Gaul and Ret destroyed

the portal in the abandoned building before we came for you. He has no immediate means of returning."

"They did what?" Bridget sat up straighter. "But Dahlia was still trapped. Ret said they were going to go back and get her."

"I don't know what Ret told you, but we didn't know there was a second portal until we arrived in that parking lot."

Bridget could feel her face turning red. "Did they get the drawings?"

"Some of them," Ivanova said, unclasping the gun case they'd retrieved from the forest. She pulled a few folded papers from inside. Bridget hadn't had time to see what was on them during the fight, but now she could see the swirling patterns.

Bridget shook her head in disbelief. They'd never intended to save Dahlia. Ret had lied; all he cared about was the sketches. If Bridget hadn't gone through herself, her sister would still be there, trapped. Her fingernails pressed into her palms as she balled her hands into fists. "If you didn't know about the other portal, how did you find us?" Bridget asked. "How did you know where Nuriel and I were?"

"You set your phone to share your location data with me yesterday. Before we went to confront Kai the first time. Remember?" Ivanova set down her coffee cup.

Bridget hadn't thought about the GPS since she'd first turned it on. Whether her text had gone out or not, it was reassuring to know that the detective had been watching.

For all of Bridget's anger, Ivanova had come through in the end. She had risked her life to protect her and Dahlia. It felt good to be wrong about her.

There was a click at the door. All three of them tensed as it swung open. Danel stood on the other side. Dirt still streaked his face, and his shirt was torn.

"What do you want?" Ivanova's voice was like ice.

Danel lifted a plastic bag as he stepped into the room. "Nuriel picked clothes up for everyone." He glanced at Bridget. "He grabbed your things from the hotel, as well. It's all in the other room."

She pointed to the floor. "Leave them."

He complied, then paused. "Thought I'd get a shower." He had dark circles under his eyes, and his blonde hair was still thick with grit.

Dahlia stood from the bed, her expression stony. "All that dirt suits you," she snapped. They were the first words she'd spoken since Ret had healed her.

"He saved our lives," Bridget reminded her in a quiet voice. Dahlia's shoulders stiffened.

"You need to answer for what you've done," she said.

"I've told you before, Dahlia, I never intended—"

Dahlia's voice rose. "Don't you *dare* make excuses, Dan. I don't give a damn what you intended. Look at what *happened*!"

"I do have questions," Ivanova said, cutting Dahlia off. She pushed away from the dresser to stand beside her.

Danel scowled. "I've already answered plenty. I told Ret and Gaul everything I know."

"You can answer a few more." Ivanova was shorter than Danel, but she seemed to tower over him.

"I don't—"

"Are we safe?" she demanded.

Danel shrugged. "For now. Tannin didn't have any other access points to Cleveland. He'd have to board a plane from Athens and go the long way around."

"Athens?" Bridget asked.

"That's where his collection is," Dan said.

Ivanova spoke again. "Does he have any other operatives here in the States?"

"Probably, but none that I know of."

"What is he planning next?" the detective asked.

"I don't *know*." Danel sighed in exasperation. "All I can tell you is he wants to get as many of those symbols working as possible."

"But *why*?" Ivanova pressed. "He clearly wants to make more of us. What for? And why now?"

"Maybe he's lonely," Danel said with a sneer. Ivanova took a threatening step towards him and he held up his hands. "I don't know. He's delusional. Always focused on 'reclaiming what we've lost' and hoarding artifacts. He sees it as vital academic research."

"Hoarding dead bodies isn't academic." Bridget suppressed a shiver.

Danel shrugged. "Whatever his plans are, it's not over. We'll see him again."

Bridget cast a worried look at Dahlia, who still stood with her arms crossed. "Why did you do it?" Bridget asked Danel. "Why hurt Dahlia? Why even work for him?"

Danel's jaw tightened, and he looked away. "I had no choice."

Ivanova cursed. "He offered you protection, didn't he?"

Danel looked away. "Can I get that shower now?"

Ivanova scowled. "You and I are going to have a *much* longer discussion soon. I want to know how you weaseled out of your other contract for so long."

Danel flushed. "Yeah, well, it's about to catch up with me." Without another word, he turned and disappeared into the bathroom. The shower squeaked on.

Dahlia rounded on Ivanova. "Why are we letting him stay? We can't trust him."

Ivanova shot her a withering look. "Stay out of what you don't understand."

"I understand plenty," Dahlia said. "I understand that Danel is a manipulative asshole."

"And you prefer we turn him loose?" Ivanova asked. "Give him the opportunity to crawl back to Tannin? Or find someone worse?"

"No." Dahlia's voice was firm. "We need to make sure he doesn't crawl *anywhere*, ever again."

Bridget flinched at Dahlia's words. She had no doubt her sister meant it—not after the way she'd shot the guard. She'd changed, that much was certain.

The glow of the television caught Bridget's eye. "Look," she said as a new headline flashed across the screen. *One confirmed casualty in Lakefront fire.* "It must be Kai." Her stomach twisted as she remembered the blood spurting from his neck.

"Hopefully burned beyond recognition," Ivanova added. She took another sip of her coffee. "Still, they'll know he was shot, and they'll trace the cars."

The vehicles belonged to Ivanova and Danel. Was there anything to tie Bridget to the scene, other than her connection to the detective?

"Shit," she said aloud, drawing both women's attention. "My phone. Kai took it from me. It's probably still in his pocket."

The detective winced. "The digital forensics team will likely trace it to you, even if it's damaged."

Dahlia looked to Ivanova. "Can't you protect her? Destroy the evidence or put her in witness protection or something?"

Bridget shook her head. "I'm not doing that. I'll tell the police the truth. Kai attacked me."

"You can't," Ivanova said. "They'll have more questions. You'd have to either lie, in which case they'd catch you, or tell the truth. And if you did *that*, you'd activate Gaul's contract."

Bridget shook her head. "I don't think the contract works all the time."

Ivanova folded her arms. "The contract does work, Ms. Keene."

"No, it doesn't," Bridget said. "Back at Tannin's place I started to tell Dahlia about you all. Nothing happened."

The detective frowned. "That's a question for Gaul. But I wouldn't test it by talking to the police." Her voice softened. "We'll protect you, Bridget. You saved us."

The words were no comfort to Bridget. Is this what her life would become? Hiding in hotel rooms and strange cities? What would her mother think? She'd already lost one daughter. Bridget couldn't bear to do that to her again.

It was too much to think about right now. Searching for a distraction, she said, "There's something I've been wondering."

Ivanova lifted her eyebrows. "Go on."

"You and Nuriel told me Grigori have multiple abilities. And I saw some of that. Like, Danel moves fast *and* causes earthquakes. But some of you only seem to use one. Like, you only *ever* use fire. Why?"

Ivanova shook her head. "I am using my secondary ability; you just can't see it. It makes me stronger, immune to my own flames. Not all of our powers are as flashy as Danel's."

"But that's not true."

Ivanova and Bridget both looked at Dahlia in surprise. She'd fallen silent during their discussion, watching the television.

Ivanova pursed her lips skeptically. "What's not true?"

"What you told Bridget. That there are two abilities."

"I think I would know better than you, Ms. Kee—Dahlia." She frowned at the realization that there were two Ms. Keenes to address.

"Then why do I have more?"

Bridget froze. She stared at her sister. Ivanova sucked in a sharp breath.

The detective strode to Dahlia. "Stay still," she ordered, grasping her wrist and turning it to inspect the tattoo there. Bridget leaned forward to watch, her throat tight.

Ivanova shook her head and dropped Dahlia's arm. Then she reached up and brushed aside her sister's dark hair, pulling the neck of her shirt down to reveal the skin between her shoulder blades. There, meticulously inked, was an identical symbol.

Ivanova hissed and released the fabric. "How long?"

Dahlia looked uncomfortable. "Since I woke up in Tannin's cage."

"And this? Just vanity?" Ivanova gestured to the marking on her wrist.

Dahlia shrugged and looked away.

Ivanova let out a thin, angry sigh. "There's your explanation, Bridget. Gaul's contract didn't activate around Dahlia because she's Grigori."

Bridget's vision swam with tears. It was true. Dahlia was one of them.

And what did that mean? Was her sister—her *real* sister—dead, like Kai had said? If so, who had Bridget risked her life for? Who had James died for?

The door to the bathroom swung open and released a puff of steam. Danel stepped out. He wore only a towel wrapped around his waist.

"What?" he asked, seeing their grim expressions.

"Dahlia is one of us," Ivanova said in a curt voice.

Danel stilled. He looked between Dahlia and the detective, then his gaze darted away.

"You knew." Ivanova shook her head, incredulous. "Why didn't you say anything?"

He shrugged. "I only suspected it. Besides, we've been sort of busy. And I didn't want to bring up..." he trailed off.

"Say it." Bridget's voice cracked.

"The fact that you betrayed me?" Fury laced Dahlia's voice. "That you sold me out to Tannin? That you let me *die*?"

He shook his head. "I had no idea he would do that, Dahlia. Trust me, I never planned any of this."

"Well, I *don't* trust you," Dahlia snapped. "Get out."

"Okay," Danel held up his hands. "Let me get some clothes on first, alright?" He grabbed the plastic bag then backed into the bathroom again.

Silence fell over them.

You let me die.

Those four words sat like a physical weight in Bridget's stomach. Everything she'd fought for fell away in the face of them. She covered her mouth as a sob threatened to bubble up.

Dahlia turned. "Bridget—"

She shook her head. "Don't."

"It's okay. I'm okay." Dahlia insisted.

"No. You're not." The words came out as a whisper.

How could someone dead be okay? After everything, she had failed her sister.

"Ms. Keene," Ivanova said, "both of you, I know this is difficult, but we do have a process for integrating newcomers."

Bridget didn't respond. Instead, she pulled her knees up to her chest and ducked her head. It was a lie. It couldn't be true. Tears threatened, but she pushed them back. No. She wouldn't cry. If she cried, it would make it real.

"Gaul will help when he comes back." Ivanova's voice sounded fuzzy as she addressed Dahlia. "He's done this before. I haven't."

There was a pause, and Bridget gulped in air, trying to rein in her emotions long enough to focus on the conversation.

"I can never go home, can I?" Dahlia asked in a quiet voice.

Bridget glanced up and saw Ivanova sit on the bed beside Dahlia.

"No," the detective said. "You both need to stay with us. Not even your family can know."

Dahlia nodded, tucking a strand of dark hair behind her ear.

"We can't disappear," Bridget said, voice thick. Dahlia and Ivanova looked over at her. "It would kill mom."

"*Going home* would kill her," Ivanova said. "Tannin will expect it. Isolation is the best way to keep your family safe."

Bridget felt sick. She wrapped her arms around her stomach. It was all too easy to imagine their mother sitting alone at the kitchen table. This time, she'd be surrounded by photos of Bridget, not just Dahlia. She'd choose one to send the police. Answer endless questions, reliving her last moments with her daughter over and over again. Over time, her initial desperation would shift into quiet resignation. Bridget swallowed hard. "Can't we at least tell her we're alive?"

"It's too dangerous. I'm sorry."

"But..." she trailed off. She was as trapped as Dahlia.

"It gets easier over time," Ivanova said. "At least, it did for me."

Dahlia bobbed her head in another nod but said nothing. The two of them lapsed into silence. Dahlia continued to look down at her lap. Ivanova watched Bridget, then turned to the muted television.

Bridget lowered her head, and her tears fell.

THIRTY-SEVEN

"Walk me through what you can do." Gaul watched Dahlia, his expression troubled. He'd returned to the hotel room with a few essentials from the house. The electricity still worked, which meant James' body was safe for the time being.

In a strangely paternal gesture, Gaul had also brought them food. An array of sandwiches from the hotel's restaurant sat on the desk, untouched. No one had much of an appetite. Danel was back with Ret, uninterested in the barrage of accusations.

Bridget watched Gaul and Dahlia from her spot near the headboard. Her knees were still pulled up to her chest, and her eyes felt puffy. She'd stopped crying, but she could feel herself on the precipice of a fresh onslaught.

Dahlia sat on the edge of the bed by Ivanova, and she regarded Gaul with a narrow gaze. He leaned against the desk, arms crossed, lines creasing his forehead. The television was still on, muted reporters discussing the possible cause of the fire.

"It depends," she said in a slow, uncertain voice. "Sometimes I have more strength than I should. Other times I can move the wind, like Kai does. Did." She paused, a frown pulling at the corners of her mouth. "I've made things appear and disappear. Illusions."

"Show me," Gaul said.

Dahlia shook her head. "It doesn't always work. I don't know how to control it. It just happens."

He considered this. His fingers tapped his arm, and he shot a glance in Ivanova's direction, then looked back at Dahlia. "Try fire."

Dahlia shook her head. "I've never done that before."

"Try it now."

Dahlia hesitated, then held out her hand. Her eyes dropped to her palm, focusing. Seconds ticked by. Bridget felt a small surge of hope. Maybe this was all a big mistake. Maybe Dahlia was wrong, and the tattoo meant nothing.

Then, a spark flickered to life, cupped within her fingers. It smoked, spurted, then fizzed out.

Bridget's heart sank, and fresh tears spilled over, rolling down her cheeks in twin streams.

Ivanova frowned at Gaul. "So she's like me?"

Instead of responding, Gaul picked up a ceramic mug

from the desk and strode to the balcony. He tugged open the sliding door and stepped outside. Bridget watched as he filled the mug with dirt from one of the potted plants. He returned to the room and handed it to Dahlia.

"Make it pull together into a ball," he said.

She stared up at him with a furrowed brow, then focused on the cup. At first, nothing happened. Then the dirt rolled itself into a clump.

Ivanova drew a sharp breath. "That's impossible," she said.

"I thought—" Bridget paused to clear her throat. Her voice was thick. "I thought you said you have two abilities."

"Not those two," Ivanova said.

Gaul nodded, taking the cup back. "We each possess an elemental power—like fire or earth—and a vital one, such as my ability to spread disease or Ret's to heal." He watched Dahlia with an unreadable expression. "We never have two of the same type."

"So what's going on?" Dahlia asked. Her voice shook. "What's wrong with me?"

"Nothing," Gaul said. "You're a mimic. It's rare. Ret knows more about it than I do. He can answer your questions when he's feeling better."

"What does that mean?" Bridget asked. "To be a mimic?"

Gaul's green eyes found hers. "It means she possesses no natural abilities of her own. She can only use the abilities of nearby Grigori."

"I've never heard of that," Ivanova said, eyes narrowing.

"That's because you're young yet, Eisheth," Gaul told her. He looked uneasy. "Be careful, Dahlia, until you understand it better. Now, if you'll excuse me, I'm going to watch over our prodigal son so Ret can rest."

"Is Viri on his way?" Ivanova asked.

Gaul flushed and turned away. "Someone has to take care of Ret's leg."

Bridget sat up straighter. She had more questions. She slid off the bed to follow him. "We need to talk."

He glanced at her, then nodded, holding the door open. They stepped into the hotel hallway. It was long and narrow, lined with swirling carpet. It smelled like lemon cleaner and furniture polish. No one else was in sight, although there was a linen cart at the far end.

"You *left* her," Bridget accused as soon as the door was closed. Her vision grew misty, and she wiped at her eyes with a jerky motion. "You brought back the sketches, but you abandoned my sister to that cage."

He sighed, keeping his voice low. "We had limited time. The sketches were easier to retrieve, and we couldn't even get all of them. We had to make a difficult decision."

His words made her cheeks flush hot. "That's your excuse?" she hissed. "You're lying to me. You trapped her there when you destroyed the portal behind yourselves. It was *deliberate*."

Gaul considered her, then beckoned for her to follow.

He led her down the hall, farther from the cart. He came to a stop by a humming vending machine and pulled a bill from his wallet. "There's something you need to understand about our people." His voice was quiet enough that she had to lean in to hear. "Our human forms can be killed, but our Grigori forms can transfer from body to body, even if we don't retain our memories."

"And?" Bridget prompted.

"I already suspected Dahlia was one of us, and that she was dangerous. So I made the call to leave." He fed money into the machine and made his selection. A soda can rattled to the drawer at the bottom.

"My sister is *not* dangerous," Bridget snapped. "She was a prisoner."

"Bridget," Gaul said in a low voice as he bent to pick up the drink, "the woman in that hotel room is *not* your sister. She may look like her. She may sound like her. She may even act like her, for now. But it's not her."

Bridget wiped her eyes again. She shook her head and said the line she'd been rehearsing in her head. "If she looks, sounds, and acts the same, what's the difference?"

He pressed his lips together. "She's drawing from your sister's memories, but her personality is her own. The Grigori that lives in her now has a past. She can't remember it, but it's there nonetheless. None of the mimics can be trusted. Ret can tell you more, but they've proven their loyalties are as unreliable as their abilities."

She scowled. "You're being a bit heavy-handed, don't you think? Isn't that how you feel about humans, too?"

Gaul's eyes narrowed. "Bridget, I'm trying to help you. Listen to me. The longer she's a Grigori, the less you'll recognize her."

She shook her head. "I'd be able to tell. I've known her all my life."

Gaul fixed her with a level look. "No. You've only just met her."

Sorrow squeezed her heart. *No.* She wouldn't accept that.

"If you'll excuse me, I have Danel to deal with." Gaul took a step past her.

"Gaul, wait—what about James?" she asked. Her voice cracked at the sound of his name.

The redheaded man paused and looked back at her. "I'm sorry about your friend."

"I don't want sympathy," Bridget pushed ahead. "I want you to save him. To make him one of you."

"Are you listening to me?" he demanded. "Even if we could, he wouldn't be the same person. And we can't. Ret showed you our book of names. There are none left."

"But we have Dahlia's sketches now," Bridget said. "If any of them are names, you can use one to bring him back, can't you?"

"No," he said, voice firm. "For one, those sketches aren't accurate enough to create new Grigori. Otherwise, Tannin would have already done so. More importantly, it's a delicate process. Binding the wrong person to a creation contract could be disastrous."

"But—"

"Not to mention it could start a civil war, or worse. Haven't you had enough fighting?"

She wiped sweaty hands on her pants. "He showed more bravery than anyone I've known. He doesn't deserve what happened to him."

"He didn't," Gaul agreed. "But it happened, and it's best you move on. I'm sorry. James is gone."

He turned and walked back to Ret's room, leaving Bridget in the empty hallway.

Bridget returned to the hotel room to find Dahlia and Ivanova sitting side by side on the bed. Ivanova was speaking to Dahlia, and they both looked up when she entered.

An all-too-familiar pressure welled up inside her chest. Grief had been her constant companion ever since Dahlia first went missing, and she knew it could overwhelm her if she wasn't careful.

Suddenly, the hotel room felt suffocating. "Getting some air," she murmured. She strode past Ivanova and Dahlia to the sliding door and let herself onto the balcony.

It was cool outside. Night had fallen, and the roof above protected her from a light drizzle. That was good, Bridget reflected. The rain would help douse the ongoing fire across town.

She wasn't alone. Nuriel sat on the neighboring

terrace in a plastic deck chair, a pad of paper balanced on one knee. He'd managed to procure a pack of cigarettes, and one sat half-smoked in an ashtray.

"Are you drawing?" Bridget asked, going to the railing between the two balconies and looking at his paper. It was emblazoned with the hotel's logo at the top.

"I am," he said, turning the pad so she could see. It was a sketch that portrayed a woman in a ruffled blouse, curls tumbling over her shoulders. Her eyes were penetrating, and her lips curved in a pert, flirtatious smile.

"Who is she?" Bridget sat in the nearby chair, watching him through the gaps in the railing. He was only a foot or two away.

"Someone I knew a long time ago." He reached for the cigarette with his free hand and took a slow drag. "I'm sorry about your sister," he said as he exhaled. Smoke wafted past his face.

"Thanks." Bridget looked out towards the city. It was too dark to see the lake, but she could make out the bright lights of the skyline off to the east. Beyond it was an orange glow from the fire. Silence stretched between them, and Nuriel resumed his sketching. The scratch of pen on paper mingled with the patter of rain.

"You saved me," Bridget said finally, eyes still on the city. The scratching sound paused. "Back at the house. You could have let Kai take me, but instead you risked your life." She turned her gaze away from the horizon to meet his. "Thank you."

"He still took you, in the end. I wasn't strong enough,"

Nuriel said.

Bridget shook her head. "If not for you, Ivanova and the others may not have gotten there soon enough. Dahlia would be back in Athens. We would've all burned up in that fire. We all did our part." They really were stronger when they cooperated. She and James had been, too. He'd helped her free Dahlia and held off Kai. If she'd accepted his help sooner, maybe he would still be alive.

"I suppose you're right," Nuriel said, but he still looked glum.

She turned in her chair to face him. Her hand slipped between the iron bars and came to rest on his shoulder. "You helped more than you know." His gaze followed her hand, then turned back to her eyes. She could see the doubt in his expression, but he nodded.

She withdrew her hand and settled back in her chair. "What happens now?"

"I don't know." Nuriel took another drag of his cigarette. "Ret and Gaul will want to know why Tannin is so intent on making more of us."

"You're not interested?"

He shrugged. "I am. But I'm more disturbed by what happened to Kai. I knew him for a long time. Centuries."

Bridget's chest tightened. "I'm sorry if you lost a friend, but that man was evil."

"He wasn't a friend. He was a teacher, and I respected his skill, but we never had much in common." He resumed his drawing, adding shadow to the woman's neck. "And the grudge he held against humanity always concerned me. But even so, he was a Grigori of principles. I don't understand what Tannin could have said to convince him to work with him."

Bridget shook her head. "Some principles."

"I know." He sighed. "At the end of the day, I'm mostly invested in keeping the peace. You saw today what happens when Grigori fight one another."

"Do you think there will be more fights like that?"

"Maybe. Tannin lost his Artist, which will delay him. But it also means he'll be searching for someone to replace Kai. I'm not sure what will happen. I'm still new to this, relatively speaking."

His words sent a pang through Bridget. He considered himself young and inexperienced, yet he was hundreds of years old. What did that mean for Dahlia's future? Would Bridget become a relic of her sister's past? Hundreds of years from now, would Dahlia sit and sketch pictures of Bridget to calm herself after a battle?

The sound of the slider opening drew Bridget from her thoughts. She looked up to see Dahlia step out onto the balcony. She paused, uncertain. "Is it okay if I join you?"

Despite Gaul's warning, Bridget couldn't bring herself to push Dahlia away. She nodded.

Nuriel pressed the burning end of his cigarette into the ashtray and stood. "I should go check on Ret." His gaze caught Bridget's again, and there was compassion within.

Then he looked to Dahlia. "If you need a listening ear, come find me." She nodded, and he stepped back into his room.

Dahlia waited until his door latched, then shifted her attention to Bridget. "I wanted to thank you," she said in a quiet voice. "For everything."

Bridget watched Dahlia, heartache and anxiety fighting for control. Turning in her seat, she gripped its plastic arms. "Why didn't you tell me?" It came out as an accusation.

Dahlia shook her head. Her eyes were glassy.

Bridget swallowed back a lump in her throat. "Who are you?" There was an edge of despair to her voice.

"I don't know," Dahlia whispered. She sank into the chair beside Bridget's. "I just don't know." Her dark eyes shone, and she sat with her shoulders hunched. For the first time Bridget could remember, her confident, brazen sister seemed uncertain of her place in the world.

They sat in silence. Dahlia lowered her gaze and Bridget looked out at the speckled lights of the skyline. She blinked hard to force back the tears that threatened to spill over.

This was the person Gaul thought was so dangerous? Dahlia twisted her shirt between her hands. Bridget had seen the same anxious gesture countless times growing up. Her heart gave a painful lurch. She couldn't abandon Dahlia. They both needed help now. Maybe Dahlia was becoming someone new, but wasn't Bridget a new person too, in a way?

Bridget licked her lips. Maybe they could help one another. "Can you fix your sketches?" she asked. "One, at least?"

Dahlia looked pained. "What do you think I've been trying to do for months?"

Bridget reached out to slide her fingers around Dahlia's. "I know. But James died helping me find you. If you can find him a Grigori name, we can help *him*."

Dahlia searched Bridget's eyes. "He won't be the same. He won't be James."

"I don't care," Bridget said. "You might not be the same, but it's better than you being gone. I owe him this."

Dahlia nodded. "I can try."

Bridget let out a slow breath, taking in her sister's scared expression. "And, Dahlia, I'll help you understand yourself—this new part of you."

"Why would you help me?" Dahlia whispered. "I lied to you."

Bridget forced a smile. "Habit, I suppose. We'll figure this out together."

Dahlia met her gaze. Bridget saw her resolve grow. Her fingers tightened in Bridget's grasp. "Like sisters," she said in a quiet voice.

Bridget squeezed Dahlia's hand. "Like sisters."

THE END

ABOUT THE AUTHORS

Jessi Honard and Marie Parks met as adults on an *Animorphs* forum—an online homage to the middle grade sci-fi books they've geeked out over since age 10.

Their friendship quickly expanded to a shared love of camping and hiking. Something magical happens in the woods, far from cell service: you get to talking about your big dreams. For them, that was creating meaningful stories. So they started co-writing.

Multiple times, they've been asked if they're sisters. And even though they aren't related, the answer is yes, because siblinghood goes deeper than blood. Jessi and Marie both believe in the power of found families, a theme that emerges in their solo and joint writing projects, along with identity, trust, and belonging.

Originally from Cleveland, Ohio, Jessi currently lives in the Bay Area of California with her partner, Taormina, and her very opinionated cat, Obsidian. Follow her at jessicahonard.com.

Marie lives in Albuquerque, New Mexico with her spunky chihuahua rescues, Maya and Mitchell. Follow her at marieparks.com.

SPECIAL THANKS

There's a misconception that writing is a solitary act. Ours wasn't, just on account of us being co-writers. But *Unrelenting* wouldn't be possible without an entire community who has helped us create the novel you have in your hands.

To Jessi's partner, Taormina Lepore, who spent countless hours listening to us read passages aloud, cheering us on, and making sure Jessi never forgot a meal, thank you. You started talking us up long before we had the confidence to do so, and we're forever appreciative for your support and encouragement.

We also want to thank our families for encouraging us to follow our passion from the time we were kids. To our parents (Robin and Mark Honard and Nancy and Barry Parks), in-laws (Marlene and Andy Lepore), siblings (Eric and Sean Honard, Katrina Lepore), grandparents, aunts, uncles, cousins... thank you. You mean so much to us.

Josh Rieken, thank you for your words of encouragement and for believing in us.

Benjamin Gorman and Viveca Shearin at Not a Pipe Publishing, we are grateful you believe in Bridget as much as we do. You helped us wrangle our manuscript into shape with such a thoughtful, attentive eye, and you've given this novel a truly special home.

We will forever be grateful to Matt Joseph Mistech and Peter Malone Elliot of Pipeline Media for the honor of making this manuscript a Book Pipeline award winner before it was even published. Thank you for your support of this book and our careers, and for introducing us to such fine people in the industry—especially the team at Not a Pipe.

Gigi Little, you took our ideas and brought them to life with magical cover art. We're particularly grateful for your work in creating a visual representation of the complex symbolic language of the Grigori. Gigi, you took the ideas from our heads and made them real, and we feel so fortunate to have worked with you.

A huge thank you to our amazing beta readers: JJ Adams, Jess Ayer, Ben Hicks, Robin Honard, Jeanette Hobbes, Taormina Lepore, Billy McDoniel, Nancy Parks, James Ranson, Joshua Rieken, and Josh Tutt.

We also owe a huge debt of gratitude to our local critique groups, who heard our story (chapter by chapter, week by week) for over a year. Three cheers for Cyberscribes of Albuquerque, New Mexico; Berkeley Writer's Circle of Berkeley, California; and the Coffee House Writers Group of Los Angeles, California! Thank you for your critique and camaraderie; it has meant the world to both of us as we've settled into new cities. And Geoff Habiger, we are grateful this project gave us an opportunity to get to know you. Thank you for believing in this project and for your encouragement and friendship.

Similarly, the Writing Excuses and Potted Plant communities have provided an incredible network of friends and colleagues. You've helped us navigate countless stumbling blocks along the way to publication, and you've been excellent friends to us. You are some of the best humans we know.

We are grateful to Diane M. Pho and @AmqueryingH on Twitter for supporting us with our query letter, synopsis, and first pages. We also want to express our gratitude to our literary lawyer, the wonderful Melissa Nasson. Our author photos are by the lovely Kamron Khan, taken in Cleveland, Ohio. To the entire team at North Star Messaging + Strategy, we are grateful for your trust in us and all you do. You're the best colleagues we could ever ask for.

Erica Hashier, Taylor Banks, and Rachel Schuster, thank you for your help with specific manuscript questions. We are grateful to all of you for your friendship and support.

We also want to give a shout out to Katherine Applegate and Michael Grant, the co-authors of *Animorphs*. You were the first professional authors we met, and you've always been the epitome of good people. Because of your early influence in our lives, we never questioned our ability to co-write, and you inspired us both to pursue this dream. Without *Animorphs*, the two of us would have never met at all, and we're eternally grateful.

To you, our wonderful readers, thank you for joining us for this journey, and for giving Bridget and the Grigori hours of your time. We've been dreaming of the day we could share this with you, and we're so glad you decided to be on the receiving end when the time came.

Finally, we want to acknowledge that this book wouldn't be possible without friendship and trust. The entire process, from initial idea to final draft, was a collaboration that required honesty, a shared vision, and a willingness to put our friendship first. We may not have been born sisters, but we're close enough.

If you've enjoyed this book, please review it and share with your own chosen family. It makes all the difference.

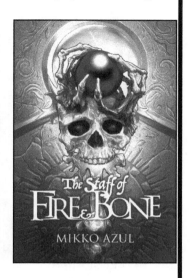

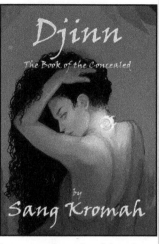

CPSIA information can be obtained
at www.ICGtesting.com
Printed in the USA
LVHW080023110422
715852LV00007B/166

9 781956 892062